Going Under

LAUREN DANE

BERKLEY SENSATION, NEW YORK

THE BERKLEY PUBLISHING GROUP
Published by the Penguin Group
Penguin Group (USA) Inc.
375 Hudson Street, New York, New York 10014, USA

Penguin Group (Canada), 90 Eglinton Avenue East, Suite 700, Toronto, Ontario M4P 2Y3, Canada
(a division of Pearson Penguin Canada Inc.) • Penguin Books Ltd., 80 Strand, London WC2R 0RL,
England • Penguin Ireland, 25 St. Stephen's Green, Dublin 2, Ireland (a division of Penguin
Books Ltd.) • Penguin Group (Australia), 707 Collins Street, Melbourne, Victoria 3008, Australia
(a division of Pearson Australia Group Pty. Ltd.) • Penguin Books India Pvt. Ltd., 11 Community
Centre, Panchsheel Park, New Delhi—110 017, India • Penguin Group (NZ), 67 Apollo Drive,
Rosedale, Auckland 0632, New Zealand (a division of Pearson New Zealand Ltd.) • Penguin Books
(South Africa), Rosebank Office Park, 181 Jan Smuts Avenue, Parktown North 2193,
South Africa • Penguin China, B7 Jiaming Center, 27 East Third Ring Road North,
Chaoyang District, Beijing 100020, China

Penguin Books Ltd., Registered Offices: 80 Strand, London WC2R 0RL, England

This is a work of fiction. Names, characters, places, and incidents either are the product of the author's
imagination or are used fictitiously, and any resemblance to actual persons, living or dead, business
establishments, events, or locales is entirely coincidental. The publisher does not have any control over
and does not assume any responsibility for author or third-party websites or their content.

GOING UNDER

A Berkley Sensation Book / published by arrangement with the author.

PUBLISHING HISTORY
Berkley Sensation mass-market edition / February 2013

Copyright © 2013 by Lauren Dane
Excerpt by Lauren Dane copyright © 2013 by Lauren Dane.
Cover photo by Claudio Marinesco. Cover design by Rita Frangie.
Interior text design by Laura K. Corless.

ISBN: 978-0-425-26210-8

BERKLEY SENSATION®
Berkley Sensation Books are published by The Berkley Publishing Group,
a division of Penguin Group (USA) Inc.,
375 Hudson Street, New York, New York 10014.
BERKLEY SENSATION® is a registered trademark of Penguin Group (USA) Inc.
The "B" design is a trademark of Penguin Group (USA) Inc.

PRINTED IN THE UNITED STATES OF AMERICA

10   9   8   7   6   5   4   3   2   1

ALWAYS LEARNING   PEARSON

This one is for Fatin Soufan,
who is so much more than an assistant.

Acknowledgments

This is a pretty solitary job at times, but it's the supporting cast of characters in a writer's life that really makes all the difference.

For my husband—who supports what I do, even when it makes me crazy and we eat far too much take-out. Forever.

I'm so lucky that I have friends who've stuck with me no matter what. Who always get my back, who tell me when I have spinach in my teeth, who keep me from hitting send on that tweet and who let me complain to them instead of respond to hatemail. Megan, thank you for being my BFF.

Speaking of friends—thanks go to my secret author illuminati ninjas at the List That Shall Not Be Named.

Laura Bradford—my friend and my agent who holds my hand when I need it.

Leis Pederson, who is such a wonderful editor—thank you so much!

Chapter 1

BURNING flesh created a smell unlike any he'd ever experienced. Sickeningly sweet, while at the same time sticky with death and pain. It was a stench Gage had hoped to never come across and yet, over the last months, he'd gagged on it more than once.

The house burned, casting orangey-yellow reflections all across the street. Over the cars parked by people who'd simply wanted to slump inside their homes and relax until they had to return to work the following day.

The red of the fire truck would delight children at any other time. But the flames made that shiny, cheery red into something more sinister. Grime coated the faces of the firefighters who'd been working to put the blaze out, but it didn't hide the resolution that there was nothing else they could do to save the three who'd been caught inside.

"The arsonists had to have used an accelerant of some type." Lark, who still favored the side where she hadn't been shot, looked on, standing next to Gage. Her sister, Helena, also watched.

This was supposed to be a visit to share information and

new spells. And now they'd have to attend yet more funerals.

"They best goddamn back off in my town or there'll be hell to pay." Helena wasn't scrappy and scary like Lark. But she had her own sort of strength, and Gage believed the Hunter in charge of Gennessee's security would indeed take out the murderous asshole humans who'd set a house on fire while the people living there had been locked inside.

People. Others. Witches, to be exact. Five of them who shared the house and attended nearby UCLA. Three of whom had been home in bed when the place had been set on fire. Strategically. At the exits, so the witches inside couldn't escape.

The firefighters had tried. Two had been hurt when part of a landing collapsed as they'd valiantly attempted to get to the second story where the bedrooms were.

Impotent fury tightened Gage's muscles so hard he had a headache. The stench of these young men's death would live in his system for days, though he believed the memory of it would live far longer. Right next to the memory of how Edwina Owen, his former boss, had looked after she'd been shot just weeks before.

"I don't know if there's a peaceful way out of this now." Helena's hands, fisted, hung at her sides. Rage pulsed from her, wave after wave. Her magick sparked from her body, even as Lark ran a hand up and down her sister's back.

"I'm not sure there ever was."

"SO you understand, of course, that this . . . *attention* you've garnered of late is detrimental to the firm."

Shafts of sunlight gleamed against the mahogany furniture in the room. Elegant. Chosen with extreme care.

Molly cocked her head, resisting the urge to lick her lips. Her hands were clasped on the tabletop before her. Her legs were crossed, back straight. They'd never know just how hard she had to work to hold herself together.

"I understand many things, Paul. This is our business,

after all. And you know as well as I know, that things like this can be spun into positive attention." Paul Weller was another named partner. Weak. She had little respect for any man who spent so much time being afraid.

Their business wasn't for the weak. Or the scared. He was both. His family money and eye for design were the only reasons he was fit to sit at the table with her.

"You can't honestly believe this will blow over." Angelica Reynolds spoke from her place to Molly's right. "I know things have been hard on you, but this is not going away. And it's costing us money."

Hard? How many people had died? How many of the ones left were losing everything else? Like she was right now. It took every bit of Molly's control not to slap Angelica's face. Now *that* was hard.

"I built this firm. I was the top earner here last year. And the year before, and the one before that too. The biggest clients are those I brought in. Whatever rabble might be making a fuss out there, this is *my* firm. I made it into what it is today."

Aaron took a deep breath before he spoke. "No one disputes that. But Angelica is right. This isn't blowing over. There have been riots in some cities. This morning Bright and Cleen called and they're going to pull their campaign if you're not fired. That makes four of our biggest clients all on the way out the door."

The others at the table she could handle. But knowing Aaron Davidson wasn't behind her—well, that was a blow.

"Because of you," Angelica added.

She smiled sweetly at Angelica before turning her attention back to Aaron. "I think it would be best if you just spoke plainly. Otherwise this is a waste of my time."

If she stayed remote and chilly, she might get through this. She couldn't stop to think about the cost of putting herself in that place over and over again for the last month. Not then.

"We've prepared a generous severance package. Let's call it a sabbatical to the public so it will appear you've left for personal reasons. After all, that's not so very far from the truth, is it?" Aaron's gaze skittered away for a moment and she successfully kept her lip from curling. Her muscles burned from holding herself together.

The nausea shifted to a cold, numb emptiness.

"You're terminating me? A named partner in a firm you all know I built. Based on what?"

"You did not disclose your . . . nationality to us. This is a direct violation of your partnership agreement." Paul stuttered the first part.

"My *nationality* is American. I was born here in Chicago, to my mother, who was also born here. In fact, my mother's family has been here eight generations."

Aaron sent a glare in Paul's direction. "Of course you are. To put it bluntly, you're in violation of several clauses in your contract. Your behavior has led to a stampede of our top clients. You're costing us money each day you're still on the letterhead."

"My *behavior*. And how so?" They would say it. She would not simply crawl out of there and let them make her feel ashamed. This was bigotry plain and simple.

"You're one of them and you never said! For god's sake, you're an abomination and you had no business thinking you'd be allowed to stay here with what you are!" Angelica's face was red by the time she finished.

"Allowed? One of whom?"

"You're a goddamned witch! How can we trust you now?"

"That is more than enough, Angelica." Aaron's mouth was in a hard line as he glared at the other woman.

Molly looked to Aaron. "More than enough? Please, Aaron, you can get mad that she says it, but by going along with this, you're giving in to it. As far as I can see, you all think it but she's the only one who has the guts to say it. As for your charge? My behavior has not changed. My *behavior* is to get up at five, exercise, come to work where I spend ten to twelve hours each day doing my job. And then I go home. There is nothing in my *behavior* that could be considered a violation of my agreement with the firm." She could add some new things to that routine like funerals, being hassled by the cops, being outed by human supremacist groups. Good times.

Aaron heaved a sigh. "The negative attention you've garnered because of your . . . whatever you'd call it, status, identity, has impacted the bottom line of the firm."

"To be clear, because of my genetics, something I've kept private because it was none of your business, is the reason I'm being fired. Or rather, because I did not give in to the blackmail of the hate group who finally outed me after stalking me, my friends and family, I'm to be terminated from this firm. You're firing me because of who I am. Which, by the way is who I was two weeks ago. Two months ago when you had me on your boat, a boat I remind you that you were able to buy after the success of a campaign I created."

Aaron's face colored. "You have been an integral part of this firm. I'll be the first one to state that. I hate what they've done to you. I'm sorry for it. But this is business."

The last three weeks had gone by in a sickening haze. She'd gotten that proverbial late night call, telling her the man she'd considered her father had simply disappeared and was presumed dead. Not only that, but his oldest daughter, Molly's best friend, sister and the girl who'd taught Molly how to put on eyeliner, had also disappeared.

Worse, then came the insanity of the reaction from humans as the world of the Others had been exposed.

Little by little, everything she'd known and counted on to keep her anchored and safe had been stolen from her. Funerals were a weekly occurrence. The human-only hate groups had begun to agitate and turn the fear the humans had into rage. Her clients, people she'd known and worked with for years had begun to ease away. There'd been write-in campaigns to get her fired. Her work suffered. Her home had been vandalized multiple times. Several of her neighbors had put up anti-Other signs in their yards and would ignore her, or worse, call her names as she left for work each day.

Work at the public relations firm she had built with Aaron

was the one thing she'd counted on, even as her clients had turned skittish in the previous weeks.

That internal wall she'd built inside began to crumble and she saw clearly for the first time in a very long time.

"*Business?* Your giving in to bigots who'd be siccing dogs on small children for daring to use the whites-only drinking fountain is *just business*?"

"It's not the same." But Aaron didn't hold her gaze.

"It *is* the same. Just because you want to be able to celebrate your bigotry and call it something else doesn't mean anyone with an actual brain should allow you to do it. If you're ballsy enough to do it, be ballsy enough to call it what it is. Own it like an adult, but don't expect me to shuffle off in shame because *I'm* not the one who should be ashamed. You all should be. I have done nothing wrong. In fact, of all of us sitting here at this table, as we're talking business and all, I'm the one who pays the bills. I'm the one who brings in clients."

Paul didn't meet her gaze. "This is uncomfortable for us all. I don't see why we can't remain civil."

"I'm sure you don't consider the fact that you're firing me because I'm a witch to be uncivil. But I do. And as such, I only give respect where it's due. And none of you deserve it."

"Don't you at least want to see the details of your severance? We're trying to take care of you. Even in these difficult times." Aaron pushed a piece of paper at her.

"You're not trying to take care of me. You're trying to cast me off because of my genetics. This is not acceptable. You know this, Aaron. Even if Angelica is too greedy and stupid, you know this. Even Paul knows this."

Molly didn't touch the paper but she saw the figures on the first page. Enough money to get her through the next year or so. Help her start her own firm, or relocate. Still, it was money to shut her up after they cast her out.

But the walls were down and all she felt was anger. No, it was past anger now. She was into rage territory and she was seeing things very clearly.

"You should send these to my attorney. He'll be in touch later this morning." She stood, brushing her skirt to rid herself of the wrinkles. She'd never let them know how hurt she was. She was better than every single person in that room. And she'd never let them forget it.

Aaron attempted a charming frown. "You can't mean to fight this. It'll only bring more negative attention to the firm."

He was quite fortunate she didn't go with her instinct to slap his face for that. "You're truly going to sit there—in a chair *I* chose—and tell me I should accept your bigotry like a good little second-class citizen to save you embarrassment? You're out of your mind."

"Be reasonable, Molly. You built this, as you've said. Would you really tear it down? For what?"

"For what?" She blinked at him, so incredulous it was a wonder she didn't start laughing hysterically. She felt her power deep in her belly and panicked for a moment that she'd do something she didn't plan. That would be very bad.

So, instead of going all Carrie on them and setting the place on fire, she took a deep breath and centered herself, just as Rosa had taught her all those years ago. Once she'd gotten her power under control again, she squared her shoulders and glared. "I'm defending myself against a completely unwarranted attack on my person. And for what? Because I'm a witch? What if I had brown skin? Or my religion was different? That's not acceptable so why should this be? And why on earth would I stand for it? Do you think I built this place so small-minded hatemongers could simply shove me out and reap my profits? You have another think coming if you believe I'll simply pack my office up and go quietly."

She'd been utterly and completely numb for weeks. Now she was awake and they'd better run.

The bitterness and hate rolled off Angelica in waves. "You can't win and you know it. Now that we know about you and your kind, we'll make sure you can't."

Molly smiled at Angelica and then over at Aaron. "See? Just business."

Molly wouldn't give anyone the pleasure of rushing away. She turned her back on that sorry trio and walked to her office on shaky legs.

Her assistant was waiting for her there, her features expectant, then falling when she caught sight of Molly's demeanor.

"Is it true? Oh my god, it is." Paige threw her hands up as she began to mutter and pace. "Those assholes!"

Well, this was at least better than the last reception she got so Molly eased into her chair to watch her assistant of five years pace and bitch about the other partners.

Molly needed to be doing something. Anything. She grabbed her phone. "I need to call Jim. Keep the bad words to a minimum." Paige snorted as Molly dialed her attorney's office and was put right though.

She laid the entire story out for him as Paige plopped into a nearby chair and gawked.

He asked a few questions as they went and when it was all over he sighed. "You're the third client this month who's been terminated for their status."

She knew it had been happening nationwide to lots of Others. Rosa, her foster mother, still reeling from the death of a child and her husband, had been asked to retire early from her job teaching middle school. Though *asked* was a nice term for the pressure they laid on her to get out. Molly's biological mother, a human, had been harassed by groups of students under the flag of PURITY. PURITY, who proclaimed to be about love and safety all while digging through trash and turning people's lives upside down by outing them, they way they had with Molly. They even had a television show and a nationally syndicated column called *Know Your Enemy* where they published lists of names of Others. They may as well be wearing white sheets; it was the same thing.

"This is a gray area, but I'm working on it with some other civil rights attorneys across the country. I'll get something to Aaron by day's end. Do you . . . are you sure you even want to stay?"

"How can I let them get away with this? If I walk away, I'm saying it's all right!" She knew that she didn't want to work with any of these people ever again. But there were principles in play here. And this was her business, damn it.

"I can get more money out of them to get you out the door. I can probably work it so they have to use a different name. As part of your separation agreement. Even if I win, and I don't know if I can, do you want to be there with them?" Jim paused, she knew, looking for the right words. "I'm sorry. You've suffered a lot over the last several weeks. I just want you to know that no matter your choice here, I'm on your side."

She heaved a sigh and fought back nausea. She wanted to go home and hide under the covers. Wanted to pretend the sickness of heart and soul hadn't beaten her down.

"Take some time. You don't have to make a decision right this moment."

"Time." She snorted. "Why should I have to? It's unacceptable. They're trying to push me out for nothing, acting like I've committed a crime or something."

"You haven't done anything wrong, Molly. You know it and so do they. I'll fight for you as hard as I can. But you also know you're not going to have anything to do but ruminate over this until you make yourself sick. Just get out of there a while and make it about yourself. Let me do the obsessing, okay? It's my job."

Molly blinked back tears of frustration. "I don't have much to do here today. My clients, the biggest ones, have fired me."

That cut deep. Some of them had cloaked it in a bunch of talk about how they couldn't afford the controversy in this economic and political climate. This after she'd saved *them* more than once. These were people who she'd had dinner with, had spent time in their homes.

"Go home. I'll have something messengered over to your place in an hour or so. I'll lay out all your options and you can think them over. I'll keep you updated."

She hung up and looked to Paige, whose anger soothed some of Molly's agitation.

"This is dumb. They can't do this. Who freaking cares if you're a witch or not? What does it have to do with how you do your job?"

Molly picked up an award statuette. She'd won it only three months before. Three months before when the world was different. She slid it into the large tote next to her desk.

"Fair or not, it's happening all over the place." She grabbed some of the photographs from the credenza. A shot of Molly with her foster family, her *magickal* family, she supposed, at her college graduation. One of her with her biological mother and her maternal grandparents when she'd accepted an award a few years back. Memories of a different world. She placed them in the tote.

"Are you really going to let them do this? None of these dicks would even have a place to work if it weren't for you."

"It makes me sad to think they're going to drive this firm into the ground. All for what? My witch cooties? They can't catch it, for heaven's sake."

"It's Angelica. She's been agitating everyone with every single newspaper article and Internet thing she can find, true or not. Like when your sister-in-law sends you mass forwards filled with things a simple visit to snopes.com could tell her were fakes."

"I'm sure she's a card-carrying member of PURITY. But that doesn't matter. Aaron is with her. As is Paul. That's three of four partners." She realized they could, and *would*, be able to terminate her contract. The knowledge was awful and unbearably sad. A whole part of her life was being taken away from her.

Sad or not, she sure wasn't going to go down without a fight. Or a financial settlement that was far more representative of her value to the firm. She'd start over if she had to, but she'd do it with the money she earned. And they'd have to change the firm's name.

Still, Paige wasn't as fortunate to have all the options Molly did. "Look, I can probably work on Aaron's sense of duty and get you on with one of the others. We approved a new-hire slot just a few weeks ago. You're terrific and they'll need you after I leave."

"You're not going to let them run you out of town like a

criminal, Molly. I'm not going to let you. Hell, you can get your stakes back and start a new firm, this one working for Others. I'll happily work for you there."

Molly paused, resting her hip on the desk and thought about that idea.

"Oh, girl. I can see you're taking that seriously." Paige sat nearby. "Want me to take some notes? Call some people? We can work out of your place for a while until we get a new office."

She smiled at Paige, who was also six months pregnant and couldn't afford to jump ship and risk losing her insurance and the healthy retirement plan she'd begun to build.

"Even if I did that, you're not in any position to up and leave this job. You need the benefits. For the baby and for Mark too." Paige's husband had been laid off from his job four months before and had been looking for a new one ever since. He had some health problems, which made any risky moves by Paige even more precarious.

"You can't possibly think I'd choose this place without you in it. After the way they're dumping you? My parents raised me right."

"Yes, they did. And I appreciate the solidarity. More than you can know. But, Paige, you're pregnant. Your husband is unemployed. I can't offer you health care, even if I did start a new firm. Hang on until you have the baby and you've used your leave and all that stuff. By then, well, at the very least I can get you on somewhere else."

Pragmatism was something she couldn't get around. Molly shrugged. "It isn't right. Not at all. I'm going to fight it, but in the end, I don't think it's going to make a difference. Oh, I'll get more money from them probably, but they won't have to keep me. And they won't. Right now, all across the country Others are in a gray area legally. And there are plenty of people who will use that."

Paige's pretty face fell as she accepted it. "This is dumb. I hate them."

Molly laughed without humor. "Yeah, me too. Now, I'm

going to take some of this stuff home. But before that, let's go to a late breakfast. You have my permission to take the rest of the day off."

WHEN she and Paige came around the corner, Aaron was waiting for her at the elevators.

"You going to check my bag to make sure I'm not stealing pens?"

"Give me a break, Mol."

"Don't." She held her hand up. "You don't get to call me that. I'm leaving for the day. I have the vacation for it. But I'm not quitting, or saying I'm going on sabbatical. That's not going to happen."

"Why don't you and I go to lunch and talk? Away from here."

The audacity! "If you really wanted that, you wouldn't have ambushed me here. You'd have spoken to me in advance."

"It was in the conjecture stage. And then Bright and Cleen called. I'm sorry." His gaze skated to Paige, hindered by her presence to say anything else.

Good.

The elevator dinged and the doors slid open. She moved to walk past and he grabbed her arm. "Molly, please. Be reasonable. You can't just end a ten-year friendship. I had to make a difficult choice. You should understand that."

"I don't understand it at all. I don't understand you and I will grieve, along with a boatload of other things, that you cared so little about our friendship and this firm that you'd give in to this absurd demand. It's terrorism, Aaron, and you know it. You do this for them and what will they ask next? Who else might not be . . . *enough* for them? Hm? Talk about slippery slopes."

She yanked her arm back.

"My attorney will be contacting you by day's end." She let the doors slide closed.

Chapter 2

"I got fired today."

Molly hung her coat up and turned to her mother, who stood at the table, pouring a glass of wine.

Eliza's eyes went wide and then narrowed dangerously. "What?"

"Partners' meeting. They ambushed me before I even had a sip of my coffee. I go in and they tell me I've violated my agreement by not disclosing my *nationality* and for bringing negative attention. Risking clients."

Eliza held out the glass. "You need this more than I do."

Molly took several bracing sips.

Her mother waited until she'd done so before she continued. "Tell me the rest."

Eliza Ryan was the strongest person Molly had ever met. Her mother was her greatest hero and role model.

"Well, you know PURITY outed me two days ago. Apparently this morning Bright and Cleen called. Said they'd dump the firm if they didn't dump me. I'm told I'm an abomination."

Eliza's brow rose. "I can guess who said that. Does Angelica still have a stick wedged up her butt? Puritans, the whole lot of them. Oh, you were just fine to get them out of trouble a month ago. But now?" Her mother sniffed before gulping her own wine.

"Not everyone is acting that way. Paige volunteered to quit and follow me to a new firm if I started it. She threatened to quit anyway. Don't worry, I told her not to. She's pregnant and she needs the benefits. It wouldn't make a difference to them if she quit and it would only hurt her. Plus the Troys— you know my neighbors with the house across the street? Anyway, they came over when I got home today. With a big basket of baked goods. She hugged me and said it would be all right."

With that, the tears came. Because it wouldn't be.

Eliza put her glass down and moved to gather Molly up into her arms. "Let it all go. This isn't right. It's not fair and it's not even American, for heaven's sake."

"I d-don't think things are going to be all right. Everything is different. Anthony is dead. Emma is dead. The guy who did my yard? Turns out he was a shifter. He's dead too. I don't think I'll be able to stave off being fired. My firm. I built that firm, damn it." Anthony Falco had been a father to her, Emma her sibling in everything but blood and she missed each one of them every damned day.

Her mother rubbed a palm up and down her back. Up and down, over and over, just like she did when Molly got sick or when she got dumped.

"*I'm* not dead. Nana Ryan isn't dead. Rosa isn't and she needs you now more than ever. We all need you, Molly. If you can't stay at the firm, you'll do something else. It's who you are. I'll help you in any way I can."

"You have your own problems."

Her mother snorted. "Thank goodness for tenure. The rest of the faculty—for the most part anyway—are supporting me. I'll get through this. Don't worry about me."

"Of course I worry about you! This is happening to you because of me." Her mother was being persecuted for no other reason than being a parent to an Other. It was absurd and horrible and Molly felt responsible.

Her mother stepped back, holding Molly at arm's length. "*No*. This is happening because people are scared. And because people with no values are using that fear to whip them up into this frenzy that's wrecking everything. You are the best thing I've ever done. I won't let a bunch of small-minded bigots make you think anything else."

Her phone buzzed in her pocket. The song told her it was Rosa so Molly mopped up her face and answered.

"Hiya, Mom." Rosa Falco had come into Molly's life when she was thirteen. She'd been the one to teach Molly about the other side of her heritage. The magickal side. The Falco family had become hers too. So much so that she'd been calling Rosa *Mom* since she was fifteen.

Together with Eliza, they'd guided her, loved her and supported her. That her biological mother shared her daughter without any apparent jealousy was a testament to Eliza's strength and love. And a powerful reminder that no matter how much Molly had lost, she still had them.

"Turn on the television." Rosa's voice held a lot of anger.

"What? What's going on?" Molly found the remote and turned the television on as requested.

"Watch and call me back."

"Okay."

She sat, her mother at her side.

On the screen, Carlo Powers, the leader of PURITY, sat across from a news anchor, smiling. That smile made Molly curl her lip. A smiling fascist was still a fascist.

"Well yes, Bridget. We love *everyone* of course. But that doesn't mean we have to tolerate their behavior, or let them threaten our families."

"Heard that one before," her mother muttered.

"A few million times." Eliza reached out to take Molly's hand.

Bridget Patterson, the local network anchor, frowned. "Mr. Powers, there are those who say your group's weekly outing of different paranormals is only adding to the increase in violence in communities across the country. They say outing is dangerous for those you've exposed. Others have been fired as a result of your show. Attacked in some cases. How do you respond to that?"

He cocked his head, the mean shining in his eyes briefly. "These paranormals are abominations. They've lived among us for all this time secretly. They can't be trusted. Can you blame decent Americans for wanting to defend themselves against that?"

Molly's stomach heaved.

"This man is dangerous, Molly."

"No shit. Um, no crap." She grimaced. "Sorry."

"You get to use all the curse words for this sorry excuse for a human being. I'll write you a note."

On the television, Bridget soldiered on. "Is that what you call it? Defense? Yesterday in Kentucky a couple's store was burned to the ground. They lived above it and the doors were blocked from the outside so they couldn't get out. They managed to escape only because they jumped from a second-story window."

He spread his hands, still wearing that smile. "Of course that's wrong, Bridget. We at PURITY don't condone that sort of violence. I'm just saying that I'm siding with decent human beings who feel threatened by these creatures. Decent Americans, *human beings* who want to protect their children against monsters like werewolves. We dealt with them a few times in our history, it's only reasonable to expect we will again."

Loathing made Molly's lip curl. "Yeah, by drowning us or burning. Is he aiming for a new Inquisition?"

Eliza squeezed Molly's hand. "Don't joke. This guy is dangerous."

And he'd been the one who outed her. This filth sat there with his smile talking about decency this and that and he'd been personally responsible for the loss of her job. Clearly they owned two different dictionaries when his definition of *decent* meant people got killed and had their businesses burned down.

It went on like this for another minute or two before the

interview was over and Molly sat back, finishing her wine in one gulp.

Her mother shook her head. "You can't stay at your house anymore. Stay here with me. It's too dangerous now."

"I'd say the same of you. It's not just Others being targeted." Molly flipped the channel and paused on a different news show. "Isn't that the witch who runs Clan Owen?"

The interviewer tapped a pen on his knee a moment. "There are those who say the paranormals are dangerous. That you've kept hidden because you have an agenda."

The Owen, as the witch who led Clan Owen was called, took a deep breath and maintained her calm. "I can't speak for all Others, any more than you can speak for all humans, but I can tell you most of us kept our identities secret in fear of this exact reaction. If protecting my people is an agenda, I suppose those making such claims are right."

The interviewer smirked. "Meriel, if I can call you that, werewolves came out several years ago. Some of the other shifters have been making that slow process. They've been all right."

"Ms. Owen is fine." Meriel smiled and Molly snorted a laugh. "*All right* is a relative term. While there haven't been the same sorts of murders we've seen recently, they've faced job, health care and housing discrimination. Unfortunately they've also been the targets of hate groups like PURITY as well. The shifters who led the original coming out have been a model of how to do it, but they've not been unscathed."

They were sidetracking her, Molly realized. "They're muddying her message."

"She needs a public relations whiz, clearly." Her mother gave her the side eye.

And then she sat back as Meriel Owen continued to be directed off the topic only to fruitlessly try to get back on track. "She totally does."

GAGE stood off to the side, gaze flitting around the studio. Meriel had received a death threat just that morning. He'd advised against the appearance, but Meriel did what she wanted. Especially when she felt it was important.

She'd finished her interview and he cleared the exit, checking in with the people posted outside to bring the car around.

"You ready?" He took position in front of her, blocking anything that might come their way.

"Dumbasses," she muttered. "Yes, yes, let's go."

Lark was there as well, and she got them all out to the newly armored car Meriel and Dominic now had to use.

"I don't think that guy likes you much." Lark meant the interviewer who'd treated Meriel like she was overreacting, while simultaneously making her feel as if it was the fault of Others for remaining in the closet about their identities.

They drove through a large protest of PURITY members, who banged on the car as they did. *Decent* of them.

"He was photographed at a PURITY fund-raiser just a few days ago. So no, I doubt he likes me much. Which makes us even. Because I think he's a scum-sucking pig."

Dominic Bright, Meriel's husband, grunted, kissing his wife's hand as he kept his gaze on the fracas outside.

Lark gave him a look when Gage moved a hand to the window toggle. He really wouldn't have rolled it down, but he wanted to.

"Ignore them." Meriel shook her head.

"I'm ignoring my impulses, Boss."

Lark laughed a moment but quit on an intake of breath. She'd been shot multiple times just a few weeks before as they'd fought off the Magister and its minions. So had Gage. Lark had been in the hospital for several days and was still healing. She liked telling everyone she was too stubborn to die and too pressed to let anyone stop her from doing her job.

Gage believed every word.

There was a counter-protest just across the street, which gave him hope, even in such a dark time. Not all humans were bad and wanted to kill them. The humans out there protesting in support of Others could be the majority if they played it right. But it was hard to play anything when every single Other on the planet had lost someone when the Magister manifested itself. Hard to be smart and rational when they were getting firebombed and picketed and attacked.

PURITY had picketed his uncle's funeral. The thought of it still outraged him.

Meriel spoke again, her voice strong and sure. "We need to continue a presence out there, keep going. Keep our message in the public eye. We're going to get a few hits over it. But that interviewer in there can't scare me."

Like so many others, Meriel had suffered a loss due to the Magister. Her mother, an incredibly powerful witch and the former Owen, had been assassinated just moments after Edwina had aided in shoving the Magister out of their world. Meriel had been trying to get her life back on track, but it'd been difficult when all this external stuff kept happening. When she had to go to funerals and meet with Clan members who'd been outed and faced problems keeping jobs and relationships.

Gage had been giving self-defense courses, along with Lark, to their membership. First it had been to protect against the bands of mages who'd been bent on stealing their magick. But that had been before the Magister. Now it was also about protecting themselves from violence and intimidation from the humans like those in PURITY.

And they'd grown more adept at using their power. All of them had. His powers seemed to have sharpened. What he'd been good at before, he was excellent at now. Desperation could do that, he supposed. Still, it seemed to be something many other witches were experiencing. Again, he wasn't sure if it was that desperation gave them all a focus they hadn't had before, or if it was some odd side effect of the Magister's manifestation in their world.

He squeezed his hands into fists. Needing the sharp pain of violence and not having an outlet. "I don't know what they expect. We're just living our lives, for fuck's sake." Maybe he should shoot a few fireballs at them, just to give them what they seemed to crave so much.

"It's fear. Fear makes people irrational. They're scared

and people like Carlo Powers manipulate that fear to their advantage." Meriel sighed.

"Whatever it is, it's got to be dealt with. They're not going to find it as easy to kill us this time." Lark's face darkened as she looked out the window.

Gage understood that sentiment very well.

Lark had them stop at the Owen offices to drop her off before he continued on to escort Meriel and Dominic home.

Once they'd arrived at Meriel's, Gage did a quick check with the guards posted full time, before heading out to do a sweep of his own around their property. Seattle hadn't been nearly as bad as other cities across the world. While Meriel and Dominic had had to deal with threats and pickets, there'd been no overt violent acts or attacks on their home. That was something, he supposed.

Still, Meriel's father had set ward upon ward, all around the property. It was a magickal Fort Knox and it had given him something to do as he'd grieved over the loss of his wife.

In addition to magickal protections, there were snipers stationed strategically as well.

They would not simply lie down and let themselves be victimized. No one was going to harm Meriel and Dominic, not without a great deal of blood and pain.

He checked in one last time before leaving and heading back to the office.

He wasn't surprised to find Lark was waiting for him there. "You need some downtime."

For a tiny witch with blue hair, she still managed to be authoritative. And she knew what she was talking about.

"Says the witch who is here as much as I am. I'm going home soon. I just wanted to do one last check-in."

She looked him over carefully. "You're here all the time. And when you're not here, you're on a patrol. Take some personal time. God knows you need it. Hook up with someone. Sex is a good way to blow off steam. I know . . . I know you've not been with anyone since Rose left. It doesn't have to mean anything. But everyone needs some affection."

Rose. He snorted. They'd barely even started to date when the Magister had . . . happened. It wasn't that he was heartbroken at her absence. She'd bailed, left town out of fear of what might come. But the guilt of her being right echoed through him.

"This is *not* me being heartbroken over Rose. In case you hadn't noticed, things got real around here lately. I don't have time for fucking. Casual or no."

Lark rolled her eyes at his tone and it made him laugh. She didn't take his shitty moods seriously. But she listened to him, was a damned good friend and someone he was proud to have at his back.

She was also good at seeing right through any crap. Which meant he got away with little when it came to her. It made him miss his old partner Nell a little less.

She tucked a pen behind her ear. "Your only stress relief can't be this job. It's going to eat you alive. And then they win. Right?"

He shrugged. "I'll probably stop by Heart of Darkness later on tonight. Maybe you can line up some suitable company for me."

She laughed. Her soon-to-be husband, Simon, was part owner of the Other-centric nightclub. Since the Magister, the club had expanded the small Others section at the back to the entirety of the space.

"Ha. I've got enough to do with this job and handling a control-freak alpha male. I can't be your pimp too. Anyway, you're too pretty to need any help."

The club was full every single night. Turns out all this drama and threat was good for business. Many Others in the community were driven to be out and public, as if to say they were part of the city and would continue to be. A celebration of life. Some came to gawk at the spectacle of the pickets outside. Most just came to drink and dance and hook up.

"How's the new security protocol going?"

All the attention had been good for business but also hell on security. They'd had to add more bouncers and the clan had to send out witches to place wards on what sort of magick could be worked there and by whom.

But none of that stopped firebombs and bullets. So the bouncers had to wear body armor and carry weapons themselves.

He was so over being on the defensive. Over being threatened. It was time for them to turn the tables. Others weren't weak. They should stop acting like it.

Chapter 3

MOLLY had been advised to stay clear of the office that morning as her attorney and the firm's attorney had been going back and forth. She'd accepted, after much discussion with her mother and her lawyer, that she had no real chance of keeping her spot at the firm. But that didn't mean she wasn't going to make them pay for it.

That was fine because she'd made a decision last night after she left her mother's house.

Really, she'd decided after she'd driven around for hours, trying to pretend she wasn't scared simply to go into her home, worried about what might be waiting for her. Even when she got home she'd checked all her smoke detectors to be sure they were working and checked her locks for the dozenth time.

The numbness she'd felt since that call from Rosa telling her Anthony and Emma were dead had been washed away by righteous anger. Anger at her termination, at losing what she'd built herself, at losing the life she'd had before the Magister had taken it all from her. And what the Magister had left, the humans she'd grown up among had been working day and night to destroy.

It was time to stand up and fight. To use her gifts to help her people. For a long time it had been that she'd been living a human life for the most part. But now she had to stand up for the other part of her identity.

It had been a while since she'd woken up with such a sense of purpose and it felt good. She took that as a good omen as she'd managed to charm her way into getting the direct line to Meriel Owen's office.

People didn't really understand the benefits of manners. Being gracious, having manners and treating others the way you'd like to be treated garnered you a lot in life. A lot more than rudeness or clumsy attempts at bribery.

She picked up the phone and made the call.

"Clan Owen, Meriel Owen's office. How may I help you?"

"My name is Molly Ryan and I'd very much like to speak with Meriel Owen."

The assistant's voice went very cool. "And what is this concerning?"

"Public relations. As in, I think I have something to offer Clan Owen."

"As you can imagine, Ms. Ryan, we get many such calls each day. Clan Owen has no need for your services. If you'd like, you can mail your résumé in."

Secretaries were key. Molly had a great deal of respect for the men and women who ran the lives of their bosses. Espccially the part where they kept away any wastes of that boss's time.

But if she couldn't get around this one, Molly didn't deserve the job anyway. Besides, it had been at least three or four months since she'd had a challenge like this one.

Five minutes later Molly found herself speaking to Meriel Owen and laying out her backstory.

"So they fired you? Really? God, that makes me so mad. This is your firm and they just tossed you out?"

"The price of entering into a partnership is that the others can toss you out if you break your contract. Of course, I tend to take exception to the idea that being a witch is akin to being a drug mule or sending harassing texts to clients."

Molly sobered and changed the subject.

"I saw your interview last night. You're good in front of a camera."

Meriel laughed. "There's a *but* coming."

"If that was all you needed to do, you'd be fine. More than fine, actually. You're mediagenic. Intelligent. Articulate. You're relatable and yet you're also aspirational. This is all good."

"Mediagenic? Aspirational?"

"You look good in front of the camera and people admire you enough to want to be like you. But what happens when these sorts of interviews are done is that you're dragged off message by having to respond to idiotic things. It muddies the point, which is what they mean to do, as *their* point is usually stupid. The interviewer had an agenda, so he pulled you off yours."

"What's the solution? And you'd do this then? Be the face?"

Molly was glad to hear the hesitation in Meriel's voice. She wouldn't want to work for someone who'd just say yes without some back up of who Molly was and what she could do. "I don't know enough about your organization there to say for sure. I'd need to dig in, get a feel for you and your clan before I could make any recommendations."

"Would you be willing to come out for a face-to-face interview? We'd need to check your references and your background first. I've been trying to figure out how to handle this better, but it's been spinning out of control faster than any of us could deal with. You might be what we need."

"I can come out, yes. I'll email my résumé to your assistant so you can start that."

"I already think you're pretty amazing to have gotten past her the way you did. She's pretty formidable."

"Part of my charm. I can do that with the media too." Just a fact. Confidence was a positive as long as it wasn't a brag.

"This is more and more tempting. Yes, email that information to my assistant and she'll get back to you with some times for you to come out."

"I'm going to suggest you do this as soon as possible. New things happen every hour it seems. You need to get a handle on this before it spins out of control and you're in the weeds." She'd already sent the email along with some links to her television and other media work.

"You're correct. Expect a call by the end of the week and if you can get us in your schedule to come out then, we'd appreciate it."

Molly hung up and didn't quite know what to do with herself so she headed over to Rosa's.

IT was hard still, to pull into that driveway and see Anthony's truck off to the side with a tarp over it. To know he wouldn't be in his workshop in the garage or out back working on his garden.

Everything was so different now.

AJ, the only other surviving member of the Falco family, met Molly at the door with a hug and a kiss to the cheek. "Good to see you. Come on in, she'll be happy to see you."

Rosa was in the kitchen, her favorite room in the house. She looked up from the counter where she'd been rolling out dough and smiled. "Hi there, doll. Come give me a hug."

Molly did, filching a slice of apple afterward. "Pie. Yum."

"Good thing you came over. I haven't been able to get used to having two less people eating my pies. I make too much." A cloud passed over Rosa's features briefly, before she went back to work.

"Not like it's a chore to eat pie. So"—Molly hopped up on a chair—"I called Meriel Owen today and offered her my services as a media relations person."

Rosa looked up, surprised. "Look at you. What did she say?"

"She asked me for my résumé and all that stuff and said

if it checked out to expect to come out later in the week to be interviewed."

"You're going to move to Seattle? Just like that?" AJ poured himself a cup of coffee and got one for his mom and Molly as well.

"Not just like that. Not really. I've been out of sorts for a while and then yesterday the other partners kicked me out of the firm. I've got an attorney fighting it, but really, to be honest, it's going to be about how much money they throw at me to go away. My life here is . . . well, it's not what it was before. And I think I can make a difference with Owen."

"I think you can too. But I worry. That's a lot of exposure to be on television as an official Other spokesperson." AJ shrugged.

"I lived a long time not really hiding that I was a witch, but not necessarily waving a banner about it either. That got me nowhere. No, that's not true. It got me slapped and humiliated by my partners and watching, horrified, as humans like PURITY have set out to destroy me and mine. What's left of us anyway. I'm mad, AJ. I'm mad and sick and tired."

He blew out a breath. "I've been talking to Mom about moving someplace with a clan. The witches in clan territories are more organized. Safer. Owen is as big as it gets in the States."

"Yeah, together with Gennessee, they control from northern Mexico up to British Columbia. I've never been to Seattle, but I researched it a bit. Wetter than here, but less snow. I don't know. I guess I feel like it's my time to do something right and meaningful. I don't want all these deaths to mean nothing. Or worse, to have people like Carlo Powers use that to do us more harm."

Rosa threw up the evil eye. "Pig."

"Yes. That interview last night, my goodness. I should send him a thank-you note for that last push into this decision."

Rosa grabbed her attention and held her gaze. "You have so much potential. Your gifts are strong. Use them to put that creature in his place. This is a good choice for you. I'll miss you. Who knows, maybe AJ will convince me at last and we'll come out there too. You were meant for greatness. I know this."

Molly knew that coming here would make her feel better. Knew Rosa would say exactly what she needed to hear.

"If I do move, I'm going to miss you guys so much."

AJ snorted. "Sweetness, you're going to be too busy saving our world to miss us."

GAGE looked up when Meriel knocked on his door.

"Hey there. What's up?"

"I just had an interesting call from a witch who lives in Chicago. She's some PR whiz." Meriel held up a sheaf of papers. "I've got her résumé and some assorted information about what she's done. Television, radio, other media and all that stuff. She called to offer her services. And if what I'm seeing here is on the up-and-up, she's exactly what we need right now."

"You want me to run a background check?"

"Indeed. Can you rush this? I'd like to get this wrapped up so we can get her out here and on the job. I mean, I'll interview her first, obviously. But I spoke to her on the phone for about half an hour. I like what I see so far. She's charming but no nonsense."

Gage held back a smile. Of course Meriel would like that. She was the same. But he'd run a thorough check because he'd had enough being taken advantage of. Their clan wouldn't be hurt by anyone if he could help it.

"I'm on it now."

Meriel paused. "Are you all right?"

He looked up from the papers he'd been given. "I could ask you the same question."

"My answer would be no. How about yours?"

He snorted. "No. Not really. This isn't the way I'd imagined finally revealing ourselves."

"Three weeks. Dozens of funerals. And I've got to deal with all this stupid stuff and it makes me crazy. I want to scream at the interviewer, hey asshole, I lost my mother, what is *your* problem?"

Gage ached for her. Hell for everyone he knew.

"Yeah. I hear you. I hope this PR lady works out because it'd make me a hell of lot more comfortable if you weren't the one out there all the time."

Meriel's smile was slightly sad. "I'd be lying if I denied the appeal of being out of the spotlight on this. Right now with all this stuff going on, our legal stuff is overwhelming. We're working with the ACLU and some other human rights groups to deal with all the employment and housing discrimination stuff. But I'd prefer to be out there fighting that fight too instead of dealing with asshat news reporters."

"We don't have to talk to them, you know. Fuck what they want."

Meriel shrugged. "We don't have to, no. But this issue isn't going away. In fact it's getting worse. We need to control the message or we're screwed."

He sighed. "All right. I'm going to get on this. I'll let you know what I find out."

Background checks were pretty rote by that point. He knew back doors into the nationwide system and into several major city and state databases. It didn't take him long to begin to build a folder on Ms. Ryan.

Molly Ryan was an interesting woman. If she was what she claimed to be, she'd be a boon to Owen. Graduated top of her class in every class he could find. Intelligent, clearly. Raised by a single mother who happened to be an economics professor at the University of Chicago. No arrest records. No record of who her father was either.

That part burned in his gut. What kind of man just walked away? Did he know, Gage wondered? Maybe the mother never told him.

He paged through the links she'd sent and those he'd dug up on his own. Awards. He was able to get her financials.

She made a lot of money. Saved it. Donated regularly to several charities. Mentored college students. Maybe she hated kittens or something.

It appeared that she'd lost several people she was close to in the aftermath of the Magister.

Hadn't they all?

She'd also been outed in a spectacular fashion by the PURITY people just several days before. That filled him with rage. These PURITY people were garbage. They didn't care who they hurt.

By the time he left many hours later, his respect of Molly Ryan had grown immensely. If everything else panned out overnight and she came out and Meriel and Dominic liked her, she'd be a great asset.

Chapter 4

MOLLY had gotten off the plane, headed to the hotel and channel surfed for three hours before finally getting herself relaxed enough to get to sleep. Things were so . . . she didn't know how to describe it. Anxious maybe. She wanted to get started on something. Hated not doing anything.

Still, when she woke up and her breakfast showed up, she began to focus and get ready. Having a purpose was something she found soothing. Doing her hair and makeup, getting dressed—it had felt as if she was putting on armor.

The walk from the hotel was as quick as the instructions she'd looked up online had said. Seattle's downtown core made sense. Molly liked it. Loved all the little coffee shops and bakeries. Loved the hustle and bustle of commuters as they landed and began to stream toward office buildings.

There was a protest and a counter-protest outside the Federal Building. But plenty of police presence kept it out of riot territory. At least during the time she'd walked past. A lot of angry faces and hateful signs, as she'd seen elsewhere. That part made her sad. But it hadn't made her fearful. And the counter-protest had been sizable. Larger than the anti-Other protest. That had cheered her.

The air was clean and her magick lay in her belly, so easily called. Not something she'd experienced in the middle of a city before. Maybe it was about the ground here being held by a clan so long. She didn't know. Didn't know a lot of things about this part of her identity.

That put her off balance a little. She liked being in control. Knowledge meant control. But at the same time, she found herself eager to learn.

The building the Owen offices were in had heightened security around it. Molly hadn't expected that. But she supposed, once they became known, they'd be a target. It also indicated that Owen had plenty of money to do that. She hoped that was a sign of stability.

She could feel the wards. Something she'd never actually experienced before. But they seemed to recognize her magick. She'd ponder that later when she had the time to do so.

She walked through two separate security checkpoints. One with a metal detector. Her bag had been searched and before they let her in the building they called up and made sure she truly did have an appointment. She'd also been told that there were spells cast to dampen the ability of other witches to use their magick while on Owen property. The guard had said it by rote, not asking if she was a witch or not.

The one who searched her last had her wait while he called yet another to escort her inside. Her escort was armed and no-nonsense and used a key to get them up to the clan's reception floor, leaving her at check in.

"Ms. Ryan, someone should be with you shortly. Can I get you something to drink while you wait?" The receptionist smiled her way. It was a business smile. A little wary at the edges. Remote.

"I had a latte already. I'm afraid if I drink any more coffee I'll start bouncing off the walls." Molly smiled, genuine and warm.

The receptionist relaxed, as Molly had intended. "I hear

you. Meriel loves her coffee extra strong, so you probably would get a big jolt."

"Always a plus in a job interview." She looked out the wall of windows, over the city, and wondered if she'd be living there when this interview was over.

BY the time Meriel's assistant came to collect her, Molly had made a friend in the receptionist, Kelly. Kelly had given her a few tips. Nothing that would be considered oversharing, but it was helpful all the same.

The assistant pushed a door open after tapping on it. Everyone inside the room stood.

The power there stirred her own, calling to her magick. Molly put a hand on her belly a moment before stepping in totally.

"Please, Molly, do come in." A red-haired witch, no doubt Meriel Owen, moved in her direction, holding a hand out. Molly took it, liking the strong, efficient shake.

"Thank you. I'm Molly Ryan. It's very nice to meet you."

"Meriel Owen, and the pleasure is ours." She indicated the others in the room. "This is Dominic Bright. He's my husband and my bond-mate." A bond-mate was what Full Council witches had. Their sort of magickal other half and the person whose magick unlocked their full potential.

There were other introductions but Molly really sort of forgot them once Meriel pointed out the blond male with the wide shoulders and the wary gaze.

"Gage Garrity. He and Lark run the Hunter team together."

When he turned to focus on her, Molly's knees went a little weak. For long moments she was surprised at herself. She didn't get weak-kneed over most anything and certainly not a man.

But as men went, the one looking her over with nearly amber eyes was a fine, fine specimen. Broad-shouldered. His shirt stretched over his upper body, only highlighting the power that lay beneath. She was sure he'd have a narrow waist and flat belly. She didn't need to see him standing to know that. She also bet he had a nice butt.

Still, he probably called women *babe* and peed on the seat.

Meriel clearly wielded the power in the room, but she did it well. She leaned toward Molly, her fingers clasped loosely on the table. "So we've checked you out and know your background and experience. I'm not exaggerating to say we're all very impressed. But our number one question is why? You didn't really do your work for Others in the past. Why now?"

Molly looked around the table, meeting eyes with each and every witch there. It was a fair question and she wanted them to know what had changed for her. "I was raised in a human home. I didn't even know I was a witch until I was thirteen. In middle school one of my teachers, Rosa Falco, noticed and spoke to me after class. When she realized I had no idea what she was talking about, she met with my mother."

Molly held back a shrug and continued. "She and my mother came to an agreement. In the end, the Falcos became my second family. Rosa taught me how to use and control my magick. I spent many weekends at their home, went camping with them, learned how to embrace the other side of myself."

"But you never belonged to the coven there?" Dominic Bright wasn't accusatory in this, but it was clear he wanted to know why.

"No, I didn't. The Falcos did—do. I went to some coven events. I finished high school, then college and then I started working for a PR firm. I worked eighty hours a week. My leftover time was for sleeping and eating. I didn't feel it was necessary to join the coven. I'm a witch. I'm not ashamed of it. Neither did I feel like I had to wear it on my shirt like a button. It was a part of me, but it wasn't my banner."

Dominic nodded and she got the feeling her answer was what he was looking for.

"So why now then?"

"I got a call in the middle of the night. It was Rosa telling me her husband, the man I thought of as my father, had simply disappeared. And Emma, her oldest daughter and my sister, had also disappeared. It was some sort of creature or being and it had taken them. Over those first days we knew of others who'd been taken. So many.

"And then the backlash began. I'm trying to help Rosa and her son get through this and suddenly these bigots are showing up at my mother's office. My biological mother, I mean. She's a professor, though I expect you know that. Anyway, they know about me and they want *her* to resign. She kicked them out. But it was the beginning. They showed up at my office too. They knew about me. They'd dug around and because I'd never really hidden it, they had pictures of me at events with the Falcos and other witches. They threatened me with it. I assured them they didn't know me at all."

"You figured they'd leave you alone?" Gage's tone told her what he thought of that reaction.

"I figured they were attempting to blackmail me. I don't give in to terrorist threats. I don't give in to blackmail. I'm a witch; I never tried to hide it and I wasn't going to. My mistake was in believing my clients, people I'd worked with for years and years and had saved multiple times, would stand behind me. I believed the other partners in the firm I'd created would back me up. I made the money, after all. These clients were mine."

Gage watched her as the change came over her features. Just a brief glimpse. Pain. So much for them all. "And you were wrong."

She nodded. "I was wrong. I was outed on PURITY's *Know Your Enemy* show. They have a show now." She shook her head. "My clients all began to give in to the pressure and leave. And then they began to go around me to the other partners."

Molly sat back, her back straight, her gaze clear. "As I sat there, the people I'd helped support, some of them my friends, wanted me to slink away in shame because of what I was—well, I realized it was time to push back. And then I was at my mother's house and I saw Powers on television and my mom said something like how Others needed a good PR campaign and I realized yes, yes, we did."

Meriel nodded. "And we do."

Molly spoke again. "You do a fine job, first let me say that. As I said on the phone with you, you're smart and well spoken and you clearly know what you're talking about."

Meriel's smile widened. "Thank you. But I know my niche. I know what I'm good at. Before this mess I'd have been fine. But with the fever pitch now, well, we need a professional to get the message out there."

"It's a full-time job and you have far more things to do than just dealing with media. The biggest task will be to keep your message on target. There will be all sorts of side tangents to get sucked into. It's human nature. And before you know it, your three to five minutes are up and you didn't make your point."

Meriel nodded, frowning. "Yes. Frustrating."

"Media people know how to do this. They do it every day. Most of the time to keep people on task, but as you saw with the reporter interviewing you, sometimes they do it to knock you off message because they have an agenda. It takes someone who knows how to avoid those traps to get a message out."

"And you think you can do a better job? Even though you grew up as a human and didn't have much to do with our world?" One of the other members of the Full Council, Sami Ellis, asked. It was clear the woman had her doubts about Molly. Sami could be very intimidating so he supposed they'd see just what Molly Ryan was made of. "What makes you think an interloper can tell our story better than we can?"

Gage was impressed by the way Molly simply turned that perceptive gaze toward Sami. The question was rude; he caught sight of Meriel bristling. But Molly kept her cool and he added a few more points to his estimation of her.

"Interloper? That's an interesting phrase. You mean because my father walked out and never bothered to tell the person he was sleeping with that he was a witch? Is that my fault too? You'll have to excuse my sore spot on this point, but I'm trying to do what's right. Not only for me, but for my people. If your clan is just PURITY with a different face,

I'll just take my services elsewhere. Because I have no need to prove my racial purity to anyone. I have lived in the human world. My mother and grandparents are human. I am not ashamed of that. Nor would I ever allow anyone to make me feel that way."

Gage caught Dom's eyebrow as it rose for a brief instant and then settled back into place. He smiled then.

"I can't guarantee this will be easy. It hasn't been for any of us. But I can guarantee one thing and that is we won't be engaging in any sort of purity tests. I grew up outside a clan too." Dominic looked toward Sami before he cast his gaze back to Molly. "And now I run one. You're a witch and you're offering your services, which we *all* know are highly desirable and effective. We'd like to offer you a position here."

"Not just as the head of our public relations campaign, but as a member of Clan Owen," Meriel added. "We've checked you out. You're everything you claim and more. We need you on our side."

Molly kept her gaze on Sami, which Gage found himself fascinated by. This was a full-council witch. Most people would have left it alone. But Molly Ryan was clearly *not* most people.

"Before I give my answer I'd like to hear from Ms. Ellis. I didn't grow up in a coven. If this is going to be an issue, I'd prefer it to be said outright and openly. I'm afraid that while I use subtlety in my job all the time, I'm not much for using it with my employer."

Meriel's gaze shot to Sami, who sat back, clearly surprised by Molly. It made Gage like Molly even more.

Sami's tone was slightly defensive. "If I have reservations, it's my duty to speak them."

Molly's posture remained confident. "And that's what I'd expect. I'd simply prefer it be laid out openly. I came here for a job interview. I expect you all to look into my background and to want to know who I am and why I want this job. That's part of the territory. But I'm trying to fight against this sort of contest to see who is more pure and if it's going to be an issue that I didn't grow up in the magickal community, it's best that I know now. Because my answer would be different than it would be if it's not an issue."

"You'd turn down a job because of that? Because of me being worried about how you'd adjust in a clan system after never having been in one? Doesn't that suggest you're not the right person for this high stress of a position?"

"What an interesting interpretation. No. I'd appreciate having a discussion on the differences between the non-magickal world and the inner workings of a clan. And I'd certainly understand your wanting to know how I'll deal with it. Which is of course an entirely different tack than the one you took earlier." Molly leaned in and Gage felt the wave of her charisma. "I have a lot to learn about clan governance and I'd consider that part of my job to get up to speed. But I'm not a second-class human or a second-class witch because my human mother raised me on her own outside a clan. Nor will I tolerate any inferences of the sort."

Sami nodded. "All right then. I do hope you accept and should you do so and want any history lessons or other information I'd be honored to help you." She tipped her chin down slightly, which of course Molly couldn't have known the importance of, but everyone else at the table did.

"Thank you." Molly tipped her chin back at Sami and then turned to Meriel and Dominic again. "I accept the offer. Of both the job and the place within your clan."

"Excellent!" Meriel beamed and then lowered the hammer. "We've already got some work for you to do. Oh and an office and an assistant. Just in case you took us up on our offer."

Molly stood and Gage couldn't help but admire her anew. Tall, but not too tall. She wore hose on her legs, not something he saw very often, but with her businesslike skirt and blouse, it worked. Instead of old-fashioned, it was sort of delightfully retro.

He wondered then if they were stockings and then made himself stop. Then he started thinking about her other underwear.

Gage had had to physically turn his gaze away so he could get his focus back.

Meriel stood as well. "I'm going to show Molly around. Dominic, can you check in with Lark to be sure we've got someone on Molly when she makes public appearances?"

Lark nodded and looked to Gage.

When the room cleared, Dominic sighed and leaned back. "So glad Meriel won't be out there all the time. Don't repeat that to her, I'll only deny it and tell her I think she's awesome. Which she is of course. So what are you two going to do to keep our new PR person safe?"

Gage and Lark had talked about this just the day before. "She's going to be the public face of this clan in a way that will attract negative attention. There's no way around having a guard on her at all appearances. She may not like that though."

Dominic nodded. "We'll need to get to know her a little. Once she finds a place to live we'll have to ward it well. I'm going to suggest the clan assign her a driver. Simon's brother, Faine, might be perfect for that. Then he can be her guard as well as her driver. He's been wanting something to do."

The Lycians had sent Faine, one of Simon's younger brothers and a warrior just like he was, just a week before. He was on loan for the foreseeable future to help. As the guy was nearly seven feet tall and broad as a truck, he would be perfect as a guard.

Lark looked to Gage to be sure he was on board with Dom's suggestion. Gage and Lark had a good rhythm. She was different than Nell, his old boss, but they worked the team in a more cooperative way. Lark was good at what she did and trusted him to be good at what he did. They'd taken the team light years ahead in the last months, even after the disaster of the Magister.

"That's a good suggestion. I'll talk with him today." Lark made a note.

Dominic nodded. "Good. Okay. Just get with Molly on it. I want her to feel included and welcomed."

Unlike what Sami had done. That passed, unspoken between them, but Gage knew Dominic, knew too that something would be said to the other full-council witch about keeping her communications with their new PR person civil.

"I'll stop by her office in an hour or so to introduce myself. Then I can go over some things with her. I don't know what her power is like, though certainly charisma is one of her gifts."

"We can talk with her about some training too, for her magick. If she needs it I mean. And who doesn't?" Lark shrugged. "I don't get the feeling she's easily offended or intimidated. But I do think she's at that *I am witch, hear me roar* stage, which is good."

"She's going to need it. The news gets worse every day. We're tossing her out there into a firestorm." Gage respected Molly's experience, but he hoped she'd be all right. They were asking a lot of her.

Chapter 5

HER new assistant eyed her from the doorway as if she wasn't entirely sure whether to kick Molly's ass or give her a hug.

Molly smiled, hoping for the latter. "Hi, Rita. What's up?"

"You're perky."

"I am. It's a terrible flaw."

Rita narrowed her eyes until she harrumphed and came into the office. "Are you a morning person?"

"Why are you asking? Just curious."

"I've been doing this job for thirty years. It helps if I know the person and their habits."

"I'm not really, but now that I'm on the West Coast I'll have to be."

"Why?" Rita wasn't rude, she was just blunt and straight-forward. Molly liked that quality in a person.

Molly sat back, crossing her legs. "A lot of the media we'll be reacting to or interacting with will come from the East first. New York, D.C., and so forth. So I'll have to be alert first thing and ready to handle any emergencies that might arise. Most likely I'll be up at five or so to read ahead, but at this time I'll be in the office by about six thirty. You don't have to be though."

"If you're here, I'm here. That's the job."

"How about you and I make our own rules instead? I write my own press releases because I'm a control freak. I generally try to do things in order. Morning is time for reading. Press releases, news articles, that sort of thing. I don't need you here for that stuff."

"All of us are."

Molly leaned forward. "What do you mean?"

Rita waved a hand. "All witches are control freaks. Oh, some of us are better at hiding it or regulating it, but we're all control freaks in some way or other."

That was good to know. It wasn't that she didn't know any witches. She did, but her circle had been a dozen or so witches and she only knew the Falcos well enough to have said if they were control freaks or not.

Rita nodded. "Including me. This is my job and if you're here, I'm here. I'm not perky though."

Molly bit the inside of her cheek to keep from laughing. "All right then. In the mornings I read. I like to be up on everything that might affect my client."

"In this case, witches?"

She nodded, approving of the way Rita started taking notes.

"Not just witches. We're all connected, all Others I mean. So I'll be reading about shifters and vampires too. I expect I'll need to meet with their communications people as well."

"I can handle setting all that up for you."

Molly looked up at the new voice to catch sight of Gage standing in the doorway. In faded jeans and cowboy boots. He was ridiculously hot as the light glinted off the hoops in his ear. Three. His hair was gold-blond, thick, but short and neat around his face. She bet it started to curl when it got any longer, or maybe when it was wet from the shower, and then slapped herself for thinking about it. She wasn't there to meet boys, for god's sake.

"Handle what?"

"The introduction to the shifter and vampire people. Do you have a few minutes to talk?"

Rita frowned at him. "Gage, she hasn't even had lunch yet. Give her a break."

Gage smiled easily at Rita. "Hey there."

"Hey yourself. Have *you* eaten? I was telling your mother just yesterday that you're getting too thin."

Rita gave him the same stern tone she'd used on Molly. Molly steepled her hands in front of her mouth to keep from smiling.

"You're the reason she showed up at my house the day before yesterday with eight bags of groceries!"

Molly couldn't help it, she let go of a delighted laugh and both the others turned to look at her.

Rita waved a hand in Gage's direction. "He's too skinny. You should see him when he's all filled out. "

Damn, he was even more lethally gorgeous than he was right then? She wasn't sure if her hormones could handle that.

Gage appeared to be counting to ten. "I'm a little busy lately."

"What? Too busy to have a cereal bar or something? This is my grand-nephew, by the way. Just in case you thought I lectured strangers this way."

Gage snorted. "Which she does."

Molly could totally believe it.

"You can take me to lunch and tell me about what neighborhoods I should be looking for an apartment in after we talk business." Molly looked at her watch. "Say in half an hour? I need to finish this meeting with your aunt."

He appeared to be amused, which looked good on his handsome face. "I'll be back for you in thirty minutes."

She turned back to Rita. "All right then, where were we?"

They went over her expectations and schedule and at thirty minutes exactly, Gage poked his head into her office. "Ready?"

"I really am." She grabbed her bag and headed for the door.

Rita was out there, guarding her office door like a teeny, frizzy-haired pit bull. She looked Molly over and then nodded. Molly felt like she'd gotten an A on a test.

"I'll be back in an hour. I have my phone if you need me."

"Take an hour and a half; it's business after all." Rita sniffed. "And be sure that one eats or I'm going to tell his mother again."

"**DO** you have a preference for lunch?" Gage headed to the elevators and she followed. He pressed the button and then looked down her body. "Maybe not walk too far."

"Why would you say that? Is it raining again?"

He laughed. "It's always raining. If you don't walk in the rain, you won't be doing much walking at all." He gestured, and she preceded him into the elevator. "Use your keycard like this." He pulled his out and put it in front of the reader on the number panel. "It'll give you access to all the lower floors. There's a food court down on five. There are several choices."

"I can walk in the rain, you know. I have a coat. I'm from Chicago. It was snowing when I left."

He looked her over again. "I bet you can. But you have heels on. I was trying to save your feet."

"Ah. I can walk in heels. These aren't that high anyway. Do you have any favorites? I should be learning Seattle now since I'll be relocating."

"Do you like seafood? McCormick and Schmick's is up the block. They've got lunch specials, that sort of thing. It'll be quieter and less . . . food court–ish than downstairs."

She fought a smile. "Food court–ish? I like that."

He didn't fight anything apparently. Instead he turned the full force of that damned mouth on her, with a smile that sent her senses into full-blown standing ovation.

"Seemed apt."

"McCormick and Schmick's sounds good." She hoped he didn't hear her gulp.

He walked to the outside, shielding her. She allowed it,

making a note to ask him about it once they'd settled in at the restaurant.

MOLLY Ryan was the kind of woman men looked at.

Not in the same way they looked at the woman at the bar in the tight red sweater and a short skirt with heels. No, they looked at Molly the way people liked to look at pretty, elegant things.

The light seemed to hit her just right. She moved with the kind of grace he rarely saw in people who weren't dancers. She charmed the hostess. He knew this because they got a great table.

"You're like a Disney princess."

Startled, she looked up from her menu. "What?"

"Birds sing, the clouds part, people turn to you expectantly. Is this part of your gift?"

The server came so they suspended the conversation briefly while they ordered.

"Am I so horrible then, Gage Garrity, that only magick would make someone turn to me expectantly?"

He paused, abashed, and then realized she was teasing. "Not horrible at all. Excuse my manners. Don't tell my aunt or she'll tell my mother and then I'll have lectures about how I speak to women, as well as casseroles and my mom's special tea blends showing up in my kitchen."

She smiled. "Your aunt is formidable. I'm glad to have her working with me. I bet people will think twice before they give her any guff to get to me."

Gage laughed. "Yes. Well, she's a tough old bird."

"To answer your question, I'm told that charm is part of my power. Rosa, she's my other mother of sorts, anyway, she said people with my gifts often go into politics or entertainment. Maybe I should be an actor instead."

He could totally see her as an actor. "Hours are probably better. Pay too."

"Weather as well. Los Angeles is sunny today I bet."

But then he wouldn't be having lunch with her and Meriel would still be at risk too.

"So is there a good reason then? For your mother to be plying you with food?" Her eyes were beautiful, probably the most striking thing about her. The blue of deep, deep water, with flecks of gold around her pupils. Long, dark lashes.

Those eyes of hers saw right through him, he realized. It wasn't entirely comfortable.

"Been a bit hectic here." He shrugged.

"I don't know much about it. About what happened I mean. What I do know is . . ." She shook her head quickly. "I know it's not the time or place."

"You'll need to know it. For your job I mean. When we get back, have Rita get me on your schedule and we can go over it. For now, let's get to the day-to-day stuff. What is your daily schedule going to look like? What sorts of events will have you leaving our building?"

He watched as she very precisely put sugar and cream into her coffee, stirring without making a single sound. She sipped and he saw it, the pleasure skittering over her features at the taste.

The moment was just a breath of time. And yet the intimacy of it shocked him. A flush heated through his belly.

She tore her attention from the coffee and back to him. "I needed that. Why do you ask? I'm assuming scheduling if and when I need security?"

He spoke under his breath and the spell dampened all sound around them. "We can hear when we're being approached, but we can speak without being heard."

Her eyes widened and the wonder on her face chipped away a little of his bitterness. "Really? Can you teach this to me? Oh, that would be brilliant."

He found himself smiling more with her than he had in some time. "I can, yes. For now, the answer to your question is yes, I need to know for security reasons."

"I expect for the next several days it'll be a lot of catch-up and getting some structure into place. Then I'll be doing the things Meriel does now. Interviews, that sort of thing. Do you have a website?"

"Hm? Uh, yes. Locked to Owen members only."

She nodded and pulled a pad from her bag and began to write.

"I apologize. I wanted to note something while I was thinking. There'll be legislative visits. But I can make the drive down to Olympia easily enough if the maps are correct. I'll probably only need your help occasionally. Appearances will take up a lot of time some weeks and others I'll be at the office. I'll have Rita let your office know in advance if I'm doing something I feel will need an escort."

He held his finger up briefly, breaking the spell as the server approached with their food and then recasting once they were alone again.

"You seem to like blunt talk, am I correct?"

She took him in, her eyes narrowing slightly. "Yes, I prefer it."

"Things are bad. We get multiple death threats weekly. Meriel and Dominic have given Lark and I the ability to run the security needs of the clan and its witches. Lark and I believe your job will be as dangerous as it was when Meriel did it. By that I mean the moment humans find out you're our spokesperson, you will be under increased threat. It's my job to be sure we protect you against that threat level. As such, *all* appearances outside the building will be with a security detail. The clan will provide you with a guard who will also serve as your driver."

"Driver? That's ridiculous. I can drive my own car."

"Three days ago, a witch in Arizona was pulled from her car and nearly beaten to death by thugs who found out she was a witch. We routinely get reports of nails in tires. A witch in Spain, part of their council, was killed just a week ago. An IED planted at the end of her driveway. You will have a car the clan secures when you are not in it and you will have a trained driver, who will be your guard as well. This is not negotiable."

One of her brows rose and she cocked her head slightly.

"Your home, once you secure a place to live, will be warded by one of the witches the clan trusts. Meriel's father is one of the best. Sami is also quite powerful at warding." He paused to eat and let it sink in a little.

"Welcome to war, Molly Ryan. It's my job to be sure you're tough enough to make it out alive." Even though he knew it wasn't a promise he could keep every time. The truth was, he couldn't protect them all.

GAGE, true to his word, had assigned her a guard and a driver named Faine. Faine, who was a great deal like a flesh-and-blood tank, was Lycian. She'd discovered Lycians were sort of like werewolves and they came from the other side of the Veil, like the Fae. *There were Fae.* She was still sort of reeling over that.

Anyway, Faine was Simon Leviathan's younger brother and once she got past the fact that he was nearly seven feet tall, she discovered he also had a very sweet way about him.

He'd been given the room next to hers at the hotel and had come inside Molly's room to give it the once-over. Apparently someone from the clan had come over earlier to ward the place as well.

Once he'd finished, she touched his arm briefly. "Thank you. I'm sorry your life has been uprooted just to be next door."

Faine smiled again and she couldn't help but respond with a smile of her own. "This is what I came here to do. I'm pleased to be able to help. Have you eaten dinner yet?"

She shook her head and took a peek at her watch. "Didn't realize it was already after eight."

"How about I order us up some dinner? We can get to know each other a little and I can explain to you just why it's necessary that I'll be your shadow for the next little while?"

She sighed. "All right."

"I'm going to shower and order the food. I'll be back over in about twenty minutes."

Molly used the time to change into sweatpants, thick socks and a sweatshirt. She called her mother quickly while she had the chance.

"I'm sorry it's so late!" she said when her mother answered.

"I can't sleep anyway. I'm glad you called. I feel better now that I've heard your voice. So tell me."

"I accepted the job. I started pretty much immediately. Wrote a press release even." She snorted. "I've got an awesome dragon as an assistant. She knows stuff and no one is getting through to my desk unless they deserve to."

"Good to hear. They're good people? These Owens?"

She smiled. People sometimes considered Molly's mother to be a bit of a stone-cold ballbuster. But underneath the ambition that had driven her to such success was a person who loved her family. Molly would be seventy years old and her mother would still worry. That filled her up.

"They seem to be. They're footing the bill for this hotel I'm in. One of those extended-stay dealies. They offered to help me find an apartment. My assistant even made me a list with places they consider safest. I have a driver and a guard."

"A what?"

Molly sucked in a breath and explained. "This is more than me being a witch and outed on television. Here I'll be associated with the clan in a much more open way. They seem to think it's a necessary thing so I'm going with it."

"I don't like it."

"Me neither. But what can I do? Hide? Pretend it's not happening? You should see some of the background material I read today. There is some seriously bad stuff happening to Others all across the globe right now."

It turned her stomach. Outraged her that it had barely even been spoken of on the news. She needed to remedy that. Humans needed to understand and Others needed to realize just how threatened they were.

Her mother spoke again, interrupting her mental planning. "When do you think you'll be back to pack up?"

"I don't know. My schedule is already full." Molly rubbed her eyes, suddenly exhausted.

"I just spoke with Rosa earlier. Why don't you let us do it? At the very least we can get your clothes and shoes packed up and sent your way."

"You're so good to me, Mom."

"I'm your mother, it's my job. Also it gives me something to do so I won't miss you so much. So . . . what's it like? I feel bad, not having you grow up knowing this stuff. I never meant—never knew it would be like this."

"Please don't apologize for the choices you made. I wouldn't change a thing about the way I grew up. I promise. It's different here. It's not that I've never been around witches. But they're very, I don't know, it's a big part of who they are. I mean, you should see this building they're headquartered in. It's like a giant corporation of witches. They have a landscaping business. A chain. A legal department. All sorts of stuff. They offered me lessons. So I can learn how to use my power in new ways. Classes on clan history, which will be helpful in my job. Some of them are wary of me. Most of them have been welcoming. I'm overwhelmed, but so busy it hasn't really sunk in yet."

"That's probably for the best. You always do better when you have lots of things to do. Anything new on the stuff with the firm?"

"I'm not going to get my job back. Which is pretty much what we knew. I mean, Jim said he could fight it and maybe we'd win. But the partnership agreement was violated in that my whatever—existence, identity—had brought negative attention to the firm and cost it clients. That was true, even though the reasons were stupid. I don't want to fight it for years, spending all that money. Their settlement to me will be double what they offered originally." And that was a great deal of money. Though, of course, money she'd made anyway. "They have to change the name of the firm, and Jim crafted a better statement on my departure that didn't cast them as saints and me as a witchy whore." She sighed. It still hurt.

"I hate them."

Molly grinned. "Thanks, Mom. It sucks. A lot. But the

money will enable to me buy a great place out here and get a car and still have some in savings. I suppose I need to look for the bright side for the next little while."

"It'd be more fun to punch them all in the throat."

"Ha. Yes, much more fun. Alas, the police look down on such problem solving."

They chatted a while longer before hanging up and she felt a lot better. More settled after she'd touched base.

FAINE came over shortly after, tapping lightly. She noted the food on the big tray in his hands gratefully.

"I hadn't realized how hungry I was until right now." She stood back and he came in. They settled at the table and he pulled two beers from a bag.

"Bless you." She grinned his way as she opened things up and grabbed a carrot.

"I didn't think to ask if you were a vegetarian or had special dietary stuff."

"You have very good manners. Your mother must be proud." She took a long drink from the beer.

"My mother would not tolerate anything else. She's not even four and half feet tall, but no one would dare to disobey her." Faine grinned.

"So was your, um, world affected by the Magister?"

"It didn't manifest on our side of the Veil. We knew it was bad. The Magister I mean. Simon and Lark came to us to warn and get our pledge of support. But we didn't . . . we had no way of . . . The night it came was the stuff of nightmares. But even though I knew about it, I still can't quite get over it. I came over with some of my family when we got word about it. Lark nearly died. I don't know if my brother could have gotten over it if she hadn't come through." He paused and then changed the subject. "You're what they call outclan, yes?"

"I don't know what they call it. I was sort of an extended member of a coven. But it wasn't part of my daily existence really. I had a life and my being a witch was like having blue eyes or a quick wit. Part of me, but nothing I really thought about a lot. And then suddenly it was everything and I didn't even know what all was true."

He pushed her plate toward her. "Won't do you any good to get sick because you're not eating."

She ate because it seemed as if he wouldn't unless she did. It was automatic, but it got the job done.

"I spent pretty much the entire day today reading reports about what's been happening. All the assaults, threats, violent attacks, people losing jobs and homes." She shook her head.

Molly was used to being good at everything she did. She was in over her head right then, needing to just go step-by-step, but having someone she could talk to was a hugely important resource. "I'm still sorry you have to be here babysitting me instead of out living your life."

"My life has been pretty much consumed with the aftermath of the Magister. Guarding you gives me something to do. I've been staying with Lark and Simon so it's a nice change of pace to have a space of my own. And room service is better than having to cook. This is my job." He shrugged. "I'm good at my job."

"As your job is keeping me safe from thrown eggs and nails in my tires, I'm grateful."

"You read it yourself. This is far more than egging or mean-spirited op-ed columns in the newspaper. We're talking death threats, Molly. Don't let yourself forget just how dangerous it is out there. Witches look human, so you're safer than some Others. But those assholes in PURITY want you dead just the same. And many have ended up that way."

She swallowed hard. "I don't want other people in danger because of me."

"I don't want you in danger because you're trying to help our people. So, we're even." He winked at her and it broke the tension.

Chapter 6

"**HOW'S** it going?" Gage tapped on her door. "Settling in all right?"

The morning sun glinted off the gold highlights in his hair, making him look like an angel. A fallen one, but an angel just the same.

"I'm just on my way out. I've got an interview at the television station." She held up some papers she'd been reading over. "This proposed legislation is abhorrent."

"Yeah." Emotion crossed his features and she knew she wasn't going to like whatever he said next.

She sat. "All right, I'm sitting. Tell me."

"I must be losing my touch if you could tell it was that bad." He moved and sat beside her. "What's your schedule like later today? I've been speaking with the Enforcer at Cascadia—the local wolf pack—and they'd like to meet you."

"Hang on." She pulled her calendar from her bag. "They're not just any old pack right? Aren't they like wolf royalty or whatever? The oldest brother runs the National Pack?"

"You did your homework."

"It's my job. I can move things around this afternoon and evening if necessary. I'll have to coordinate with Faine as well; I assume I'm supposed to take him to things like this? What time did they want to meet? And then you can tell me what gave you that look."

"The meeting will be with Lex Warden, who is their Alpha and he's also the representative to the Council of Others so he'll be speaking for not just Cascadia but all wolves."

"Good to know."

"Four, if you can do it. Faine . . . well, the wolves and Lycians have a tense relationship. It's best if I escort you. They tend to spend lots of time on dominance displays. It's sort of tedious."

"Interesting. Shall I have Rita call to confirm then?"

"Yes, that's good. I'll check with her on my way out to be sure she has the contact information. As for my look . . ." He heaved a sigh. "Nice piece in the *New York Times* this morning. You work fast."

"Part of my charm." She shrugged. That and the issue was a hot one and she was willing to talk about it. She knew who to call and what buttons to push, which also helped.

A glimmer of a smile and then it was gone. "You got your first death threat. Record time. Only two full days of employment."

She sat back and swallowed, hard. "I've always been an overachiever."

"You're well protected, Molly."

Nausea rose, making her skin clammy. "Was it a call? Letter? Is it credible?"

He reached out and squeezed her hand, more than a little impressed with her ability to continue thinking about the big picture. "An email sent via the website. It ran through an anonymizer program but we're working on it. Lark and I have assessed it; we don't believe it's credible, no. In fact, in the days before . . . well, before all this, we wouldn't have even told you."

"This needs to be reported to the police." She sat up straight and took a deep breath.

"We don't involve human police in clan matters."

"Yes, well, they know about us now."

"They don't care, Molly. I'm sorry, but that's the truth of it."

She shook her head. "You misunderstand. I don't care about that part. I'm not surprised. But they're trying to remove our status as citizens just one state over. We will report this officially or I will myself. We are citizens and we will expect the same service from the government as anyone else."

"Why? So they can ignore us and we can waste our time reporting it? You're overestimating how much humans care about our lives, Molly."

She narrowed her gaze and he saw fire there. So much that it sent a thrill through him. "Listen here, I am many things, including in over my head. But I am *not* stupid. Or naïve. We need to report because we are citizens. We can't let them allow us to feel otherwise or in fact, to legislate otherwise. It's not that I want a lollipop and a teddy bear from them because I've been frightened. It's that I am a fully vested citizen of this country and I will be treated as such. Anything else is wholly unacceptable. We need to stop acting as if it is." One brow rose as she took him to school.

"Underneath the subtle but feminine perfume and the pretty clothes you've got the heart of a predator." He smiled.

"I'm not going to allow anyone to make me feel inferior. If a human received a death threat, they'd go to the cops. Why should I do anything different?" She held a hand in his direction. "Let me see it."

"No. It's ugly. Hateful and ugly and you don't need to see it. I'll handle it with the police."

"Here's another fact about me, I don't like to be handled or managed. I may be new to the death threat game, but I'm not going to pass out because I'm fragile. Let me see it. I'm the one making the police report, I have to know what it says."

Stubborn. Damn, he liked it.

He handed it over and she scanned it. He'd have been lying if he denied being impressed with how she took another person threatening to disembowel her and let crows eat her guts. She read it calmly, though he caught the way she'd paled and made notes before looking back to him.

"Tell me why you feel this isn't credible. I'm not arguing, I just need to know your process."

"Partly it's the energy of the message. Hate, yes. If the sender saw you on the street he or she might yell at you, might picket outside a building you were in, but there's no intent."

Her eyes widened and she leaned closer. "You know this how?"

"It's part of my gift. It's not infallible, it's a gut feeling and it needs to be backed up by other evidence. Sometimes it doesn't work at all, especially when it's a letter or over the Internet. But when it pings my magick, it's usually because it's got a lot of intent. We have a checklist of things we use. This particular threat is one we've received a few times already. Pretty much word for word. It's almost like an Internet meme. He's hateful, but not serious."

"That's incredible. What an amazing gift you have. And of course it's a gut feeling, that's where your magick lives." Her eyes looked so damned blue. The expression of wonder she wore made her even more beautiful.

He was struck by the sudden and intense desire to haul her close and kiss her senseless.

He shoved that desire far away and decided to stick with amused and flattered. Far less likely to get slapped that way.

"I never really thought I'd have call to use it. It's not something we had to deal with before. Death threats and the like, I mean."

She sighed and folded the paper into her file. "I'll take this to the police with me." She stood and he caught the scent of her magick, just a brief breath of it. Enough to bring the hair on his arms to stand from the electricity of it.

He followed, standing too close, but not moving. "We'll call them and have them come out. Let's get you to the studio first. Faine and I are switching places today and probably tomorrow."

"Is he all right?" She cocked her head, looking up at him.

"You're a very public face on Owen. You're a high-profile target for a lot of attention. Meriel came by with Dominic to discuss this issue. Lark and I feel you'd be better with one of us. Faine is great and damned good at his job." He took her hand and squeezed it briefly. "But I'm better. I have magick, he doesn't." Though certainly one couldn't underestimate the power of shifting into a giant wolf with razor-sharp teeth and claws.

"I'm sure you have better things to do with your time than babysit me."

"No, not really. This meeting later with Warden is huge for us. It's important I be there anyway. And in the wake of the piece in the *Times* today, it's important you continue to represent us in the media. So my being there is important too."

"That's a lot of important, right there." She said it low, with a teasing smile on her lips and the air between them thickened.

He stepped back. "It is."

SHE sat across from the interviewer and clicked into her job in a way she hadn't thus far. *This* was familiar territory at least. Here she didn't need to dwell on the sick dread she'd been choking back since she'd read that death threat.

Molly didn't get death threats. Sure, being in the PR biz had exposed her to negativity on multiple occasions. That came with the job. People wanting to kill her didn't. Her brain couldn't process it and so she put it in the place she'd been shoving all the other stuff she couldn't process over the last month or so.

"Before we get started, are you familiar with how this all works?" The PA hooked Molly's mic up.

"Yes, thank you."

"Do you need anything to drink?"

"I'm good, thank you." Molly smiled and the PA smiled back.

"Good luck." The PA took a look around before leaning in close. "Just . . . hang in there."

Well now, *that* wasn't hopeful.

The same interviewer who Molly had watched with Meriel just days before bustled into the studio. He didn't look at or speak to her at all until moments before the cameras went live.

He looked up, focused on her and began the interview without so much as a how-do-you-do. Clearly his mother didn't teach him any manners.

"I'm here tonight with the new public relations minister for the coven here in town. Ms. Ryan, some might wonder what you've been hiding."

She cocked her head ever so slightly and stared at the interviewer, a piggish-looking fellow whose bias against Others was blatantly written all over his posture.

Her smile was perfectly measured to convey how silly she found him. "Minister? Oh my, that's grand isn't it? I'm sorry to say I'm a regular old communications person. Not nearly as exciting as a minister. And we're Clan Owen, named after the Owen family who runs the organization of witches situated here in the area. Did you know the Owen family is one of the oldest established families in the area? Right up there with the Denny, Terry and Yesler families. They helped build up Seattle. In fact, one of their mercantiles is part of the Underground Tour. Deep ties to the land here, to the people." She wanted to convey that over and over. They might be witches, but they had roots in the country. She wanted humans to understand that while their gifts had been hidden from them, their presence hadn't been. They weren't a threat; they were an asset.

Molly shifted, crossing her legs. "But to be serious a moment, I'd like to talk about the new legislation being written in Idaho. We're naturally—"

He interrupted. "You suddenly appeared this week. Why haven't you been here before? Just what are you hiding?"

The only way to defeat a troll is to not feed it. This asshole had an agenda and she'd be damned if she'd descend to his level. Plus it amused her to ignore that and poke at him. She sent him an amused smile, though it was amused at his expense.

"My mother would be puzzled by that, as she would beg to differ about how I just suddenly appeared. I'm still paying back my student loans so the University of Chicago might beg to differ as well." Deftly, she got back to the subject. "This legislation seeks to change the constitution of the state to say a citizen would be defined as a human being. Others would be stripped of their citizenship."

"What are you hiding, Ms. Ryan?"

"This is an interesting theme. I'm sitting here on television in the middle of the daytime. You and your station have been provided with my CV. Where I've been is clearly stated. In fact, it's available on the Clan Owen website where I've started doing video updates and posting pertinent news and information." She looked to the camera and gave the URL and then shifted her attention back to him. "Now then, legislation such as S1046 is dangerous on many levels."

"What makes you say that?"

The man was so stupid she wanted to laugh. Instead she stuck to her points. "First, such legislation is unconstitutional. It's a waste of taxpayer dollars to have legislators writing legislation they know will not survive a constitutional challenge. Things are hard for Americans right now; why on earth would we want our elected officials working on this time-wasting nonsense?"

Gage watched her, impressed as all get out. Christ, she was a shark. This Briggs Anderson guy didn't know what hit him.

She adjusted herself, looking delicate and pretty as she did so. But not in a helpless way. There was something so self-assured about her. It drew him in, made his heart beat a little faster.

She spoke again. "In addition to those very important facts, this is America. At the very heart of what this country is, is the melting pot. We're all different in some way, yet we share more in common than the sum of our differences."

"You're not human beings." Briggs baited her with his tone and she easily stepped from the way, never ceding control of the interview for a single moment.

"We *are* Americans though. That's the point." She smiled and refused to get pulled into his angry little trap. "I was born here, in this country. The doctor who delivered me also delivered my mother, which I think is pretty awesome. I went to elementary school and made macaroni picture frames for my grandparents. I went to high school and college. Weezer's *Blue Album* was the first music I bought with my own money. I am an American. Like you are. Like the Others in Idaho are."

Damn, Gage wanted to give her a standing ovation. Briggs just gaped at her in silence, still not quite getting that she'd just totally dominated him and made her points.

"But you are *not* Americans. You gained your citizenship by deceit."

"No, Mr. Anderson, that is not true. I gained my citizenship the same way you did. I was born here. As was my mother. And her mother. My grandfather fought in Vietnam, his father in Korea. This is my country as much as it is yours, or any of the legislators pushing this bill."

The red light went off to the right and the cameraperson made the *wrap it up* move with his wrist.

Molly didn't cede any time to Briggs though, she continued on. "We are the same people we were before this tragedy. We are your neighbors, your teachers, your friends and family. We have harmed no one and we just want to be left alone to live our lives as we did in the past."

She drew it out right to the very last moment and sat back with a smile. Even Briggs was caught up in it for a second until it was too late for him to say anything but "So you claim," which seemed rather petty in response to her genuine appeal.

Chapter 7

GAGE shielded her as he walked her to the car. There was a small group of protesters outside the studio but none close enough to get to them.

"You did a great job."

"He's an asshole." Though luckily, like most assholes, he was a stupid one.

Gage laughed and she liked the sound. "He is." Gage opened the door and looked around before he motioned her inside. "But you dominated him in that entire interview."

She smiled as he got in on his side.

"He's small potatoes. That was a softball compared to what we'll face out there from now on. Anyway it wasn't live so we'll see how it's edited."

Her stomach growled and he gave her a sideways glance. "You hungry? We don't have a lot of time before the Warden meeting but they'll probably have snacks. I've got protein bars in the glove box."

"I can wait." Though when this was all over she had some ice cream that needed eating. "I need to give Meriel a quick debrief." She pulled her phone out.

"Tell her I said you kicked ass."

Warm with his praise, she ducked her head and called Meriel to fill her in on what had happened.

Molly liked Meriel. She was unerringly competent, intelligent and ran the clan well. They were tight-knit without being cliquish. Close without being into each other's business. The people she'd met from Owen had been an eye-opener. Molly had all sorts of preconceptions about clan life, and none of them had been correct.

Meriel told her she'd sent some recent news via email so Molly made a note to check it out when she finished up with the wolves.

Once she'd finished, she turned to Gage. "Thank you for guarding me today. I know things are busy in your office."

He nodded. "It was nice to get out, actually. Gives me a chance to get to know you better too."

She could not lie. She wanted to hear that little flirtation in his voice. He made her sort of . . . breathless and giddy. As this wasn't a usual state for her she preferred to pretend it was the novelty that she liked so much. When really it was that she had the beginning of a crush on him. A crush was wholly fun and silly. Something to cleanse away the negatives that surrounded her all the time.

"How are you settling in? I mean, you've only been here a few days I know. I imagine it's hard to leave everything behind."

An understatement. But really, she'd lost so much that she still reeled from it. So she tried not to think on it, instead pouring herself into her job.

"I miss my family." She shrugged. "I've been so busy it hasn't been as bad as it could be, though. My mom and Rosa, my other mom, they went to my place and packed my clothes up and have sent them. I have to find the time to look for a place to live before I can get everything else dealt with. I guess it just falls to the bottom of my list."

"If I can be honest, it's better to have you at the hotel anyway. We know the owner and most of the employees are Others. We can keep you safer there."

It was turning out to be too busy for her to look anyway. She'd been there only a few days and already had travel plans for work. "I'm looking forward to a time when I can have my own place, but I'm so busy just now I don't have time to miss my stuff."

"We're glad to have you and I think you're a great asset to us. This will be over. Someday. And when it is, you can build a life here. I'm sorry yours was so abruptly altered."

"Everyone's was." She desperately didn't want to go there just then. She needed to keep her focus on the meeting. Bringing the Others together, at least in some way, was her priority. Falling apart wasn't even on her to-do list.

"Tell me about the wolves." Changing the subject would help and she needed the info anyway.

"They're smart. Well organized. Especially now with Cade Warden at the helm of the National Pack. They have a good public face. Each pack has liaisons with local law enforcement, which was revolutionary at the time. Still is now, I wager. Anyway, Wardens run every influential pack in the U.S. The sister in Portland. Another sister and brother-in-law in Chicago."

"They speak with a unified voice then?" It would make it easier if they did. That is if they weren't crazy. She'd done some homework on Lex Warden and his family and from what she could tell they'd be good allies in this fight.

"They're all attuned to their members. Each pack has its own challenges and strengths. But they do have a unified voice, I'd say yes. They went to the brink of war several years ago. Cade unified them. He's one of the smartest people I've ever met. He understands politics; he's sharp. Brutal when necessary."

She raised a brow at him. "When necessary? When is that?"

"Don't tell me you think this can be handled if we all just love each other enough. We're not humans, Molly. To pretend otherwise is why we're in this mess to start with."

"I was under the impression we dealt with this earlier. I'm not stupid. Or naïve. I asked a question. If you can't answer it, you're in the wrong job I'd say."

He was quiet for several minutes, which made her nervous but at the same time, if he was thinking over his answer that meant he was more thoughtful than she gave him credit for, which was important.

"You look so soft and sweet."

She snorted. "Is that a compliment or an insult?"

He laughed again. "An observation. Though you're no chore to look at. What I meant was that at first glance you look like butter wouldn't melt in your mouth but you're no soft touch. I shouldn't have assumed you were attempting to insult me or being naïve."

"I don't ask questions idly. Not usually. If I'm to do this job, it's best if I do it with as much input as I can get."

"To answer your question, brutality is rarely necessary, but when it is, it's best to not hesitate. In this specific context, I believe there's at the very least a significant percentage of the human population that would happily dance us all into our graves. So brutality may be necessary to underline just how unacceptable that would be."

She nodded. He was smart as well as muscly and handsome.

"You're quiet over there."

"Just listening." Molly felt that listening was more important than talking. Many people didn't seem to get that.

"So are you teasing me then? What's your take on brutality?"

She shrugged. "As it happens I agree with your take. Mostly."

THEY really couldn't talk about it much more as Gage got off the freeway and they arrived at the huge gates at the bottom of the drive to the Warden estate. Two ridiculously large guards came from what appeared to be thin air before verifying who they were and that they were supposed to be there.

Once they'd parked and had gone inside, Molly didn't bother to hide her appreciation of the beautiful home Lex and Nina Warden lived in with their children. Expansive views from every window, wraparound decks—the place was insanely gorgeous.

Much like the Alpha couple.

Lex was dark haired with dark eyes, broody, sexy and big. The guy was massive and when he shook Molly's hand, hers was dwarfed.

Though this was totally a new thing for her, she wasn't nervous. First of all, she'd begun to think of Others as just like any other client. Even if they did turn furry or need blood to live. Plus, Gage stuck close as they went through the introductions. He only spoke to give her little bits of information she might need. He was pretty good at that part and she made a mental note to thank him when they left.

Nina Warden had beautiful, long dark hair she'd braided back away from an equally lovely face. "Welcome to Cascadia land." Nina waved them toward some chairs set around a large table. "Please come and sit. I wish we were meeting under better circumstances."

"Me too. Condolences on the loss of your father." Molly addressed Lex and then Nina. The death of Lex Warden's father had been a blow to the Other community, she knew from all the background material she'd read. And she knew as much from her own losses.

Lex nodded, the pain on his face. "Thank you. I understand you have your own losses to bear. Condolences to you and yours as well."

She nodded briskly; best not to dwell.

They got down to business right away. "I spoke with Cade, that's my brother and the Alpha of the National Pack, earlier today. He's empowered me to be the spokesperson for the wolves here in the United States. As such, I'll be your liaison with the different packs." He turned a charming smile her way briefly. "If you have any advice on how to get a bunch of grumpy wolves to mind, let me know."

Molly tried not to snort. "I'm afraid I'm not much of an expert on how to get anyone to mind, much less wolves."

Gage spoke up then. "Don't let her bullshit you. She's been with us only a few days and she's already instituted a clear channel for all communications from other clans and covens."

Molly waved it away. "Well, it makes sense to have one point everyone knows to start with when they need to report something or ask a question. That's common sense."

Lex looked over to Nina, who smirked. "It is, but I didn't think about it until just now. Though my lovely mate did bring the issue of having a communications director up to me just this afternoon."

"I'll try not to lord it over you. Too much anyway." Nina turned her attention back to Molly. "You're that, right? The communications director?"

"Yes, apparently. Though today I was referred to as a PR minister, which sounds better than communications director."

"Briggs Anderson interviewed her. You should have seen her kick his ass." Gage tipped his head in Molly's direction.

"Oh him." Nina rolled her eyes. "Okay, so things are bad. I don't see the use in not just laying it all out there so we can work together. We've got wolves all across the country who are being discriminated against. Attacked. They're receiving threats, vandalism to their businesses and homes. We've made an effort to keep things calm, but each day that passes means there is more of this nonsense."

"And each day that passes means Others nationwide are coming out of their grief-filled stupor and realizing just how bad it's getting." Lex added with a raised brow. "It's only a matter of time before we start fighting back."

"And what's wrong with that?" Gage demanded.

"Well, to be honest, nothing is wrong with it. We should be allowed to defend ourselves." Molly looked over to him. "But I'd prefer to find solutions that don't involve us having to defend our homes and families from being firebombed. It's not good for our children to have to fear all the time. It doesn't *have* to be lying down to be killed or doing the killing ourselves. Not yet anyway."

She spread her hands on the table and looked Lex and Nina square on. She'd been reading up on how to address shifters and she hoped she didn't mess it up. "I'd like the opportunity to provide a unified front with all the Others, to stand together and strong. There is all this stuff going on and as long as we remain in our camps, we're weaker."

"No one speaks for wolves, but wolves." Lex nearly growled it.

Gage moved closer. Close enough that Molly felt the warmth of his magick as it came from him in waves. It made her a little light-headed.

Molly contented herself with a raised brow and a sniff in Lex's direction. "I don't want to speak for you. I have enough on my plate; I don't want to run your pack. I don't want to tell you what to do. This is war, Mr. Warden. We can make a far less attractive target if we stand together. You can do what you want. Working with us isn't mandatory. But I'll be making this same pitch to the cats and to the vampires."

Slightly chastened, Lex nodded. "Just what is it you're pitching then?"

"Two things—they're actually connected I think. For practical reasons, I'd like Others to have wide-open lines of communication with their people so they can be updated on a regular basis. Others need to feel heard. We need a place to report the things we're experiencing. A place where we can connect them to help and services and be sure they're getting the help they need. Meriel has been gathering legal resources and I'm happy to share that."

"Makes sense. God knows how many Others have had something happen to them but didn't know where to turn to get help." Lex took a quick note. "The other thing?"

"You need a council of Others. A governing body of sorts. And then at the top of that, we need representatives from each group who will accompany me to different appearances and press conferences. Humans need to see us. They need to hear our voices and be reminded we are the same as we were before the Magister came. They need to hear that we understand their fear and upset, but are unwilling to be their victims. It's an easier message to hear if it's delivered right."

"And snarling, seven-foot-tall werewolves, even in nice suits, make it harder to hear?" Nina's mouth twitched as she studiously avoided her husband's gaze.

He snorted though.

"They knew about some of us. You've been out for a time, the cats were working on it, vamps too. But this is different. They found out about us in a terrifying way."

"Did they lose their father? Their uncle or their children? How dare they get scared of something that didn't hurt them at all!" Lex pounded the table and Molly was proud she didn't jump.

"Don't raise your voice to her." Gage spoke calmly and simply, but he was just as scary as Lex had been.

The two males locked gazes as the room got very, very silent.

"She's making apologies for what's happening," Lex said at last.

"Bullshit," Gage countered.

"If I may." Molly rapped the table with her knuckles. "There's a difference between making apologies and understanding motivations. How can we begin to make peace with the humans if we don't even take into account how they're feeling? How can we address it and still get our point across that we are not going to take this nonsense if we don't even understand why they do what they do? It's stupid, in my opinion, to go to war with anyone without a basic understanding of who and what they are and what makes them tick. If I make an apology, I do it openly and honestly. I do not appreciate being accused of something I have the courage to do without pulling punches. I was raised to believe that sort of thing was insulting."

Lex heaved a sigh. "Why do all the females I know give me lectures?"

"She's right." Nina arched a brow at him.

"I'm testy. These are my people, my land, everything I need to protect and I can't. I'm not much interested in making nice with people who burn down houses with children in them. But," he added before she could speak, "I know you're not saying that. My buttons got pushed but you're right about the importance of understanding motivations."

She understood it. Everyone had been shocked. Everyone had suffered staggering loss. It was more important than ever to keep their heads right then.

"For what it's worth, I'm not interested in making nice with murderers who kill children either. In fact, I'd love to be sure we hold them accountable so they spend their lives in prison for it. We can do it. I think. But it's going to take planning."

"So what's your plan then?" Nina spoke at last.

And Molly told them.

Chapter 8

"BEEN a long day for you. How 'bout you let me buy you dinner?" Gage kept his eyes on the road as they got off the freeway and headed to her hotel.

"I wanted to thank you."

"For what?"

"Back when Lex was so angry, you defended me. Thank you."

Gage was outraged anew at the memory of how she'd flinched, just a little bit. "He was out of line."

"He lost his father."

Beneath the cool, together exterior she had a big heart. "So did you. We all lost people." Gage's mouth hardened. "No call to terrorize someone you invited into your home and who was trying to help him and his damned wolves. He's not a bad guy. He's good at running his pack. People look to him for leadership. That you won him over the way you did will mean something to them. And to the Others also thinking of joining your little road tour."

She blew out a breath. "That's the idea anyway. I hope it works the way I envision it."

He wanted to soothe away the tension around her eyes. Wanted to take care of her a little. She was so far away from home. "Do you like burritos? One of the witches in Owen runs this Mexican joint just ahead. They make the best burritos in the state."

"All right. Sounds good."

"Let's get you back to the hotel first so you can change. Put on something warm. It's cold out there tonight."

"I won't argue with that."

He checked her room and the wards out before leaving her to get dressed. He told her to knock on the connecting door because he needed to check in with Faine anyway.

He didn't know why she got to him the way she had, but she did. He mother always said he was a nurturer. Of course his mother was a hippie-type witch who loved to use words like *nurturer*. But Molly was half a country away from home with no friends and family around. It had to knock her off balance.

She'd handled herself so well with the wolves that afternoon. Anyone, big or small, powerful or not, would find it hard not to cow to a powerful Other like Lex Warden. The male was a freaking nuclear reactor of energy. But Molly had met his gaze without flinching. And even when he'd pounded the table, she'd hidden her distress. Her response hadn't been more anger, it had been reason. She was cool as a cucumber, but Gage wondered what she was like when she finally lost the reins on her emotions.

Faine had returned from the job Gage had sent him on that morning. "So I watched PURITY HQ all day. I've forwarded you all the film of who came and went. A few took the back way. Those ones you'll likely recognize quite easily. Including a federal court judge and two members of the county council."

Gage's lip curled. "Fucking ridiculous."

"Yes. But now we know. How'd she do? I saw the interview, by the way. Don't think they cut too much. She held her own."

"She said they had to agree to curtail editing for only

specific things. Part of her contract to speak. She's smart, our Molly."

"Totally. What'd the wolves think of her?"

"They agreed to her plan to have a council of Others and they'll send one of their people with her when she does public speaking events. Hell, she even showed them how to do video blogs to update the pack members via their website."

"I noticed she gets people to agree to things they probably had no intention of agreeing to before she walked in. And the aftermath of the death threat?"

Gage shrugged. "She's shaken up some. Who wouldn't be? But she did that interview right after she was told. We still need to go to the police to report the death threats. She got Meriel to agree that we'd report them all. Still don't know how effective it'll be. But I get her point."

Faine shrugged. "We won't know until we try I guess. I like her. Molly I mean. She'll fit in here just fine. Just wish it was under better circumstances."

"Yeah. I'm taking her to grab dinner. You want to come with us?"

"Sounds good."

EVERYTHING had been . . . manageable until they'd finished what had been a pretty delightful dinner.

Gage on one side, Faine on the other, she was protected by a wall of giant, muscly and admittedly gorgeous man flesh as they left the restaurant and hit the sidewalk outside.

"Shit. Hang on, Molly." Faine touched her shoulder. "We've got a whole group of protesters to get through."

"Let's go back inside, we can head out the back door." Gage's face had hardened, leaving her breathless and fascinated.

"No. Unless you think it's too dangerous. I don't think we should turn tail and hide." Part of her knew how much they both hated the idea.

Maybe it was the fear. Or her exhaustion. Maybe it was

the way the death threat had turned her world upside down but whatever the cause, she didn't want to back down.

Gage locked his gaze with hers. "Are you sure? This could get ugly."

"Uglier than a death threat? Uglier than losing my job because my clients, who I thought were friends, turned on me?" She hadn't meant for that to come out, but it did and he took it in, emotion flooding his features for a brief moment until he hardened again.

That's when the tussle happened.

A wall of protesters surged forward and Molly nearly lost her balance. She stumbled back into Faine, who shored her up, allowing her to keep her feet. Gage snarled something, shoving forward. The magick flowed from him, surrounding her, bringing the hair on her arms to stand.

The crowd was screaming stuff. She didn't register most of it, but the tone was enough to convey their hate and fear. Molly dimly registered that things were being thrown, but not what. She kept her head down.

They held signs with crude and hateful words. Some used the signs to batter the group as they tried to make their way through. She should have gone out the back door like they suggested.

The sidewalk was full. People spilled out into the street. Cars screeched to a halt to keep from hitting people. Horns sounded.

Chaos ruled, and for what?

Molly's brain shut down everything but essential functions like keeping her feet and letting Faine and Gage get her through the crowd and to the car.

Faine shoved her in and followed, shielding her with his body. Gage scooted across the front to the driver's side, cursing as he jammed the key into the ignition and started the car. They were surrounded by protesters banging on the hood and windows until Gage did some sort of magick stuff and they parted enough for them to get free.

They drove away quickly, Faine on his phone with the

woman who owned the restaurant telling her they were sending some people over to guard the front entrance.

Molly stared out the window and barricaded the walls around her emotions. They trembled and she whispered in her head to hold it together until she got back to her hotel room.

The rage radiated from Gage as he drove. Faine made calls and gave orders, punctuated by short directives from Gage as he went. Neither of them said anything to her, which was good because she was beyond speaking anyway.

Back at the hotel Faine turned to her. "Hold on, I'm coming around to get your door."

She nodded, numb, her hands loose in her lap.

Gage turned in the driver's seat to look at her. "Are you all right?"

If she spoke she might laugh. Or worse, cry. So she nodded again.

"Did you get hit with anything? Harmed in any way?"

In any way? A laugh bubbled up. One of those not-quite-sane laughs and she choked it back, shaking her head and scrambling out when Faine opened her door.

One foot in front of the other and she got to the elevator and then down the hall. She managed to blurt a thank you to Faine on his way out of her room to be sure everything was fine.

He paused, clearly about to speak, but must have seen the panic in her eyes and touched her shoulder instead, before leaving.

She locked up and methodically took her hair down, throwing the pins across the room so hard they pinged off various surfaces. Her watch followed, whether it broke or not when she threw it she didn't know. Or care.

One shoe knocked over a lamp, then the other better aimed at the closed bathroom door.

Gage knocked on the door. "Are you all right, Molly?"

Fuck no. She wasn't all right.

"Fine," she nearly snarled as she headed toward her bathroom, pulling her clothes off as she went.

The nearly scalding water filled the room with steam. Enough that she didn't have to look at herself when she got into the shower. Enough that she wasn't sure where the tears began and the water ended.

She didn't get death threats! She didn't have people screaming that she was a demon from hell. Didn't get things thrown at her. Even when she'd dealt with the worst kinds of scandals she hadn't seen this sort of violence aimed at her.

She was far from everything. From Chicago, from the road signs and rooftops she knew best. Far from the way her mother's front walk curved ever so slightly before it reached the front steps. Far from Rosa's porch swing and roses.

She had no one to talk to. No one who could understand her. Her life in Chicago was hours ahead. Too late to call. Too late to be listened to.

Molly was not a wallower, but it seemed like it was all she could do to try to scrub the day from her skin as she wept like an idiot.

GAGE heard the thump and then another and then a crash. He pounded on her door. "Are you all right, Molly?"

There was no sound and then the tiniest intake of breath. Admittedly he used some magick to boost his hearing. She was on the edge, that much had been clear by the way she'd held herself on the way to the hotel.

When she answered with a terse "Fine," it was threaded with anguish. He put a palm against the door, not knowing what to do.

"Leave her be." Faine jerked his head toward his door.

"She's clearly upset. We can't just leave her be." He stayed at her door until he heard the rush of the shower and then headed to Faine's room.

"We have to let her decide if she wants to share or not." Faine shrugged as Gage locked up.

"She needs friends right now."

"She does. And they're a thousand miles away. Or maybe two. Whatever, it's far from here to Chicago. This is all new to her. She's essentially lived as a human. *Nothing* is the same for her now."

Gage's stomach hurt. "Which is why we need to go to her now."

"No. It's why we need to let her decide when to let us in. Dude, I know a control freak when I see one and the lovely lady next door is the biggest control freak I've ever met. She's precise in nearly every way."

Gage remembered the way she'd laid her napkin out, the way she'd cut her burrito up into equally sized pieces. "And your point?"

"My point is, when people like Molly lose their shit, they may not want to do it in front of a total stranger. She might see it as a weakness, being affected by all this crazy. If we push our way in, she's going to be embarrassed. Or worse, feel like she has to keep holding it together when I'm going to venture a guess that she needs this little breakdown more than even she understands."

"You went into the wrong field. Should have been a psychologist."

Faine lifted a shoulder. "I have many talents. Anyway, go on home. I've got things covered here. I'll check in with her tomorrow morning to make sure she's all right. I doubt she takes days off. Then again, neither do you."

"Too much to do." Gage headed to the door again. "I told her I'd take her to the police station tomorrow to report the death threat so I'll be by at ten or so. I can take tomorrow with her so you can have the day off. Hell, take the weekend. Spend some time with Simon and Lark."

"I got it. She's not that much work and when she's at the office I have plenty of time to finish my other work."

"No arguing. It'll be good for her too. I'm going to give her some training on Sunday anyway. Defensive magick. She should know more about how to take care of herself in this new world she finds herself in. Probably give her some sense of control too."

"All right then. I'll talk to you later."

Gage didn't go straight home. Instead he headed to Heart of Darkness. He needed something. Company maybe. A drink definitely. Chances were Meriel and Dom would be there so he could brief them on the situation.

And maybe to keep from being alone.

Chapter 9

"YOU sure you want to do this?" Gage looked her up and down when she opened the door to her room the following morning.

"Where's Faine?"

"You're going to give me a complex, Molly. What am I, chopped liver?"

"Liver's gross."

"I suppose that may have been a compliment. Anyway, Faine has the weekend off. I'm on Molly duty. It's better that I go to the SPD with you anyway. I've had some dealings with them and we've got sort of an established relationship there."

Molly took one last look at herself, grateful for the wonder of modern makeup and the few awesome glamour spells she knew to get rid of under-eye circles. She'd slept pretty hard after her shower wallow and that huge bowl of ice cream. Before the makeup and hair she'd looked every inch the person who'd been up too late.

"Yes, let's get this over with. I have a conference call in

two hours. Do you think this will take that long?" She grabbed her bag and he helped her into her coat.

"Shouldn't, no. They may have questions, but it shouldn't take them that long."

"So glad it's a snap to report a death threat," she muttered.

He guided her to the elevator and then out through the lobby where his car waited. She didn't want to talk about the night before but he had that look men got when they knew they should probably mention something that had upset the woman before. But they didn't know how to do it and they were uncomfortable with it anyway. If she'd been dating him, it might have been more amusing than annoying.

She headed it off. "I'm fine."

He gave her a sideways look as he snapped the seat belt but thankfully left it alone.

"This cop we're talking to is pretty all right. He's someone the wolves have dealt with in the past I'm told. So he's not unfamiliar with Others, nor is he a bigot. At least not any kind that could be turned up after a search of his background."

"Do you do that? Routinely check on people?"

"Yes. Especially now."

"Like how?"

"Do you really want to know? Don't you want plausible deniability? Or whatever."

She held her eye roll in check. "I'm not your attorney. I need to know. I'm fine not answering a question if I feel that's what's necessary. And I don't need to know every little detail. I just need to know what you're doing. If it comes up I should have the information. It vexes me when I should know things and I don't."

He blew out a breath. "We want to know what all the powerful humans in the area are up to. What their affiliations are. Lark thought it was best to keep an eye on PURITY headquarters to see who came and went."

"Smart." And it was. These people had a big say in whatever direction all this went. It was important to know who they were inside. What they supported and believed in.

"So that's pretty much it. We look into donations for the big anti-Other organizations. Who goes to dinner with whom. That sort of thing."

"Have you connected with your counterparts in different, um, Other groups? I don't even know what to call it, them, jamborees, packs, nests, whatever."

He snorted a laugh and pulled into a spot next to a parking meter.

"Lark has made some connections. I've worked some with Megan Warden, she's the Enforcer for Cascadia. Smart. The vampires aren't as open to us as the shifters have been. They're scared of Lark though."

Molly could believe it. The woman may have been tiny and blue haired, but Molly knew a predator when she saw one and Lark was that.

"Well, I'm meeting with someone from the local nest next week so I can bring it up then."

He groaned. "You are? Did you clear it with Faine? You can't go unescorted."

"Rita made the arrangements. She told me she'd clear it with your office."

He got out and moved to her side to open her door. His gaze never stopped moving as she got out.

"By the way, that spell you did last night—outside the restaurant—what was it?"

"Do you want to learn it?"

She nodded.

"I'll teach you tomorrow."

NO one looked at them twice as they were met by Detective Alder. When he saw Gage he glowered a little and Molly watched him, learning him as he took them back to his desk and had them sit.

"Detective Alder, this is Molly Ryan. She's the one who received the death threat I told you about."

"Why didn't you report this yesterday?"

"It's nice to meet you, Detective." Molly held a hand out

and, as she suspected, he was raised well enough to take it. "I appreciate your seeing us today." She brought her chair a little closer and changed the pitch of her voice slightly. He'd have to pay closer attention, which is what she wanted. "Shall I be totally honest about why we didn't come in yesterday?"

He looked surprised. She sensed Gage's surprise as well, but he let her go without interruption.

"Yes, that's the point, Ms. Ryan."

She smiled charmingly. "Oh please, do call me Molly. We did report this yesterday of course." She flipped open her notepad. "I've got the details here. We called it in and as no one was available to come to us, we made this appointment for today. I'm sure you understand what it is to have so many things to do at work you can't stop for anything else. I had several prior engagements and then of course after dinner we were assaulted by PURITY protesters outside the restaurant. Busy day. That's why we came in today."

Detective Alder wanted to dislike her. She could sense it. But she needed to make that impossible. Needed him to see her as a person. Clearly he saw her as an Other, and that was fine. She was an Other after all. But she was a person. He'd help a person; he was a police officer after all.

He cleared his throat. "Assaulted? Did you report this?"

"We called it in once we got Ms. Ryan to the car safely. Dispatch said they'd send someone over. We had guards posted outside the restaurant and by their reports no one showed up for an hour. But the officers on the scene did speak with the owner and make sure the protesters didn't block fire exits or harm anyone coming or going."

Molly leaned in just a little. "Seems to me, Detective Alder, that it's bad for business, bad for the city and bad for her citizens if they can't even eat a burrito in peace. If we can't express our beliefs without harming other people, what does that say about our beliefs? We don't expect their rights of free speech to be violated, of course. We just don't want to be physically attacked. The two things are not mutually exclusive." She used a little bit schoolteacher, a little bit librarian and a little bit mother. It was a lecture and a tease all at once.

There was a little upward movement at the edges of his mouth. Just for a brief moment, but she knew she was winning him over. "Yes, ma'am."

She pushed the copy of the email they'd received his way. "We sent the original with the header information to your email address here."

He read it, his face darkening as he did. Once he finished he looked up at her. "I'm sorry you had to see that."

"You and me both, Detective. I'm not used to death threats. Heck, I'm in PR and I've never received one before."

He looked her over and shook his head. "We'll look into it. I can't promise you much. We're short staffed and a lot of this email stuff is a dead end."

"Used an anonymizer. We tried to track it as well."

Alder looked to Gage. "You keeping an eye on her then? In case?"

Gage nodded. "Yes, she's being guarded at all times. As are many of our leadership. This isn't the first death threat we've received since the Magister."

Alder blew out a long breath. "Did you report any of them?"

"After the first you mean? When one of your compatriots told me I was lucky no one had killed us yet and to keep my head down and it would blow over?"

Molly sat straighter, shocked. She'd have to speak with Gage about not springing that stuff on her.

"Who said that to you?" Alder's eyes went hard, his jaw tightened. He was offended by that sort of thing. She knew he'd do the right thing, even if he was uncomfortable with the whole coming out of Others.

Gage gave him a name and Molly made a little note to be sure to follow up as well. It was not to be tolerated.

"My apologies Ms. Ryan. Molly. I promise you I'm taking this seriously. I'll do what I can. But you need to stay vigilant. There are plenty of kooks who don't bother with threat notes. They just cut straight to the point. Gage, I'll get back with you on the other threats. I'd like to see them all. Just get them into my hands directly and we'll be sure they're taken seriously."

They stood and Alder walked them out, shaking her hand before turning to Gage. "We should make some time to talk about all this. Maybe work on liaising better."

Gage relaxed his spine just a little. "I'd appreciate it."

HE walked her out, not saying much until they'd pulled away from the curb and headed away.

"You're fucking amazing. That's all I'm saying."

She turned her body toward him. "What makes you say that? I mean, thank you and all."

"It's not only your magick. You have a great deal of personal charisma and charm. That's one thing and it opens the door for you to make a point. But it's the way you use your charm and then your brain and posture and what you say and how you say it to totally get past people's defenses. It's brilliant."

"Oh. Well." She ducked her head. "Thank you."

"What's your plan for the day? Where to next?" He didn't want to embarrass her but he definitely planned to go to Meriel to tell her what an amazing job she'd done that morning.

"I have some phone calls to make, but those notes are here with me so I can do them from my hotel room easily enough. I have some press releases to write. I want to update the website with a little statement about what happened last night."

"All right. How about you come with me out to my mother's house today? I want to check on her. She lost her brother, my uncle. Well, you knew that part."

He found himself talking more than he'd planned to with her. At first he'd suspected her magick, but it was more that she was a good listener and maybe just a little bit that he wanted her to know him. She was new to Seattle after all and needed friends. He could do that.

"You can make your calls first and then take your laptop to her place. I can guarantee you she'll have a fire going and some soup cooking. She's got a big glassed-in porch that overlooks her garden and the Cedar River down the hill. You can work on your press releases there, right?"

"I don't want to be in the way. I can work from the hotel and you can go see her. I promise not to leave or do anything silly."

"No. I think she'd enjoy having you there. She needs a visit and the company and really it gives me an excuse to drop in. I can tell her *you* need the company. She's a doctor as well as one of those nurturers. She likes being useful."

"But chafes at the idea of being a burden?"

Shocked that she was so spot on, he held his words back for a moment. "Yes. I want to check on her but I don't want her to think I'm only checking on her because I'm worried."

"All right. It should take me an hour or two to get the calls taken care of. So let's go to the office. I'll do them there and you can get all the information to Detective Alder."

"Deal." He'd be able to watch them both.

"Rosa, my foster mom? She's a nurturer too." Molly spoke as they got onto the elevator at the Owen building.

"She's a teacher. Or, was a teacher I guess. They're trying to fire her. Her union is protecting her, thank goodness, but there's a lot of pressure for her to retire early."

"You said she came into your life later on?"

"Yes. I was thirteen. She was my humanities teacher in seventh grade. She knew I had magick. She asked me about it one day but I didn't know what she was talking about. Lucky for me, she called my mother and they met. It was hard for us to believe at first. But when someone shows you they can do magick and then helps you do some yourself it's sort of impossible to deny."

The elevator doors slid apart and that openness fell away, replaced by her reserve. He wanted more, damn it.

"This is us. I'll text you when I'm finished, all right?"

Reluctant, he nodded. "Yes. See you in a bit."

He wandered back toward his office but veered off to see if Meriel was around, which of course she was.

He tapped on her door and she looked up, tiredness all around her eyes. "Hey there, do you have a few minutes?"

"Yes, of course." She pointed to the table near the windows. "Sit and I'll get us both a cup of coffee."

He did, staring out over the city below. This high up the rain was still snow and it fell past his gaze, easing his anxiety a little.

"Loving this thing Dom gave me." She indicated the single-cup coffeemaker as she put a mug in front of him. "I'd offer you milk but I know you don't use it. Sugar is right there." She sat. "I tell myself I don't actually drink more coffee every day since I got it. I do have tea and hot cocoa and stuff." Meriel sipped with a happy sigh. "Oh, the lies we tell ourselves."

He laughed.

Molly eased back in her chair, watching him carefully. "I saw the interview with Molly. She's really good at this stuff. Briggs had zero idea what to do. She cornered him so well."

"She did. She was that way just a bit ago at the police station. Alder has been all right so far. But she charmed him past all right and into downright helpful. Even outraged on our behalf."

"So it went well then? The cop thing?"

"Reported the death threat against her. The others too. In fact when I mentioned the reception we got the first time we tried to report he was *not* pleased. Asked me to send everything we had directly to him. That's next on my list. I have to hand it to her, I was really dead set against even bothering with the authorities and she's turned me around. Reported that bullshit from last night too."

"Molly and I had a talk about it yesterday. Reporting things to the cops and FBI I mean. She sees it as our right as citizens and she's not going to let them shirk." Meriel shrugged. "She's right of course. I think her perspective is important. Especially now. She remembers what it means to be human in a different way than we who've grown up in clans do."

"You made a good choice when you hired her."

"She handling it all okay? You see her more than I do."

"Death threats are no fun. She was shaken up last night when the protesters rushed us. But she refused to take the back way. She's strong."

Meriel nodded. He filled her in on everything else and by the time he'd left, he felt better. Meriel had that way about her.

Chapter 10

BY the time they headed back to the hotel it had been a very, very long day. Molly had enjoyed her time at Gage's parents' house. His father had been warm and welcoming, interested in what Molly did for a living. His mother, well, she'd been overjoyed to see Gage when they'd arrived.

It'd been easy for an outsider to see how much Shelley had needed the visit from her son. She'd tutted over how thin he'd looked and the shadows under his eyes before she turned her attention to Molly.

She'd fed them both. Repeatedly as the time had worn on. True to Gage's word, Molly had been able to work and finish her press releases in the sunroom that had overlooked the garden. No one had bothered her except to bring her a cup of tea here and there.

And when she'd finished up, they'd all ended up watching a movie and gorging on pizza and popcorn. It had been the first time in well over a month that Molly had actually relaxed. She'd really needed something delightfully normal and it had been that in spades.

"You were good to my mom today. Thank you." Gage

came into her room to do his usual checking under the bed and testing the wards.

She put her shoes in the hall closet and hung her coat up as well. "She was the one who was good to me. I was thinking on the way back here that this evening was the first time I felt truly relaxed since . . . well, before the Magister."

He stood in her entry and she waved him all the way inside. "Are you staying here tonight?" She blushed. "I mean, next door? If so, I've got a bottle of wine if you'd like a glass."

He'd reached out to her when she'd really needed it. Plus she liked being with him. He smelled good. Made her feel safe and there was no denying he was nice to look at.

And she wasn't ready to be alone yet.

He smiled. "Yes. I sent Faine home for the weekend. A glass of wine sounds good."

"I'll be right back. I'm going to change out of these work clothes. There may be some cheese or something like that in the fridge. Meriel sent over a basket yesterday."

She ducked into the bedroom and then stood there as she tried to figure out what to wear. Sweats? No. Yoga pants? Yes, that would work. She didn't look herself in the eye in the mirror because for heaven's sake, the man did not care what she wore! But she did.

She carefully hung her work clothes up, thankful for the washer and dryer stacked in a nearby closet. It wouldn't be that hard to live in the hotel for a bit, especially when she could wash her clothes and make her meals.

When she emerged he'd opened the connecting door to the other room and he'd kicked off his boots, padding around in his socks. She paused, arrested for a moment by the sight and not understanding why. He wasn't naked for goodness' sake.

"There you are." He smiled her way as his gaze moved up her body, lingering at her breasts, making her glad she wore the snug long-sleeved shirt. He cleared his throat. "I took the liberty of uncorking the wine and getting the glasses."

They ended up settled on the small couch in the living area. She tucked her feet beneath her and grabbed her glass.

"Wait." He held his aloft. "To successes. Big and small."

She clinked her glass with his before sipping.

"I'm a little superstitious. I like to make a toast when I drink spirits. It feels like I'm wasting magick if I don't."

She smiled. "I like that. So, what made you decide to be a hunter?"

"Family business. My father was a hunter. He only retired a few years ago. Before that it was my grandfather, his brother, and so on. There's been a Garrity in the Hunter Corps since the first years of Clan Owen. Hell, since we all lived on the East Coast. That or Hunters. That's Nell's family."

"Nell is the hunter out on maternity leave now? The one who was kidnapped just shortly ago?"

He nodded, the anger on his face drawing deep lines into his forehead. This Nell was clearly important to him.

"Yes. She and her husband have faded into some well-deserved obscurity. He was wary about her job before. But after the kidnapping, well, let's just say he is *not* enthused about the family business at this point. Though he is part owner of Heart of Darkness still. They have a newborn so that's rightfully their focus. A little girl named Libby."

Babies helped you remember what was important in ways nothing else could. "I get that. And I understand why she'd back off. You two were close then?"

"She's like a sister. I'm just glad she and the baby are all right. But I miss having her around. Lark and I work well together, don't get me wrong. I like her. She's smart and capable and I think she and I run a tight crew."

"But it's not the same."

"No. It isn't." He snorted. "Do you have a best friend like that?"

"I did. She . . . the Magister." Molly licked her lips, suddenly unable to control her emotions.

He took her hand and she shook her head. "No. I can't. Not now."

He kissed her knuckles and her lids flew up. He filled her vision.

"You don't know me well, but you don't have to be strong

every single moment. Not on my account. I understand it. The loss. The anger."

If she let it go, Molly was afraid it would fill the room and drown them both.

"So Rosa found you at thirteen and then took you under her wing?"

He was good at this. Changing the subject enough that she could fight past the knot of emotion in her throat.

"I pretty much lived at their house a few weeks a month and most of the summer. She and Anthony, that was her husband, they accepted me like I was theirs. Taught me how to use my magick. I remember the first time I did a spell successfully. A protection spell." She smiled remembering that moment when all the symbols she'd drawn in the air had worked, come together and she'd felt it all the way to her toes. "Rosa taught me a lot of healing and protection stuff. Anthony showed me that I didn't have to do sigils to use my magick. That was later on, when I was nearly out of high school."

"So you were part of their coven then?"

"Sort of. I went to barbecues and picnics, that sort of thing. My mother insisted I participate on some level because she's always felt it was important I understand the other side of my heritage. I never really felt connected to it. Not the way you all do to Owen."

"Maybe you will too, someday."

"Maybe. It's different now. I've changed. This thing has given me a different perspective."

"My first week on the job I got my nose broken. My mom could help some with it, but it still hurt like a bitch. Worse, I was humiliated because I got it after making a stupid mistake. My dad said to me, as he picked me up off the sidewalk, *'Kid, some lessons are best learned the hard way.'* Not that I'm saying it's good you had to go through this, that any of us did, but I'm hoping that we can all learn from it. And never fail that way again."

She shrugged, suddenly so very tired. Instead she held her glass out as he filled it again. "Do you have a girlfriend?"

Oh god. Did she just say that?

"No time really. I dated someone, but she left after the Magister. Wanted to get out before the heat came down. I guess she was right to go."

"Look, it's not like I was the poster girl for witchcraft and my entire life was destroyed. Not by being a witch. But by scared, cowardly people. She can hide, but I don't think that's much protection anyway."

"You used to think so too, didn't you?"

Annoyed, she sent him a raised brow. "I wasn't hiding. Just because I grew up in a different way doesn't mean I'm incapable of understanding reality."

"I deserved that."

"You did. I never much thought about it before one way or the other. Which is a problem of a different sort and one I have to deal with now. I wasn't active in the coven not because I was ashamed of being a witch or felt like it was bad. But because I had a life I was happy with. I had a business and a home and friends and family. I was a witch, same as I am now, but it didn't define me in the same way it does now. But that's not me misunderstanding what I was, what I am. That's life changing not only the way others view me, but the context of what I am too."

Abashed, he realized how much more self-actualized she was than he. He, who'd grown up with all the clan had to offer. Connection, history, education, the collected skills and information of generation after generation of witches.

"I'm sorry. It's not what you think. It is in some ways, I admit. You're an outsider and"—he paused as the irony hit him—"I guess we both know how that goes now. Anyway, are you dating anyone?" He probably could have changed the subject better, but he wanted to know anyway.

"No. I've been busy with my firm. Building my professional life. I dated here and there, but never anything serious. I just didn't have the time, or the interest to put anyone before work. Now I'm glad I didn't. I guess."

"You'll find the time here after a while. This can't go on forever. At some point we'll get to back to normal. Woman like you? Smart and pretty, talented—you'll find yourself swimming in suitors."

"Don't know if *back* to normal will ever happen. We'll have to find new normal. And ha, suitors. You sound like my mother."

"Did she never marry then? I mean after your father . . . though I guess *father* is a relative term. Can't abide a man who abandons his family."

"To his credit, I don't think he knew when he left. They were only together a few months. She had a boyfriend for nine years. She said marriage wasn't in the cards for her at her age. Though for goodness' sake, *her age*, like she's ninety instead of fifty. Anyway. They broke up two years ago and she hasn't really been looking. She's a little, um, daunting. I've never met anyone as awesome, ambitious and totally in charge as my mother."

He appeared to be looking at someone who was as awesome, ambitious and totally in charge, but he didn't say that. "Did you ever want to find him? Your father I mean."

"Rosa has wanted me to for years. But I don't know. He's not really anyone to me. I had a man in my life. I had a father. Even my mom's boyfriend was more of a father to me than the one who made me." She shrugged. "Anyway, my god, let's talk about something good. What do you do for fun, Gage Garrity?"

She leaned in, a smile on her face, and it lightened his heart. Though also, undeniably, other parts got a little heavier.

"I don't know, do you want the PG answer?"

She laughed. A different laugh than she'd given him before. This one was husky, sensual. He liked it.

"Well, it's been a long day and I've had some wine so let's go big or go home. Give it to me."

Then she blushed, putting her fingers over her lips as she laughed again.

He started to laugh and kept on. She was so much more than he'd imagined at first. She kept surprising him, which was unexpected and wonderful all at once. Not much was surprising to him those days. Not in a good way anyway.

"I'd scare you all the way back to Chicago, missy."

One of her eyebrows rose ever so imperiously and he dug it like an idiot. "Is that so? Hm. I think that might just be the other way around. I might give you gray hair. Just because I don't date on the regular doesn't mean I don't know how to get my *hobby* on."

"Oh my god, you're a menace," he said through laughter. But he'd be lying if he denied he hadn't gone there when she'd said it. Hadn't wondered just what she meant.

She started laughing and within moments the two of them were doubled over on the couch, laughing so hard they couldn't speak.

"I haven't laughed like this in so long." She wiped her eyes with a paper towel. "Thank you."

He grinned. "Right back atcha. Just remember how much you like me now tomorrow when I'm working you."

She started laughing again. "You're what?"

"Teaching you defensive magick! Gah, you are a total perv, aren't you?"

"You started it!"

He hadn't laughed like this in so long either. God knew he needed it. And he really liked that it was with her.

Chapter 11

GAGE had cornered Faine and sent him off on an assignment. One anyone else could have done in his place. But he wanted to escort Molly to the local nest to meet with Franco Pendergast. The local vampire bigwig had agreed to meet with her and she had no idea what she was dealing with.

Not that he'd tell Molly that. Or, well, he'd tried in nice ways, but she'd given him a look that had sent his balls up into his body in fear.

So he'd escort her and shoot anyone in the face if they tried to touch her. It worked for him.

"I really can't believe I'm going to visit a vampire at his lair. Nest. House. Whatever. Honestly, it's silly for me to be surprised, given the fact that I'm a witch and all, but vampires seem so much more fantastical than anything else."

"More fantastical than men who can shift into wolves?" He grinned as he drove.

"I didn't profess my surprise to be rational. It's just so . . . well, werewolves aren't like in the movies I guess."

"Don't expect vampires to be in polo shirts and jeans with backward baseball hats."

She laughed. "Check that one off the list. Though it would be really funny if they were. I know they're predators. Lark took me aside a few days ago and gave me a big brief about them. She's awesome. I wish I could dye my hair blue."

Random. Women were so damned random sometimes. He just nodded and hoped she'd wander back to the point soon.

"Anyway, so I know not to stare into their eyes. Not to make sudden movements. She gave me a list of topics to avoid. Not that I would have been discussing any of them with strangers anyway. And frankly, who *does* discuss that sort of thing with strangers?" She sniffed, outraged, and he tried not to laugh. "In any case, I'm more curious than frightened."

"Good. They smell fear. Of us all, Others I mean, they're the most, um, different than humans. They've been around a very long time. A lot of the really powerful ones are hard to relate to so they keep to themselves. The one you're meeting with today, Franco, is only a couple hundred years old. He's all right. He knows we're not victims. I'll set him on fire if he gets out of line. I find that helps move things along."

She looked over at him and shook her head. "Lark told me about the last run-in with them. Still, I'd like to think I could do this on my own. I'm not totally helpless."

"We've gone over this many times before, Molly. You're not totally helpless at all. But this world, well I'm more familiar with it. And I know how to set shit on fire. I'm handy to have around if things get out of hand. Just think of it that way. Never, ever deal with vampires if you're not armed. Consider me your weapon."

"That and the two rather large side arms you're wearing."

"You saw that, huh?"

"Yes." She wore a smile, one he thought . . . well, it couldn't be a sexy smile. She was amused by him. Which worked better than sexy. Right? They were better off as friends and nothing more. They'd work better that way. Even if he was fighting off the urge to sniff her, or smooch her every time he got her alone these days.

Stupid hormones.

It was the way she made him laugh. That's all.

"Look, there's going to be a little push and shove here. They're going to want me to show my belly. And that's not going to happen. It's mainly ceremonial anyway. Just let me handle that part." He pulled up to the gate and stopped, rolling his window down. A burly human guard muscled over and gave them the eye.

"Molly Ryan here to see Franco Pendergast on behalf of Clan Owen."

"She's on the list, but you're not, Garrity."

"He's my interpreter." Molly leaned over, hovering over Gage's lap, her hair close enough to his face that he had no choice but to breathe her in. Goddamn, she smelled good. And right over his cock. He held his breath before he said or did something stupid. Oh, and he probably should pay attention too. "Wouldn't want to make a mistake with so much at stake, now would I?"

The guard looked down at her, a surly expression, which faded quickly as he caught sight of her. Another one bites the dust. The woman could seemingly win over everyone. But the PURITY people, anyway.

"Do you have identification?"

"I do." She braced a hand on Gage's thigh to sit up to grab her bag and he ground his teeth together. Shortly she produced her wallet with her driver's license, which the guard decided was enough.

"I recognize you, Gage. Go on up to the house. You'll need to leave the guns in the car. You know he doesn't allow them in the house."

Fine. He could still be a weapon without side arms anyway. And they both knew it.

Molly knew Gage didn't need to be there. Lark had told her Owen and the Vampire Nation had a peace accord. One Lark had brokered herself just a month before.

But she had no trouble admitting she liked having Gage around. This was all totally foreign to her. Being out of her element was one thing. Dealing with vampires was something totally different. Lark had had to break noses and arms and stuff to be taken seriously. Molly could be a badass, but breaking things was most assuredly Gage's arena.

Plus he looked unbelievably hot in those snug, dark utility pants with his combat boots and those damned guns strapped to his thighs. Really, really nice thighs.

Okay she had to stop thinking about his thighs. Or his belly, which she caught sight of when he bent to put the guns in a locked case in the trunk.

"From here on, they can hear what we say. Even if we whisper it. So save anything important for later, all right?"

She tore her gaze from his ass, guilty and totally busted. He wore the glimmer of a smirk, but straightened.

"Yes. Yes. I got it." She'd been careful about what she'd chosen to wear. Too much hiding of the neck and it only emphasized it. Too much exposed skin and the result was the same. So a shirt with a collar worked.

The front door opened as they approached. More guards. "Franco is waiting. Come in. I need to pat you down."

Gage stepped in front of her, putting himself between them. "No, you don't. I put my weapons away as requested. I'm not going to allow you to put your hands on her."

"Then you can't come in."

Molly shrugged and stepped back. She really didn't want this guy's hands all over her. And if Gage didn't want it, well, then she didn't want it even more. "All right then. Good day." She turned, speaking to Gage over her shoulder. "Let him know when you call later that this opportunity is only available so long. I have other things to do. He can of course deal with the humans alone. Or face them in a coalition with all Others. I know our preference. Mr. Pendergast needs to figure out his."

A male came out into the main room, skirting the light at the front door. "Back off, Mike. Let them pass. Mr. Garrity understands what would happen if he tried anything."

The vampire male wasn't handsome. Not really. But he was compelling. His eyes were so brown they were nearly black. He wore a soft sweater and trousers. Nice watch. Nary a hint of crusty blood at his lips or anything like that. No cape either.

He bowed slightly. "Ms. Ryan, the Vampire Nation welcomes you to our nest."

She did the same, her gaze focused on his eyebrows. "Thank you, Clan Owen is grateful for your welcome."

He smiled. "Well done. Come in. I've just had coffee brought in. It looks cold and wet out there. Warm up and give me your pitch."

THAT had gone amazingly well. Molly smiled as she waited for Gage to open her hotel room door and do his thing.

That's when she saw the boxes had finally arrived from Chicago. She managed to withhold her little dance of joy, but the sight of her mother's concise handwriting on the address labels comforted her anyway.

"Looks like your stuff arrived." Gage turned to her with a smile.

Faine showed up. "Hope you don't mind that I brought it all in for you. It arrived at the office so I delivered it here. Figured you'd like to go through it all here rather than there."

"Thank you, Faine. I appreciate that very much." She turned back to Gage. "Thanks for guarding me with the vampires today as well. Go on, have a life. I'm safe in my gilded cage."

"You did an awesome job. I can't believe they extended an offer to let Meriel address their Convocation. And to send a representative with you when you to testify too. You have a way about you. Honestly, it's fun to go with you just to see what you'll get people to give you."

She blushed, the warmth of Gage's compliments washing over her. "I'll see you both tomorrow. I plan on a pizza and a lot of unpacking."

Gage nodded and Faine lifted a hand as they both backed from the room and left her alone.

She knew exactly which box she wanted to open first. Thank goodness her mother hadn't been offended by her

rather precise instructions. Molly cut the top open and carefully unpacked the turntable. She placed it on the counter
and went back to get the Bose dock that would also serve
as her speakers until she moved into a real apartment and
had the room for her whole setup.

She found all the cords, neatly labeled by her mother,
and got everything hooked up before she found the box with
all her non-work clothes and opened it, changing into jeans
and a T-shirt before returning to grab a glass of wine and the
box with her records.

Molly knew exactly which one she wanted. The orangey
glow of Led Zeppelin's *Houses of the Holy* greeted her as
she pulled it out and slid the record from the sleeve.

Ah. She cleaned everything and placed it down, putting
the needle at the beginning of "The Ocean" and stood back
as the crackle spilled into the room over the speakers and
she felt a million times better as the song started.

She'd been scared spitless at the very first when they'd
driven up toward Casa de Vampire. Ha. But being with Gage
had made it better. The way he'd consistently helped her
through things, given her advice and even taught her some
awesome new defensive magick spells—had all combined
to build her confidence in this entirely new world she found
herself in.

Also, her crush on Gage burned still within her. Man, he
was so . . . hot. Smart. Sexy. Strong. Powerful. He was all
manly and protective and it rang her bell. Not her type at
all. But apparently she'd been doing it all wrong because
hello.

When he'd gotten in between her and the bodyguard earlier that day her entire body had come to attention. She really
shouldn't be thinking of him in the way she was just then.
But whatever, it was in the privacy of her hotel room and she
could objectify anyone she wanted in her fantasies!

The song ended and she flipped the record over. Strange
to think that her life had settled in such an odd way. Adrift,
away from everything she knew, she was beginning to find
her way. It gave her some measure of comfort and right then,

her records, her cupcake socks and a glass of wine did the trick.

THE woman who stood just at the table wasn't the giggling witch he'd drunk wine with just two weeks before. This woman was not silly. At all. This Molly was totally in charge. It sent a flash of heat through him. Her hair was back from her face, captured by two barrettes at either side of her head. The rest had been held in a pretty but not fussy knot at the back of her neck.

He stared at that bun, wondering what it would feel like when he pulled the pins out. What the cool silk of it would smell like as it tumbled around his wrists and hands.

He tore his gaze away and it snagged on her suit. A skirt, not too short or too fitted. It had a flare so it moved as she walked, hitting the top of her thighs. Her blouse was the color of deep, cold water and it made her skin look . . . Christ, what the fuck was he doing? She looked nice. Yes, that was it. She looked nice. Pretty but not too pretty. Sexy, but that was probably just his twisted mind. She wasn't showing anything! She had on pearl earrings for god's sake. He was just broken and bent, that had to be it.

She wore heels, but they weren't too high. Just right. Not dowdy, but not the hot sexy ones women wore a lot of the time. Not that he complained about such things. He *liked* hot and sexy high heels.

She nodded to the person next to her and sat, only to have the guy next to her push her chair in. Gage frowned. He could have done that. But she'd have been pissy, he knew. He noted the slight tightening around her mouth and wanted to laugh. She was pissy then as well, she just hid it better with the human next to her. Ha.

He'd seen her be interviewed. He'd seen her give video press releases, but he'd never seen her testify before any legislative body. He settled back, his gaze never stopping for long, moving around the space. There were metal detectors and security here in the wake of 9/11. But he wanted more. They'd told him it was fine. He hoped they were right.

"Ms. Ryan, Mr. Sawyer, Ms. Freed, welcome." The chair of the committee addressed them. He turned to the person who'd just entered. Ugh. It was the state PURITY leader, Alison Moore.

Moore smirked. "I apologize for being late. It took me some time to get through the throng outside. All those concerned citizens you know."

Gage had his game face on, but it was a challenge not to smirk right back. He was surprised she hadn't giggled like that character from Harry Potter. *Concerned* citizens his ass. Thugs. Just like the thugs who showed up anytime anyone from PURITY would be anywhere.

Molly smiled, her hands clasped loosely on the table before her.

"Let's take this alphabetically, shall we? Ms. Freed, would you like to go first?"

Lani Freed was an attorney. A civil rights activist who'd been working in the Puget Sound for most of her life. She spoke about the uptick in the number of cases she was seeing regarding unlawful terminations, evictions and general harassment at local businesses.

Sawyer, also a human, married to a shifter, spoke about the impact of the harassment on his family. They'd lost his mother-in-law and a child when the Magister manifested. Two local businesses refused to host the wakes and his wife had been attacked outside their home as she was bringing groceries in from the car.

No one on the panel had any questions for either Freed or Sawyer. And then it was Alison Moore's turn.

"Thank you so much, Henry, for having me today."

No one else had used first names. The senators on the dais had used *Ms.* or *Mr.* with the people testifying and those testifying had used *Senator* this or that. This woman had a serious set of stones, Gage had to give her that.

"I came here today to give voice to those so blatantly

ignored by the media and our legislators. *Honest*, hardworking human beings. No one seems to care that our neighbors have been monsters this whole time. None of the elite seems to worry that our children could be infected and turned into wild animals. Well, I'm here to tell you we human beings, the *true* citizens of this country, are worried and we want you to protect us."

A few heads on the dais nodded and Molly took mental notes. She'd remember them. Also, Alison Moore made Molly want to punch her. Every time she heard this hateful rhetoric it made her crazy.

"We're tired of protecting these special-interest groups at the expense of the majority. At the expense of all the decent *human* beings in this country who are rightful citizens. All these *lawyers*. What do they need lawyers for? Hm? If you're innocent why do you need them? All we're asking for is for you to classify these . . . *creatures* so we know who they are. All we're asking for is for *us* to be protected instead of harmed at their expense. Don't we have a right to know if our neighbor is a witch? Many of our community are concerned at the satanic rituals and demon-called walking among us. We're God-fearing and this is our country."

It went on this way for a few minutes more until her time was up and they gave her an extra minute.

"Ms. Ryan, if you'd like to go next."

"Thank you, Senator Albright, for having me here today. I'm thirty years old. Up until a few weeks ago I was a lifetime resident of Chicago, Illinois. Though I hope you won't hold that against me." She smiled. "I've even stopped carrying an umbrella and I can order my coffee like a real northwesterner now. I was born here, in this country. My mother and father were born here. My grandparents were born here. My boss Meriel Owen's family has not only been here in the country for generations, but they helped build this entire region. We are not creatures. We are not monsters. We don't call demons and we don't worship Satan. What we are, are citizens of the United States. Just like Ms. Freed, Mr. Sawyer and Ms. Moore."

Moore snorted. "You're pretenders and liars."

"I allowed Ms. Moore her time plus a minute. It's my turn to speak and I'm sure we can all agree, no matter our perspective, that democracy means we don't speak over each other. How can we understand each other if we don't listen? Now, back to my points. We understand why the human community is uncomfortable and afraid. We're happy to be as open as we can about what we do and who we are. We want nothing more than to be left alone to live our lives as we did before. Yes, before you knew about some of us."

Senator Albright gave her a considering glance. "Just why did you keep your existence a secret? If you're not a harm to the rest of us?"

"Senator, all you need to do is look back over recorded history for your answer. We've been burned at the stake. Drowned. Tortured to death. Imprisoned. Every time humans found out about us, they tried to wipe us out. So we learned from that and kept what we were private. Not to trick anyone, but to protect ourselves. And as many of us have begun to suffer from the reaction to our existence, yet again, it can't be that hard to understand why we did it."

She sipped her water. "We too understand your fear of the unknown. Of finding out overnight that not only were there werewolves, who you've known about for several years, but witches and vampires too. And yet, you can also look to see we have not harmed you. When you didn't know about us we did not perform satanic rituals in your yards. We did not steal your children. We lived our lives just as you lived yours."

"How do we know you didn't? How do we know all our criminals weren't witches or vampires or whatever else unholy things? Animals disappearing, serial killers, war, famine! How do we know you people aren't responsible for everything bad?"

Molly looked at Alison Moore, not surprised by her ignorance, just exhausted by it. "This is small-minded and petty nonsense. We're not trying to track humans or take away *your* basic human rights. We're simply asking the same of humans. Anything else is a waste of precious time and energy. And as someone who has lost loved ones, along with Mr. Sawyer and pretty much every single Other I know, we understand just how precious that time is now. This is our moment, as Americans, to shine. To set an example, as we have over and over through our history. It is not time to crawl back into factions and throw rocks. We want all that we had before the Magister showed up. That is all."

Molly took up every last second before she let go, knowing many of the senators on the committee had another meeting right after this one ended. It worked as they thanked everyone for their testimony and headed out.

"Ms. Ryan."

Molly turned to face the woman coming toward her. Her stomach clenched and it felt . . . wrong.

Gage shoved her from the way so hard she hit the corner of the table on her hip, sending a shock of pain through her body.

"Back up, right now."

Power radiated from Gage, and Molly again found herself fascinated by how Gage used his magick.

Police had come around, weapons drawn. Gage put his hands up. "This woman has something in her right hand."

The police moved toward Gage and Molly was not having it. "Did you hear what he said? No! He's not the issue. She is. At least get whatever she has before she drops it." Molly pulled every last bit of authority that had been hanging in the air and drew it around herself. It worked as one of the police officers moved to the woman.

He held it aloft. "Looks like paint or ink. Maybe blood."

The woman spit at the cop, who really got pissed off, spinning her and cuffing her wrists.

Molly's would-be attacker began to scream. "She's a monster. They're going to kill us all! How can you all just sit there calmly while they take over? Every last one of them needs to be killed. They are ungodly. An abomination on our lands."

"Do you see what you've done, Molly?"

Molly turned to face Alison Moore, who wore that damned smirk again.

"Excuse me?"

"There is no excuse for you. You are unholy, a blight sent upon this land sent to test us. We will not fail."

"Ms. Moore, I did this. Back in third grade. I believe *I know you are, but what am I* would be the next line. But I'm not in third grade anymore and neither are you. So let's be absolutely clear on this. We will not allow you to terrorize or threaten us. We want peace. We want to help you understand us. We don't need you to love or accept what we are. We just won't tolerate being assaulted. You need to understand that point."

"Or what?"

"I'm not being coy. It would serve you not to be either. Lastly, it's Ms. Ryan. You don't know me well enough to use my first name." Molly turned back to Gage, who'd just finished speaking with the police.

"She's one of those flour-bomber types. They're not going to punish her for it. She'll be fined. Are you all right? I pushed you out of the way a little hard."

She rubbed her hip. "Oh, that little bit of fluff didn't scare me. I just . . . it felt wrong. I don't know why."

"I could feel it too. She projected menace pretty clearly." He smiled. "You listened to your gut pretty well there."

"Hm. Let's go before they get out the blood and try to make it a scene from *Carrie*."

"I don't know," Gage murmured as he ushered her from the room out into the chaos of the hallway, "might be nice to see that scene where she started blowing up cars and shit with her mind."

People pressed in on all sides, but she'd be damned if she allowed any of them to make her afraid. Or at least to look it in public. She held her head up high, kept close to Gage and Faine and hoped she didn't trip.

"Next time we do this we'll need more security and to leave by a different door," she said as they finally got to their car.

"Next time? What the hell do you mean?"

"Testifying. Not just here, but I've been asked to go to D.C. next Tuesday with a group of Others to address a new committee they've established to deal with the Other issue."

"Issue? Like we're measles." Gage snarled it and she was glad Faine was in the car behind theirs.

"Look, this is reality. We can't pretend it away. Some of them do think of us as akin to a communicable disease. We can't get anywhere until more people *don't* think that. And the only way to do that is to be out there countering what those PURITY people say about us."

"Why bother? I could have shut her up with the flick of my wrist."

She rolled her eyes. "Oh yes, that would have been peachy keen. Then she could have talked about how we used magick on her to shut her up."

"So?"

"So then she can get everyone wondering just what we do to *them* without their knowing it. We can't give them anything else to use against us. She's dangerous, Gage. PURITY is dangerous. They will do whatever they have to to harm us."

"So why are we wasting our time on diplomacy? Fuck this and those assholes. Why are we even letting them get close enough to throw ink on you? They're not worthy of your time."

"Of course they're not worth my time. But that's not the issue here."

"So what is the issue here then? Don't you think your talents would be better utilized elsewhere?"

"Oh, for goodness' sake, Gage! What do you think my talents are? I'm not a big badass witch like you or Lark. I'm not some whizbang, awesome-at-everything witch like Meriel and those other full-council witches. The God's honest truth is that this is *exactly* where my talents are best utilized. I am good at what I do. Better than that hack Alison Moore, that's for damned sure. The issue here is that the walls are closing in around us and fast. Every day there's something new. More dumb legislation aimed at stripping more of our rights away. The issue is, I've got to work to stop it and I can. I am totally capable of doing it. Better than most anyone I can imagine. And that when I do I will be slapping the spit out of those thugs in PURITY is just icing."

"Your talents could be better utilized for something good. Where people don't want to hurt you all the time. That's all I'm saying. Those PURITY people aren't going to change their minds. They like to hate something. They lost Russia and have been looking for something else as the big-bad-evil ever since. We're it."

"I don't care about PURITY. No, we won't change their minds. Small minds are often closed anyway. It's everyone else. Do you want PURITY's voice to be the only one out there? Where we're Satan worshippers barbecuing the family pet to call demons?" She snorted. "God, they're dumb. Anyway, if there is no answering voice, that's who we are. And I refuse to let that hang out there without being the counter to it. A woman with my taste in shoes would never eat a kitten." She sniffed.

Molly was hot with anger. It filled her body and fired her up. Oh, she was mad now and it didn't happen very often. But when it did, well, she didn't stop until she'd won. Until she'd vanquished the person who made her mad.

Only the situation was far beyond a cheating boyfriend or someone who stole a client. This was big and she was quite sure she'd never felt like this. More than anger, she was offended by the hateful things she had to deal with every single day.

"Also, PURITY has, oh, I don't know, offended my something. In a big way. I'm so angry at them I'm not articulate. That horrible, evil bitch is going down. Satanic rituals? Oh my god, fuck them sideways!"

He laughed then. "You're going to make me get into an accident with the stuff you say."

"Before I continue, I believe *your* next line is, "But you're right and I'm sorry for being such a jerky dookie head.""

"'Dookie head'? You just said 'fuck them sideways' and I get 'dookie head'?"

"Rosa can't abide insults to family. Or to people you like in general. So she'd get so mad if you called your brother or best friend stupid or anything bad. Dookie head was as rough as it got around their house."

"So you like me?"

"Most of the time." She gave him the side eye.

"Well, a guy like me can't ask for much more I guess."

"I don't lose." She said it quietly, but he heard it straight to his heart. She sounded angry, yes, but maybe just a little bit lost too.

"I bet." This woman sitting next to him nearly vibrated with magick. That ambitious, hyperintelligent hardness, smoothed out by something else. A softness in her sense of humor. Something she had already, but now it was more. He'd found himself charmed by her several times a day. In fact, he thought about her an awful lot during his waking hours.

So he felt the difference in her magick then. Hotter than before. Sharper.

"But you'd bet wrong because I did lose. I lost my dad, my sister and best friend. I lost my firm. Something *I* built. Losing sucks. I don't like it in any way. So naturally I can't allow Alison Moore to beat me. I've dealt with some icky people. Part of the job sometimes. But she is . . . well, I can't even think of a bad enough word for what she is. She is a soul-sucking, dead-hearted, joy-killing, walking, talking bag of hate. And for that she must be destroyed." She picked a piece of lint from her skirt and sighed as she said all that so matter-of-factly.

"You're sort of scary right now."

"I feel sort of scary right now. How dare she show up there and say all that stuff right after a man talked about the pain of losing a child? She's a piece of work and she is not smarter than me at all. Also I have better hair, skin and I'm totally prettier. I win, Gage. I simply can't allow an inferior being to beat me this way. One of us is going down and it will not be me."

"You are most definitely smarter and prettier. And better

spoken. And you have a good heart. You also, because you missed this one, smell better and have a nicer rack."

There was silence for a moment and he desperately hoped she'd say something very soon.

She laughed and he mentally blew out that held breath. "I do, don't I? Anyway, I don't normally have the urge to completely destroy someone and salt the earth afterward. But I think I've been pushed that proverbial last step."

"It looks good on you. I, for one, can't wait to watch you destroy PURITY."

He didn't tell her her magick had grown and sharpened somehow. She felt it, or maybe she didn't, but she would. She'd taken a very big step into their world.

Chapter 12

MOLLY had just managed to escape the lovely and earnest college students who'd thrown a reception for her after her afternoon speech about Others in Seattle, when Faine materialized like the ghost he sometimes seemed to be.

He escorted her to the car and she began to check on her messages to see what she'd missed while she was speaking.

"Before you do that, Molly, I've got some bad news."

She turned to him as he ably drove them through the U District and back south toward downtown Seattle. "Oh god. What?"

"A family was driving home from an afternoon soccer practice. Witches. Mom, dad, two kids. They were run off the road. The car was set on fire after the father was beat nearly to death. He's in intensive care right now. If the beatings don't kill him, the burns just might. The daughter is also in intensive care with several broken limbs, a collapsed lung and smoke inhalation. Son, who is eight . . ." His voice choked up for a moment and she reached out to squeeze his hand.

Her heart ached. She hadn't even heard the whole story

yet and her heart ached anyway. What was the world coming to?

"The son is dead."

That aching heart leapt to her throat as she gasped, her hand over her mouth. "No."

"I wish to God you were right. But you're not. He's dead. Gunshot wound to the head. The mother is missing. The cops are playing this very close to the vest. They won't tell us anything more right now."

"Jesus. Oh my god. They shot an eight-year-old boy in the head?" She reeled, trying to understand, but she just couldn't wrap her head around it. "So are they out looking for the mother? What's going on with that?"

"Authorities won't give us any information. It was actually a big deal that Alder called to tip us off at all. But Gage and Meriel are on it now. They'll find out who these witches are."

Her head spun. "All right. I'll have Rita get working on media contacts so we can get this info out there. See if we can't find out who did this."

Faine drove up the block toward the office and she groaned when she caught sight of the picket in front of their building. PURITY people had found out where they were and each day they now had to run the gauntlet of protesters to get to the doors. Luckily, Owen owned the building so they didn't have to worry about landlords getting annoyed. But some didn't have that luxury.

"I'm going to use the garage entrance on Third." Faine pulled into the parking garage and her head seemed to hum the entire time.

It just kept getting worse. When would it stop? She wasn't even sure she was doing any good. Not if families were . . . god, it didn't bear thinking about but she had to. It was unavoidable, this new, horrible situation.

He escorted her back upstairs and she went her own way and he the other.

"Rita, can we talk, please?"

Rita looked up from her computer screen, grabbed a pad and followed Molly into her office.

"Are you all right? Can I get you something? You look pale. Too pale. You need more sleep. You work all the time."

Molly smiled. She knew people were afraid of Rita, but Molly thought she was awesome. Sure, she was crusty and no doubt scary, but she'd been so much help and support to Molly and beneath that exterior there was one hell of a big heart.

"I take it you haven't heard yet." She filled Rita in on the news and then asked her to see if she couldn't set up an interview or two for that evening's news cycle.

"I'm going to do a press release with what we have. Rumors aren't going to help. Can we get a tip line started I wonder?"

"I'll touch base with Gage or Lark on that one. If we can, I'll get it to you as soon as possible."

"Thank you."

Rita stood, pausing for a moment. She closed Molly's door and turned back to her. "I know it's been . . . hard for you. You're so far away from home and your mothers. If you need a shoulder, a lecture, whatever, just know I'm here. All right?"

Molly choked back her emotion. "That means a lot to me, Rita. You've already been wonderful to me. You've helped me so much with all this stuff I didn't know. I appreciate it more than I can say."

Rita left her alone, closing Molly's door in her wake. She put her head down and closed her eyes, trying to control her breathing. Things were spinning out of control. Molly was a fan of control. It gave her a sense of surety and security. But none of that existed anymore and she didn't quite know what to do.

First things first. She sat back up and sucked the emotions back, putting them in the box that already strained at the corners. Time to get working on the press release.

GAGE found her at her desk, hair back from her face, a pen between her teeth.

"Hey."

Molly started, looking up. She warmed, her smile, though ragged at the edges, revealed that hidden Molly so rarely seen. He'd come to her when he hadn't needed to. But he wanted to. Wanted to see her. She'd ask a million questions anyway so it was best.

This is the lie he kept telling himself instead of admitting he'd just wanted to see her.

"Any news?" She looked tired and he wanted to make it better.

He sat and put a file on her desk. "I forwarded it all to your email but I thought you might want an update in person. The little girl is in intensive care, as you know. The father is in recovery from his second surgery. She's stable, the father is more touch and go."

She blew out a breath. "All right. I'm scheduled to go on camera in an hour. I'll leave for the studio in forty-five." She made notes absently in her ever-present pad.

"I'll take you. Faine is off doing something else just now." Or he would be when Gage went to him and sent him off.

"You're a busy person, Gage. Someone else can give me a ride. People offer to help me all the time. I'm fine."

"This is dangerous. You're a public face now. I'm better than Faine is so I'm taking you. I'll be back here in half an hour." He got up. "The police have no suspects. At first no one would even talk to me, but Meriel did something, faxed something, I don't know, shook her legal stick at them and they shared some. We have an ID on them now so Dominic is in touch with their family as well."

"Any news on the mother?"

"Still missing. But they haven't ruled out a nonviolent cause."

She burst from her chair, her fist coming down on the edge of the desk. "Are you kidding me? The woman's car is run off the road, her son is murdered, the father and daughter have burns and gunshot wounds! We know the father wasn't in the driver's seat, the mother's blood is there and they're not going to rule out what? That she got out of the car and decided to shoe shop? What the hell else could it be? They've taken her. Or she's in a ditch somewhere dying."

Molly when she was being smooth and elegant was a sight to behold. A sight he'd taken to reimagining every time he closed his eyes. But this Molly, eyes ablaze with anger, mouth a hard line, well, this furious woman was beautiful and terrible at the same time and the sight of it shocked through his system like a drop of water in a hot skillet.

"We're in agreement. Lark and I have sent a group of our people out to look for her."

"Good. If we can't get the help we need from the authorities, we need to do it ourselves. I can bring it up, if you like, when I address the press later. You know, a call for volunteers."

She stopped ranting for a moment and took him in suspiciously. "Why are you looking at me like that?"

"I guess I just expected you to insist the human authorities would help."

But that was the wrong thing to say. He knew it right after he said it. He hadn't even meant it the way it came out. But it was too late; the damage had been done.

Her eyes, full of the heat of passion, went flat and cold. "Thank you for the update. I'll see you in half an hour."

"I'm sorry. I didn't mean it the way it sounded."

"Please go. I don't want to talk about this. I have to finish a dozen things before I leave." She turned her back, dismissing him.

He sighed heavily, feeling like a dick, and left.

OUT of camera range, Gage put the phone into his back pocket and looked straight at her. She knew, before she even heard the words, that they'd found the mother and the news wasn't good.

So she finished her spot and gave the information out to anyone interested in volunteering in any way with Clan Owen. The cameras turned off along with the lights once she'd finished.

"Thank you for allowing me to come and speak today." Molly appreciated the kindness of the news staff at the station. Briggs was at the rival network just across the street and two blocks down. From what she'd been given to understand, he'd used his muscle there to veto Molly or anyone from Owen being allowed to speak there on this issue. Their news coverage had said it had been an accident and was under investigation.

Bitterness washed through her as she took her bag from Gage and allowed him to lead her out. He'd tell her once he felt it was safe.

"We found her. She'd made it to a nearby business. From the looks of it, she pounded on the back door but no one answered. When someone arrived for a later shift they found her unconscious. She's in a coma. They don't know if she'll make it or not. Her family has given the cops permission to speak to us and give us details."

"When they can, obviously."

He paused as he opened her door. There was an angry crowd just beyond the gates they were parked behind. A constant these days. She could pretend it was so rote she didn't even notice. Sometimes anyway.

"What do you mean by that?" His tone was sharp. Suspicious.

She mentally counted to ten. "I mean they're going to obviously keep some things close to the vest. They don't know if we're part of it or not. I imagine once they figure out we aren't we'll hear more. At least from Alder."

"Yes, we're obviously so guilty in this situation."

She sighed, so tired, pushing past him to get in the car. She'd have preferred to have walked at that point. It would have really only taken about ten minutes. But the damned protesters . . . dangerous obviously. Hemmed in.

Damn it.

Still, she had shit to do and it didn't include playing this same old tired game with Gage and his anger. Like she wasn't angry? Like he was the only one who got to be mad at stuff?

He kept quiet until it was obvious she wasn't going to speak either. As he got her to the elevator of the hotel he punched a button a little harder than he needed to. "You could talk to me instead of glaring."

She gave him a look from the side of her eye. "I could. If I wanted to." She got in and allowed the doors to close.

"Just tell me I'm a dick and I can say I'm sorry and we can get back to being friends."

"You know you're a dick. You don't need me to tell you that." She unlocked her door and stepped aside to let him check the room. She took a call as she waited, not trusting herself to tell him just exactly why she was mad right then.

He did the check and stayed in her living room.

"All clear?"

"Yes."

She stood at her door. "Okay then. Thanks. I'll see you tomorrow."

He walked around her, closed and locked the door and turned her to face him.

"Talk to me."

"You've said enough today, Gage."

The emotion was clear in his eyes and she may have felt bad for a few moments.

"I know I hurt your feelings. I'm sorry. I'm sorry I was a dick."

"What *exactly* are you sorry about?"

"Oh god, really?" He shifted from foot to foot, looking exactly like a man who is so pretty and beloved by the women in his life that he probably always got off with just an *I'm sorry* and never had to truly apologize.

Well, *she* wasn't his mother or his aunt. And while he was undoubtedly hot, he was also a jerk. So if he wanted her to accept his apology, he really had to make one first.

"You surprise me." He licked his lips and she raised a brow. "At least let me have a drink first."

"Are you kidding me? You need a drink to truly apologize to someone you call a friend? You have been dreadful to me on this issue. I have *never* done a thing to make you believe

I'd do anything but my very best for my people and yet you treat me like those humans protesting outside. You suck."

He hung his head for a moment and when he looked to her again, it shot straight to her toes. He placed warm hands on her shoulders. "You're right. I'm . . . I'm so damned mad and sometimes you get in the way of that. But you absolutely have never done anything but your very best for our people. I do suck."

"I'm not the enemy."

His gaze sharpened at the wobble in her voice and she wished she could take that moment of weakness back.

"I'm so sorry I made you feel that way. I am. I was a dick and I took out all this rage on you. It's not your fault. It's mine."

And then his mouth was on hers and he was kissing her. Not a friend kiss. Not at all.

He pulled back and her mouth tingled. She licked her lips and tasted him, having to gulp at how good it was.

"I can't apologize for that. For the kiss I mean. I've wanted to kiss you for . . . well, since the first moment I clapped eyes on you."

She tipped her head, ready to ask him something, and he moved in again. Her words were lost as his tongue slipped into her mouth and she didn't care to do anything but wrap her arms around his neck and kiss him right back.

HEAT raced through him at her taste. Like everything else about Molly Ryan, it was sweet, but then spicy. She knew her way around a kiss, that was for damned sure. He had to lock his knees to keep them from buckling when she sucked on his tongue before releasing it to nip his bottom lip. Her body, strong and soft in all the right places, pressed against his. His thoughts scattered to the four winds and all he felt, smelled and tasted was Molly. And that was more than all right.

He spun her, backing her against a nearby wall where he could ease into another level of the kiss. He slowed it down, kissing her deeply until he felt her spine ease as she gave in and let him taste.

She smelled so good. Her perfume was one thing, but as they kissed and her skin heated, her magick began to warm as well, scenting the air between them. His rose to respond, swirling around them, making him dizzy.

The phone in her pocket began to buzz and she sighed softly, breaking the kiss.

He was unable to tear his gaze from her mouth as she answered, his body still caging hers to keep her in place. Once she finished that call he had some more smooching in mind.

"Yes, yes. I'm going to look now. Thanks for the heads-up. He's here with me. I'll tell him." She hung up and looked up, her lips swollen from his kisses. Christ.

"You're going to tell me something that's totally going to kill the mood, aren't you?"

She nodded. "Several windows in the lobby of the building have been broken. The protesters. They discovered the back exit too and are now blocking the driveway. Meriel's car was damaged. That was her calling. I need to update the website. We've already been urging people to travel in pairs. I'll have to reiterate that."

His phone started buzzing too. Lark, he realized when he pulled it from his back pocket. He answered and slid into hunter mode as she began to give him details.

Molly's hands shook a little as she fixed her hair and got her makeup reapplied.

Holy hell, Gage Garrity was an Olympic-class kisser.

She was a sucker for a good, slow kiss. It was like he read her mind as he'd crowded her against that wall and his mouth had found hers. His arms around her were tight but not restrictive. And he meandered. Tasting. Teasing. Seducing. He even made several deep moans of appreciation as she'd held on tight, giving as good as he gave.

He'd also apologized. Genuinely. Shown her a bit of the man behind all that anger. Something else she was a sucker for.

And really, she realized as she blotted her lipstick, she was apparently a sucker for Gage.

She sighed.

Her computer was booted up and she issued a brief statement about the new information about the Borache family's condition and also the recent violence and vandalism at the Owen building, urging all of Clan Owen to remain vigilant and to travel in groups. She then called Gennessee to let them know. They didn't really have their own media person so she'd done some stuff for them as well. She had an assistant of sorts down there so Molly gave her the URL for the update she'd just given.

The news from Los Angeles wasn't any better. There'd been a record number of assaults and harassment complaints that week. Since PURITY had started outing Others, they'd also created a gallery of sorts on their websites and had joined with multiple affiliates. And now they were including information like home addresses and work information. Two Gennessee members were currently in jail for a fight they'd gotten into outside a popular nightclub. At least the humans involved were also in jail.

Small things. She needed to hold on to the small things.

HE came to her as she was finishing up.

"I'm sorry for the interruption. I have to go. We're going to help the cops canvas the area around the crash to see what we can find out."

"Of course. I hate to be the bearer of more bad news, but did you hear about the stuff in Los Angeles?"

He blew out a breath. "Yes. I checked in with Lark and she told me."

He paused and she realized that if he apologized for the kiss, she would have to kick him in the shin.

"I'll see you tomorrow."

"No. I'm flying to Sacramento tomorrow. I'm going to a luncheon and then testifying at the state house. There's a dinner reception deal that night so I'll be back day after tomorrow. I'll check in with you then."

"I'm going with you. The protesters . . . well, they know

you're here. I've taken the room on your other side here tonight."

My.

"I like to be at the airport nice and early." It stressed her out to even contemplate being late for something. But he didn't need to know that part.

"Oh shit, did no one tell you?"

She narrowed her eyes at him. "What?"

"Cascadia is loaning us one of their planes and a pilot. She's apparently hot shit. A veteran and a jaguar shifter too. Anyway she's flying us down."

Private plane? Well, that would make things a lot easier, she supposed. But she didn't like that she hadn't been consulted or even notified of this change until that moment.

"Nice to be told of such things." Rita was usually better than this.

And then he just kept talking like he hadn't been busted. She had to give him points for sheer will to pretend she hadn't caught him meddling in her business and not telling her about it.

He even leaned in a little, crowding her. Goddess help her, it totally worked and it was sort of hard to remember she was annoyed at him.

"It's far safer and quicker too. I don't know if my office told Rita. That's my fault."

It was the jaunty smile that pushed her back into annoyed. It would not do to let him get away with such a thing or he'd do it more. He was bold that way and he liked to be in control even more than she did. And it was entirely too tempting to let him take control, to take over and make things happen.

"You're damn right it's your fault." Molly stood, to get some space and a breath he didn't fill up with his magick. "You can't just make all these choices for me without even consulting me! This is my job. Pretty much every minute of my day is scheduled so I need to know this. Rita needs to know this so she can keep my calendar."

"Hey look, my office is busy!"

Oh, he had to make it easy. "*You're* the one who takes

the calls. A call about *my* transportation should come to *my* office, not yours. You treat me like . . . like I don't even matter. I'm not your charge, for goodness' sake. I probably could have fit a meeting in tomorrow morning before I flew out. I turned several down because I thought I had to be at the airport. This isn't just courtesy, this is part of my job. As such I expect to be kept in the loop."

He growled and parts of her tingled. Her brain and the logic part of her body had to constantly wrestle with the senses, who really, really liked Gage Garrity.

"It's my job to protect you. You *are* my charge in that way. And I forgot. Sue me."

"Sue you? Is that all you have for me?"

"You're determined to be mad. Maybe I should kiss you again to shut you up."

"Is that right? Well, give it a try if you're feeling particularly brave."

He got very still and focused on her with such intensity it made her rather dizzy. She'd just pushed him and she waited to see how he'd respond. It was so irresponsible of her. She should be all business but man, oh man, he was like Fran's salted caramels. He made her mouth water and she knew he was bad for her in large doses but she was going to eat that next piece and she knew it.

His anger washed away as he took a step toward her and swept her into his arms, the warmth of his mouth settling against her lips. She sighed, giving over to the pleasure of it, making a mental note to continue her point later. First it was time to kiss.

Her mouth was heaven. So soft. Her lips opened to him immediately as she wrapped her arms around his neck. Her body against his lit him up. He wanted so much more than this kiss. Wanted what he should not even be contemplating. But he couldn't stop thinking about it as her taste slid through his senses, taking over.

Need beat at him and he wanted to back her to the couch and get down to a little bit more than kissing.

But he had to go.

Damn it.

Reluctantly, he broke the kiss and gave her another—just a quick one. "I like that. Maybe I need to make you mad more often to get a little of this."

Her smile was genuine and he felt a little better. "Saucy. Seems that once you put your lips on a gal you loosen up a bit."

He snorted a laugh, liking this side of her. "Well, it tends to do me that way. Your lips anyway. Faine is here so I'd like it if you left the connecting door open once you were ready to go to sleep. I've also got some people outside who'll patrol past several times a night. Don't open your door to anyone but people you know."

She blew out a breath but didn't argue. While he was relieved, he was sad too that she'd come to accept that as reality.

He licked his lips and shoved his hands in his pockets before he reached for her again.

"I'll see you tomorrow morning to take you to the airport. And I promise to be better about coordination with your office." He paused.

"That wasn't hard at all now, was it? Stay safe, Gage."

If only she knew just how hard it, *he*, was just then . . .

Chapter 13

SHE hadn't realized how fortunate she was to live in Seattle until they got closer to the state house in Sacramento. The crowds scared her.

Gage looked her way. "I've touched base with some local Others. They're working with the police to handle our security. I'm not going to let anything happen to you."

Admittedly, she felt better.

"This is . . ." Molly didn't even have words for it. There was so much energy humming in the air. So many passionate feelings in one place. The volume of it began to build as they drove through. Precarious.

"Why aren't there more police?" There had to be thousands of people on both sides of the Other issue. And not nearly enough police. Already things were tense, she wasn't sure how they could hold a riot off if one should break out.

"There should be. Lark's sister, Helena, is coming up for the day from Los Angeles. She's a hunter too. Anyway, she's coordinating with the local shifters. We've got a good personal detail." Gage held her gaze the entire time and while she was reassured, she couldn't stop thinking about how he kissed.

"I trust you."

He nodded. "Good. If and when I tell you to do something today, I need you to do it immediately. Even if you think it's stupid. All right?"

She blew out a breath. "All right. Just don't tell me to do anything stupid."

A smile hinted at his mouth. "I'll try."

Maybe they were understaffed there at the capitol, but it really just felt like they didn't care. She let out a long sigh and went back to her notes. She had a lunch meeting with a few key legislators, then she would testify and then later that evening she had a dinner to attend. She needed to get her head in the game. It didn't matter why there weren't more police there. She just had to put it out of her mind.

They pulled the car as close as they could. When Gage opened her door and got out first, she heard it. The tone buzzed in her head. So much anger in the crowd. It surged and then moved back and she shoved her fear as far away as she could. It was go time and there was no place for fear in what she had to do that day.

"I don't like this." He got closer to her, keeping at her side to shield her body. Which was difficult, as the crowd seemed to move like the tide.

Just a few steps from the main doors and the crowd surged again, seeming to suck Gage away with great force. It was during her alarm for him that she lost her focus. Until she nearly fell. Hands touched her. Some trying to help, Others, not so much.

It was hard to keep track of everything happening because it all seemingly happened at once. Molly heard the sound first, the ripping of her suit jacket and then felt the cold on her skin. Then the pain as her hair got pulled. In those seconds of confusion, Gage shoved his way forward, pushing the crowd back, managing to grab the person who'd thrown . . . whatever it was. He'd been so strong and so fast, his magick had seem to rush off him, nearly scalding hot. A moment of panic chilled her as she took in his ferocity. It calmed her even as she worried he'd really hurt someone because they'd harmed her.

The police managed to get her into the building, closing the doors, and the noise of the crowd dimmed enough that she could hear the pounding of her pulse and her strained breathing as she attempted to get herself back together.

"Are you all right?" Helena—Lark's sister, it was clear from the resemblance—shouldered over while Gage had a very terse conversation with the police as he handed the person, still screaming insults at Molly, off. His rage billowed from him and even the police, who couldn't see his energy, could sense it. One kept touching his side arm.

But then they turned their attention to the woman who'd attacked Molly and their distrust of Gage eased back enough that she was relatively sure no one was going to get shot.

With a slightly shaky sigh, Molly looked at herself in the reflection of the glass doors. "No, as it happens, I'm not." She pulled her jacket off. Covered in white powder of some sort as well as ripped in several places. Ruined. Damn it, she loved that suit. "This was a favorite."

"I'm sorry. This shouldn't have happened. It's a great jacket. Color is perfect for you. Dumb cow." Helena looked toward where the cops had the woman.

"I don't expect you to be perfect." Even as she spoke to Helena, Molly couldn't tear her gaze from Gage.

"It's our job to protect you."

She did turn back to Helena then. "You did. There are thousands of people out there. When the crowd surged it was impossible to keep any space around me. That's when she grabbed me. You have to trust that on some level the human authorities did their job too. You can't be everywhere. I'm not physically injured so that's a plus."

"I don't think the human authorities did do their job."

"What if it was some sort of bio agent!"

They turned to take in Gage as he got right in the cop's face and Molly realized she'd never even considered that. Her stomach dropped and she clamped her teeth together, breathing through her nose.

"This person threw white powder all over Ms. Ryan. How do we know what it is? Why are you not arresting her?"

"It's flour. She's disturbing the peace but your boss wasn't injured."

Molly was now angry. Far more angry than scared. She stalked over, pushing her way between them. "You'd know that how? As far as I can tell you've not even asked after my condition."

The cop looked her over, his disgust clear on his features.

She pulled her pad out and uncapped her pen. She needed to control something. So why not her job? She could do this and maybe give this asshole a little fear of God while she was at it.

"You look just fine to me."

"Oh well, that's an accurate measure I'm sure. You are? I'll need your badge number as well."

"I don't need to tell you anything."

She raised her brows and then looked to Helena and Gage before turning back to the cop. "Well, as it happens, you do. I'm a citizen requesting this information." She peered at his name tag and wrote it down. "So, Officer Phillips, how about it? Your badge number?"

He rattled off a number and made sure to sound extra insolent.

But he wasn't done. "You're not a citizen. I don't owe you shit."

Molly cocked her head. "Oh, but I am. I'm imbued with all the rights and responsibilities therein. Your *personal* opinion of me is of absolutely no concern. You either do your job, or you don't. I don't know how your department is run, but if any of my staff doesn't do their job, they get fired." She held his gaze, letting him know just exactly what she meant before she moved on. "Now, I plan to press assault charges so you'll need to do your job or I can certainly find someone else who will. It's your choice, but I will not be ignored or bullied into letting you turn this person back out into that crowd."

Another police officer burst into their circle.

"What the hell is going on here, Phillips?"

Molly turned to that officer and told him.

"Excuse me, ma'am." That officer yanked Phillips off to the side, clearly chewing him out.

Phillips shuffled away without even a look over his shoulder. The other officer returned to them. "Now, Ms. Ryan, I'm sorry you had to go through that. I'm going to take your statement. Would you like to freshen up? The building is secure inside."

"No. I'm going in now. Can you take my statement as we go? I don't want to be late for the luncheon."

The officer nodded. "More than likely there's also video footage. She also admitted what she did to Officer Phillips."

"I'd also like it known, officially, that your officer was rude and refused my request for his badge number. I do not give a fig what anyone thinks of me. I do, however, give a very large amount of importance to people managing to do their sworn duty."

"Yes, ma'am. I agree." His manner was solemn and she quite liked that.

She began to recount her memory of what had happened outside the doors and then the situation with the cop. Before he left, Officer Lynde gave Gage and Helena his card, urging them to contact him so they could better coordinate any other events they'd be involved in while Molly was in the city.

Gage watched her as she walked down the hall, her head high even though her hair had been partially ripped from her usual chic bun thing. Her jacket had been a ruin of egg and flour but she held it, folded over her arm.

He'd come very close to punching the stupid bitch who'd attacked Molly. In fact, he had used his magick to shove her away from Molly and then to bring her close enough to grab and haul into the building so she could be taken into custody. He'd never had that sort of power and range in a spell before. Again he thought about the way his power had ramped up since the Magister. Thank goodness he had it then, though he'd had to use all his control not to leave the bitch a bloody, twisted mess.

He leaned in close. To a casual observer, she looked

together, though disheveled. But he saw the cracks in her demeanor and knew she was struggling with her composure. "You sure you don't want to fix up?"

She kept her voice down. "I want them to see me this way, Gage. They need to be confronted with this insanity. They can't be in the hospital to see Eric Borache's daughter. They won't be at the funerals. But they should not be able to avoid all evidence of just what is happening out there."

Damn she was smart.

"I'll need a new suit; there's one in my bag back at the hotel. After the lunch I'll go back to get it."

"No. You'll tell me where it is and what you need and I'll have someone get it for you. I don't want you running that gauntlet out there again."

"I won't argue with that. Thank you."

"I'm sorry."

They arrived at the luncheon room and she turned before going in. "For what?"

"I told you I'd protect you and I didn't."

"I didn't get shot. I didn't get stabbed or otherwise physically harmed. I said the same thing to Helena, but I want you to listen because I get the feeling you're taking this personally. You can't protect me from everything. Especially in these types of crowds."

"No one should be allowed to do that to you."

She smiled. "No, but it happened." She shrugged. "Let's be glad it wasn't worse. *You're* the reason why. I know you used your magick to get her back, to protect me. You did your job and I'm thankful for it. Now, let's go in. Keep your fingers crossed for cheesecake."

THE people in the room took one look at her and stood immediately. "What's going on? Is everything all right?"

A tall man in a navy-blue suit approached. From the news, Gage knew this was Toshio Sato, one of California's two members of the United States Senate.

"A scuffle outside with an unstable woman armed with

hate, eggs and flour. There's quite a large crowd out there still with not too many police to keep them in check. I do hope the security will be heightened for our hearing later. For now, please tell me there's some coffee." She smiled up at Sato and Gage fought his frown. She wasn't flirting in any way. There was nothing intimate or sexual about how she was acting. But Gage liked it when she smiled at *him*, not other good-looking and successful dudes.

"I'm going to have my aide connect with the police here." Sato nodded at Molly. "For now, sit. We'll get the salads out and definitely a cup of coffee."

"Thank you. Oh, Senator Sato, this is Gage Garrity, he's the head of security for Clan Owen. Helena Jaansen, who holds the same job only down in Los Angeles for Clan Gennessee."

Gage shook the man's hand, as did Helena. "Perhaps I can speak with your aide regarding security?"

The senator looked up and indicated that the man in the far corner come over. Sato made the introductions.

Molly put her ruined jacket on a chair and sat at one of the tables, tucking her hair back up quickly as she was introduced around to the others. Gage moved to a corner of the room with Helena and the rest of the team to coordinate with the senator's aide.

When they left, some four hours later, it was after a truly wonderful lunch and some pretty good testimony in front of the joint committee Sato had begun to set up. The members were made up of state and federal legislators, most of whom seemed to want to make peace between Others and humans. It was the first tangible step that had given her real hope since she'd started this job.

THEY'D been able to get her out a back door and to the car without any further insanity. And when she got back to her hotel room and had a moment alone she called her mother to tell her about the events of the day before she saw it on television.

"I don't like this, Molly. You could get far more than flour thrown on you. These people . . . Rosa's going to kill me for telling you, but you need to know."

Molly sat. "Tell me."

"Their house was broken into and trashed. Windows broken, graffiti all over the place. Moll, they shot the dog!"

Molly gasped. "They shot Jellybean? Is she all right? Is Rosa all right? Was anyone hurt? When did this happen and why didn't anyone tell me?"

"Jellybean is dead, honey. I'm sorry. Rosa is physically fine. She's staying with Anthony Junior for the time being. It happened last weekend. She didn't want you to know because she knows how stressed you already are. She did decide to take the offer of early retirement, so that's a relief to her at least."

Molly tried very hard not to cry. "And you? How's your job?"

"The union isn't going to let them screw me over. Not until or unless they have no choice."

"I read about the proposed new rules." There was a new law moving its way through state legislatures across the country, barring Others from holding teaching jobs at public elementary, secondary and postsecondary schools without a waiver. All Others had to declare their *origin* and agree to an entirely different set of employment rules before they'd be hired. Molly knew it was a way to fire teachers whose positions were protected from this sort of nonsense.

"I'm thinking of coming out there. With your grandparents. There's not much left for us here. I was going to ask Rosa too. We can help you with house hunting while you're working and though I know you're busy, I'd get to see you."

Molly ached for them. For all they were losing. Because of what she was. The unfairness of it left her struggling against bitterness more and more often. Each time she wrestled it back, it got harder.

"I don't want you to have to give up everything you've worked your whole life for."

"It's not worth much if I have to keep fighting for it at

my age. Come on, Molly. I can teach lots of places. I can go into the private sector. I can work for a number of policy organizations. Your grandparents are getting too old for this shit. At least in Seattle they could be anonymous."

"Don't be too sure. We've got PURITY there too. They leaked my hotel to the media and now there's always a picket. One creepy guy with an orange ski hat who has these signs about the whore of Babylon and the other is a woman who looks like her face would break if she smiled. At least it's just two on a rotation I guess."

She got herself on track again. "Outside work too. It's . . . I can't even explain what it is to have to run a gauntlet of people who hate me and want to harm me multiple times a day. I don't want you to have to face that here. Maybe you guys should go to Maine to be near Uncle Andrew. Then you'd be far away from me and you could have some peace where people only know you as humans."

She should want that for them. It was the best thing. The safest. But it made her sad to even imagine her mother being so far away. It made her sad such a thing was even an option. Powerlessness was not something Molly liked, not one bit.

"I don't like to hear tears in your voice. That settles it. I'm going to start making plans to move. Do not argue. I'm your mother and you're supposed to respect me."

She laughed, feeling so much better she should have felt guilty. Her mothers and grandparents had lives in Chicago. But having them close? That would be . . . marvelous.

"I don't like them in my voice either. I'm trying to keep my game face." It slipped a little more and a sob threatened.

"You can cry in private. I hate that you have to. But I understand it. I'm your mother, I've wiped your bottom and cleaned up your vomit. You can always cry in front of me. I wish I was there with you right now. I hate being so far away. Just hang on."

The words made it better and a million times worse at the same time. But she was happy to have them anyway. "It's enough that you're with me over the phone right now. I needed it."

Her mother's laugh had its own tears. "I'm glad I can help at least that much then. So tell me about the rest of your life. The good parts."

"I'm making friends. Since I have full-time guards it helps that I like them both. Faine is this huge guy, former military, um, well, he was in the military a long time." She didn't want to say he was Lycian over the phone. They couldn't risk PURTY figuring out there were even more places beyond the Veil, and phones of various Others had been tapped several times in recent weeks.

"Anyway. He's good with magick and his hands and he's cute too. He makes me pancakes in the mornings. Sweet huh? And then Gage, he's the other one who guards me. He's the boss though so I see him less. He's really gorgeous as well as being a bad 'mamma jamma,' as Pops says. Plus he's really funny. I like the people I work with. I . . . I have to admit I had some preconceptions about what witches in a clan would be like, but I've been wrong. They've welcomed me." Most of them anyway. "I've been so busy every minute of the day but they stop in to teach me things to hone my magick. Gage makes me go to the shooting range. Shooting stuff is really fun. I had no idea how much fun it would be. That's my social life now." She laughed, but it was real. "Anyway, I like Seattle, even with the crazy anti-Other people around. They like good food, good coffee and good beer, you really can't fault that in any way."

Her mother laughed and they shared some more small talk until Molly hung up.

It wasn't all the way better by any stretch. She was still raw and shaky from what had happened earlier. But there wasn't much in the world your mom couldn't make at least a little better.

And for right then it was enough to get her through another day.

Chapter 14

SHE looked ridiculously beautiful.

Despite the stresses earlier in the day. Despite the crowd they had to drive through to get to the home the dinner was being held at, Molly moved as if she was waltzing. Or some other sort of dance where the women look like they're on air. Or whatever. She was full of grace and femininity and his gaze continued to return to her over and over as she set about charming everyone she met. She laughed with them and listened to their stories and then she told her own. Educating them even when they probably didn't know it.

Her pretty blond hair had been swept up off her neck, held up with sparkly things that caught the light as she moved. The dress was simple. No frills or bows or anything. Navy blue, it swept over her body like a caress. Hinting, but not overtly broadcasting the body beneath. The only real skin was at the back where the dress draped into a vee. She wore necklaces backward there, several of them. She was elegant and lovely and he hungered to possess her.

He wasn't the only one, that was also clear. Gazes lingered on her as she put out that magick of hers. It was personal magick that she gave off, so much more than any spellwork. You simply liked it when she spoke to you. Or he did anyway. And it was clear Sato did too.

Gage withheld an annoyed frown as he kept his eye on the room from a far corner. He wanted to stay out from underfoot, to let her enjoy the evening without the constant reminder that she needed a bodyguard. Even if it was pretty much all he wanted to hear her voice and smell that perfume of hers.

The dinner was pretty rockin', he had to admit. Some sort of fish with a fancy sauce he probably never would have ordered in a restaurant, but it was really good. Swanky dessert. All kinds of wine and stuff, though he noticed that even though she had a glass of wine, it was the same one all evening.

She gave a speech. Heartfelt, of course. She gave credit to everyone else, thanked people by name, remembering bits and pieces she'd most likely learned from all the research she did on people. She put a human face on the plight of Others. That was important, he knew. Even as he wanted to argue that they didn't need to beg humans to not persecute them, he knew it was integral that they unite with those humans who cared about their basic civil rights.

When it was over she said her good-byes, handed out a lot of business cards and he gathered her up at the cloakroom, helping her into her wrap.

She held his arm as they made their way to the car that'd been brought out.

"How you holdin' up?" he asked, never taking his gaze from the road, though always totally aware of her there next to him.

It wasn't until they drove away from the house, through the neighborhood and out the other side that she turned to him with a smile. "Maybe I'm adjusting to this insanity as the new normal. In any case, I'm so hungry. I can never really eat at these things."

"Too bad. It was pretty awesome, though I'm really hungry now that you mention it."

"We should totally get a burger. And some beer. Yes, a beer would be so good right now."

"I know where there's an In-N-Out and there's beer in the minibar in my room."

"Score. Double-double with cheese. I'm also having a milkshake. I will, however, eat the fries first, on the way back to the hotel. They're best hot. And really it would be un-American any other way."

He laughed. "Do they have In-N-Out in Chicago?"

"No! Travesty isn't it? But every time I come to California or Las Vegas I make a stop. Maybe lots of stops but we don't need to examine that too closely."

"I'm going to have to take you to Red Mill when we get back home. They have rings to die for."

"You're on."

WHEN they got back to the hotel he took her up the service elevator. They had a suite, which meant he was just in the bedroom next door, not a whole different hotel room.

She wasn't the *kicking off her shoes* type, but she did pause in the entry to toe the delicate heels off with a sigh. "Man, these hurt."

She had great feet. He wasn't a foot guy usually, but hers were as lovely as everything else about her. "They're pretty though."

"Indeed they are. I'll be right back out. I need to change so I don't get cheeseburger on this."

While she was in her room, he dashed to his to change out of his shirt and tie and into something way more comfortable. Namely anything that wasn't a tie.

He'd finished putting the burgers on plates and opening the nine-dollar beers from the minibar by the time she finally emerged. He still wasn't used to the change in her when she wore casual clothes. One minute she's buttoned up and the next, even in nothing sexier than yoga pants and a long-sleeved shirt that was open at the throat exposing some mighty fine cleavage, she was a far more relaxed Molly.

"I'd be so happy if I never had to wear anything with a waistband or a zipper." She sat, tucking her feet under her ass as she took the plate he handed her.

They ate in silence for a while until they'd both filled up a little.

He knew the day must have set her on her ass. Hell, he'd had more than one day like that over the last year and it still got to him.

"You had a rough day. How are you?"

Her gaze met his. "This hasn't been my favorite day ever. But I think we made some significant friends. The dinner was a rousing success. I've been asked to hook people up with local Others who'd be willing to share resources and information. The hearing? Well, that was bound to be less clear. We have enemies too."

"Good to know who they are."

"Yes. And to figure out if any of them can be swayed to our way of thinking or if they're never going to change." She patted her belly. "Oh my god, that was so good. Now I want to nap for a million years."

She avoided the subject, he noticed.

"You have a look. Should I be worried?" She quirked a smile.

"I don't know." He wondered if he should push it or let it be. "Do you want to be worried?"

"If that's your way of suggesting you might be offering up some more kisses, yes."

He put his plate aside and moved closer. He'd wanted her pretty much every second since he'd left her room the night before.

"This is totally inadvisable." Which may have been a tiny part of why he had to do it.

Her smile was far more sexy all the sudden. "I know. That's what makes it so hot."

He brushed his lips over hers and she sighed, relaxing into him.

"I'm totally glad I didn't get onions on my burger now."

He couldn't help but laugh. "I'm pretty sure that wouldn't stop me from wanting your mouth."

She leaned in and kissed him quickly. "That's good to know."

Molly's breath caught at the way his pupils grew. So intent, his expression, that shivers of delight and anticipation broke over her skin. She was fairly sure she'd never wanted to be kissed more desperately than she did right then.

His mouth, at first, took over hers slowly. His lips were warm and soft as he tasted her. He didn't crowd her, but she wanted him closer so she was the one who moved to close the gap between them. The satisfied sort of growl he made flowed into her and she swallowed it eagerly.

Then he took it deeper, his arms wrapping around her body to keep her close. As if she'd go anywhere else. His tongue slid across her bottom lip and then dipped into her mouth. Hers danced along it, tasting him in return. He was so good at this. Good enough that she wondered what he was like naked and horizontal.

She arched into his body, needing more contact and he broke away from her mouth. Her disappointment was dashed when that mouth of his made its way across her jaw and then down. He paused just below her ear, kissing and nibbling until she was boneless.

"Damn, you taste awful fine, Molly," he whispered into her ear before he nipped the lobe and went back to work.

She swallowed hard as she slid her hands up under his shirt. Oh sweet baby Santa, his skin was hot and taut over muscles she really wanted to taste.

He hissed when her nails scored up his side.

"Careful there." When he lifted his head, his eyes had gone all sleepy and sexy.

She caught her bottom lip between her teeth as she considered whether or not she should just take this for a nice make-out session and go to bed . . . alone.

She ended up snorting at the very idea. "I've been very careful in my life. Careful is great and all. But right now,

I'm feeling distinctly un-careful. Right now I'm thinking about you naked. With me. In my bed."

He paused for long moments and she prayed he wasn't trying to find a way to let her down easy.

And then he stood and held a hand out.

She took it and he hauled her to her feet.

When they reached her bedroom door he paused again. "You sure? Now's the time to speak up. Otherwise I'm going to be far too busy ravishing you."

She grinned. "Oh, thank goodness."

But once they were in her room he got very serious.

"I want to see you. Take your clothes off."

Molly pulled her hair loose, shaking it out as she grabbed the hem of her shirt and pulled it up and over her head. She'd been cold earlier back when she changed out of her formal clothes but carbs, beer and the promise of sex had warmed her up just fine.

But it was the way he stilled, like a predator looking at his prey, that sent a burst of heat through her. Her nipples beaded as she shimmied from her bra.

He closed the gap between them, his hands sliding up her belly to cup her breasts. "These are fucking magnificent."

She couldn't even joke at that point. Instead she wanted to preen at the roughly spoken words. She arched into his touch like a cat, wanting more.

He bent to kiss the side of her neck. "You're so much more than I'd imagined at first glance. Each little thing reveals more of you. And each time I learn something new I want you even more."

Who'd have guessed this man was so capable of compliments like these?

"You have your clothes on."

Smiling, he stepped back and whipped his shirt off. Her mouth dried up at the sight. Holy crapdoodle.

"Wow." She flapped a hand in his direction. "You have pierced nipples and tattoos. That's, wow." Molly moved to him to kiss his chest as she toyed with the bars through each of his nipples.

"I know the feeling." He thumbed across *her* nipples until she moaned.

"Pants."

He stepped back and she watched, unable to move as he popped open his jeans and slid them down revealing a trim waist and powerful thighs. Oh and that too. Shew! Once he shoved his boxers down his cock sprang free, clearly as invested in the encounter as he claimed he was.

She got rid of her yoga pants and underwear and circled him. The tattoos on his belly and chest were nothing compared to his back, which was covered by a very large pentacle with detailed Celtic work. In the center was the tree of life.

"Astounding work." She drew a fingertip along the edge.

"Runes and protective sigils are woven through it." Strain left his voice a little hoarse and she smiled, loving the way she affected him.

"I really love it."

He turned and slowly backed her to the bed. But he didn't immediately follow her down. Instead he simply took her in from head to toe. "You're unbelievable. So beautiful and feminine. Your body is . . ." He shook his head and blew out a breath. "Amazing. Gorgeous. Your tits make my mouth water and your hips, good lord, you've been hiding this bounty under those clothes this whole time."

She smiled up at him, flattered and flustered.

"Like a delicious secret only I know."

Then he moved to the bed, at her side. "I'm torn between wanting you all right this very instant and taking it slow and savoring every last inch."

"You can do both. I'm not going anywhere."

"Thank God for that."

And then he rolled her on top of him and she set to kissing along his jaw and then down his neck. He kept his grip on her ass though, which was pretty hot so she wasn't about to complain.

"You throw off magick like pixie dust when you're turned on," he murmured as one hand broke free and his fingers tiptoed up her spine and then across her shoulder. She'd never considered such a thing sexy, but however he was doing it sent warm pulses of sensation through her system, dizzying her.

"I do?"

He flipped her onto her back and she looked up into his handsome face and fell into his gaze. It seemed that he saw right through her.

"You absolutely do. It's fucking delicious. Irresistible. Luscious." To underline his point he licked up her neck and then to her lips for a brief time. "Like caramel. I want to eat you up."

"If you keep saying stuff like that, I'm going to pass out and then I'll miss this."

He laughed, right as his mouth found her nipple and she squirmed, her fingers sliding through his hair and holding on.

He drove her relentlessly toward orgasm just with that! But when he moved to lick over the swell just beneath her breast she thought she'd have a few moments to get herself back under control.

Until he kissed down her ribs and then over the hollow of her hip—who knew that would be so hot—and then nibbled her belly button until she may have squeaked.

And that was all before he dropped to the floor on his knees, pulling her ass to the edge of the bed.

"Oh!"

He laughed but he sounded like a pirate and then he got down to the ravishing he'd promised just minutes before.

Gage had to tamp down the need the best he could. She was so much. He wanted to gorge and gorge on her. She was the best thing he'd ever tasted. He wanted *more more more*.

And when she came it was worse. Once he tasted her skin, once he knew what it was to watch a flush pinken her belly and breasts, once her magick washed over him he knew without a doubt he couldn't quit her. Not for a good long while.

He managed to get back in bed with her. She slowly came

back to herself and he found himself mesmerized by the way her lips quirked up into a smile.

"Secret smile." He kissed her.

"Secret smile?"

"This smile, it's like you've got a secret." He traced over her bottom lip and she surprised him, taking a nip of his fingertip. But then she sucked his finger in between her lips and he forgot what he was saying for a bit.

"I suppose I do have a secret." She sat up and moved, straddling his waist. "He's a very gorgeous blond. A witch who wears weapons and frowns a lot."

He laughed.

"Please tell me you have condoms."

Panic crossed his features. "Um."

She squirmed, brushing herself over his cock, impatient now that the opportunity had presented itself.

Then she giggled and embarrassed herself.

"You're going to kill me." He rolled her off. "I'm going to check my bag. And if there is no condom in it I will run downstairs to buy some. Do. Not. Move." He got to his feet and then bent to kiss her again.

She levered up onto her elbows to watch him leave the room. "Man, oh man, you're no chore to look at naked."

"Thank you!" he called out and she fell back to the mattress, blushing and grinning like a moron.

"He's got superhero hearing apparently."

He sure as hell had a superhero mouth. This thought made her laugh again and she realized it had been a really long time since she'd laughed that way after . . . during . . . whatever while sexing.

"You only drank half a beer. You a lightweight?" He strolled back in holding a foil packet victoriously.

"Ha! I'm just drunk on sex chemicals. So get on over here before it wears off and I fall asleep." She grabbed the condom, setting it on the pillow before she turned back to him.

"Not much use over there."

"I have plans first. Patience."

She grabbed him, fisting his cock a few times to underline her point. His gaze blurred and he cursed. He arched into her grasp as she kissed her way across his chest, tasting his skin.

He was spicy, electric as he filled her, driving her crazy. She licked over his left nipple, loving the way the bar felt, loving it even more when he moaned.

"That's enough. I want to be in you."

She kissed down the flat belly, down the pale gold line of hair that led just exactly where she wanted to be.

He watched down the line of his body, a light in his eyes that she felt to her toes. She licked over him and he made a sound laced with so much need things tightened low in her belly.

He was quite honestly the hottest thing she'd ever been up close and personal with. Like unbelievably hot.

He reached back to the pillow and grabbed the condom, tearing it open and moving her aside. "I want to be in you right now. If you keep that up, I'm going to come and while that'll be just fine the next round, I want to be in you, with you all around me when it happens this time."

She frowned but let him get suited up.

"You look like a toddler who just had candy taken from her. I kinda like that."

"Hm."

He flipped her over and he was above her, blocking out the light so that all she saw and felt was him. She breathed in deep and his scent tickled her nose and woke up her senses.

"Ah, look at you. Goddamn, how lucky am I?"

He teased her a few moments before she had to get proactive, wrap her legs around his waist and pull him closer.

"You just got luckier."

His laugh faded into a groan as he got settled.

Of course, as she'd suspected he was just as good at this as he was everything else. He set a pace that was just shy of relentless, rendering her to a panting, nearly begging mass of woman.

And that was before he shifted her thigh to get his fingers close enough to brush over her clit, lighting her body up as she arched into his touch.

His lips wore a smug smile and she couldn't blame him. He had every reason to be smug as he drove her toward climax. Thrusting in time with his fingers on the heart of her. His muscles bunched and rippled against his skin, his sweat seemed to make him gleam and when she did come, it was hard and fast as she saw stars against her eyelids.

He snarled and pressed so deep it was as if he tried to climb inside. He jerked inside as he climaxed, collapsing on her, but not entirely so as not to crush her. But her heart seemed to pound against his skin as his answered with its own frantic beat as they caught their breath.

HOURS later he found himself staring up at the ceiling. She lay next to him, naked, warm. Her magick hung in the air, soothing even as it slowly stoked his want.

Gage hadn't expected it to be so fucking glorious. They fit so well. She was fearless in bed. She made him laugh. Took what she wanted, gave just as easily.

He hadn't expected a lot of things, like how good it had felt to fall asleep with her. Or how natural it was to just be there with her.

He didn't know what the next day would bring, but for right then, he could enjoy it. And he planned to.

Chapter 15

MOLLY finished a call while he sat, waiting for her to finish up. He tried to pretend he wasn't eavesdropping but he totally was. He liked to watch her at work. So intent and intelligent, it only made her sexier. Though he didn't need to share that part.

They'd woken up the day after they'd had sex that first time and she'd just gone about her day. There were no talks about relationships or emotions or any of that. Which he'd admitted was a relief and saved the awkwardness he'd been hoping they could avoid.

But it hadn't prevented two more scorching hot interludes in the week and a half following that trip to California. Which was fine with him in every way.

She hung up. "Sorry, I was working out some schedule issues with Tosh. What's up?"

"Tosh?"

She blushed, smiling. "Senator Sato. He told me to call him that. It's a shortened version of his first name. Anyway."

Gage kept his frown in his head, pretending he was all right with the blush. She blushed a lot. It could be that she felt bad for using a nickname in front of Gage when *Tosh* was a United States senator and all that.

"Do you have some time? I wanted to do a little work with you on your defensive spells."

Her smile got bigger and he couldn't help but respond with one of his own. "Yes! I'd love to. I have to check in with Rita. Can you give me about twenty minutes?"

He stood. "Yep. Meet me on the roof when you free up."

"Got it. Thanks!"

He paused at her doorway. "And have Rita coordinate with my office on coverage for your trips. I want to rotate a little with personnel."

Concern immediately replaced her smile. "Is Faine all right?"

Faine had been helping Lark out with improving the scheduling and training of their Hunter Corps. He'd been a warrior for his father's pack back home and he had a lot of great ideas.

That and Gage liked guarding her himself. It was becoming increasingly difficult to assign her safety to others, even when they were as good as Faine. He didn't want to examine that too closely.

"I like to rotate them all around, give him some time off. He's also helping me and Lark with our team. We lost eight members of our team when—after—the Magister so we have to train new people."

"Of course. I'm sorry."

He stepped to her desk and put his hand over hers. "No need to be sorry. You're not at fault here. None of this would be necessary if people could control themselves and use their fucking words instead of threatening us. I'll trade off with him. It's not a big deal. I like to travel." He lowered his voice. "And there are other benefits to being alone with you."

The smile she gave him was one she never used with anyone else. It made him feel special.

"All right then. I'll see you in a few."

He backed away but didn't turn until he'd reached the door, liking to look at her.

* * *

HE flustered her in ways nothing and no one else ever could.

Molly really liked Gage. He made her laugh and he was really good in bed. On the couch. Standing up—and *that* had been a very pleasant feat of strength on his part. Sitting down. Even on the kitchen table.

She liked the way he made her feel. But he was busy and filled with a lot of stuff she didn't know if she had the ability to help him through. Or even if he'd want help. A lot of anger. Which made him very good at his job, she realized.

Truth was, she had a lot of stuff too—stuff she wasn't ready to unpack just yet. Or ever. So sexy fun was good. It wasn't serious, but it was enjoyable and that was exactly what she needed right then.

She checked in with Rita about trips and scheduling before she changed into her sneakers and headed up to the amazing gardens on the roof where Gage would be waiting.

When she arrived she paused to take him in. He sat on one of the steps leading down to the garden, his face tipped up to the pale sunshine filtered through a brief break in the clouds. The muscles in his biceps bunched as he leaned back on his arms. A golden god.

She had sex with that man. *Holy cow.* All badass and tattooed, he was delicious and she wanted to take a bite.

He opened his eyes and looked her way. "Hey you."

"Hey yourself. Sorry to disturb you."

He stood, brushing that stellar butt off as he did. "Nothing to disturb. Just having a quiet moment before you arrived. You don't want a heavier coat?" He cocked his head, concerned, and her belly warmed.

"I'm fine." Really, back in Chicago it was snowing. It was forty degrees in Seattle, which was cold and wet, yes, but it wasn't something she couldn't bear. Plus he made her all hot and stuff so it worked out anyway.

"All right then. It'll warm up in a moment or so as we move into the garden anyway. So you've done some of the defensive spells well enough that I think you're good to go on them. But I want you to focus a little on magick in general."

He led her down into the plants that bloomed as if it were summer. She'd only been up there at night so it was the first time she'd really gotten a good look. "This is amazing."

"Isn't it? Meriel's dad is responsible. He's got a gift with green things. The magick we give off feeds the plants up here, keeps all this flourishing. The only time I've ever seen it look like winter was after Edwina was killed. He shut down for a while. And there was less magick flowing into the Font too."

"Less witches, less magick?"

"Yes. But less magick because less Others and the ones left alive were reeling. Only recently has this garden really come back to life. And the magick going into the Font has blossomed to far more than it was before."

It was warm all the sudden and not only because he made her hot. She shrugged from her coat.

"Yes, once you leave the platform and step down here it warms up."

She breathed deep and everything smelled so good as she drew it into her body.

"That's magick."

She opened her eyes and looked to him. "What is?"

"The reason you lit up when you took a deep breath and drew in a big old hit of Owen magick. It smells really good right? Even maybe tastes good?"

She thought for long moments. "Yes, it does have a taste. I never noticed that."

He stepped to her, putting his hands on her hips. "You haven't? When I lick your skin I can taste you. Your magick is part of it. It rises in the air when you're emotional, when you work, when we're . . . together. It's delicious."

She probably gulped. It couldn't be helped.

"You taste good. I just figured it was, well, the way you tasted. I mean, you look good so why wouldn't you taste good too?"

He smiled and all sorts of stuff zinged around her belly. He took her hand and kissed her upturned palm.

Molly took a shuddering breath. "You're a menace."

He licked then, against the sensitive skin at her wrist. "Am I?"

She nodded. "The good kind."

"Your magick changes when you get turned on. You're sweet and sort of lavender and roses and then when you get hot, there's pepper and spice there. Drives me nuts."

She knew she blushed but it couldn't be helped either. He simply made her feel stuff she couldn't get around. Her entire life was off balance. In unmapped territory and she was so off balance the confusion and fear she'd mess up were like constant white noise.

But *this,* this thing with her and Gage was unfamiliar in the best sort of way. It was new and thrilling and she wasn't afraid of it, just excited.

She took his hand, the one that had held hers and turned his palm upward to kiss him there, breathing in deep. Then she licked at his wrist and he groaned.

"Do you see what I mean?"

"I don't lick anyone but you, Gage, so it's hard to tell. I've never been with another witch. A lot of this is new. I'm not used to not knowing stuff." She hadn't meant to say it all.

Surprise skittered over his features briefly and then he laughed. "You'll have to trust me. And keep licking only me." He got serious again. "Every Other has their own unique magick. You know we do. It comes from the earth, from all around us. Witches have the ability to filter and gather it and transform it. Shifters' magick exists in their ability to change. When they take on their animal, they have their own magick to unlock their other form and let it take over. Vampires, it's a little more difficult to say because they keep their business so close to the vest, but their ability to transform the life force of others to sustain and enhance their senses—strength, speed, lifespan—is a particular kind of magick. And each one of us has our own unique magickal signature."

"Really? Fascinating. I mean, I knew some of this. Rosa

took me to an awesome series of lectures at the coven about the history of witches and magick. Is it like a fingerprint? So you can get very specific information about the Other based on that signature?"

"Damn, you're smart. Yes, exactly. So when we get to the scene of a crime and there's magick there, it's a very specific signature. But unlike a fingerprint, you can't really keep it in a database. It's not that portable. But you can compare if you've seen the signature before, or if you have the witch nearby. I've got a lot of signatures stored in my head. I have notes I keep about specifics. Sometimes it's colors or scents."

"Wow. *I'm* smart? That's brilliant. Can you show me? How to do the signature thing, I mean, I don't expect that I'll know it like you do, but it might be helpful to understand. I mean, I guess I can tell when I meet another witch. Is it like that?"

"How is it you know?" He took her hand and walked her through the gardens.

"I can see—maybe not see. Not with my eyesight. But I can sense? The wording is imprecise for what it is."

"The word you're searching for is *othersight*. It's viewing things through your magick instead of through your human parts and senses."

He stopped once they got to the middle of the garden and turned her to face him.

"Othersight is not solely our thing. It's also been referred to as the third eye and in that sense it's using that extra level of perception that humans rarely do or can't quite unlock. Only what we have is more than that. Did you learn to see in any other ways when Rosa was teaching you about your magick?"

"No. I don't think so. She taught me how to tap the energy at my feet, how to pull it up and into myself so I could use it. But nothing about seeing differently."

"You don't need to use othersight to work your magick. But it helps you be aware of how your energy moves, and how it's all around you. You don't have to only get it through your feet. I'm going to show you something. Do you trust me?"

"Are you going to show me something naughty?"

He grinned and then shook his head. "Maybe later if you do well with your lessons."

"Fine. Party pooper. And yes, I trust you."

"I want you to be aware of your magick. You already know it's here." He pressed a hand over her belly. "I want you to think of it as a living thing. Close your eyes and focus on it."

She did and was immediately calmed as it welcomed her.

"Now, I want you to totally relax. Your magick knows what to do. It's part of you like your blood and your skin. Just *let* it be part of you. Feel it filling you down to your toes. Everyone's magick is different. Mine sort of shoots down and out, but yours, well, I bet it sort of fills slowly like honey." He hummed and parts of her she was supposed to relax came to life again.

"Stop that. I can't concentrate when you flirt."

"You're frowning." He kissed her quickly and her magick filled her to her toes and then up her torso out to her fingertips. "Ah, I can see it. Hmm, it responds to my magick."

Her magick was as easy for him as the rest of her apparently.

"Now, let it fill you all the way to the top of your head. Once it does I want you to use it to see. When you open your eyes, keep relaxed, let the magick do the work."

Gage knew that with other witches who hadn't had a few lessons, the first time using othersight wasn't always successful, or it only worked halfway. But the witch he faced was the biggest control freak overachiever he'd ever met. She'd get it because she'd never allow anything else from herself. Her magick had to be just as bossy as she was.

He felt it, the rush of heat as her magick began to radiate outward. Her aura was clear and blue with some green here and there. Her scent seemed to envelop him in a wave, sucking him under as his own magick rose. She called to him in ways very few others did.

Probably no one else.

Then she opened her eyes and her mouth, that luscious, delicious mouth of hers made a little *O*.

"Wow," she whispered. "It's like a filter you use with digital pictures. The colors are . . . different. Everything is, I don't know, layered maybe?"

"You're seeing magick all around you. The plants give it off. Partly because they're living things and are conductors for our personal magick, which is sort of a key to our lock. But also because they're here on Owen land and witches come up here all the time to meditate and work. There's a lot of recharging going on up here. Powerful witches too. So if you look carefully you can see that, the smudge of all sorts of magick up here. Meriel's has its own signature just as mine does. As yours does."

"Can I turn it on and off at will? Does it use up my energy like a lot of spellwork does? Should I only use it in emergencies?"

She continued on with the questions. On and on as she thought and he answered as they went along. Of course she'd want to know everything. That was who she was.

"Will people know if I'm using it?"

"A lot of witches, especially those who grow up in a clan will use it at least occasionally. I use it all the time, just to check things out. Like when I go into your hotel room I check to see if any magick but yours and mine has been used. Let it become second nature when you enter a room. I'll have you use it when we go testify the next time. Plenty of villains when we do that so you can see what negative energy looks like too. That's why I'd like you to practice and use it all the time. It's not going to wear you out like a lot of spells would. But I would also encourage you to come up here and recharge at least once a day."

"I don't even pull magick from the Font. I don't use that much magick to deplete my own. Are you sure I need to?"

"When you come up here it's more than just charging your battery. You're cleansing yourself and your energy. It's good up here, can't you feel it?"

She nodded slowly. "Yes."

"You're dealing with a lot of negative stuff right now. Coming up here will help you."

She chewed her bottom lip. "I don't know how. Is it the same as pulling magick from the earth at my feet?"

He took her hands. "Sort of, yes. Can you see all the wisps in the air? Sort of like little ribbons?"

She blinked and looked all around, nodding.

"That's magick. Just hanging in the air. Lots of witches don't realize how much ambient magick is all around them. Up here it's supercharged. To bring it into yourself you just call to it. Like you do through your feet, only through the air. I always just sort of breathe it in and it sticks to me and absorbs. But that's just the imagery I use. Try it."

She took a deep breath and he used his othersight to watch her draw all that magick to herself.

"It feels like snowflakes." She smiled when she said it and he noted the magick seemed to melt against her skin before it disappeared.

"That was beautiful. You did great. How do you feel?"

"Awake. Alert. Like I just drank a quad espresso only without the jitters."

He smiled. "You did it right."

"This is the coolest. Thank you for showing this to me. I feel like even though I know how to use my magick in the basic sense, there's so much I missed."

"Your power is second nature. Really it's about letting it do what it needs to. Like I said, it's part of you. Witches make the mistake of thinking they have to control it and then they blunt their power. You're not going to blow up the gym or anything. I'm happy to show you things, but the key is to trust your magick. First and foremost. Everything else is a matter of style."

Chapter 16

SHE walked side by side with Meriel as they headed toward the door of the restaurant they'd be having their meeting in. The Others had all created a unified governance council and Meriel was their representative. Molly was, in turn, the media person who was the liaison to them and from them to the media and humans in general.

Faine and one of the others who stood in for Lark were also along for the trip serving as guards. Gage and Lark were just a few feet away in a smaller dining room meeting with the enforcement arms of different groups of Others.

No matter how much she knew it was necessary to have guards, it was still something she had difficulty getting used to.

Meriel interrupted her thoughts. "You get used to it. I'm sort of shocked at how easy it is to get used to."

Molly started. "Am I that easy to read?"

"Not really. Not usually anyway. Lots of adjustment for us all of late though. I'm not sure how we process it all without losing our shit half the time. I'm glad of it, don't get me wrong." Meriel gave her a quick smile. "As for guards, after a while you do let go of the knowledge that they're there and you can get past it. Or that's how it's been for me."

"You're like the head witch. Haven't you had guards your whole life?"

"Not really, no. Until the last year or so it's been pretty safe and mellow here for us. My mother"—Meriel paused to lick her lips before speaking again—"she never had guards either. But after the mages and then the Magister, well, we had to do it."

"I get the whys of it. And I know they're doing their job and stuff. But it's . . ." She stopped, not wanting to continue this conversation in front of anyone else. "It's a reminder of how much things have changed I guess. My life won't ever be the same."

Meriel's smile turned up a thousand watts and Molly had no idea what she'd said to merit that. "You're making me nervous, Meriel."

Meriel hugged her quickly. "That's the first really personal thing you've shared with me. I'm just happy. Because I like you and I like being your friend and I want you to share stuff with me. Selfish I know."

"If I shared it all I just might start crying and then not know how to stop. I'd be a red-faced puffy mess. We're better off that I don't, trust me."

"Thing is, I do trust you. And I want you to trust me too. This isn't the place, I know, but why don't you come over for dinner tonight? Dom and I wanted to do a check in with you anyway and this can be away from the office. You don't have to share anything." Meriel grinned. "But I'd like to get to know you better and Dominic likes to cook so you'd give him an excuse."

"All right. I'd like that."

THE room was full of Others once they walked into the small private dining room. She used her othersight but even without it she would have guessed those in the room had magick of some sort.

She couldn't wait to tell Gage about it. Through her othersight she detected the musk of the cats and the loam of the wolves, even the cool taste of the vampires.

Othersight was the coolest thing she'd learned about her magick in years.

Meriel's power seemed to vibrate from her and Molly realized she was just as powerful as any Other in the room. She just wore it differently. She didn't need teeth or claws. Meriel had a metric ton of magick.

The thought buoyed Molly. She had magick too. Oh sure, not on the same level as Meriel did. But enough to defend herself if she needed to. It was the first time she really understood it and the relief rushed through her.

The vampires took up a great deal of time until Meriel sighed heavily and shifted, as everyone else was. They were losing momentum.

"If I may?" Molly stood and several different Others, clearly relieved at the interruption, recognized her.

"All your points are good ones. But to keep this moving forward I'd like to suggest we address the items on the agenda. And then if we have time left we can take up these issues afterward."

That was quickly approved and Meriel indicated she continue. "There are two major pieces of legislation I want to speak to you about today. In Virginia there's a bill set to register all Others with the state. Sort of like the draft. They claim anyway. No one will say with any clarity just how this information will be used or go into any detail about the penalties for nondisclosure. I'll be testifying there next week, but I've prepared talking points and sent copies of the legislation along with any supporting documentation to each one of you." She pulled out folders and pushed them across the table to each group. "And I brought hard copies today as well. It would behoove us all to get working on this. Letters, emails, calls, visits to legislators on all levels."

"And what good will that do? They're already just doing whatever they want," Franco, the verbose vampire, interrupted.

"We need to be in their faces. We need to help them understand we will not let this happen to us. We will not sit idly by while they legislate us into second-class citizenship. Or worse. Right now, those of us who were citizens before the Magister are still citizens. We need to act like it."

"She's right." Nina shrugged. "I'll speak with National and we'll get some of our people down in Virginia working on this. Get some opinion papers written. I see you've included a sample. You're really anal."

Molly started and Nina snorted a laugh. Megan, Nina's sister-in-law and the Enforcer of the pack, sighed. "She's got a weird sense of humor."

Nina just smiled. "You're organized. It's a good quality. The Alpha female of National is just as much of a tightass as you are. She's a bitch in heels and a scarier female I've yet to meet. So you're in good company. We're on it."

"The second piece of legislation is actually something happening in four states right now, the result of which would nullify union protections for Others in public positions. So teachers and other public workers would be terminated and then *reclassified*. They would then have to reapply for those positions and be hired by a panel of appointed citizens. They'd lose pensions and retirement funds and any seniority they've built up over the years."

"Why aren't we just killing them all?" Franco shrugged. "We're stronger and faster. They'd certainly get the point, no? We can spare the ones who aren't trying to harm us, of course."

"That's a refreshingly old-school solution. But how about we try it without the killing part first?"

He smiled her way, amused, and she breathed a little easier. Vampires were wild cards, one never knew just how far they'd go on some issues.

Franco wasn't quite done though. "We won't be lying down for humans who come onto our property trying to harm us. We've conveyed this information to the local authorities, who informed us they couldn't be there to protect us at every moment and suggested guards. We suggested they remember that should anyone break into our homes intent upon doing us harm, they would meet harm in return."

"That's fair. And as it happens, the law anyway."

They spoke about some of the other legislation and she was able to mobilize them with promises of action. Gage and Lark were just next door dealing with the different security groups for the Others, talking about how to keep everyone safe. She bet it was far more interesting over there.

"HOW'D it go?" he murmured as he met up with them outside the dining room.

"You know if you have a meeting in a dining room one expects lunch."

He tried not to laugh but failed. "You're food focused. I like that."

"I do require sustenance to survive." Molly's expression was prim but humor danced in her eyes.

"Shall we stop somewhere then? To grab you some sustenance before you fade away into nothingness?"

Meriel reached them. "Don't get too full. I texted Dom that you're coming over for dinner and he's already at the grocery store. Prepare for a feast. Lark and Simon will be there too. Gage, you're invited as well." Meriel waved over their shoulder to Nina Warden as she left.

Well, if Molly was going she'd need a guard anyway. So it would be smart for him to be there. Though of course Simon and Lark would be there along with Meriel and Dominic and of course they had full-time guards around the entire property. But none would be *her* guard specifically. It was responsible of him. Plain and simple.

"Sounds good. I can give Faine the night off."

Meriel smirked for just a brief moment but said nothing else. She leaned in to kiss Molly's cheek and squeezed her hands. "You did an amazing job in there."

Molly blushed. "Me? No, all of you have such bigger jobs than mine. I just helped people stay on task, that's all."

Gage snorted as Lark approached. "Ready to go back to work, Boss?"

Meriel had a full-time guard. Two of them actually. But Lark or Gage accompanied her to meetings like this one as well. Her safety was paramount to the survival of Owen.

"You have that town hall meeting, right?" Meriel turned to Molly.

Molly looked at her watch. "Yes, in half an hour."

"We're going to that. There'll be a pretty large Owen turnout I think."

Lark sighed, knowing it was part of the job, but she and Gage hated the exposure. Not just for Meriel, but for Molly as well.

"I hadn't realized it was that late. I have protein bars in my bag. I can make do. But I need coffee."

Meriel grinned and joined her arm with Molly's. "Me too. There's a place on the way. We can walk."

"Do you think that's a good idea? There's bound to be a crowd gathering already near the town hall." Lark glanced to Gage briefly.

"I think I'm sick of being caged up in a car with bullet-proof windows. Especially on a rare sunny winter day. It's full daylight. We've got four guards."

Molly spoke up. "And I don't think we should allow the PURITY people to push us off the sidewalks of our own city. We have the right to enjoy it like everyone else." She allowed Gage to help her into her coat, which held her scent, and he had to work to keep from leaning in and sniffing her at the nape of her neck where her magick seemed to gather.

"You're right." Lark nodded and looked back to Meriel. "Let's go then." She called over the other guards and they all headed out. The car would meet them at the event, which was truly only blocks away.

But those blocks nearly gave him a heart attack. The sidewalks were crowded with other Seattleites who wanted to take advantage of the sunshine too. So there was much jostling. Six months ago it wouldn't have caused him a moment's concern. But now? Well, things had changed. He and Lark combined their magick to form a protective circle around the women as they walked, talking and laughing. Molly looked particularly beautiful, her hair shining in the sun, a big smile on her face.

He was glad as hell when they arrived at the coffee shop.

"Oh, I need that muffin." Molly smiled up at the counter guy, who nearly tripped over himself to give it to her. He also drew a pretty design in chocolate on the top of her latte. Gage sent him the eye, but he missed it because he was staring at Molly so hard.

He and Lark sat with them at the table, backs to the wall, eyes always moving.

"I try to pretend I'm in a movie of the week. Like a princess or something who is trying to live a normal life in the United States while she goes to college."

Meriel cocked her head and then laughed. "What?"

Molly waved a hand toward the guards. "You know with all the guards around. It's better than knowing they're here to protect us from whatever crazy loon who wants to harm us because of who we are."

Meriel nodded. "I like the way you think. I just think it's nice to look at Gage and Faine and the others. Lark makes me laugh and when she's around; Simon often shows up and he's definitely nice to look at."

"Well yes, that too. I was trying to be more subtle about that part because Gage is here and all. Oh and also because Lark is pretty badass and I'm afraid of what she'd do if she knew the thoughts her man inspired."

It was Lark's turn to laugh. "I can't lie, he *is* mighty fine to look at. I could tell you what a handful he is, but that doesn't even begin to blunt the visual impact." She winked and Gage would have frowned if Molly hadn't agreed so readily to him being nice to look at too.

"I'd like to think things will be normal again at some point." Meriel looked out the windows. Across the street and half a block up, a crowd was building around the town hall space.

"There'll be a different kind of normal I think. But I think what we had before? It might never be the same again."

It got quiet for a while as they finished up.

"Let's go to it then." Molly stood and Meriel followed.

Molly stood tall but kept close to Gage.

"Use your othersight," he murmured. "It's going to be fine."

That comforted her more than she could admit out loud.

Inside it was already standing room only and there was a bit of a misunderstanding about where Gage would be while Molly was up on the dais.

They wanted him to sit in the audience but he wouldn't let it go. He was like a bulldog and she was very grateful for it. She'd not admit it out loud, but the crowd in the room freaked her out.

There was a lot of hostility. But it wasn't all bad. There were plenty of friendly faces. More curious ones, open to change. She could sense that; it had always been something she was good at.

Mayor Stimson was the moderator and she tapped on the podium and introduced herself and then each one of the panelists.

There was a lot of question-and-answer stuff and Molly was grateful for all her years of preparation and practice in similar situations. Though nothing quite like this.

Molly was all for new learning experiences and all, but this wasn't quite what she had in mind. Still, she was proud of herself for keeping a straight face through it.

Until.

She could see before the woman in the audience even spoke that it was going to be bad. Her features were set, eyes narrowed, the hate coming from her like a blast of heat. So it wasn't really a surprise when she got her question out. "How do we know you're not controlling our minds right this very moment? There's a reason witches were burned."

Molly tipped her head in a *bless your heart* way. "Believe me when I tell you that if I had the power to control your mind, I wouldn't use that power to have people break the windows at my place of work and assault me at public events."

That got a laugh and Molly realized that when she used her othersight, she could gauge the energy in the room better. The magick rose, yes, but also humans had their own sort of energy, far more faint, but when they were passionate, it was easier to spot. She could use that.

Use it to grab this event and wrestle it back before it went off the rails. "And on a historical note, we got drowned a lot more than we got burned. Though we were also tortured and raped." The room quieted. "There's something that frequently gets missed in these discussions and I want to make it clear here today. The Magister happened to *us*. To the Others as we're now known. We lost mothers and fathers, wives and husbands, children, friends, cousins. None of us came out of this untouched. We're trying very hard to get through the fact that we lost so many so very suddenly. We're mourning. We were not hiding our magick from you to trick you. We were keeping our magick private because past history has taught us to be careful or get dead."

"Maybe you should be." Alison Haterade from PURITY spoke from across the stage. "Not dead of course, we'd never advocate such a thing. But this being culled your numbers for a reason. Maybe it's because you're a threat."

So much hate. The energy poured from her, dark and sticky and if Molly had been closer she may have recoiled physically to avoid it.

The mayor pounded her gavel and called for order as the room went crazy. In the corner of Molly's eye she saw Gage tense and move closer.

"If I may." Molly leaned close and made eye contact with as many people in the audience as she could. "This sort of hateful speech isn't helpful or useful. It is divisive and seeks to destroy rather than unite. I tell you of the loss so many of us have been hit with and this is no more than a cudgel to Ms. Moore. And it's a prime example of just why we've hesitated to come out all these years before. We are not a herd to be *culled*. Which by the way means to kill, so spare me the dishonesty about how you don't mean exactly what you're saying."

Alison squawked but Molly kept speaking until she shut up.

"We're happy to answer questions and deal with very real and honest fears humans may have about us. We're happy to talk about what exactly we are and what we do. But we won't be targets for talk of *culling*. I'd thought this basic fact was so easy to understand it didn't need to be repeated. But apparently it does."

"You're twisting my words!" Alison acted like a woman offended when she was a hateful charlatan. Molly had nothing but disgust for her.

"They're *your* words so I suggest you either use less loaded terms to be clear or own what you say."

Molly was angry now. Angrier than that day when she'd been in the car with Gage. Culling? How dare this bitch even utter that?

"We deserve to know when we have monsters living next door. This has been foretold. Demons walking the face of the earth. You all bring the end."

Molly mentally centered herself. You couldn't argue with people's religions. She had no desire to. Alison would believe what she believed and it wasn't any of Molly's affair unless and until it had *kill all Others* as its bottom line. Which it did in this case. So now she had to deal with the concept and weave around the religious part. She sure as hell wasn't going to admit there were actual demons and push this lady even further into crazytown.

"As we've existed as long as humans have, I don't think a very good case for us bringing the end can be made. We want a peaceful resolution to all this upheaval. We don't need to be loved by all. We don't need to convince you we have souls. Your beliefs are your own." Molly looked back out to the audience and pulled them in. She felt it in her gut, knew her magick drew their attention. What she did with it was up to her. She had a gift and for the first time since the Magister she *understood* she had a purpose. She was standing there for a reason. She could make a difference, a real difference.

"We are here. We are citizens and we care about our communities, human and Other alike. If you have questions or concerns, please bring them forward and we will do our best to resolve those honestly. But do not ever make the mistake of believing this is a referendum on our right to exist. That is not up for a vote. It is not up for a debate. We don't want to control your thoughts. We don't want to infect you with lycanthropy against your will. We want to live in a world where our houses aren't set on fire while our children sleep and where we aren't run off the road and gunned down on the way home from soccer practice. It seems incompatible with anyone's stated wish to protect children to support what happened to Jeremy and Missy Borache just three weeks ago."

She sat back and the stunned silence burst into applause from Other and human alike. It wasn't unanimous, but it was enough.

Chapter 17

"**DON'T** forget dinner at my house tonight." Meriel hugged Molly when they pulled up at the hotel. "You did such an amazing job. Closing the way you did? Goddess, I think I nearly cried."

Lark snorted. "I totally cried."

Gage watched her, proud. He wanted them all to go so he could tell her in private.

"We'll see you guys in a few hours." Gage got out, checked the area and then held a hand out. She took it, allowing him to help her from the car.

Of course her phone started ringing and she answered, even as he ushered her through the lobby and she smiled and waved at the desk staff, who adored her like everyone else.

"Already? Well, that's interesting."

They got into the elevator and he pretended not to be annoyed that she was doing her job. Because it was her job and all and it was silly to be annoyed over that.

"No, it was standing room only. But they did have a lot of police there so that's a plus."

She laughed and Gage just bet it was Sato on the other line.

"PURITY continues to be an issue. Today she said we were bringing the end. I reminded her we'd been around as long as humans have been and haven't brought it yet. I'm sure that's just another plot on our part."

She laughed again and blushed.

Gage pushed past her. To protect her of course. But also so she could see his butt. He knew she looked. Goddess knew he looked at hers.

"Yes, we'll be there. Thank you. Yes. Bye."

He unlocked the door and did his usual walk-through but when he turned, he found her staring at him, an amused smile on her face.

"What?"

She put her things down exactly where they went and he had the childish urge to muss her papers and move her phone. But he didn't give in.

"What's bothering you?"

"What do you mean?"

She laughed as she put her shoes in the hall closet and hung her bag. "I mean you're prowling around, frowning. Not that your frown is hard to look at. Your brow gets all furrowy and I imagine you're growling in your head."

She made him wary. Women could be wily about stuff. This one was very smart. "You seem like the type who'd never say these things."

"I know. It's my secret weapon." She sat on the couch and looked up to him again. "So?"

She really was something else. "I think that's a very accurate statement. You were mighty and fantastic today." He moved to sit next to her, putting his arm around her shoulders and pulling her close. She snuggled in.

"Yeah? I *felt* mighty and fantastic. I have to tell you, I used my othersight and it seemed to click with my magick in this whole new way. I could gauge the whole room. Not control it necessarily, but when I could read it so well I could tailor my responses far better. Also, the urge to punch Alison's face grows and grows. Bringing about the end? Fuck her. And fuck her hate. I am sick to death of it. She's a vandal, that's what she is. She wants to tear this country apart to make some stupid point. She doesn't care who she hurts either. Disgusting."

He was proud. But he didn't know how to say it without coming off condescending so he pondered just how to say it as he settled for kissing the top of her head. "You did punch her in the face. Metaphorically I mean. She got up there and was all smug and hateful and you never sunk to her level. You did us all proud."

"I did threaten people though. I wondered if it was too far, but at the same time they need to understand we're not going to line up to let anyone hurt us. God, I think about that family. About that little girl recovering to go back to a life without her mother, father and brother. She'll need more skin grafting for the burn injuries. And what for?"

Her bottom lip wobbled just a little and it tore at him. He kissed her, holding her tight.

"For nothing. But it's not your fault. You're working to make their deaths mean something. That counts."

"You're being very nice to me. It scares me."

He snorted. "I'm always nice to you."

"When we're naked."

He was going to joke but then she said *naked* and his words sort of fell from his head as his blood all rushed south.

"I'm trying to comfort you and you go mentioning sex. You're a pervert."

The wobble was gone and she climbed into his lap instead. "Is your virtue threatened?"

With this woman in his lap? Oh yes. He gave her a wolfish grin and she tipped her head back, laughing.

He took that invitation, leaning close to kiss up the creamy column of her neck as she hummed her pleasure.

Her blouse was soft as he flicked each button, opening the front to expose another layer, this one a lacy tank-top thing. Beneath that she wore a bra.

"You're like Christmas morning." He slid the blouse from her arms and then pulled the other thing up and over her head.

"You want to crawl down my chimney?"

"Honestly, no one would ever believe me if I told them how you were behind closed doors." And he'd have been lying if he'd denied how much that appealed to him. This Molly was all his.

One more little movement and her bra was gone and those breasts were in his hands.

"Mmmm. I like where this is going."

"So many layers to you. Not just your clothes, which is what I meant by Christmas morning. As in I get to unwrap you."

She freed her hair and then sat upright. "Can I confess something?"

"Hell yes." He leaned in and licked over her collarbone and her fingers dug into his arms.

"I have a thing. A thing I wasn't aware of really until I met you."

He licked over a nipple and she writhed with a little squeal. The heat of her against his cock as she moved began to blot out everything else. Need for her swept through him. He bit down and she arched into his mouth.

"You like that."

"Why do you sound so surprised?" She made another sound then and her magick rose, teasing his senses.

"Not surprised." He did it again on the other nipple. "Delighted. So tell me about this thing of yours."

"I quite like it when I'm nearly naked and you still have clothes on. I'm sure that makes me a filthy wanton." She laughed again and he joined her this time, his hands pushing her skirt up to her waist so he could get at her panties to pull them off.

"I'm always happy to oblige the filthy wanton living just beneath your skin."

She had to lift up for that part and he missed her heat even for those few seconds. Smart girl that she was though, she got his pants unzipped and freed his cock. "My. What have we here?"

He shifted forward to get at his wallet where he'd stashed a condom exactly for moments like this one. He never wanted to have to wait once they were alone and this far along.

"I had plans for that first." She fisted him, pumping up and down a few times, sending him very close to the edge.

"I like fucking you. I want to fuck you right now. Work with me."

She rolled her eyes but grabbed the packet and rolled it on him quickly.

He slid his hand up her thigh, keeping her gaze. "Just want to be sure you're ready." And she was. So gloriously hot and wet he sighed happily, tickling a finger against her clit until she made another one of her sex sounds.

"Love your everyday voice, but the sex voice has it beat hands down." He traced around her, through her folds, teasing her gate until she took him by the root, got to her knees, positioned herself and sank down on him.

"Want something done right, do it yourself." She grinned at him and began to move.

He captured that mouth of hers for a long deep kiss as she slowly rode. "Should have known you'd be a control freak in bed too. Not that I'm complaining or anything."

That made her laugh and hug him. "We rarely make it to a bed. And you did say you wanted to fuck me."

"This is true. On both counts. Mmmm, you feel good."

She did. So hot and snug. Her hair a tousle around her face and shoulders. That crisp skirt tucked up around her waist the only clothing she wore. Damn.

He slid a hand between them, finding her clit again and slowly built her climax as she rose and fell. The winter sun setting, casting shadows against the glory of her skin and hair. His free hand wandered over a breast, palmed the arch of her neck, and found the cool silk of her hair, tipping her head just so.

She moaned as he tugged slightly, making him chuckle. "You like a little hair pulling."

"Mmm. From you? Yes."

"Keeping that in mind. Now, let's set this off." He

increased his speed and pressure and her inner muscles rippled around him, squeezing until he nearly cried at how good it was. And then she exploded on a whispered cry, dragging him along with her as he slid his arms around her, holding her tight.

"I do love this house. You two work well together. I can see you both in the design and layout." When she and Gage had arrived at Meriel and Dominic's house, they'd given Molly the grand tour.

It felt like a nice evening with friends and she decided— clearly still drunk with sex chemicals from her time with Gage—to try to forget the world outside and just enjoy herself.

Dominic looked toward Meriel, his face changing when she turned back and smiled. They shared a moment and through each of them, he saw another side to this couple.

He shifted, handing Molly a glass of wine. "Thank you. She had an apartment. I had an apartment. But this is our place. It feels like our refuge at the end of all these crazy days."

Molly sipped. "This is really good."

"Thanks. It's from a winery one of our witches runs in Eastern Washington. Tough day today, I hear. I was there, in the audience I mean. If I could have thrown flowers on the dais after your closing comments I would have."

It was Molly's turn to say thank you. "I had no idea you were there. Appreciate the support." She thought he'd also be a good face for the clan in certain media events and he'd reluctantly agreed. But he'd done a great job. People feared him for good reason. But they respected him too and that balance was a perfect compliment to Meriel's more cool and efficient outward persona.

Dominic Bright was intense. A powerful witch, but a powerful man as well. His personal energy simply took over whatever space he was in. He wasn't just handsome, he was riveting. And like his wife, he'd been very kind to her since she'd arrived.

"I like to be incognito sometimes. Sit with people who may not know me so I can see what people do and say." He shrugged.

"He's very sneaky." There was admiration in Meriel's voice. This couple was leading the clan during some really difficult times and doing it well. That took a lot of energy, brainpower and strength of will and conviction.

The doorbell rang and Meriel waved them to sit. Gage took the lead, giving her a lecture about letting him handle the door answering. The two bickered good-naturedly down the stairs to the front entry.

"Hard for you. Coming here and leaving your life behind. I know people have said so before, but . . . well, I understand very well just what it is to have grown up outside all this. To be an outsider in the world of clan witches."

She shrugged. "People have been quite welcoming. Gage has shown me a lot of stuff. How to use my magick more effectively. In fact he showed me how to use my othersight and it's been pretty awesome. I wish . . . in many ways I wish I'd grown up within a clan. Sometimes it feels like I'm a stranger to my own history." It was overwhelming sometimes, just how much she didn't know about witches and her own potential.

"That sounds ungrateful and it's not that I grew up sad or had a bad life before. I had a good life before I came here. I had . . . have family and friends. It's not like I didn't know I was a witch. I know how to use my magick." But this Molly was so much more. The woman—the witch—she was now was a universe away from who she'd been six weeks ago. It was hard to put into words how many feelings and fears all of that evoked.

"I get that. And I agree. I didn't even know I was a council witch before I met Meriel and then suddenly I'm her bond-mate and that means I'm this powerful witch and so I guess I'd been using such a small portion of my power and all that wasted potential kept me up sometimes. Made me wonder what I'd been missing. Sometimes I resented my dad who'd kept me away from all this stuff. To protect me of course, but still." He lowered his voice as the sounds of Lark and Simon's voices got closer. "I just wanted you to know you can always talk to me. We have a lot in common and I know this world can be overwhelming sometimes. Meriel and I want you to feel welcome here. We're your family in a way. It's got to be lonely sometimes. I know you work a lot so that cuts into the time you need to establish a life here in other ways. I'm probably messing this up, but I just wanted you to know you weren't alone."

"Feeling that way less and less each day. I appreciate it. The reaching out I mean."

He nodded. "Meriel tells me your family is moving out here. You must be excited to have them close again."

"Yes. My mom, grandparents and my other mom . . foster mom, whatever you want to call it—they're coming out to look for places to live and work. Chicago has been difficult for them. Since the Magister I mean. I'll be glad to have them here."

"Rosa, that's your other mom right?"

She nodded.

"She's welcome in Clan Owen. As is her son. Your mom and grandparents as well. We'll have to be sure to introduce them to the human members of the clan too."

Molly sometimes forgot the size of the clan and that there were mixed families so there were human members too.

"My nana will love that. She's the most social person I've ever met. You can't go anywhere with her and not have her end up in a conversation with the bagger, a random person in the parking lot, the server, whoever. She's impossible not to respond to."

Anthony Falco had been that way too. He'd been short. Barrel-chested with salt-and-pepper hair and an infectious sort of joy. You liked being around him. The ache of his absence sliced through her, reopening wounds she wished would finally heal over.

"What are you up to over here?' Gage approached in that way of his. Smooth, like a predator.

"Drinking wine. Talking shop. How's your mom, Gage?"

Molly liked that Dominic let their talk remain private. He seemed to understand she needed to process this all on her own terms. Which had equated pretty much to *maybe at some point in the future when she was alone and had a week or a month or maybe a few months* to let it go and let herself feel all she'd been pushing away.

"She's getting better. They're being great at work so that's a big relief for her." Shelley Garrity was a doctor for a local health co-op, Molly had learned when she'd met her.

"I'm glad to hear that."

"Work keeps her busy. When she's busy she doesn't dwell." Gage grabbed one of the crackers and loaded it with meat and cheese. He looked at Molly. "How's my great-aunt working out?"

"Rita is awesome and I don't know what I'd do without her. She scares away any casual interlopers. Manages my schedule like a bulldog. She knows everything about everyone. She's like my own personal superhero. And she brings me sweets. But don't share that. She likes it that people think she's mean and scary."

Gage grinned. "She *is* mean and scary. You just pass muster."

"I imagine taking care of you keeps her mind busy too." Dominic pushed a glass of wine Gage's way.

"I'm on duty."

Dominic snorted. "There are some pretty badass witches here and a giant wolf. Not to mention the four guards outside the house. I think we'll be all right if you have some wine."

"Peer pressure!" Lark approached, laughing. "Dominic, you're being such a bad example."

"I was born to be a bad example, Lark." Dominic attempted to look stern but his laugh spoiled it.

Molly grinned up at Gage, who looked at her like he did no one else. She had this . . . potential that had been missing since before the Magister. It was normal. And hopeful and romantic and silly and she hadn't had that in what seemed like forever.

She had to grab the counter tight to keep her knees from

buckling as the realization hit. "Excuse me." Molly put her glass down and headed back to the bathroom.

Once she had the door locked she ran the sink and avoided looking at herself in the mirror as she washed her hands and tried to gather herself back together.

She needed to think about her upcoming schedule. About where she'd stay and how she'd structure her time between meeting with Others and dealing with humans and the media.

Calm came after the fifth hand washing, after she'd planned her upcoming trip to Washington, D.C., with precision that ran down to fifteen-minute buffers in some places.

At last she dared to look at herself and then cursed. In her head of course. But she looked like a woman barely holding herself together.

Probably because she *was* a woman barely holding herself together.

She had a touch-up kit in her purse. Some powder and lipstick. Blotting cloths so she didn't look like the sweaty mess she was just then.

The hard-won control slipped a little.

Even after some tissue blotting and a finger comb of her hair she still looked ill.

Molly opened the door and went straight to get her bag.

"You all right?" Meriel called out.

"Yes. Thanks." Molly headed back into the bathroom. The women would simply assume she had to deal with some sort of period-related issue. That thought allowed her to unclench her jaw.

One breath after the other, she managed to pull the pretty black bag from her purse and unzip it.

The touch-up kit was something she'd perfected over the years in public relations. A collapsible brush, a sewing kit, hairspray, stain pen, mini lotion and an array of basic cosmetics.

She redid her hair and mentally made the city of Seattle into a grid and began to rate the pros and cons of each neighborhood for possible places for her family to settle in.

By the time she closed the cap on her lipstick Molly had managed to get her mask of control back into place.

GAGE looked toward the hallway again. She'd been gone a while.

"Don't." Lark patted his arm. "She's fine."

"You sure?"

One of Lark's brows rose just a bit as one corner of her mouth quirked up. "Well now, Gage. Aren't you a wild card?"

"Don't poke at him, Lark." Simon bent and kissed the top of her head and she leaned back into him.

"It's adorable."

He should have known even Simon couldn't stop Lark from poking once she was onto something. "It's my job to protect her. Also she's my friend. I'd be worried if it was you in there. Or Meriel."

Lark looked to Meriel and both women snorted.

Finally Molly emerged with a smile that was uptight at the edges. She moved like she did when she was on camera. Precise and totally in control. Graceful. But there was a difference when she relaxed and opened up. A softer sort of Molly. One that had more humor and more than a little bawd.

She put her bag back and joined them around the kitchen island once more, grabbing her glass.

"So when are you finally going to Lycia to perform the binding ceremony?" Meriel simply continued their conversation as if nothing had happened.

But there was a difference there and it niggled at the back of his brain.

She gave him no single moment of longer than a minute or two to get her alone so he could talk to her about it though and by the time they'd finally left Meriel and Dominic's, she seemed pretty much back to herself.

Chapter 18

GAGE really hated the way Toshio Sato looked at Molly. There, he admitted it. The senator would lean in close and give her all his attention as she spoke. He saw her for the intelligent and well-spoken woman she was.

Currently they were having a rather intense discussion while Gage and Helena pretended they weren't watching.

"You have to be patient," Sato urged.

Molly sat back and shook her head. "Tosh, how patient do we have to be? Hm? How much more should we take? This is all unconstitutional and you know it. You can't just kick people out of apartments and fire them en masse because they're Others! I'm out of patience. More importantly, my people are out of patience. How much do you think a were-wolf is going to take when his business is repeatedly vandalized and his son is assaulted *on the school bus* in full view of cameras? You really think I should tell him to not fight back?"

"We're trying our best. If he reacts, we lose integral public support."

"Please do excuse me for this. But fuck that. Fuck that

bullshit and fuck you for even suggesting that Others should let themselves continue to be assaulted and harmed and treated this way and to continue to be patient when this just gets worse every day. What would *you* do if that boy was your son? Hm?"

Helena's brow rose. So much like her sister that in that moment. She nodded, also like her sister, bloodthirsty.

Gage was impressed. Molly rarely used really bad words so when she did the impact was explosive. Sato's body language reflected that. He was being dressed down by one pissed-off, frustrated woman.

"I'm saying if they go all vigilante, it makes anyone trying to support them think twice."

Molly stood, hands on her hips. "*Vigilante?* Excuse me? So the people burning crosses on lawns and breaking windows are doing what? Defending yourself from that makes the *Other* a vigilante? Not the other way around? This argument is beneath you, Tosh, and you know it. Don't waste my time with this another second."

The senator sighed, abashed. "You know better than most the way this works. I'm not saying the humans doing this are right. You know how public perception reacts to this stuff."

"What I know is that I've got my own support to worry over. I've got my own people who are scared and angry and still grieving over their losses. None of us has even had a spare moment to mourn our own dead. And we keep being told to be patient and in the meantime Others keep on taking the hits. I'm telling you, totally up front here, that if things don't change very soon, this will not end well for humans because there's only so much patience a vampire or werewolf or witch has when our families and lives are on the line. You get me? Time's a-tickin' on this and we need to see a lot more, totally open support from humans in power. I can only hold people back so long."

Sato sighed heavily. "I understand. You know I do. But you know how this works. Just hold on. Keep your people in check so I can get some things done. Each time one of these horrible things happens, more humans begin to realize this has gone too far."

"Really? I could have told them all that six weeks ago. Eight weeks ago. I've given you nearly all the time I can. I'm telling you without any embellishment that this is just about ready to explode. Get that stuff done before it's too late." She looked at her watch. "I have to go. I'll see you on Wednesday."

"We still friends?" Sato asked.

"Yes. And I appreciate all you do for us, I truly do. But that's not going to stop my people from getting fed up." She looked to Helena. "See you Wednesday too?"

"Yes, I'll be there. Nothing like Washington, D.C., in late February. Wheee."

Molly grinned. "Ha. I'm just getting used to how nice and mild the winter in Seattle is and now I've got to dig out my big coat. Be safe, all right?"

Helena nodded.

Gage opened the door and checked the hallway first before gesturing her out.

At the entry where the car was, their guard had grown. The cats had sent along some of their best, along with Gennessee.

"This is not incognito."

He opened her door. "No. It's 'if you even try to fuck with us, we will crush you.' "

She paused and then nodded, buckling her seat belt.

"Too bad you don't get frequent-flier miles for all this."

"Maybe National will give me a pen or something."

At least she could joke. That was something. He'd seen her put people in their place before, but this was the most tense exchange he'd seen between her and Sato.

She hadn't lied about the pressure she was under. Others were impatient. Sick of being told to wait. Some didn't. Some had met violence with violence and Meriel had been working overtime on getting legal representation for all the Others they got reports on. They tended to throw Others in jail first and asked questions later.

She fielded one call after the other, even as they'd gotten on the plane and strapped in.

"Two and a half glorious call-free hours. Think on it that way."

She gave him side eye but sat back with a sigh and closed her eyes as they took off.

He wanted to talk with her but she was so exhausted she dropped off to sleep before they'd even reached altitude so he put a blanket on her and watched her for a while before doing his own work.

"WHY are you turning here?" She looked up from her phone to ask. Once they'd landed and she'd turned her phone on she'd been on it nonstop.

She was a machine, but even machines needed to be powered off sometimes or they'd break. He decided to do his part in that.

"I'm taking you to my house where I'm going to feed you, make you sit in my hot tub and then I will smooch you and make you get nine hours' sleep."

"I have work to do. I need to go to my office."

"Rita has forwarded everything pressing to your email. I have a nice work setup at my place so you can check in then."

"I don't have time for this, Gage."

"For what? Shutting down for a while so you can recharge? Molly, you're pale. You have big dark circles under your eyes. You're impatient and snappy. Cut yourself a break. Let me fucking take care of you for a few hours. The world won't end if you let yourself turn off for a while."

"But it might!" Her voice rose, nearly breaking and the full brunt of just how on edge she was hit him.

"I know better than most that you can't protect everyone. You can't. You can only do what you can do. And you will fail some people. But you won't help anyone if you're so strung out you can barely speak. Your work will be there tomorrow. And more the next day. I hate seeing you like this. If you won't do it for yourself, do it for me."

She sighed, leaning back in the seat. "Fine."

"That's a start. Thank you."

He hadn't brought her to his place yet. He'd known her for nearly two months and they'd been . . . involved for nearly a month of that time. They'd been in hotel rooms in multiple states but never his bed.

"It's not as big as Simon and Lark's house." He opened his front door and ushered her in. No one had been here since he'd been there a few mornings prior to get fresh clothes for the trip they'd just made to Sacramento.

"Your view." She moved to the windows overlooking downtown and the Sound off in the distance. "Wow."

"The building is old. The heat is mercurial. The hills are impassable when it ices up after snow. But the view keeps me here. In the summer I like to walk down the hill to downtown. It's only about fifteen minutes."

"My apartment . . . my old apartment that is, had a nice view too. I guess everything is packed up and being shipped out here. Maybe someday I'll have a house to put it all in."

He came up behind her, pulling her to his body. "You want to talk about it?"

She tensed up. "No."

"You need to."

"Trust me, no, I don't. Not here and not now. Didn't you say you were going to make me dinner? I'm starving."

"I'll call for take-out. There's not much here fresh since I've been living at the hotel so many days a week. You like Thai?"

"Yes, that'll do nicely. I like it hot."

He turned her slowly. "I know."

She smiled in her secret Molly way. "Dirty."

"All for you." He kissed her and moved to the phone to call the food in.

"You're staying over tonight so you may as well get comfortable." He drew her down the hall to his bedroom.

"You have weapons on your walls." She stared at them all.

"I do. Easy access if necessary."

"And a reminder of who you are and what you do."

He paused a moment, his hands in his dresser as he looked for a shirt that wouldn't drown her.

She understood him better than most. It made him uncomfortable, but he couldn't deny it also made him feel as if he belonged.

"Here's a shirt. I'd pretend to give you some of my boxers but we both know I'd have you out of any underpants in moments anyway so let's skip that part. My shower is right through there. Go on. By the time you're finished the food will be here and then we can go up to my hot tub."

"I can't sit in your hot tub without underpants. Ew."

Gage burst out laughing. "You're right. But as it happens I've got a swimsuit here. You can use that one."

"Why do you have a swimsuit?"

"Why does Toshio Sato look at your mouth too much?"

One of her brows shot up. "Are you joking?"

Ooops. "It's my mom's suit. Like two years old. They house-sat for me and she left it here. It's been in a drawer all that time. It's clean."

"I just remembered I have an overnight bag with sweats in it. Not for your hot tub." She paused. "He doesn't look at my mouth. And you know, if you didn't think it should be such a secret that we're together, maybe no one would look at my mouth because they'd know I was taken."

Oh god, not this. They'd briefly discussed it in the past and he'd told her it was best if they kept their involvement quiet. That wasn't the same as keeping it secret.

"What? He totally does. He gets very close and he looks at your mouth. And I'm not keeping it a secret. I'm just not announcing it. It puts me in an odd place. I'm your guard. It's a bad idea to sleep with the person you should be guarding."

"Are you really standing there telling me the reason you pretend we're not sleeping together is professionalism? Really?"

"You're having a rough day. You're tired. You're grumpy. You'll feel better after you clean up and eat."

"Boys are so dumb. I'm taking a shower."

Molly snatched the shirt and stomped into his bathroom, slamming the door.

How was it they were having a fight anyway? She'd been fine and a little horny. That always suited her. And suddenly she was pissed and he found himself turned on? God, she was right. Boys were weird.

GAGE was lucky he was so nice to look at. That's all she had to say.

She washed her hair and all the travel grime from her skin. She smelled like him and it shouldn't have made her smile to use his soap but it did. She was the dumb one. But damn it, she liked Gage. A lot more than she probably should. But he was someone to her.

Which didn't erase his being a jackwagon. Oh, so Tosh looked at her mouth? Really? If that were true, he had the chance to end it by just giving the other person a look that said *back off she's mine*. Oh she knew he claimed it was professional and safer to keep things quiet.

Hell, maybe it was and she was just being unreasonable because she was beyond tired and no small bit of hopeless.

His bringing her to his apartment was nice. He liked taking care of her. And heaven knew she craved just letting go and leaning on someone for a while. But it had only been a few months since they'd met and only a month since they . . . well, whatever it was they were doing. It was more than whatever they called it, fuckbuddies or what have you. And it wasn't that he was ashamed of her, she got that too.

She sighed, turning off the water. It had been extra hot, which was bad for her skin, but it finally chased the chill from her bones and burned off some of her stress. She needed to turn off her work brain, just for a while. She was overwhelmed and she knew it. Worse, Gage knew it, and that was not a good sign. She did need a solid night's sleep. Maybe a movie or something.

She had her bag so she changed into the T-shirt he'd given

her and some sweats after she braided her hair back from her face and brushed her teeth.

When she came out, he handed her a glass of wine. "Drink. Food should be here shortly. They're only a few blocks away."

She sipped, sighing. "Thank you."

"You're in bare feet." He frowned.

"I didn't have any socks." Well, she did but they were her nighttime lotion socks and they were beat up and ugly and they had a while to go before she'd consent to ratty clothing around him.

He snorted and left the room, tossing her a pair of socks when he returned. "You don't need to be cold."

Like she'd done it on purpose to irk him. "Thank you. Why are you grumpy?" She sat and put the socks on.

"I was going to ask you the same thing."

"We bicker a lot."

She closed her eyes, smiling. "Because you're entirely unreasonable sometimes."

He snorted a laugh. "That's me."

"Tell me about Rose." She immediately wished she could dig a hole and crawl into it. She wasn't even sure where that had come from. She opened her eyes. "Or not."

"I'll tell you about her if you share some of yourself with me. It's only fair."

She licked her lips. "All right."

"People like to make a bigger deal out of it than it was. She worked at Owen in our tech department. She's smart and I liked how tech savvy she was. We'd only actually gone out on a few dates when the whole thing with the Magister came about."

"She left the clan?" That had seemed so drastic to Molly. Now that she'd found Owen and had been part of a clan it was sort of difficult to imagine having this and giving it up voluntarily. This membership meant something to her. It had become her family in such a quick fashion.

"She felt like the only way to stay alive was to keep her head down and not be out as an Other." He shrugged.

And that bothered him. The question was, why? And should she push him and then risk getting an answer she wouldn't like?

"And that bugs you."

He pushed to stand and began to pace. "I can't protect everyone. It's entirely reasonable given what we've seen in the last months to want to get away from all this danger and keep your head down. She made the choice she needed to make for herself."

It wasn't that he'd been sweet on the woman who'd left then. It was that he felt he'd failed. And she got that one, big time. Still, he gave everything to the clan to protect them. He was a witch, not a superhero. There was no way anyone could protect everyone. That wasn't how things worked.

"Is that what you think? That you have to protect everyone?"

"It's my job. Now what about you? How are you holding up?"

She let him evade. After all, she was doing it too. "I'm used to a high-stress job. I can handle it. I just need some rest."

He turned to her, shaking his head. "That's shady, Molly."

"What? Shady how?"

The buzzer sounded and he turned to deal with it.

He refused to let her even give him a dime for the food and laid it all out. The weight of his disappointment hung between them the entire time.

She sighed. Then sniffled because true to his promise, the curry was hot like she liked.

"I'm afraid that if I really let go and tell you how I'm doing that I'll lose my shit." There. She said it.

His gaze snapped up from his plate and to her face. "You think I'd judge?" It wasn't accusatory, just a question.

She didn't know the answer. Maybe if she lost control she'd never get it back. Maybe if she unleashed all that bubbling fury and pain she'd be nothing more than a mess. And she couldn't afford it.

"Maybe. I don't know. It's certainly not the only reason

I'm worried." She ate for a few minutes more until her system started to feel better with the infusion of calories. "I've had an easy life. Maybe this is my punishment for that."

He snorted. "Really? You think all this death and utter chaos is because you had a happy life until now?"

"Self-centered of me, I know. It's stupid." She looked down at her plate and he put his chopsticks down, reaching out to take her hand.

"It's not stupid. And it's not self-centered. But this is not because you had a good life as a kid. Tell me how is it now? Now that you're here in Owen."

She might be able to do that. Just a little bit of unloading.

"I like the feel of Owen. It had always seemed like sort of a snooty yacht club or something. From the outside I mean. But it's nothing like that. It's like one big family. Sure, some of the family members are jerks who always get drunk at weddings and cause fights. But there's a sense of unity I've never really experienced before."

"You never felt that with humans?"

She sighed, thinking. "No, not really. It's not like I felt bad. Or like an outsider. But the fact is, I *was* an outsider." And that had become painfully clear when she'd lost everything she'd gained in her human life.

"I never really imagined this is how they'd react. Humans I mean. Oh I figured some would freak out and make a fuss. But a fuss isn't setting shit on fire and killing defenseless families in their sleep. It's not a world I feel much affinity with anymore."

"They're not all that way."

"Why do you always defend them? They stole your entire life, Molly! They came in and when it got hard, they dumped you and stole your life. Your job. Your clients. Your friends abandoned you."

She flinched because he'd been right. No one spoke to her the way he did. It was frustrating and exciting all at once.

"That might be true. But my mother is human. She raised me, Gage, not my witch father. And when Rosa discovered me and went to my mother, she shared me with another family to be sure I got what I needed. She's the one who urged me to come here to Owen. My grandparents are human and they've never done anything but love and support me. Tosh Sato is human and he's risking his career for Others. They're not all Alison Moore or her puppet master Carlo Powers. So I think my reply to you is why do *you* always attack *them*? You say you hate it when they do it to you and then you turn around and judge all humans by the acts of a few crazy people."

"Yeah, so where are those non-crazy people when Others like the Boraches are run off the road and murdered? Huh? Silence is just as bad as what PURITY is doing in some cases."

"Yes, it is a problem and connecting with those silent majority humans is a big task, but necessary. What is it exactly that *you* think will solve the problem? Should we go to war? Just kill as many of them as we can while they do the same? And what's the end game there? What is the point?"

"We should stop coddling people like Sato who flirt with our rights but then give out lectures about being patient while Others are being discriminated against left and right. When our businesses are being vandalized and our homes aren't safe? He can't call himself a friend to Others while he gives *you* a dressing down about vigilantes. And by the way, you rocked that meeting today."

"I don't even know how to process you, Gage. You're pissy and grumpy and unreasonable and then you compliment me."

He grinned, clearly caught off guard. "If I keep you on your toes, you're too busy trying to figure me out to pop me one for being a dick sometimes."

"Hm."

"When you do that it only makes me hot."

He was so charming. Good gracious, the man was a handful, but she really did enjoy him on so many levels.

"Toshio Sato is a good man. He is so get that sour look off your face. You're ruining all that pretty."

"You think I'm pretty?"

"Are you fishing for compliments?"

He shrugged. "Of course not."

Liar. "Yes, I think you're pretty. Well, maybe not pretty. You're too masculine for that. You're brutally handsome. Your body is, well, I do like to see it naked. Or not naked. I just like your shoulders and your arms."

"And my ass. Don't think I haven't noticed you looking."

She laughed, blushing. "I'm weak. And your butt is spectacular. I can't not look. It would be un-American not to look at a behind as fine as yours, Gage."

He blushed then and she laughed harder.

"You blush!"

"I do. But not very often. About Rose." He licked his lips and she thought about how much she liked his mouth and that tongue too. "She was nice and fun. But this thing." He waved a hand back and forth between them. "Is more. On a whole different level."

She wasn't asking him to say it, but she was glad he did. "Yeah? So why hide it?"

"I'm not hiding it. Not exactly."

"That is such a guy answer."

"As I said earlier, I shouldn't be guarding someone I'm sleeping with. It's not a good choice."

"So you're not saying anything about our relationship so you can keep guarding me?" Partly she got that. It made sense and it wasn't like she wanted him to take out a billboard declaring that they were . . . whatever they were.

"I'm also a private guy and I work with women who would never let me hear the end of it. And Toshio Sato better man the fuck up and back us like he should. Otherwise he's not a good man. He's just a guy giving lip service and we're still getting screwed over."

He confused her so much! He didn't have to say that about Rose and the difference between that and what he had with Molly. That had been sweet and it had made her sort of gooey inside. But then he'd circled back to Tosh?

"I agree. And he's not the only one."

"You're getting lines on your forehead again. Stop

thinking about work. I'm sorry I brought it up. When is your mom coming out?"

"She and Rosa are coming out next week to look at some houses. They've got a real-estate agent and everything and I've sent them information about the different neighborhoods. My mom has a job interview too. I hooked Rosa up with Owen. They've done a great job reaching out to her." It was a relief to know they were coming. A relief to know they'd be close.

"Good to know. We're glad to have you. You know that right? I know things were rough at first. But now that people know you it's smoother."

She sipped her wine and considered whether she should share everything. "For the most part, yes."

"The most part?" His magick rose and hers stirred. At first it had startled her. She'd never dated a witch before so her magick hadn't done anything when she was around a guy she got naked with. But with Gage . . . things were different. Her magick always rose to meet his. He touched her and she was often flooded with the warm rush of her power.

He seemed to evoke a response in her. Provocative even in that.

"Not everyone is excited about me. But I don't need everyone to be. The ones who count are."

"Like who?"

"It doesn't matter."

"Um, yes, it does. Tell me."

He was so fiercely protective of her. It overwhelmed her at times. But right then it made her feel safe and cared about.

"It's just a thing that happens sometimes. It's not like anyone has harmed me. Some witches at Owen would be happier to not have anyone with pro-human sensibilities in any position of power." She shrugged.

He frowned. "Who?"

"We've already established that I'm not going into it. I'm just saying, not everyone is happy. But that's life, Gage. Not everyone likes you."

"I don't know why you have to be so stubborn about things."

"Because it's none of your business. You can't change it. Or help it. It is what it is. No amount of frowning or brow-beating is going to make everyone like me. So let it go."

"Or, you know, you could try sharing with me and letting me take some of your burdens. That's what friends do."

"This isn't about you. It's not even really about me. It's about worlds colliding and all this grief and fury, angst and longing for a world they will never ever have again. It's the only way some of us can mourn without falling to pieces. I understand it."

He took her in and it was like he saw right to her very core. Uncomfortable and yet, part of her needed it and responded with relief.

"And what do you do, then? To mourn?"

"I fight."

"Fair enough. Ready for the hot tub?"

As a matter of fact, she was.

"The bathing suit is on my bed. I'm going to put the food away and get us a glass of wine to take up."

She hustled off and got changed quickly. It would be good to have time to unwind with him. To look at the stars and let go of the day.

He led her up a spiral staircase to a small patio. "This is another reason I keep the apartment. It comes with this." He took the cover off and it steamed up into the cold darkness.

"This is all yours? I figured it was a community tub."

"All mine. I haven't used it much lately."

She put her towel down and got rid of her shoes before she let him help her ease into the hot water. The air around them was so cold it stung against her skin as not-quite-snow fell lightly around them.

She leaned back into his body and let the stress go.

"I like having you all to myself. Just Molly and Gage. No clan, no PURITY, just you and me in this hot tub with the promise of hot sex when we get out."

She laughed, reaching over to grab him through his trunks. He arched in her hand. "Don't know that we even have to wait until we get back inside."

"I sure do like the *sex on a rooftop* Molly." He nuzzled her neck and she sighed, relaxing against him.

He slowly spun her, lifting her to place her butt on the ledge. Steam rose from her skin, but she was anything but cold as he eased her suit bottoms off and to the side.

Anything but cold as he kissed his way up her inner thigh until he spread her open and began to devour her hard and fast until she broke, coming so hard she would have cried out if they weren't outside.

But the restraint only made her hotter as he stood and pulled a condom from the towel he'd set on the nearby ledge, getting it on quickly, moving back to her, guiding himself to the heart of her and working his way into her body.

"Pretty sure of yourself."

"I like to be prepared for any sex you decide to let me have with you."

And he was in, so deep it felt like the beating of his pulse echoed through her inner walls.

But always inside her. Always lodged inside and she wasn't sure he was a man she could ever be totally over. So she just had to enjoy what they had and hope she never had to experience that pain.

Chapter 19

"**YOU'RE** stronger now." Rosa looked her over after giving Molly a big hug.

"What do you mean?"

"Your magick. Interesting."

"They've been giving me lessons. On how to use my power I mean. Maybe it's just that."

"Maybe. But I don't think so. In any case, I'm so happy to see you." Rosa held Molly's face between her hands, smiling.

Molly and Rosa had had a series of long phone calls about the move out to Seattle. She didn't want her family moving half a country away because they were worried about her. She didn't want anyone giving up anything else, damn it.

But Rosa wasn't a pushover and what she wanted was to wash her hands of Chicago and try to pull her life together again in Seattle. She'd told Molly that seeing her husband in everything, every restaurant, their home, all that had been too much. Especially when she had to deal with so much crap for being a witch.

Gage knocked at the door, poking his head in briefly,

smiling when he caught sight of Rosa. "I just wanted to check in. Sorry to interrupt."

"Come in." She kept Rosa's hand as they turned. "Rosa, this is Gage Garrity. He's the hunter here. Sort of like the head cop, though it's so much more than that. Anyway." She knew she blushed and it was so amateurish she was surprised at herself. She was usually better at schooling her emotions at work.

Gage stepped in and took Rosa's hand in both of his. "It's a pleasure to meet you. Molly speaks of you often. Welcome to Seattle and to Owen." He inclined his head slightly.

Rosa sent Molly a raised brow but grinned back Gage's way. "Thank you. It's nice to meet you too. Thank you for protecting Molly. Her mom and I appreciate it. It's hard when she's so far away." Rosa looked him over in that way she had.

"My mom will be here in a moment, she just needed to freshen up." Faine had accompanied them back from the airport but he'd disappeared shortly after they returned to the office to run back to the hotel to get Rosa and her mother checked in.

Not that she was disappointed to see Gage. Things had changed between them—deepened—in the week since that night in his apartment. More trust. She knew she could rely on him. And she was way past crush territory and well on the trip into falling in love.

It was hard when the world was falling apart all around you to make excuses as to why you should deny your feelings when it was something good and important.

So she didn't.

Her mother came in and her gaze went immediately to Gage.

"Mom, this is Gage. Gage Garrity, this is my mother, Eliza Ryan." She'd told her mom a little about Gage and her sort-of relationship with him. It was clear her mother knew it when she took him in carefully.

"Nice to meet you, ma'am." Gage shook her hand, smiling in his charming way. "Do we need to get their luggage any-where?" he asked Molly.

"Faine went to the hotel to get them checked in. When he gets back we'll go meet with the real-estate agent. They already have several places to look at."

"I'll go with you all. Faine has some other things I need him to do."

He did that from time to time. She knew because he wanted to be with her, even if the stubborn man wouldn't say it out loud.

"Oh my, we don't need a guard. We can have the real-estate agent pick us up here and have her show us around. She can drop us back at the hotel. We know you have work to do." Rosa looked back and forth between Molly and Gage.

"If Molly is with you, you'll need a guard."

Rosa and her mother both narrowed their gaze her way. "You said things were all right."

"She receives death threats on a weekly basis. She's been flour bombed, shoved, had insults hurled at her and this building has been vandalized. We have every reason to believe they're tracking her movements. So wherever she goes, one of us goes."

Molly widened her eyes and then narrowed them. The nerve!

"There is *nothing* for you two to worry about. The guard thing is a backup but there's no reason to think there's any harm in going house hunting. I want to come along. Don't forget I need to find a place to live as well." She smiled, soldiering on, but when she got Gage alone there would be a reckoning.

"Sounds to me like if you have twenty-four-hour bodyguards, there *is* something to worry about." Her mother wasn't having any avoidance of a subject she wanted to talk about.

"My job has some dangers, yes. But going to look at houses is totally fine. We'll have Gage with us because that's what his job is. He decides such things. But I'm right here. Fine."

"Mr. Garrity, can you please enlighten us?" Her mother turned and every female eye in the room landed on him.

Molly threw her hands up. "About what? He's already told you everything."

"If you don't, I have to."

He couldn't have actually said that out loud!

At that moment, if her mother and Rosa hadn't been right there she would have thrown the stapler in her hand. His gaze went to it, knowing exactly that. But the butthead didn't even flinch.

"Your daughter is the public face of the clan. And more than that, of Others in general. That's part of her job."

"And one I do rather well."

He nodded, solemn still. "Yes, she's right about that. But the better she is at it, the more people in PURITY and Humans First focus all that hatred on her. That makes her a target. It's my job to be sure that she's protected as much as possible. I don't think you or Mrs. Falco are at risk, but when Molly is with you, it's best to be cautious and careful. For everyone's sake."

"I'm rather unhappy that you haven't shared the full extent of this with me." Rosa sighed heavily.

"I'm sorry. I didn't want to worry you. I'm sorry *I* wasn't the one to tell you as well."

Gage got it then. She knew from the look that flashed across that criminally handsome face.

Faine walked past and she waved. "Faine! I thought you were off doing something else. Perfect timing. We need to get over to the first house. Can you accompany us?"

Gage narrowed his gaze at her for a moment and she shined him on, still beyond angry with him.

Rosa and her mother stared at her, but her mother wore a little smirk so on top of the whole bit about how much danger she faced, now her mother knew there was something more than a budding romance between them.

"Um." Faine looked back and forth between Gage and Molly. "I have something I need to do. I was stopping by to tell you that."

Gage sent her a smirk and her grip on the stapler tightened so much the plastic may have groaned.

"If you ladies are ready?" Gage indicated they all leave the office. When Molly passed him, he reached out to touch her but she flinched away, shooting him a look.

She then sat in the backseat, in the middle, rather than up front with him and kept up a conversation that would wall him on the other side. He wanted to play some stupid game? He needed to be schooled, apparently, that he wasn't the only one who could do that.

Gage tapped into his patience. What he wanted to do was hustle her pretty ass off to the side and have it out. But her mothers were here and it was clear he'd already fucked up. So he'd bide his time.

It was hard not to be impressed with what an icy bitch she could be when she put her mind to it. Her manners toward him were perfectly civil. But nothing more. He missed the way she smiled at him, warmth and a little mischief in her gaze.

She turned on the charm with the real-estate agent, though. He was an Other, which she'd done on purpose, Gage would wager. He checked the guy out of course. He wasn't going to let anyone near her or anyone she cared about without a thorough background check.

They looked at houses but it wasn't as if Molly's phone stopped ringing. She had to excuse herself over and over and her mother frowned. Gage wanted them to know how hard Molly worked and that she wasn't being rude.

In the end, her mother ended up liking a waterfront condo in downtown so much she put in a bid on it. It was big enough for her parents to live there with her if they wanted, which made Gage like Eliza Ryan all the more. Rosa saw a few places she liked, but none that really knocked her socks off. But there was time and she could afford to be choosy.

Molly smiled at her mother, spoke in her ear and then motioned to Gage to speak with her off to the side.

"So now you want to talk to me?"

"No, as it happens, I don't. But I figured I'd give it a try rather than go around you and call Lark. But if you'd prefer that, I'm happy to do so. This is about my mother's safety and I'm not going to play games."

"I deserved that. What do you need?"

"Is this defensible? Will she be safe here?"

He'd gone into each place asking himself exactly that question. But it didn't erase the warmth in his belly that she'd come to him, trusting him that way.

"I've checked this building out in the past. It's got a doorman, which is nice. These floors can only be accessed by a key. Her view is toward the water so there's no one directly across from her who could do harm. The balcony is positioned out of the direct line of sight from any of her neighbors. I think it's a good choice."

She nodded. "Thank you." And turned, moving back to her mother, speaking in her ear again.

Finally, four hours later, he took them to the hotel.

"I've got some meetings I need to go to so I won't be back until after nine or so. I'm sorry."

Her mother looked her over carefully. "Are you getting enough rest?"

No. But he kept his mouth shut.

"I'm working on it, Mom. But stuff keeps happening and I have to address it before PURITY does."

Eliza took a deep breath. "All right. I'll be waiting up for you. We're all going to have some tea when you get home."

Gage accompanied them to their room and checked it over before he turned and let them know it was safe. "The hotel is owned by Owen. Staffed by our people. You can't get through the lobby unless you're a guest or approved by a guest. Still, don't open the door to anyone you don't know." He handed them both a business card. "My direct number is on there. Call that if you need anything. Don't hesitate if something feels off."

Molly hugged them both and turned, striding past him to the elevator without a second glance.

Once the elevator doors closed he turned to her. "Clearly you have something to say."

She pushed the button for the lobby. "Not here. Not now. I have to meet with city officials in twenty minutes and if I said all the things in my head right now, we'd both be unable to do that. Mainly because you'd be limping."

"Oh, you think so?"

"Yes. And so do you. You moved over a little. Girl doesn't have to be a hunter to notice things like that. Now back off and leave me alone. I have to get into the right head space for this meeting."

He shouldn't have been amused. But he was. "You can't avoid it forever."

She snorted and proceeded to ignore him quite pointedly for the next several hours as she went from meeting to meeting.

He got plenty of his own work done, as guarding her meant a lot of waiting off to the side. At one point, she'd approached, handed him her tablet and gone back to work.

He resisted the urge to read through her stuff, instead hopping online, answering email and dealing with anything that had cropped up since he'd left the office earlier that day.

Once she'd finally finished up for the day it was impossible not to see how beat she was. It was one thing to be her bodyguard. But this was another level of protection and he needed to fix her.

"I'm stopping for dinner." He said this without looking her way. "Why don't you call your mom to let her know you'll be late? Maybe she'll want to eat and we can bring something."

"I have food in my fridge."

"You won't eat a meal. You'll eat an apple and a breakfast bar and call it a dinner. You've been away from the office since before eleven. You haven't eaten this whole time. I'm starving and I know you have to be."

"My mother is already here. Oh and I've got a spare too. Thanks to your lovely description of just how dangerous my job is earlier today, they're both already going to be worried. I can't be later than I already am. I'm sure Rosa has baked something already too. I'm fine."

"Look, I'm sorry about that. I didn't mean to alarm them. I just wanted them to know how things were."

"Yes, you did. You even said so. I had planned to go over it bit by bit while they were here. You know, ease them into this world. But you just threw them into it without any context. That was shitty."

"They need to understand, Molly. It's not fair of you to keep them in the dark."

"Fuck you. Fuck you. Oh and fuck you. How dare you think you get to decide any of this for me? Those two women are pretty much all I've got left. Rosa has lost *everything*. Her husband. Her daughter. Her job. With the exception of her son, her whole life. The last thing she needed was for you to dump all that on her. That wasn't your choice to make. She's barely holding on. This trip was about her getting some normalcy in her life. Finding a new place to live. Meeting witches in the clan. Finding a home. And you just stomped in with your fancy boots and pooped all over it."

He swallowed, hard, knowing she was right and in his zeal to let her family know how dangerous her job was, he'd mucked things up.

"I just wanted them to know they had a reason to be proud of you."

She exhaled sharply. "You could have told them I've met television personalities and lawmakers. You didn't need to say their daughter was being threatened day and night. It's hard enough to *be* threatened day and night but it's easier when my mother doesn't know. That just adds more stress to my schedule and, in case it's unclear, I have enough."

Her voice broke and he felt it, the trembling of those walls she had up. Wondered, not for the first time, just how much she had ferreted away. And what might happen when they fell away.

"Goddamn it. Just let go. It's killing you. All this stuff you push down inside. It has nowhere to go. One of these days—"

She pounded the seat with a closed fist, her face in a tight expression. "Stop. Just stop. I can't. Not right now."

"So when then? Huh?"

"What is it with you? Do you want me to have a break-down? Would that make you feel better? Why does it matter?"

"Because *you* matter, Molly." He hadn't meant to say it out loud, but now that he had, he felt better. "Do you think I can't see how hard you work to keep it all together?"

"Then why are you trying to make me lose it?"

He pulled off the road, into a small parking lot. Once he'd turned the engine off he turned to face her. "I'm not trying to make you lose it." He brushed hair away from her face. "I'm telling you it's safe to let it go with me."

"I keep telling you I can't do this and you keep pushing."

"Because you're about to crack and break apart. Baby, I want to catch you if you fall. I'm afraid it's going to happen when I'm not there or when it's a bad time." He cupped her cheek and she leaned into him, closing her eyes. So much tenderness flooded him his eyes swam.

"When is it a good time to lose your shit?"

"When I'm here with you." He leaned in and brushed his lips against her temple. "You have a lot of burdens to carry. All this grief. Not just yours, but everyone else's. I can see how it weighs on you. Every time something happens you take it personally. You own it and want to fix it. But you have enough of your own grief inside. At some point, where do you put it all?"

"I can't take it when you're nice to me." She started to cry.

He tried not to laugh, he was so alarmed for her, but she always made him smile, even when she was being stubborn or was on his nerves.

"Do you want me to be mean?"

"If I'm mad I'm not choking on my grief."

He pulled her close, as close as he could with the center console between them. "Let it go."

"I can't! I have to go and deal with my mother and Rosa, both of whom don't need me to be like this. Don't you see?" She pushed him back and he allowed it. For the moment.

"Let's make a deal."

She snorted and then sighed. "Does this include being naked?"

"Maybe, if you're lucky. Let me make you something to eat. Go and have some tea with your moms. And then come back. I'll be waiting with something to eat and then we can talk."

She looked at him warily.

"Please?"

She sort of growled, which made him hard and he probably should have been embarrassed to be turned on by her when she was mad and upset, but his cock didn't care about any of that. It knew what it liked and she sat right there, smelling really good and needing a cuddle.

"All right. But that is not an invitation for you to poke at me until I lose my mind. I'm not going there just now. Got me?"

He nodded, but didn't agree exactly to every part of her statement. She raised a brow, but didn't say anything else as he pulled back out onto the road and took her to the hotel.

Chapter 20

"SIT. Here's a mug of tea." Her mother said nothing more as she got settled. She'd gone to her room and managed to clean up her eye makeup so there wasn't much of a trace that she'd been crying.

She obeyed and Rosa came out, frowning. "You look pale."

"I'm just tired. I wanted to stop by because I said I would and I didn't want you to worry. And because I've missed you both so much."

"Tell us about Gage." Rosa arched a brow.

"What about him?"

"Oh really, Molly? Aren't we past that?"

She sighed and sipped her tea. "There's not much to tell. You've seen him so you know he's gorgeous and charming. Also bossy."

"You're clearly involved. No one else would have spoken about your safety that way. And you'd have never allowed yourself to get so miffed by anyone else. Not in public anyway." Rosa shrugged.

"Yes, we're involved. Sort of. He doesn't make a deal of it

in public. Not that he hides it either. Anyway. He's the most vexing person I've ever met. Opinionated. Bossy. Utterly overprotective. We bicker pretty much incessantly."

Her mother laughed. "Oh well, that just means the sex is amazing and that you two are compatible. We know you, Molly, you don't bicker with anyone but the people you love and trust most."

Rosa nodded.

She shrugged. "Maybe. But he was out of line today. He shouldn't have told you all that."

"No. *You* should have." Her mother sent her a raised brow.

"I've told you both my job is dangerous. I've made no secret that I have a bodyguard. But how could you have done anything in Chicago? Or here for that matter? Why would I burden you with worry when there is absolutely nothing you can do about it? I shared the basics. It's not like I hid it from you entirely. He and I had it out. He apologized but I have no doubt he'd do it again if he wanted to. He's . . . unruly."

Molly frowned. How on earth she got herself tangled up with an unruly man she didn't know. They were a lot of trouble. Though the benefits were pretty nice too.

Rosa laughed and Molly realized it had been months since she'd heard that sound. "They're the best kind. Anthony was unruly. You need a little unruly, honey. Muss up all that starched-up expectation you have that everything in the world will be exactly as you would have it be."

"It would be a lot easier if it was."

Her mother only shook her head, smiling. "That and he's proud of you. He wanted us to know how much you were doing. And we are too. Proud of you, I mean. Now drink the rest of your tea and go to bed. We'll have breakfast tomorrow and we can talk more but I'm worried you're not resting enough."

Molly was so glad they were there. So glad to have that support and love. "I've missed you both so much. It's so selfish of me to want you here, but I'm glad you are."

She smiled, but the emotion surged through her and both women in the room knew her very well.

Her mother hugged her, and then Rosa. "Then do what we tell you. Go to sleep. We'll see you tomorrow."

She hugged them both and paused at the door. Her mother walked her out to the elevator. "Tell Gage I said hello."

Molly blushed. "Okay."

SHE got back to her room and true to his promise, Gage was there making dinner in her galley kitchen.

"Smells good." She didn't lie. Her stomach growled.

"They settled in all right? Faine stopped in and said he escorted them to dinner."

"He did? That was very nice of him." She walked past the kitchen. "I'll be right back."

She quickly changed and returned to the main room.

"It's nearly done. I hope you like omelets."

She looked at him over the rim of her juice glass. "You know I do." He'd made them for her once or twice before when he'd slept over.

"I do. I just wanted to fill the empty space I guess."

"I guess I thought our silence was pretty comfortable by this point."

He slid the omelet onto a plate and then her way. She salted and peppered it before giving it the Tabasco treatment.

He sat next to her at the kitchen island. "They are when you're not avoiding the topic."

"My mom and Rosa know we're seeing each other." See how he liked that topic.

He leaned in, rubbing his shoulder against hers. "All right."

She ate, feeling better with each bite until she finally put her fork down and rubbed her belly. "Oh my god, so full."

"Good. You look better, actually. Imagine what eating regularly would do. I know how much you like good food." He put the dishes and the pan into the dishwasher and turned his gaze on her again.

"I'm usually better about it than I was today."

"You regularly do this, Molly. You run yourself ragged."

Too much. Before she realized it, her magick had filled her, spilling out through the room.

"Look, I'm doing my best. I can't help it that in my old life people weren't trying to assault me every time I went outside. Back then I could go to lunch without a bodyguard!"

"And yet you still make excuses for the people doing this to you."

"Yes, that's so very true. I make excuses for PURITY every day. You should find that transcript you keep citing so we can go over it. Oh. Wait. You can't. Because I don't ever make excuses for the people responsible for doing this to me."

"So stop letting them rob you of rest and eating right."

The man thought he was so clever with that reverse psychology thing.

"Oh really? You're going to try to play psychologist with me now?"

"Someone needs to." He paused. "Doesn't it make you mad, ever? That they've stolen your life too? You talk about how much Rosa has lost. But what about you?"

"I said I don't want to talk about it!"

"Yes, because swallowing it helps."

"How about you? Hm? What have you lost?"

"My uncle for starters. Friends. More members of the clan than I can count."

"Your girlfriend." Wow, that sounded petty.

He shook his head. "You're usually so smart. She wasn't my girlfriend. She was a woman I liked and had dated a few times. She left. But *you*? You're more to me than someone I like and date. Watching you punish yourself over and over makes me want to shake some sense into you."

"Even when I say I don't want to talk about it? Repeatedly?"

He grinned and she sighed at his appeal.

"Especially then. Because you're a liar. That's the problem. Normally you're strong and take charge and it's hot. You're good at your job and everyone loves you and all that. And that's hot too. But when you try to pretend you can just

ignore the welling emotions inside, that's dumb and you're
not. Your magick just overflowed in reaction. That means
something."

She stood, trying to keep her cool, but her hands shook
and she knew he noticed. "I used to have a simple life. I had
a good job. A firm I built with great clients. I had a beautiful
apartment with a beautiful view. I wore nice clothes that no
one ever threw flour on. No one ever called me a whore or
a demon. I used to have lunch in quiet little places with linen
tablecloths and servers who called me Ms. Ryan. I used to
have lots of things I don't have now. It sucks. I'll get over it."

"But you're pissed off, aren't you, beautiful?"

"Hell yes!" She took off her bracelet and threw it, instantly
embarrassed. "See what you do to me?"

He laughed. "Tell me more. What do I do to you? To all
that careful reserve? Hm?"

"You poke and poke and you think it's funny but one day
you're going to pull back a stump. Fair warning."

"You throw things when you're riled up. Goddamn, I love
that."

She threw her hands up, seeking patience, but she had
none left. "I'm so glad I can entertain you."

"You know what this is about. They've stolen your life.
You talk about how angry it makes you that they've stolen
Rosa's life. Or other people's lives, but how about yours?"

"I don't have time to be angry."

"Liar."

She chewed her lip, losing the war inside to keep everything back. It would serve him right if she just unloaded it
all over him.

"You want me to go first? Huh? I'm fucking outraged
that I can't go to a family dinner and hear my uncle telling
one of his stories. I'm even more outraged that humans are
treating his death like it doesn't matter. Some humans," he
amended. "I'm sick at having to watch the toll on people I
care about. You're losing weight, Molly. I can see that look
in your eyes when you're approached by someone new. Wary.

I've watched you change over the nearly two months you've been here. Gotten harder."

"I'm so tired." She scrubbed hands over her face, knowing she was making a mess out of her makeup and not caring. "I'm tired of having to be on guard all the time. I don't know how people do it. I used to love meeting new people. Now I have to worry if they're going to attack me. Verbally, physically, whatever. I hate the look on people's faces when they find out I'm a witch. Hate that change from friendly to distrust or outright dislike. I hate that I have to be guarded every minute of the day. It takes so much energy just to leave the room here. I hate that I lost my father and my best friend and I'm expected to move past it because somehow their deaths didn't count. My life never used to be like this."

"Doesn't that make you mad?"

He whispered those words and she felt them as if he'd screamed instead.

"Yes. Does that make you happy? It fills me with rage I can do *nothing* about. It feels futile sometimes. Like I'm just going through the motions of life and not actually living it. It feels like I'm not doing anything at all. Just treading water. I feel totally unnecessary and useless. I'm failing. I hate to fail."

The tears came in a hot rush, blurring her vision as the first sob tore through her.

"And yet you get up and leave this room every day. You go out into hostile crowds and tell the truth. And they believe you. You *do* make a difference. You're not failing. Molly, you're my hero. I'm not lying. I admire you so fucking much."

"You're the only thing that feels real."

And it was true. Right then Molly discovered something about herself. She loved so hard. Harder than she'd ever imagined she could. She loved this man who pushed her so she broke with him and not out there where no one could help her. It was so much and too much and not enough and she couldn't seem to do anything but slide down the wall and cry big ugly tears.

And he was there, his arms around her, holding her tight as he rocked back and forth, just letting her cry.

It tore him apart to see her this way, even as relief that she finally let it go filled him.

She shook with sobs as she wept and he wanted to go burn shit down on her behalf.

"Shhh, I'm here. Just let it all go."

He didn't want to feel this way about anyone again. Ha, again. What a fucking liar he was. He'd never felt this sort of intensity for anyone. Ever. There was no one in the world quite like this woman he held in his arms.

No one who made him ache so much. Or who made him laugh, even as she exasperated him. Who argued back with vigor—just as easily as she defended. She had honor. And courage.

She'd become someone to him. Her silly jealousy over Rose had made him laugh. If she only knew how much she was on his mind. How he made up stupid crap for Faine to do so he could take over and be with her.

Her admission that he was the only thing that felt real to her only made him want her more.

And he shouldn't. He had enough to do. Many people to protect. Edwina Owen died on his watch. Lark nearly died. Rose ran off. His uncle was dead. He should have protected each of them and he didn't.

He would enjoy this woman. Protect her the best he could. But he could not love her. She wasn't for him. They could be together. Hold on during these rough and dangerous times. It didn't have to be more, because it was enough.

Chapter 21

SHE had a crying headache. Served her right for sniveling all over Gage's shirt for what seemed like hours.

At the same time, she felt . . . lighter.

By the time she'd finished getting dressed, Gage came out of the bathroom looking gorgeous and wet and she checked her watch, bummed that she didn't have a good fifteen extra minutes to get some of that.

"Just give me three minutes."

"It's all right. We're just having breakfast in my mother's room. Unless . . . well, unless you'd like to come and get to know them."

He pulled his boxers on and she frowned.

"If you're sure. Since it's here in the building and we've got the whole thing locked down you're fine to go down there on your own. Stop looking at me like that or you're going to be really late for breakfast and you'll have to redo that pretty makeup."

Well, at least he didn't want to run out the door at the sight of her after she'd flipped out the night before. That was a plus.

He got into jeans and stalked over as she stood, rooted to

the spot like prey. Banding her waist with one arm, he hauled her close. "You know what it does to me when you blush." He kissed the corner of her mouth and she took a deep breath to get as much of him into her system as she could.

"How about you come down in like fifteen minutes? The coffee will be ready and we'll have time to talk about you. I may actually objectify you, so if I'm red-faced when you arrive, you'll know why."

He laughed, kissing her again. "Fine. I'll see you in fifteen minutes."

She hugged him tight. "Thank you," she managed to say, eyes closed.

"For what, beautiful?" His hands slid up and down her back, soothing.

"For being there. Last night I mean."

He set her back a little so he could look into her face. "You have nothing to thank me for. That's what . . . friends are for."

Friends. He was so dumb. Friends was what he was with Lark. He didn't have sex with Lark. He didn't make her tea after she cried all over him and then make love to her until she was so tired and pleasure fuzzy it was all she could do to fall into a deep sleep.

She doubted quite surely that Gage would consider it friendly if Tosh had done all the things Gage had done the night before.

But knowing he was being a dumb boy instead of actually pushing her away amused her. And maybe gave her a challenge.

She sniffed, smiling. "Sure. Friends."

He ducked his head and stepped back. "I'll finish getting dressed and check in with Faine. See you in a bit."

"All right." She grabbed her bag and headed to the door, but before she could open it to leave, she found herself spun and backed against it, his body pressed to hers.

"You forgot to kiss me good-bye," he murmured before he bent and began to kiss the sense right out of her. Taking over in the way he tended to do, sending her hormones into a tizzy as all his sex chemicals buzzed through her system.

He broke the kiss with that smile of his. Knowing exactly what he was doing to her. The rogue.

"I'm going to have to reapply my lipstick now." She licked her lips to taste him once more.

"Good." He opened the door and looked out into the hallway, satisfied everything was safe. "See you in a few minutes."

MOLLY looked up when Meriel tapped on her door. "Hi there. Do you have a few?"

"As a matter of fact, I do. I just got off the phone with Senator Sato's assistant. We're set to testify in front of the new committee next Tuesday."

"Good. That was fast." Meriel hesitated at the door and then motioned Molly out with a jerk of her chin. "I need coffee."

"You're singing my song."

"I hear rumors of donuts in the kitchen along with the coffee. You haven't had the joy that is Top Pot yet, have you?"

"No." They meandered down the hall. "But Gage has been singing their praises. He just took me to Red Mill last week. I can't even believe I've been missing that since I moved here. Of course it's probably for the best, as I'd probably never do anything but eat onion rings and drink milkshakes instead of doing my job. I can't believe how many great places to eat highly caloric foods the man knows about. Not that you'd know it to look at him."

"Did your mom and Rosa get back to Chicago safely?"

Her mother had put in a bid on a place and had ended up signing a contract two days later. Rosa decided to rent for a while, until her place in Chicago sold. Anthony Junior still lived and worked there anyway so it was complicated, though he too wanted to get away from his past and be in a place where he felt more welcomed.

They'd spent nearly a week in Seattle and had returned home the day before. Molly missed them both already.

"Yeah. My mom will be back with my grandparents in a few weeks. Hopefully Rosa will be back around then as well with Anthony, her son."

She poured coffee into mugs while Meriel grabbed donuts for each of them and they settled at a little table near the windows.

"Please let me know if there's anything Owen can do to help. It's got to be hard trying to help them when you're working so much."

"Sure. Because your schedule is so light and all."

Meriel laughed. "Well, but I'm in charge so I can delegate that stuff to people who can help her. I just wanted to check in with you. It's been a few months now since you've been here. Are things okay?"

She snorted and managed to get half the donut in her mouth around a moan of delight.

"Things are what they are." She shrugged. "This new Senate committee is totally divided already and it's only been in place two weeks. Tosh has been a great champion of our cause and I had a great conversation today with Senator Sperry too."

"Sperry is the shifter, right?"

Molly nodded. "Yes, that's her. There are others in the House. Other *Others* I mean. Carroll is one, he's from Georgia. But some of them haven't revealed it yet. It's only a matter of time so he's trying to help them make that move now before it's out of their hands. PURITY is sniffing around trying to find anything they can."

"I hate them. I hate them and Carlo Powers and Senator Hayes too. That smug asshole."

"Guy was just some jerk from poodlebutt nowhere and now he's got all this power because he's been courting all the crazies from PURITY and Humans First. He's got himself a bully pulpit and he means to use it. He's dangerous, Meriel. More dangerous than Powers ever could be."

"I'm pretty sick of hearing how dangerous people are." Meriel rubbed the bridge of her nose and Molly knew she needed to share something, but let her do it on her own schedule.

"Yes, well, me too."

"So you and Gage." Meriel quirked up a grin.

Molly grinned back. "Yes?"

"He talks about you constantly. He used to duck the subject when it came up. You know, *are you and Molly together?* Now he just smiles. He's less . . . intense. You're good for him."

"He's a good man. I enjoy him." Molly shrugged. "He's meddlesome and grumpy too. Luckily for him, he's handsome so he gets away with it."

Meriel patted her hand. "Oh gurl, I hear you. I've got one of those myself. He really likes you, by the way. Dominic I mean. I think it helps that you're an outsider of a sort as well. It's a perspective the clan needs to hear more of."

"Ah, that's what it is. Just tell me."

"You're good at this."

Molly grabbed another donut. "It's really just about watching other people and listening to what they say as well as what they don't say."

"Pfft. You're good at this," Meriel repeated. "You know how to read people. And you're right. There's a group—a small one mind you—who have come to me with concerns. Up front, before I say anything else I want to say I support you totally. I think you do your job excellently. I think you're the best thing to happen to Owen in a very long time. But this group is concerned you're too pro-human. At the expense of Others."

"In the old days. Back before the Magister came and took so much from me. I was a lot nicer. I could have sat here eating these magic donuts and drinking coffee and told you that of course people have concerns and I would be happy to discuss those concerns with them to come to a better understanding."

Molly sat back. "But now I'm not so nice. Not so understanding. Mainly because I work about fifteen hours every day and I travel every single week to speak to hostile audiences of people who want to harm me and mine. So what

I'm going to say right now is that if this group has an issue they'd better bring it straight on and have something more than hurt fee-fees because I have a job to do and that is to keep us all from tipping into a war neither side really wants. I spent a lot of time with Others of all kinds. Listening, watching, learning. I have nothing to say to people who run behind my back to you when they could just as easily come to me to give me their concerns. Like grown-ups. I don't have time to play all this telephone game nonsense. So if you have a specific problem let's get it dealt with so I can be on my way."

Meriel raised her brow but Molly didn't waver.

"They'd like to have one of their representatives on your team."

"No. Next?"

"My mother would have loved you." Meriel sipped her coffee. "I really miss her. She would have handled this whole thing . . . better maybe. Different."

"From what I understand about your mother, she handed the seat over to you because she believed you were best to lead. And that the seat wouldn't recognize anyone who wasn't. So, while I get second-guessing yourself—and please believe me, I really do—I think you're handling an incredibly difficult situation the absolute best way that's possible. But I still don't need anyone in my way when I'm doing my job."

Meriel's laugh was rueful. "I already told them no, by the way. You don't need a committee. You have enough to deal with and you get your direction from me and the governance council so that's what needs to happen. I just wanted you to know. I've got your back. Dom has your back. We believe in what you're doing. They're nothing."

"But a distraction." She arched a brow at Meriel.

"Yes. But they're *my* distraction. It comes with the job. You should hear some of the things people come to me with." Meriel shook her head. "Anyway, you just keep doing what you're doing. You have your own distractions to deal with."

Ha. That was true. "I had a two-hour long conference call with a bunch of Wardens earlier. The wolves are really organized, which helps me with my job as they've essentially let me be their surrogate at these legislative hearings."

"But they're also very . . ."

Molly laughed. "Yes. They like to know what's happening. And I get it. It's their issue, they have their own people to inform and deal with. But I encouraged them to send someone with me next week when we go to D.C. Since the National Pack is just in Boston the trip won't be so far. They're going to send their number two, Jack Meyers."

"I've seen him. Ridiculously gorgeous. He'll look great on television."

"Exactly. Nina said, and I'm going to quote her because she's pretty freaking priceless, *Ovaries will be exploding all over the country when the cameras pan over to him.*"

"Truth." Meriel paused a moment or two. "Are you doing all right? I find myself, even though this has been sort of like the frog in the pot and I'm almost used to it, sort of having mini-breakdowns. You didn't grow up this way. This was thrust upon you and you've been going at it full tilt since you got here. That's a lot. And you're here, away from everyone you were close to. I just know it's got to be hard not having anyone to talk to."

Molly had been seriously struggling with sharing. "I had a best friend. She was also like my sister. We used to stay up late and talk endlessly about everything imaginable. We went to college at the same time and rented an apartment. We lived in that same apartment for six years until my firm took off and her relationship with her girlfriend got serious enough that they moved in together. I spoke to her on the phone that last day. She'd come to my apartment to borrow a sleeping bag, as they were headed off camping. I was in between meetings so I had to hurry her. I told her I loved her and that we'd catch up on the weekend. I never got to catch up. The Magister happened that day. I never heard her voice again."

Tears burned her eyes.

"Anyway, she'd have been so great to bounce stuff off. She had this way about her, she got people on an instinctual level. She had more mercy and compassion than anyone else I've ever met. Sometimes when I am just so disgusted and filled with resentment I think about her, and how she'd have told me to not classify all humans or all Others the same way. She was my reality check in a lot of ways. And I don't have that anymore. And I'm not sure I can stave off the bitterness."

Meriel said nothing, just listened.

"I feel like I've been in a bad dream and I've sort of shut down. Just getting up and working and going to sleep. I need to make friends here. New friends. People I can talk to when I need the reality check. Dominic has been very kind to me. You have as well. I appreciate it more than I can say. I'm not okay. Not really. But I'm less not okay today than I was yesterday."

Meriel nodded, tears in her eyes. "My mother was my reality check. Along with Nell. I lost my mother the day of the Magister too. Nell has retreated from clan life because she nearly lost her kid and her life and her husband—understandably—wants her as far from it as possible to keep her safe. I have Dominic. And I have Lark and Gage too. But it's not quite the same as your best girlfriend." She reached out to squeeze Molly's hand. "Wanna be my friend? We can work it through together."

It took everything she had not to sob right then.

"You're so very kind. Thank you, Meriel. I need all the friends I can get just now."

"GAGE. Hold up."

He shifted his bag, turning to catch sight of Lark approaching. He'd been at the range for a few hours, working on his aim. He was good, but he wanted to be better. Needed to.

"I just got off the phone with someone at the National Pack. There was a fucking pitch battle on a two-block section of Holson, Indiana, last night. A group of humans busted into a shifter bar and started shit. It spilled out onto the streets. Three structures burned down because the fire department was held up by the cops, who simply cordoned off the area while the fight happened. Burned-out cars. A few humans in intensive care. The cops made arrests. Others only."

He blew out a breath. "What the fuck? The humans started it? Who's on the ground there?"

"The local pack, they were wolves, has lawyers involved. The FBI may be called in. There's a mediator at National who is an expert on all this stuff. He's involved as well."

"Damn it. All right. What can we do to help?"

"Their next call was going to be to Molly, so I guess they have that part handled. They already spoke with Meriel. I think we should put out a general all-clan notice about it. Dominic is going to be dealing with stuff for Heart of Darkness I wager."

They walked back to his truck. "I'm heading back now. You need a ride?"

"Simon is here with me. He's finishing up inside. I'll go back with him."

"I'm going to coordinate with Dominic on extra security at Heart of Darkness. Just let Simon know I'm doing it."

"He went to Lycia yesterday. They're sending some of their warriors here to protect him. He's vexed but I laughed. Until they said it was about me too."

"Take all the help you can get. If they're all as big as Simon, we can use the muscle. Faine has been awesome so I can't imagine it's going to hurt."

"These warriors live, eat and breathe this stuff. And they have for hundreds of years. I have no doubt they can work with Faine and teach us a few things."

He nodded, already thinking about Molly.

But it wasn't until he got back to the office and found everyone gathered around the big television in the conference room that he realized just how much more he needed to worry.

Chapter 22

"**WELL,** now I hope at long last the true Americans in this country can understand the threat we've been talking about for the last several months. These supernaturals, Others, whatever you want to call them, they're absolutely out to kill you and yours. They want to harm your family. They do not care about morals or values or the rule of law." Carlo Powers sat back, a smug smile on his face.

Without thinking, Gage moved to Molly, putting a hand on her shoulder. She looked up and his stomach clenched at the expression she wore.

Molly put her hand on his and went back to watching the screen.

"The unprovoked attack on humans beings last night is a perfect example of this." Powers lifted his hands. "We must act now. To protect the decent people in this nation from these demons."

Molly tightened up and he squeezed her shoulder.

The newscaster finally spoke. "There are reports, Mr. Powers, that contradict the claim that the attack was unprovoked."

"If that was so, why didn't they arrest anyone else? I'm sorry to see you're so naïve, but we can't afford not to face facts. Gangs of animals hunting through the streets of small-town America, attacking humans beings. One of these men, a family man, is in the hospital fighting for his life. Heaven knows if he's been infected with their disease. They are a *threat*. Like terrorism, only inside our borders. They need to be dealt with. For our safety."

"Why isn't there a spokesperson there from the pack?" Meriel muttered, twisting and straightening the bracelet she wore as she jiggled her knee.

"They weren't asked. Or that's my guess. I'll call when this massacre ends." Molly never tore her gaze from the television screen. He knew that expression. Molly was planning.

Like a war. He knew she was lining up plans of attack and defense, even as she watched Powers for any weaknesses she could exploit.

Powers rattled off the number for the White House switchboard and then for Congress. He urged the decent hard-working Americans who were not going to be threatened anymore to call their president and their congressional representatives.

When the segment was over Meriel already had her phone to her ear and within moments she began to speak with someone Gage figured was affiliated with that local pack in Indiana.

One-handed, she grabbed her pad and pen and began to take notes as Meriel quietly gave orders on the other side of the room. People rushed out and those left in the room waited quietly.

Dominic snarled as he burst from his chair and began to pace. "This is bullshit."

Molly sighed. "Yes, it is. So, no one was invited to speak from the pack. Two of their wolves are being held in solitary confinement at the jail. They've had a hell of a time getting their attorney in to see them."

"We sent a letter an hour ago to the Justice Department

asking them to get involved. These wolves' rights are being violated right and left," Meriel added.

"I'm headed to D.C. day after tomorrow. But I think we may need to move it up so we can meet beforehand and get a strategy together. The vampires are on the verge of pulling out of this confederation and declaring war on humans. The wolves are justifiably angry and are having trouble keeping their people in check right now. The cats have been waiting to see what the wolves will do so if the wolves decide to pull out of our group and declare war, they'll follow."

"Which leaves us where?" Sami asked. Gage hadn't even noticed her in the room until then.

"It leaves us bowing down to humans because we've got a mouthpiece who doesn't care about witches at all." David Collier spoke from his place in the doorway. Collier did administrative work for the Hunter Corps at Owen. He'd lost several members of his family, including his fiancée, because of the Magister.

"What are you talking about?" Sami's tone made it clear she had little patience.

"I'm talking about her." Collier pointed to Molly, who cocked her head at him, taking his measure. "She's so human you can smell it on her. She's working so hard to protect humans she's endangering the rest of us. Why isn't she asking us what we think? She just goes off and meets with these humans in private. We don't even know what she's promising them."

"You're out of line, David." Meriel shook her head in Dominic's direction. Gage hadn't even noticed the wave of anger radiating from Dominic until that moment. "I told you when you came to me last week that Molly gets her direction from me. She's following very careful plans laid out by the Full Council."

"Because she tells you what to think."

Gage stepped forward but Molly touched his wrist. Just a ghost of a touch, but she meant for him to stand aside so he would. For a moment or two.

Sami snorted. "You can't mean to stand there and tell me I'm so stupid I need to be told what to think."

Collier looked to Sami. "You were against her from the start. Why are you letting her sell us out?"

"I wanted to know where her allegiances lay. I found out because I made it a point to work with her. I'm beyond satisfied that Molly has this clan's best interests at heart. So much so she's got a twenty-four-hour-a-day guard. You're wrong. And more than that, you're rude."

"What is painfully ironic is that I have to face humans telling me I'm an evil beast set out to eat their infants and kick their puppies and when I get back here I'm being accused of selling out witches to humans. I'm beyond sick and tired of it. From them and from you. You have an issue? Own it. Be an adult and come talk to me. This silly sixth-grade tantrum is not impressive. It does not speak well of your intelligence on this or any other issue. I don't see you at any of the community meetings I've set up to hear concerns from members of this clan. I don't see your comment cards or your emails. I've never even seen your face until this very moment. What's keeping you from speaking to me? Or would you rather just whine and stir trouble behind the scenes? I'm busy, you see, so excuse me if I don't take your whining seriously. I'm working on big-girl stuff with all the other adults."

Gage had argued with her more times than he could recall. He'd seen her disagree with people pretty much daily. Even people she didn't like. But the set down she'd just delivered to Collier was the harshest he'd ever seen from her.

Damn. She made him tingly all over.

Utter silence ruled the room for long moments as David tried to figure out just what had happened.

Then Molly brushed her hands down the front of her skirt and turned back to Gage. "So can you please get in contact with Cascadia about flying me out early? I'll need a guard, obviously, so you'll need to arrange that too."

Meriel interrupted. "I'll get on the phone. I know a few

people at Justice. Maybe I can help. Do you think I should go to D.C.?"

"Not this time. But there are other times coming up that I think you'd be good for. I'll get you the information on that later today." She walked past Dave, who still stood in the doorway.

Gage touched her arm to stay her. "I'm going to get in contact with Cascadia. I'll let you know what I hear."

She nodded absently, plotting, always plotting in her head.

Once she'd gone around the corner he turned back, pinning Collier with his gaze. "You, in my office in ten minutes." Gage kept walking before he did something remarkably stupid like punch him.

Shortly after he'd arranged for their flight to D.C., Lark strolled into his office, grinning. "Looks like Sweet Molly Ryan has claws."

"She does."

"I know you're mad at David, but I think you should be careful how you handle this." She tossed herself into a chair.

"He was insubordinate. That's not to be tolerated. Molly or anyone else he works with, or under as in her case, deserves civility."

"All right. I buy that. What's your solution?"

"Clearly you have an opinion here. Spit it out."

Lark rolled her eyes. "Touchy. I know she's your girlfriend. So does everyone else, especially after the way you were with her today. So however you deal with him, take that into account. Don't undermine her. She kicked ass today. She shut him down. Broke his spirit. God, I love her. Anyway, so I vote you put a note in his personnel file along with a warning. We can't fire him. He's good at his job and until now he's only been an irritant. Can't fire someone for being a dick. Or for not liking your girlfriend."

He knew she meant how people would perceive it. But man, he wanted to fire David Collier so much.

He sighed. "Fine. I suppose punching him is out of the question too?"

She kept grinning and he deliberately did not rise to the bait.

"You may as well stay. He's due in here in like three minutes."

"Fine, fine. By the way, send Faine. That way you don't have to go. I know you have meetings here."

"I can video call for those meetings. I'm going to D.C."

"Really?"

"No offense or anything. I believe he's great and a super warrior. I've seen Simon in battle so I really do mean that. She's out there, exposed to a greater threat each day. I'm the only person I trust with her at this point. He can come along though. I'm happy for the backup."

"Come to Heart of Darkness tonight. Bring Molly."

"She won't want to go. The night before she travels she's got a routine. She's going to want to listen to Led Zeppelin, drink red wine and make note cards."

"Led Zeppelin? Molly? I totally underestimated her, clearly."

"On vinyl no less. Anyway, she won't want to go out to a club. Maybe I'll stop in, though. See what's going on."

He had no idea why he'd even said that. He knew he wasn't going to leave her alone. In fact, he liked to sit on the couch while she worked, reading a book while she made her cards. He'd refill her wine; they might bicker. They'd definitely have really hot sex.

Lark just looked at him. "Don't even think you can play that this is casual." She said it in an undertone as David's voice came down the hallway toward Gage's office.

"It *is* casual. I like her." He put his hand up to keep Lark quiet. "We're having a good time so it's not like I'm denying that. But we're not engaged or anything. And not joined at the hip either. I think it's best to keep things slow and easy. Now isn't the time to go getting serious. I'm sure I'll stay home though. I should pack and stuff."

"Now is exactly the time, dumbass. What else do we have other than a scary, uncertain future? Oh right. Packing." She rolled her eyes before hardening her gaze as David came into the office.

RITA popped her head into Molly's office. "Senator Sato's office just called to tell you to check your email."

"Lovely. That sounds just swell," she muttered, turning back to her computer to open her email.

"His assistant said to tell you to read Senator Sato's note before you read the bill." Rita shook her head. "I can only guess. I've got coffee brewing for you now. I'll be back shortly."

"Thank you," Molly said to Rita's retreating form. She turned back to her screen.

HR 877—The Domestic Security Act.

That wasn't a header that made her feel any better. She opened it up.

Molly, this just hit my desk a few minutes ago. There's a Senate version being shopped around now as well. We'll talk about this tomorrow. I will do all I can to block this.

Call me when you arrive. I've put you on my calendar at two. Come here and bring your people with you. We'll go over it then.

Tosh

She opened the attachment and began to read.

GAGE stopped by her office when he hadn't heard from her in hours. It was already nearly eight and he wanted her to eat and rest before the trip tomorrow. Wanted to get her fortified.

"Yes, I'm aware you're busy. That comes with your job, doesn't it?"

Well. Today was her day for being the ice queen obviously. Gage got himself situated in a chair near her desk and watched her in action. She tapped her pen on a thick sheaf of papers dotted with Post-it notes of varying colors. Her mouth was a flat line. His sweet Molly was pissed.

"No. I don't understand. I'm out of understanding today so you'll have to come up with a better reason for not contacting me about this ridiculous legislation than *I'm busy*. It's impossible for the show to air without even a comment from my people. To do otherwise would be irresponsible of you."

She listened and blew out a sharp breath. His aunt Rita came in, putting a mug of something at Molly's right hand. Losing the hard expression, Molly smiled up at Rita in thanks. She patted his shoulder on the way out.

"Yes, that's more like it. I'll be happy to be interviewed then." Molly hung up and Gage had to laugh, imagining the face of whoever the hell she was talking to as she disconnected without a good-bye.

"It's your day for smackdowns."

"If people didn't act like jackwagons, it wouldn't be necessary to call them at home at"—she looked at her watch—"eleven at night. Imagine the media not even consulting us about this situation in Indiana? Or worse, this new legislation? I shouldn't have to smack anyone down. They should have called me right away. Or someone from the pack. Or anyone to give a reaction from the Others."

"Legislation?"

She held up the sheaf of papers. "House Bill 877. They're calling it the Domestic Security Act. Sounds promising though slightly ominous. What it does? Well, I'm glad you asked. It strips all Others of their citizenship and gives them a new status. *Domestic Threat*. Lovely, isn't it? We're anthrax or dirty bombs now."

He blinked, stunned.

"Oh, but that's not all!" Molly looked down at the papers, flipping through until she found the right page. "All Domestic Threats will be tracked for the safety and well-being of

United States Citizens and put into one of five installations across the country where their numbers and activities will be managed by the newly formed Department of Domestic Threat Surveillance."

Shock made his skin cold and then a fire of outrage began to build in his belly. "They want to put us in camps?"

"They want to chip us with GPS trackers. They want to forcibly sterilize all of us so we can't procreate and yes, they want to put us in camps. Reservations. Whatever you want to call it. Our property would be taken by the government and put into accounts for us to use while *being hosted*."

"This is a fucking outrage, Molly."

"No kidding. So that was the big Sunday morning politics show I was just on the phone with. I'll need to meet with the Others when I get to town. The studio will be the day after. I'm on the panel now. Apparently Carlo Powers and Senator Hayes were already scheduled. Tosh told me he was on it too, so at least there's that. His office sent me the bill and then called about the show. I guess he made a fuss that I wasn't invited." She riffled through other things on her desk as he tried not to frown.

Toshio Sato was like a damned bad penny. He kept turning up. Usefully, though Gage wouldn't admit it out loud.

"I'm sure Rita already told you this, but we're set to fly out at six. Are you nearly done here? It's after eight and I know you haven't eaten."

Her annoyance faded as she gave him her best Molly smile. "You're sweet."

"Don't tell anyone. They all think I eat nails for breakfast."

"Give me ten minutes. I need to gather up some supporting documentation to take with me."

He stood. "I'll be back in ten minutes and you'll be coming with me."

"I love it when you're forceful."

"I know you do." He waved over his shoulder as he left the room.

"Make sure she rests."

He paused at Rita's desk. "Says you. Who's here at eight at night."

"I'm old. I don't need as much sleep. Also, I'm not being pummeled on every front twenty-four hours a day like she is. I'm counting on you to not only protect her, but to take care of her. I know you're sweet on that girl. She needs it. Needs something to think about other than this job."

"How'd you know?"

"The way you look at each other. The way you take care of her. The way she looks for you in a room when she enters it. The way you touch her. I'm old, I'm not dumb or blind."

He smiled, bending to kiss her cheek. "You totally aren't. Why don't you go home too? If you leave, she'll find it easier when I come back in eight minutes."

"I don't leave until she does. It's our deal." Rita patted her hair and sat straighter.

"All right. I'll be back in eight minutes and you're both leaving. I'll drop you home too."

He moved out of there quickly before she could argue, heading to his office. He wanted to leave notes for Lark. Turns out he didn't have to as she was still working.

"Hey, I figured you'd be out on patrol or home."

"Full crew is out on patrol tonight. I promised Simon I'd be home before nine for a change."

He told her about the legislation and about how Molly had browbeaten the journalist on the phone about not being on the panel.

Lark shoved both hands through her hair, sending it all over the place. "You've got to be joking. These people won't be satisfied until we're all dead."

"I agree."

"Her options are more limited each day." Lark meant Molly.

"Yeah." He hated that it was true. Knew she wanted peace. Hell, even he wanted peace. But that option was less and less certain as the days passed.

"She's no dummy. Certainly not weak. She'll do what she needs to. Even if she wishes she didn't have to." Lark sighed.

"I think so, yes. I've got to run. I'm giving my aunt a ride home before I get Molly back to the hotel. I'll keep you updated."

"Be careful, Gage. Listen to your gut."

He'd shared with her the way his powers had grown in recent months. His ability to go into a crowd and sense a real threat seemed to grow each day. The problem was in crowd situations it was harder to tell the direction of the threat. Especially if more than one person truly wanted to harm them.

"Count on it."

Lark held his gaze. "I do."

Chapter 23

SHE settled in with her note cards and Gage put a glass of wine on the table where she could reach it.

"Thank you. For everything."

He paused. "I like taking care of you. You reward me so nicely."

It was more than the sex. She knew that to her toes. He could skirt around it all he wanted, but he protected her in a way that was far different than how he protected Meriel. He touched her like she was special.

"Mmm-hmm. You going to stay over?" She asked this absently, knowing his answer, while she began to put together a map for all the things she needed to do the following several days.

"Easiest that way."

"It's a really far trip from your room next door, yeah."

He snorted a laugh. "I gave that room up a few days ago."

She looked up from her work. "You did?"

"I sleep here every night and when I'm not here, we're at my place. Or traveling. Waste of resources." He blushed as he shrugged his shoulders.

"Oh. Resource conservation." She nodded her head like he wasn't a dumbass and looked back at her cards.

"I like being with you."

Well, that was far nicer than resource conservation, she had to admit. She locked gazes with him. "See? That wasn't even hard. Also, I like being with you too."

"I should pack." He hurried from the room as she snorted and went back to her work.

This thing they had brought her no small measure of comfort. Of stability. He was something so positive in a life filled with negativity. Despite their bickering, his heart was good. His convictions were strong. He talked a good game because he was grumpy, but he wanted peace if they could have it.

Their little tiffs kept her on her toes, and she needed that. Because the humans she had to deal with didn't.

This time in D.C. was pivotal. She could feel it to her toes. Or rather, in her gut.

He wandered back in the room and settled on the couch with a book.

She kept writing, putting her thoughts down, organizing them. The more she did, the more her color-coded ink filled the paper and the greater the number of stacks, the better she felt.

Two hours later she stood to stretch and caught him watching her, wearing his sex look. It shot straight to her lady bits and she waggled her brows at him. "I was planning on a shower."

She padded from the room, smiling to herself when she heard him get up to follow.

Gage had become more than a guy she had sex with. She craved this time with him. When it was just the two of them, naked or not, but certainly naked was the most fun. She could let down all her barriers and just be Molly.

She pulled off her clothes, putting them in her laundry basket before going into the bathroom where he was already naked and had turned the shower on. A shiver went through her at the sight.

Gage was beautiful. Masculine. Hard and toned. Naked

he was even more impressive than when he had weapons strapped all over him. He was a weapon. A physical manifestation of the most badass gun, knife, whatever.

And when he looked at her, all that hardness, all that furious defense of everything she held dear softened.

Well, not *everything*. Some parts of him got harder.

"That smile scares me, beautiful." He moved to her, pulling her close so they were skin to skin. She shivered, sighing into his embrace, letting the heat of him settle into her bones.

"Nothing scares you." She kissed his shoulder.

"Lots of things scare me."

The tone he used caught her attention as she let him dance her into the shower. She groaned as the water hit her, warming the chill.

She shampooed and conditioned her hair first and then did his, loving the feel of his scalp against her palms.

"Like what?" she asked. "What scares you, Gage?"

He poured soap in his palm and rubbed his hands together as she watched, captivated by the sensuality of the slow, purposeful movement. Then those hands found her skin and she closed her eyes, opening her senses to the way he made her feel.

She was aware part of his motive for these awesome sex moves was to take her mind off his earlier comment and to keep from answering her question. Sometimes they did this. This careful dance of opening up and being vulnerable to the other.

It helped when there was sex. When they were naked, hands on the other, lips on the other, it was easier to unleash the words they kept so tightly.

His soap-slicked fingers tugged on her nipples until she made needy sounds. When she opened her eyes she found his gaze on her face.

His hair, wet and slicked back, exposed the masculine beauty of his face. Of those movie-star cheekbones and the full, luscious lips.

"So beautiful." He leaned in to kiss her. A tease of contact, pulling away and going back to soaping her body up.

"Me? Ha. You look like a television commercial for exercise equipment."

He grinned and she found herself backed to the tile, his body pressed to hers. He slid his arms around her, big hands on her ass, cupping, tipping her hips just exactly how he wanted.

He made her swoon sometimes. The way he just took what he wanted. Knowing it was what she wanted too. She was no virgin. There'd been others who'd rung her bell in the sex department.

But this was something else. More. So much more that every time he touched her she ached. Needed. Craved. She thought about sex with him pretty much all day long. Which made interminable meetings more amusing, certainly.

His fingers brushed against the heart of her, sliding through her pussy, sending ripples of sensation through her body until all she could manage was a stuttered breath.

"So hot and wet. I think about this." He punctuated that with a quick, relentless flick against her clit until she gasped a *please*. "Every time I smell you. Did you know your perfume hangs in the air like a siren song? Your magick and your skin—powerful combination. I walk down a hall and I know you've been there. My whole body gets hard and all I can think of is being in you. Of the way it feels when I slide inside and you hug me so tight."

She leaned back against the cool porcelain but it didn't help. His words dazzled her, rendered her into a pool of need. When the head of him brushed against her she didn't jump. She arched to get closer, going to her tiptoes to take him, her fingers digging into the steel of his biceps, urging him on, in.

"Impatient."

She nodded and tried not to snarl when he pulled back a little.

He let go of her butt, sliding his hands around her body, testing the weight of her breasts in his palms. "All mine."

Goddess, yes.

Then his hands slid down, fingertips teasing her belly button, a light touch over the seam where thigh met body that sent a shiver of anticipation through her. He spread her open as her hips jutted forward to get more.

"You're soapy still. I should rinse you off."

He unhooked the showerhead and rinsed her, slowly, methodically and she had to bite her lip to keep from begging him to get on with it.

"What I think I love most about you is the way you're so controlled out there in the world. No matter how pissed off or annoyed you are, you never let anyone get under your skin. Your responses are so sharp and cold sometimes, slicing right through the ego of your enemies. You're calm and collected. But here with me? When the door is locked? You're not so controlled at all. You know what you like and you're fearless about demanding it."

Helpless against his appeal, she took in the way he watched her, watched the soap slide down her thighs.

"That Molly is my secret. All that fire and passion just beneath the skin. Mmmm." He dipped his head to lick over her shoulder and then spread her open again, this time aiming the showerhead at her clit.

She sucked in a breath as the sensation began to build. Her muscles burned as she worked to keep standing as the relentless brush of the water over her clit dragged her up and up, closer and closer to climax as he watched.

His gaze was nearly as physical as the water, as the fingers holding her open. And when she broke, it was on a breath and a gasp, his name in her head.

And then he was pressing into her body, pulling her thigh up over his hip, even as her inner walls continued to flutter.

The way she peeled back, layer after layer, each more complex than the last made her irresistible to him. He wasn't sure when or how it had happened, but what he was most scared of was losing this woman whose body took his so eagerly. This woman who had a sense of humor most people rarely saw. This fierce, powerful advocate for her people with a great big heart.

He could not afford to feel for her this way but that didn't stop it from happening anyway.

He thrust, over and over as she wrapped an arm around his neck, her calf wrapped at his ass, pulling him closer, holding him in place as he loved her.

He lost all his patience when she was involved. He wanted to gorge himself of her before he even managed to get her alone to touch her. And this way, just the two of them? He pressed deeper and deeper as their magick rose and mingled on the steam.

When he came, he knew he'd want her again within minutes.

HE lay in bed as she brushed her hair out. His muscles were pleasantly loose; his skin smelled of her. He smiled, utterly satisfied.

They'd gone to sleep an hour or so after their shower sex and he hadn't woken up a single time. It tended to be like that if they made love before they went to bed.

"You're better than warm milk," he murmured as she pulled a pair of underpants on.

She laughed. "Um. Thank you?"

"It's a compliment. I was just thinking about how well I sleep when we fuck right before."

"Ah. Well, I agree. Not that I'm akin to warm milk. But it does tend to unknot my muscles. You're good with magick and handguns and sexing me into unconsciousness. While I love Faine, he's not nearly as fun as you are as a guard."

He rolled from bed, pausing to kiss her on his way to the bathroom. "Good to know my services are so unique."

He brushed his teeth and washed his face, listening to her as she got dressed and began to prepare to leave. Shortly, the scent of coffee began to waft through the air.

She looked crisp and feminine all at once as she smiled up at him. "I figured I'd have to make coffee to wake you up."

"I smelled your perfume. That's what woke me first." Well, in total truth, he woke when she got out of bed. It was as if his system came to full alert when she wasn't next to him.

He poured them both a mug and got the milk out.

"Do you want a bagel? There's fruit and cheese here too. I won't ask if you want hummus. There's cream cheese in the fridge."

"Yes to a bagel."

He settled in across from her. "I like those earrings." Her hair was pulled back, as she so frequently wore it. The earrings he knew had been a gift from Lark. Deep blue beads dangled below a pearl. Nothing showy, but feminine like their wearer.

"Thank you." She chewed on her lip and he knew she wanted to say something but was trying to figure out how to put it. He wasn't sure if he should brace himself or tell her to just say it.

In the end he waited for it, trusting that she'd say it when she was ready to.

"I feel really dumb for not knowing this. But, does your magick get stronger as you age? Or if you train more?"

"Don't feel stupid about not knowing. To answer your question, yes, in part. You don't have much magick you can use when you're a child. It grows as does your awareness of it, once you hit puberty. You have however much power you have. But like many skills, you can harness your power more and use it more effectively if you train at it."

"I . . . I think my magick has gotten a great deal more powerful since the Magister."

He paused because he'd had the same thought. Many Others had related the same thing over the last weeks.

"It's more than being trained and knowing new spells. I feel like"—she sighed, looking for the right words, he knew—"yes, I can do more things, but my ability is stronger. At first I thought it was being taught how to use my othersight. I had all this stuff but really didn't know how to use it. But even the stuff I did before seems to work better. My signal is boosted, I guess. Or that's how it feels. When I'm addressing a crowd I've always had the ability to adjust my message, to know in my gut how to do it and make myself heard. But now? Now it feels like I'm a conductor. I can see how they're all feeling, or I know it." She shook her head and ate for a few minutes.

"The problem with magick is that the terms to describe it all seem so imprecise."

He laughed then. "I know how that bothers you."

She sent him raised brows, underlined by a haughty sniff. "Nothing wrong with liking precision. When I reach down to use my magick, the well of my power seems deeper."

"Many of us are feeling the same thing. Meriel says her magick has grown by an order of magnitude."

"Nina Warden told me she can shift back and forth with far more ease and less pain than before. I heard a rumor that the vampires need to take less blood now."

Wow. Not just witches then. "Did you tell Meriel this? Or Lark?"

"I'm telling you."

"This . . . well, it's interesting. I need to consult with Meriel. Do you mind if I share this with her?"

Molly shrugged. "Of course not."

He knew it was early. But he also knew Meriel rose at five anyway so he called.

"Meriel Owen."

"Meriel, it's Gage. I've got Molly here with me and you're on speaker. I need to talk to you about something Molly just told me."

"Well, that got my attention." In the background Meriel said Dominic's name. "Go on."

"You know how we talked last week about the rise in our power?"

"Yes. And I've heard the same from other witches as well."

"Molly tells me there's a rumor the vamps need less blood now. And that the wolves have had an easier time with multiple shifts."

"Hi, Meriel. Nina Warden also told me that young wolves, ones who often have trouble resisting the call of daytime moonrises, have had an easier time resisting over the last two months as well."

"Well now. This is all quite interesting. I'm going to have Simon contact the Fae to see if they can shed any light on this. They're the only ones who know much about the Magister. The people who came to us a few weeks after the Magister left have moved on, trying to find it so they can't help us."

"Seems to me it's a question of chicken and egg. Did the rise in power or magick happen because of the Magister? Or something the Magister did? Or defeating it?" Dominic spoke for the first time in the call.

"Yes, or some variation of that. The Kellys might be a good place to start with this." The Archives had put two witches on researching the Magister full time in the wake of the final confrontation with it.

"Good idea." There was a brief moment or two of silence and Gage knew Meriel was taking notes so he just waited for her to finish.

She finally spoke again. "You're on the way to D.C. this morning?"

"Yes. We've got to leave in about ten minutes."

"I'm going to send my notes about the call I had last night with the attorneys for the wolves held in jail in Indiana. I want to know right away what you hear about this bill they're floating. Camps. I think not. Please do feel free to speak on my and Simon's behalf on this issue. In my absence you speak for the Owen. We are diametrically opposed to this legislation."

Molly nodded, though Meriel couldn't see her. "I've prepared a statement so check your inbox. I've got a meeting with the Council of Others when we arrive and then I'm on my way to the television station. I'll be checking my mail frequently. Rita has my schedule so you can always check in with her to see what's up."

"Good luck. Keep her safe, Gage."

He disconnected. "You ready to go to D.C. and kick ass?"

"Ready as I'm gonna be."

"Pretty much all you can ask for in life."

Chapter 24

WHEN they landed it was to find that the Senate version of the Domestic Security Act had been introduced. Molly fixed her hair and makeup on the way over to the hotel where the rest of the Others would be waiting.

As she did that, she also put in a call to Tosh.

"I've just arrived. On my way to the meeting now."

"I take it you got my message about the Senate version of the House bill?"

"Yes. You need to be aware that none of us is going to be pleased about this. And by not pleased, I mean we do not support any provisions in either bill."

"I know. I know. I'm working on creating an opposition coalition here. We've got a solid group forming. Then again, there's a sizable number in support of the bills in both houses, on both sides of the aisle. And a lot of undecideds. Our hearing has been moved to Monday. They want to fast track the legislation."

"Has anyone even contacted my office to see if I'm available? Or does it just not matter at all what the perspective from those who'll be affected is?"

"Molly, I want you to know that I will fight this with everything I have. This is not my country. This is not what we do in America. I knew you'd be here so when they called my office I figured I'd just tell you when you arrived."

She huffed a sigh. "Fine. I'll see you later today. I've sent the information about my escort to your assistant."

"Can you get that number down a little? Things here have tightened up since the riots in Indiana. One guard would suffice. You'll be here. It's safe here."

Gage narrowed his gaze at her, shaking his head. "No, Molly. You've been assaulted at the capitol more than once. You've had death threats. We can't trust anyone but our own people. You have three guards. Period."

"Did you hear that?" she asked Tosh.

"Yes. I'll see what I can do."

She disconnected and closed her eyes, finding her center. Now was not the time for upset. Now was the time to let anger make her a weapon. Her brain and her magick would do that for her if she just didn't let herself get twisted up.

"I'm not even going to comment on how he doesn't take your safety seriously," Gage spoke to her in an undertone as they arrived at the hotel.

"I don't have the energy to argue with you right now. I think you judge him unfairly."

"Why would I do that?" He took one side of her while Faine got the other.

"Because you're jealous." She moved ahead of him before he could reply to deny what was so totally obvious. Molly did allow herself a smile though.

MOLLY sat in that room of angry Others and never lost her cool a single time. Sometimes Gage wondered if she was a robot or a superhero. Hell, he'd wanted to punch people at least a dozen times, but she maintained her calm and because of it the room would back off from the edge over and over.

Using his othersight, he watched the magick pour from her, mix and combine with the Others in the room. She *was* a conductor it seemed. The energy moved through her and she seemed to sort of guide it, push it when necessary. He'd never seen anything like it. She seemed to get better at it each time, perhaps as she'd gotten her legs on this new job. Or maybe, maybe it was connected to the way magick seemed to be growing more powerful for many Others.

Whatever the case, she was brilliant at it. So brilliant he pretended her little jibe about being jealous of Sato wasn't true.

"If we can stay on task, please." Cade Warden, the Supreme Alpha of the United States, attempted to keep the meeting on track. He and Molly worked well together.

"What are you doing about these illegal arrests in Indiana? I've got to tell my pack something. Everyone is nervous and angry. How much are we supposed to take?" One of the wolves from a Midwestern pack spoke.

"We've got an entire staff of attorneys working on it. Because of Meriel Owen and Gabe Murphy from Pacific, the Justice Department has sent people in to investigate the situation. The wolves have been able to finally see their families and speak with their attorneys. It's our goal to get them out by the end of this week."

"What about the humans? Why haven't they been arrested?"

"Because their police department and prosecutors are bigots." Molly spoke, still remaining seated. "I wish this weren't so, but it's clear to anyone with half a brain. The location of the bar that was attacked, the property that was destroyed, all in a shifter-dominated part of town. There's surveillance video of the humans entering the bar that the police have *lost* twice now. Senator Sato and Representative Carroll are working on this from their end as well."

"Working? How? How long do we have to wait? You told us to defend ourselves at a meeting last month. And now three of us are in jail for it. Why should we listen to you at all? What's your agenda?"

Gage fisted his hands until Faine snorted, clearly amused. He leaned in close. "Your female is made of tougher things than to let herself get ruffled by such silly commentary."

Gage let go of some of the rage. "People have no idea how hard she works on their behalf."

"It's easier to complain than to understand."

Lycians were a lot more complicated than Gage had thought at first.

"I understand that you're upset and frustrated. We all are. Every time I hear about kids being picked on in school, Others losing jobs or being kicked out of their homes I get frustrated too. My agenda is the same as it's been since the first time we all met. I'm working to broker an equitable relationship between Others and humans. There are times this seems more possible than others. But for right now, it is my continued, stated agenda to continue to secure our rights as American citizens. I don't mean to push this topic aside, but I have another meeting to get to and I wanted to bring up the reason for it. House Bill 877 and its Senate companion."

He watched, amazed, as she unraveled the bills for them, pointing out what each provision would mean and the possible cascade of other events. The picture she painted was bleak.

And at the lowest point, she had them all in the palm of her hand. She stood, her voice still calm and sweet. She looked out over the room as it seemed like everyone held their breath.

"My friends, we will not stand idly by as groups of bigots in this nation tear it apart by stripping us of our rights. They are, most assuredly, the rights and responsibilities we were born with. We were Americans before the Magister and we are Americans now. They expect silence and compliance? They'll have our voices, and the strength of our will. We helped build this nation and we will not tolerate the dismantling of it by heartless vandals. One of my foremothers, upon coming to this nation and deciding to build a home for witches where we could be safe, once spoke to the largest convocation of witches ever held. *We are kings and queens, handmaids and blacksmiths. We are more than the filth they try to make us by their actions and we will underline that for them until they remember that once and for all.* Rebecca Owen was right then and she's right now."

Cade Warden stood and began to clap. People joined until the entire room was filled with deafening applause. Magick pulsing through the space. She drew it back into herself, probably not even purposely. But she shone through his othersight like a star.

"YOU'D make an excellent Lycian." Faine spoke to her as they hustled back to the car to head toward Tosh's office. "Should you ever want to come visit us, I have no doubt the males who would find you appealing would fill an auditorium."

Molly laughed, patting Faine's arm. "That's a very wonderful compliment. Thank you."

Gage frowned, but kept his gaze roving over the landscape outside. "You handled them well."

"I get their anger. I wish I had better news to give them."

"You're doing all you can. And you're effective."

She squeezed his hand and he kept it, not caring if Faine saw.

"I don't know if I'd say I was effective. I feel pretty useless right now. Pissed off too."

"Anger is a gift. That's not a quote from my foremother, but it's a Rage Against the Machine lyric, which I think is just as important."

She laughed, leaning into him for a brief moment.

TOSH'S assistant had her hold back, ushering her through a side door. "The senator would like to speak with you privately before the meeting starts. Can you please wait here? He'll be right in."

Molly turned to Gage and Faine. "I'll be right out."

"We're not leaving." Gage's mouth was set.

"Yes, you are. I appreciate that you want to do your job. But some things need to be said in private. He's asked that of me and I can respect it. You're right outside the door. I'll be fine. Also I'm a witch; it's not like I'm defenseless if something should happen."

He heaved a sigh, but went out. "If I hear as much as a raised voice, I am busting through the door."

"Thank you."

Just moments later Tosh came in. She paused to admire him. Tall and broad shouldered, the suit he wore fit him perfectly. His dark hair and eyes only framed his face. He wore his power like his tie, or the suit coat he had on. If it hadn't been for the witch outside the door and more to the point, the witch whose boobs he kept sneaking looks at, she might have pursued something romantic with him.

He was courageous. Starting off his work career in the military, like his father and grandfather before him and then ending up in law school and as a JAG. By the time he was thirty he'd ended up running for a Senate seat in his home district. There was a lot about him to admire.

"Thank you for meeting with me." He clasped her hands and kissed her cheek. "I won't take too much of your time, but I wanted to assure you about this bill. My family was sent to an internment camp. My grandmother and her sisters and her father. My grandfather enlisted to prove his loyalty to this country. They took his home and put his family in a camp where my grandmother nearly died having my father because there was a shortage of medical care. My father was career military, as were two of my uncles, and now me and my sister. I love this country very much. But I don't pretend to love its mistakes, like interning the Japanese. This is not what we do. This is not how we act. I will not be silent and watch this happen to anyone else."

Tears pricked her throat but she kept them back.

"Thank you for that. It does help, knowing."

"This is unfair and wrong. I have spent my life trying to do the right thing and I will continue that. I'm not the only human being who will. Please be patient and have faith."

"Thank you for sharing that with me. It means something. As for faith? I'm trying. But when shifters who were attacked in their own neighborhood are in jail while the humans who burned homes and businesses down are being hailed as heroes, it's hard to keep that faith. Moreover, it's hard for me to convince Others to keep that faith."

She considered telling him about their growing power, but decided not to. The time might come when they needed that secret as a weapon.

"I understand. You're good at what you do, so I have faith in *you*."

"I need to say this and I hope you'll take it in the spirit I'm offering it in. We are not cartoons. Push a shifter too far and it's going to end badly. They're up against the wall. They've held back time and again. But they're not going to much longer. So if this stuff goes forward, they will defend their family and their land. The vampires are already on the fence, they tend to stick to themselves so the fact that they're actually listening to me and agreeing to this Council of Others thing is unusual. They may be old, but they do not have unlimited patience. They don't mess around and so far they've been left alone for the most part. Make sure you keep it that way. The stakes here are a lot higher than humans seem to realize."

"Are you saying we have a problem?"

"I've been saying that from day one. It's like humans turn their hearing off. You can come up with all the cages you want, but if you think we're going to go into them without a fight, you're so sorely mistaken. I'm being as plain as I can here with you because I respect you. But we are not victims." She held his gaze for long moments, letting it settle in. There seemed to be some sort of impression that because they looked like humans and had been quiet before the Magister that they were malleable and easily controlled. She needed to dissuade that perception without overdoing it and freaking them into a knee-jerk reaction.

He sighed. "Fair enough. Thank you as well for sharing. Let's go in. I ordered some food so I hope you're hungry."

Chapter 25

"**SAY** that again?" Molly blinked, reining her temper in the best she could.

"The chair of the committee has chosen the panel of speakers. You're not on it. Senator Sato and Representative Carroll are working on this now." Sato's aide sighed.

"There's not a single Other on this list." Molly held the page up.

The aide blushed. "I know."

"How can you have a legislative hearing on concentration camps for Others without the voice of a single Other being heard? This is outrageous."

Gage paced just behind her, his anxiety battering her. Faine just stood like a big giant boulder of dude a few inches away.

Representative Carroll came into the alcove where they'd been standing. He clasped her forearm and bowed his head slightly. "I know." He held up a hand. "I've spoken with a few others in my caucus and we've banded together to give you our time."

"Can you do that?"

"This entire hearing is . . . a new take on the rules. It's in violation of established rules, but as you know, many rules are being broken right now. So because of that, yes, we can do that. You won't be sitting at the table in front though. But there'll be a comments portion, you'll come up then. My aide will escort you up. We're going to keep that as a surprise, all right? I'm not giving these bigots another chance to silence us."

She thanked him and turned back to Gage. "Did you hear that?"

"Yes. I don't like this, Molly. This feels all kinds of wrong."

Molly nodded. "Yes. I can't believe how this is all playing out. It's like a bad cable movie."

Gage stepped close and spoke in her ear. "There are a lot of people here who want to hurt us. You, more specifically. I can feel it. We should go."

"If I go, this whole debacle goes unchallenged. How can I do that? They want to put us in camps *and* not give us the opportunity to rebut that. If I go, who'll speak for us?" She put a hand on his arm, locking her gaze with his. "They have metal detectors here. You're here. Faine is here. Cade Warden's team of bodyguards is here along with an assortment of other big paranormal badasses. We'll leave as soon as we can."

"I don't like this." But his back lost some of its tension and she knew he'd relent.

He escorted her in, Faine at her back. The hostility in the room made her slightly ill.

Senator Hayes caught sight of Molly and sneered her way. She simply stared back, holding his gaze until he broke away. "He should be ashamed of himself."

"He has no shame. His aura is dark and full of thin spots and holes. He's sold his integrity for power and he wants to cloak it in self-righteousness." Faine's lip curled as he said the last.

The outsider perspective from a being as old as Faine and Simon was really useful. It enabled Molly to see other facets of these issues.

Hayes was the chair of the hearing, which meant he was running the show. So he gave a long, sanctimonious speech about how there was always a balance between the right to safety and other sorts of rights.

But that wasn't the worst part. The humans on the panel were like textbook villains. Beyond the blatant bigotry and anti-Other rhetoric, there was a liberal smattering of nonsensical fabrications about what Others did and didn't do. A bunch of outrageous drivel about bands of wolves tearing through small towns and stealing pets and infecting humans against their will. Humans had been, from time to time, infected without their permission. But not a single documented case had occurred in the last year. And they sure didn't rampage through Mayberry to eat Fluffy and the kids.

Sato, to his credit, along with several other people on the panel, did manage to ask the right questions and set the record straight, but the damage was done and she knew the things said by the humans on that panel of so-called experts would be passed off as facts in the PR blitz for this bill.

Finally, Representative Carroll spoke from his seat. "It was under protest from our caucus today that this hearing went forward without a single Other on the incorrectly named expert panel you see here. This caucus is made up of men and women, human and Other, from both sides of the aisle. We have a total of twenty-five minutes for comment. As such, we cede that time to Molly Ryan."

Carroll's aide came up to escort Molly to the front as Hayes and Sato disagreed on procedure. She was going to say her piece no matter what or they'd have to drag her out.

She didn't need notes so she reached the podium with nothing but herself. The humans on the panel started hooting and hollering about rules and the pitch in the room got higher as the arguing worsened.

It was so loud she couldn't be heard and that was not going to happen. She'd come thousands of miles with the hopes and dreams of her people riding on what she had to say that day and Molly wasn't going to let them down.

So she tapped on the mic to be sure it was hot and then

she gave a loud whistle, which did get everyone's attention.

"Now then. My name is Molly Ryan—"

"You have not been recognized by the Chair of this committee. You need to be quiet!" Hayes barked at her.

She knew she did a little head whip at his tone, like she was a wayward animal.

"Senator, with all due respect you either have to give me a seat on your *expert panel* or let me speak now. You changed the rules, but either way I can speak."

Without really even doing it on purpose, she knew she worked her magick to be heard. Which, she supposed, was better than using it to send this asshole through the wall.

Her othersight revealed a human who was devoid of much heart and soul. Faine had been right about that. But he was afraid as well. More than he'd been at the television studio the day before when he'd called her a power-hungry whore of Babylon. They'd cut that from the West Coast feed, but it had left her so angry the top of her head nearly blew off.

"Turn her mic off!" he screamed into his own. Molly looked to Sato, who was as confused as she was.

"Senator Hayes, this is a violation of your own procedure. She has time ceded to her by members of this committee. She has a right to use it to speak." Sato remained calm as he attempted to speak over the rising din.

Molly knew when her mic was turned off and rage built from the tips of her toes. Enough was enough. She called her magick then and used it to be heard.

"You cannot take away our voice. I will not allow it. This is our country as well. I was born here. I am a citizen of this nation and you will not violate the Constitution to keep me silent."

· Her voice rang clear and strong throughout the room.

"Have that thing arrested," Hayes called out to the Capitol police, who began to move toward her. When that happened, Gage was at her side in moments and Faine blocked access to her up the aisle.

"We need to go right now." Gage put a hand on her arm.

"I will not. He just called me a thing!"

Gage's anger wisped away for a moment, replaced by amusement. "Baby, I promise you can make mincemeat out of him once we've gotten you out of here. Things are dangerous. I can feel it. We need to go right now. They've already taken Cade from the room."

"I can't imagine he did so willingly."

Gage's hesitation told her she'd been right.

"In the end, he listened to reason. Just like you have to."

And then it was as if all the air was sucked from the room. The pressure changed, making her ears pop. Terrible knowledge ghosted over Gage's face as he shoved her to the floor.

She put her arms over her head protectively, up to her knees to watch as she could. All around her dust and debris flew. Glass seemed to flitter to the ground like rain. Chaos reigned. They were being attacked, that much was obvious. But how bad it was she didn't know.

Another punch in the air and she left the ground and flew a few feet. This time there was white-hot pain like she'd never experienced before and even though everything around her was deafeningly loud, she heard the crack of her bones as they broke.

Gage shoved the podium to the ground next to her, using it to shield her. "Hang on, Molly! It's going to be all right."

The pain grew and grew, worsening each time Gage shifted, jostling her. Waves of heat passed over her and she realized it was magick. Gage was throwing his magick at whatever, whoever had attacked.

She tried to move, to shift, but Faine put a hand in the small of her back. "Stay," he snarled so she did. She kept her focus on Gage's face, so intent as he protected her. And she tried very hard not to think about what might happen if he got hurt, or how many people in that room had been hurt. Or worse.

And then one more boom, this one from a different direction, sending more debris up into the air and across the room. She had a hard time wrapping her head around exactly what was happening. The entire thing was surreal. A surreal capper on a surreal several months.

She might have laughed until something heavy hit her left leg and the bone snapped. The scream she heard came from her lips and that made her very sweaty. Her vision went sort of gray at the edges.

She looked up at Gage, trying not to panic at the panic on his face. He was scared. That was bad. Molly wanted to say something. She might have actually done it, but then she couldn't say anything at all as consciousness fell away.

Gage and Faine shoved the heavy oak desk from her leg. She'd passed out just moments after it hit her. He'd been looking at her face, and then horrible pain flashed over her features. Her scream still echoed through his ears. She'd whispered, *ow*, before she'd gone white and her eyes had rolled back.

He'd had to choke his fear back until he verified she had just fainted and wasn't dead. He managed to use his magick to keep her unconscious for a little while. Once she woke up the pain would be pretty bad and he didn't want that for her.

The room had descended into chaos after the first explosion, people running everywhere. It had been his plan to get her the hell out but he didn't want her to get trampled in the process.

Screams. The stench of burning flesh. Cries of pain and rage. He'd spooled up his magick so fast and hard he tasted it on his tongue as the smell of ozone came. He thought of nothing but her has he sent blast after blast in the direction of the bomb.

The second explosion had injured her and he'd been about to bend to pick her up when she'd grabbed her arm, blood everywhere. The scent of it had wrapped around his magick. Viselike, it held him, driving him to protect and defend.

Then the third and more injuries as he'd been helpless to do anything but keep her unconscious.

Finally, the Capitol police managed to secure the space and Gage stood, noting the carnage.

"Bombs." Faine's voice rumbled from where he knelt, next to Molly. "Three of them from what I could tell. They all smell the same."

"Gonna guess they were all the work of the same people." He looked Molly over. "I want to pick her up but I don't want to hurt her any worse."

One entire wall was gone. The hallway beyond was full of cops, debris and gawkers. Investigators had already started work in the hearing room; paramedics had begun to stream in and were dealing with the wounded.

Gage didn't want any human doctors touching her. Didn't want any humans anywhere near her.

"Fuck. Fuck. Fuck."

Faine nodded. "Succinctly put. We need to get her seen to."

Sato made his way through the rubble between where they stood and where he'd been shoved out a back door by his security people. "Over here!" he shouted to the medics.

"No. I want an Other seeing to her." Gage nearly snarled it, his rage made the words bitter on his tongue. He wanted to burn shit down, she'd been so hurt.

"There aren't any here right now and she's clearly in need of help." Sato weighed his words. "I understand your anger. Just let us help. We're not all Hayes."

"Fat lot of good it does Molly."

"Be pissed at me all you want, but let's get Molly treated. Please."

Faine stood, looking to Gage. Gage knew the Lycian would back him no matter what he decided.

"Fine. But she's not leaving my sight."

The paramedic who'd paused at Gage's anger moved in and another joined him. Gage scanned them both and got nothing but some fear and a desire to help.

"What the fuck happened?" Gage demanded of Sato while they began to look Molly over.

"We don't know yet."

"I will have someone's head if Hayes claims it was Others. And why aren't you getting video of this?"

The men turned to look at Molly, who'd regained

consciousness and valiantly tried not to wince as they cleaned the wound on her neck. She was all right enough to issue orders. At least there was that.

"Hush you. Let them fix you up. Then you can make threats." The words felt like such a lie. Not that she shouldn't let them fix her up, but his upbeat delivery. Like it was no big deal.

When what he really wanted to do was start kicking the shit out of everyone in the vicinity.

"We need—" She broke off on a whimper and he and Sato both knelt down. Gage wanted to touch her but he wasn't sure where he could without hurting her more. He should have known even broken bones and bombs couldn't stop her from doing her job. "Use your phone. Don't know how they will spin it. We need truth."

"Didn't I just tell you to hush? Bossy woman."

She smiled sideways and he got his phone out and began to film the outrageous destruction all around them.

But that didn't mean he wasn't going to be sure she was taken care of. "Can't you give her something for the pain?"

"Yes, in a moment. She needs to get these broken bones set and casted. We need to transport her to the hospital. She might have a concussion. She's got multiple lacerations on her face and neck from the flying glass." The paramedic spoke into a radio at his shoulder, requesting an ambulance and a gurney.

"Not yet. We need to set up a press conference. Right now."

"You're out of your mind if you think I'm going to let you have a damned press conference instead of going to the hospital."

The paramedic spoke with her briefly about any allergies she might have and the gurney arrived. It was easier—slightly—to watch it through his camera on his phone.

"I'm not"—she swallowed hard as they put in an IV—"out of my mind. They need to see this, Gage. Every damned human in this country needs to see the price of their silence, indifference or, worse, their bigotry. There is a cost. We've been paying it over and over since the Magister. They need to be confronted with it."

He turned the camera off for a moment, leaning in close to speak to her quietly. "You're killing me, beautiful. How about this? We get you to the hospital and patched up and then you can go straight into a press conference. We'll know more, at least a little more by that point. I can call Meriel and fill her in so she can tell you if she wants you to say anything specific." He knew the last part would be an appeal to authority and that it would work with her. It was dirty pool, but he'd do whatever he had to to get her into that ambulance.

"I broke a few things."

He laughed and found himself kissing her forehead. He turned the camera back on before he did anything else like that.

"Molly, I'd be honored if you'd allow me to help these males get you onto the gurney." Faine spoke to her in a gentle voice.

"Fine. Thank you." She looked up at Sato and Gage knew by the way her face had relaxed that the pain relief had kicked in. "Are you all right?"

Faine helped get her up onto the board. There was so much debris all around that they would have had trouble otherwise. But a giant Were could pick her up easily and transfer her to the board carefully. Even so she winced and gasped a few times.

"On our way."

Sato walked next to the gurney as they pushed it quickly through the cleared path and out the hole in the wall to the hallway.

Sato looked pained as she paled when they hit a bump and she got jostled. "I'm better than you are. Listen to Gage and the doctors. I'll be at the hospital shortly. I have my own press conference to give." Sato turned to Gage. "I'll have my aide send you everything we can as we know it."

Gage nodded and jogged next to the gurney as they got

it outside to the ambulances lined up. A crowd of PURITY protesters tried to push close but Gage was beyond caring. He filmed them all with one hand while he used his magick to shove them all back so they could get through.

"Nearly there." He dared the paramedics to tell him he wasn't allowed to ride along. Luckily for them they didn't. Faine got on her other side and they closed the doors and headed off.

"I need to call Meriel; she's already called and left voice mails. It's made the news."

But first he had to get himself together. Back from the brink of falling apart. He could have lost her. His hands shook a moment, but when he looked to Molly, she wasn't falling apart so if she could do it, he could too.

"Faine, I need to speak. Can you get my phone and film me making a statement?"

Of course she waited until Gage was waiting for Meriel to pick up on the other line before she did it. He could hear the pain in her voice. She *could* just rest and let herself get treated. But no.

When Meriel picked up Gage started speaking. "I'm sorry it took me so long to call you back. I'm guessing the bombs were on the news. Lark is my next call. We're on the way to the hospital now. Faine and I are all right, just a few scrapes from the flying glass. Molly . . . well, she's got some broken bones. They want to check her out more thoroughly."

Meriel sighed explosively. "It's all over the news. Keep me updated. Have you heard about the rest?"

"About what?"

In the background, Molly stopped speaking and he knew she was listening to their call.

"Bombs have gone off in several major cities. All targeting Others. Lark will call you in a few minutes. Just take care of Molly."

"Did they go off there? Is anyone in Owen hurt?"

She paused. "Heart of Darkness was hit. Dominic was there checking stock. He's fine. Thank goodness he's made of granite. There have been casualties in a few states. I've got to go. Have Lark fill you in on the rest and keep me updated on Molly, all right?"

He scrubbed a hand through his hair. "Yeah."

"Heart of Darkness was hit. I need to get on with Lark to get updated. Others have been targeted nationwide."

Molly looked at him, pain on her face that wasn't just about her physical wounds.

AS it happened, breaking a bone really hurt. Breaking two really hurt a lot more. She also had a broken rib, a sprained wrist and lacerations from flying glass and splinters.

The painkillers she currently surfed to avoid the bulk of that pain also made her grumpy as Gage paced around the room on his phone, barking orders and cursing under his breath. Faine calmly took it in from his place in the corner.

She waited for Gage to head down the hall to see if she could leave before she made some phone calls he'd squawk about.

Faine sent her a grin as he shook his head, and she blushed.

Once she hung up, Gage came back and verified that she could leave. He was still angry, that much was easy to see from his features. Part of it was her, she knew, but the details that kept coming about the other attacks, not only in the United States but across the globe, were frighteningly brutal.

"How is it you two are relatively unscathed? Don't get me wrong, I'm happy that flying glass didn't cut up your pretty faces."

"The podium you stood at was close to the blast point. Gage and I were off to the side, the post we stood near shielded us the first time. The others? Luck I suppose." Faine paused. "And I believe the bomb was aimed at you directly."

"Lay off the scaring part," Gage said before going back to his call.

"He's a multitasker. Now, the nurse says I can go and that's what I want to do. I don't like it here. First, a press conference. I managed a few pulled strings and they're going to do it out front in thirty minutes."

"I'll call you back." Gage put the phone back in his pocket and glared at her. "You'll do no such thing."

She sent him a raised brow. "I will, yes. And I'll need you to brief me in the meantime. I need to be totally up to speed by the time the press conference starts."

"Molly." Gage looked heavenward for long moments, clearly marshaling all his patience and she tried very hard not to crack a smile, but it was really difficult, especially with the painkillers in her system.

"Gage."

"You're being a smart-ass now?"

"I get to be. I have two broken bones, a broken rib and a sprained wrist. And a lot of great drugs in my body too."

Faine stood, hiding a smile behind a cough. "I'm going to check in with Simon. I'll just be right outside."

"You can't have a press conference. Molly, one hundred and thirty-seven Others have been injured today. Including you. Six have died. You're going to be a target outside. A big neon arrow pointing at you. I'm not going to allow that."

"Others died today, Gage. Dominic and Simon's business was bombed. A hearing in the United States Congress was cut short by bombs. Homes. Businesses. A pack *school* in Utah was bombed. Three children are in the hospital and when they get out, they'll have one less teacher. Of course I'm going to have a press conference."

She tried to sit up a little straighter, but the cast and sling weren't much help in that department. Gage sighed, moving to her to assist. "Baby, please listen to me. All those losses are terrible. But you're a loss I can't . . . please."

Tears sprang to her eyes. "You like me."

He sighed, kissing her forehead, over each closed eyelid and then her cheeks before he got to her lips. All just the barest of touches, all filled with so much emotion she couldn't choke all of it back.

"You make me all sniffly and messy," she mumbled.

"You make me all terrified and annoyed," he countered.

"I'm not going to do this exactly right because as I mentioned, drugs. In fact I'd rather be with you in your apartment naked in your bed watching movies. You protected me today. You threw yourself in front of me when a bomb went off." Her bottom lip wobbled and she started to cry but she dabbed at her eyes with a tissue he handed her. "I want to hold on to you and let you take me home and tuck me into bed and never come out of my room. But I can't do that. You know I can't. Things are bad. Like really bad and we can't trust the humans in charge not to make this our fault."

He paused a long time, swallowing hard. He looked at her face as if he were memorizing each and every feature. Finally he spoke. "I hate it when you're right."

She managed a smile. "I know. But it's a cross you'll have to bear. Go tell Faine he can come back in and then brief me while I fill out all this discharge paperwork."

Chapter 26

HE noted that her hand shook slightly before she clenched her fingers into a fist. On the right only as she wore a cast on the left and a splint on that wrist as well. That rage bubbled up and he did his best to stoke it back.

She needed him to be calm and alert. Needed to lean on him because she was hurt and scared. He'd already failed her once that day, he wouldn't do it again.

Molly stepped to the mic and cleared her throat. He noted the way she drew magick up through the ground and also through the air all around her. It seemed to be second nature to her by that point. Her aura glittered as the power rolled from her and projected outward over the crowd.

The noise hushed.

"Good afternoon. Or evening I suppose. My name is Molly Ryan and I'm a witch. More specifically, I'm the Media Relations person representing Clan Owen and the Council of Others. Today at approximately half past one in the afternoon, the hearing room I was in was attacked. Three bombs the authorities are now saying were improvised explosive devices went off consecutively. Those bombs blew out an entire wall. Part of which fell on me." She motioned to her arm and the cast she also wore on her leg where her femur had been broken.

She had to adjust her weight and he had to will himself to let her. She refused a wheelchair so she leaned on a crutch. She was pale. Her blouse was dirty, ripped in several places and blood spattered. Her skirt was in similar shape.

"At the same time, all across the globe, bombs went off in buildings, marketplaces, *schools* and places of public discourse like government offices. All told, as of twenty minutes ago, one hundred and thirty-seven Others—your neighbors, your friends and family—were injured in these attacks. Seven of those Others are children. Six people have died. One was a teacher at the school in Utah where four children were also injured."

"How do we know you didn't do this? You're blaming humans with no proof." A yell from one of the crowd.

Molly got closer to the microphone. "My proof is common sense. Everyone targeted was an Other. Everyone injured or killed was an Other. Organizations like PURITY and Humans First have been preaching hate and violence while smiling at cameras. They like to talk about decent Americans? *I'm* a decent American and I'm calling them out. And shame on *any* Americans who call themselves decent who don't stand up and condemn this sort of violence. First it's camps, then it's summary execution? Who is Carlo Powers to decide this? Hm? Did any of you vote for him? This isn't prewar Germany. This is the United States of America. This is a nation built on differences and our common goals. We do not execute people for being different. We do not put our citizens in camps and chip them."

"You were testifying before Congress. How can you claim you're oppressed?" The same voice.

Molly sighed. "As a matter of fact, the chair of that committee had a panel of experts on this bill that would strip Others of their citizenship and put us in camps. On that panel there was *not a single Other*. In fact, Senator Hayes changed the rules at three in the morning and then when the other members of that committee ceded their time to me so I could speak, the bombs went off. I call having a wall fall on me, breaking my bones oppression, yes. What would you call it?"

Silence.

"Yes, as I figured."

"How do you respond to those who say that if the Others weren't stirring up all this trouble, none of this would have happened?"

"That's an absurd way to look at it, don't you think? If she hadn't talked back, I wouldn't have had to hit her? Hm? If she hadn't worn that skirt, she wouldn't have been raped? That's rhetoric we reject in every other case. Because it's called victim blaming. Did my refusal to let my people get shoved into a concentration camp cause some violent bigot to try to kill me? That's an astonishing thing to say, don't you think?"

They got very quiet. Her magick flowed steadily, surely across the space. He realized she had it in her power to actually control their actions, but she didn't. Gage knew she'd never even consider such a thing, even if it wasn't a violation of the ethical rules that bound witches to do no harm.

Unless in self-defense.

He hoped like hell they never had to test that.

SHE took questions for another five minutes or so, but he knew she was about ready to fall over. Luckily for her, she figured it out too, and ended the thing before he had to do it.

A car pulled around and Gage noted the number of National Pack wolves who had shown up to guard her. He liked that allegiance. Liked that the humans would see they weren't going down easy either.

Molly just sent him a raised brow but said nothing as he gently got her settled and they headed to the hotel.

But that didn't last long.

"I don't want to be in a hotel."

"You're about to pass out. You're white as a sheet. You need to rest, damn it. The capital is closed for the rest of the day anyway, you know in case you thought you could start lobbying or something like that."

"I want to go home." She snorted and settled back, wincing as she did. "I want to sleep in my bed tonight, such as it is. I don't want to be here a second longer than I have to."

Oh.

"That can be arranged." The shifter driving the car was Cade Warden's personal bodyguard.

Molly sat forward with a gasp. "Is Cade all right? I can't believe I forgot to ask that."

"You were a little busy getting your bones broken." Gage rolled his eyes.

"Even so." She would have brushed a hand down her skirt, as she tended to do when she got prim with him, but she flinched and pulled her hand back. The leg that hadn't been broken had a great deal of bruising from the huge oak desk that had landed on her.

The bodyguard spoke again. "He's fine. We'd gotten as far as the elevators when the first bomb went off. He wanted to come back to see if you were hurt but we overpowered him down the stairwell and got him out of the building. He's pretty pissed about that."

"I'm glad you did though. It was bad enough that I got hurt. If more Others had, it would have been worse."

"He wanted to be here, by the way. But Grace wanted him home and in the end, she persuaded him. We'll take you directly to the airport. They're getting the plane ready now."

"Check in with Lark, I know you need to. I'm fine."

"You are not fine. Fuck." Gage shook his head.

"I'm as fine as I'm going to be. And that's all I can be." She turned to look him in the eye as she said it. Her unspoken *and it's all you can be* rang out as clear as if she'd shouted it.

"When we get on that plane you're taking some more medication and going to sleep. Got that?"

She nodded and leaned back again, closing her eyes.

MOLLY woke up as Faine picked her up. She'd been dreaming about the bomb. She screamed, beating at him, bringing tears and a well of pain so deep she nearly passed out again.

Gage was there, whispering in her ear. "Shhh. It's okay. Molly, it's Gage and Faine. Wake up, baby."

She opened her eyes on a sob and then mortification. "I'm so sorry!"

Faine shook his head. "It's all right. I startled you. I should have woken you up first."

Molly couldn't seem to stop crying, which frustrated her greatly.

"Faine, can you give us a moment?" Gage asked as Faine put her down carefully. The Lycian nodded.

"I'll be right outside."

Gage handed her some tissues. "Take a minute to get it out of your system."

"I was dreaming of the attack. And then I was in the air. I just . . ."

He cocked his head. "I'm sorry."

"For what?" Goddess, she hoped she wasn't all snotty and puffy and goopy.

"Today. I didn't protect you."

"Are you kidding?" Suddenly the tears were gone and she was astonished.

"Look at you, Molly! I *knew* something bad was going to happen. Damn it."

"You did and you warned me multiple times. You tried to get me to leave. I stayed, knowing I could be hurt. But they heard me. Every one of those fucking assholes who tried to silence me has just given me a platform far greater than I would have gained from sitting on that panel."

"You're going to kill me." He heaved a sigh. "It's late. Come to my apartment tonight. I'll make you something to eat and you can get some rest."

"All right."

Of course once they'd arrived at Gage's apartment, people began to call and ask to come by. So she agreed to let him get her set up on the couch and to allow Meriel, Lark and Rita to visit. Rita was going to bring Shelley, Gage's mom, who was a healer and wanted to see if she couldn't help.

"I can't even believe Sato today."

She huffed a sigh. "What now?"

"The guy is all over you until you get hurt and then he's nowhere to be found?"

Yeah, so being in a room when three bombs went off had given her a moment of clarity. She'd bitten her tongue enough. This *friends with benefits* thing never worked. Ever.

"You can't have it both ways."

"What do you mean?"

"I mean, you get mad when he's nice to me. And then you get mad when he backs off when I need to go to the hospital. He didn't abandon me. He called to check in but he has his own work to do. And anyway, that's not the issue here."

"I know I'm going to be sorry for asking this, but what exactly do you think the issue is then?"

"You're jealous."

The look on his face was all the confirmation she needed.

"Jealous of what? He's being a dick. He's supposed to be your friend."

"Jealous because you think he's interested in me romantically. You don't like the supposed competition."

This painkiller thing was kind of cool. She could say all sorts of things.

"He's no competition!"

"Exactly. No one is. Do you understand me? There's only you, Gage. This fuckbuddy nonsense is stupid. You want to be with me, not just horizontally."

"What are you getting at?"

She blinked at him. "Don't insult me. I'm in love with you. I don't want to pretend you're just my guard. You're so much more to me than that."

He put his hands up. "Whoa. Look, this is not the time to do this. What we have is perfect. I don't deny we're involved. But I keep it mellow in public and I've told you why."

"So all of my life I've been ambitious. I've never let anything stop me from getting what I wanted. I went to school. I built my firm. I'm damned good at what I do. The damned Magister threw a wrench into all that. But the basic fact is that I'm the kind of person who doesn't do things halfway. I've been with men before you, obviously. Some even very seriously. Serious enough that I thought I was in love.

"But the way I feel about you? Well, I don't know why I'm surprised, but I love the way I do other things I want. All the way to the bone. I'm in love with you. I don't want to be a friend you fuck. That demeans us both."

"Molly. This is not the time to go changing things or thinking you're in love. You nearly died! Things are a stressful just now. We can do this talk once things have calmed down."

She sighed. "And when will that be? Things are a runaway train hurtling into really bad territory. Who the hell knows if or when it will stop. Now is exactly the time to accept what is already true. I have tampons in your bathroom. I used your razor the other day. We're already in a relationship. You already love me. Stop denying it. I want to be your woman. You're already my man. You protected me today, like you do every day. You stayed with me the whole time, you even threatened them when they tried to make you leave."

"But I didn't protect you. I didn't protect Edwina. I didn't protect Rose. I didn't protect my uncle. I'm not a good bet, I keep telling you that."

"You do because you're being dumb. You're going to take responsibility for a being older than recorded history and so powerful it simply made thousands of Others disappear by an act of its will? Do you think you're so powerful you can will people into not trying to kill me with your magick? This job is inherently dangerous. That's why I have a body-guard. Why you want to make it your fault that people get hurt I can't figure out. The people at fault are those who planted the bombs."

"It's my job to protect people. People died. So I didn't do my job."

"That's *so* overly simplistic and you know it. You have a ridiculously impossible job and yet you do it. Every. Single. Day."

"Don't romanticize me."

She may have snarled, but she knew he was trying to push

her away so she kept it reined in. "You act like a man worthy of my love. What's more? You love me too. If you didn't, you wouldn't get all pissy about Tosh and his supposed flirting with me or whatever. You wouldn't care if we were just friends." She paused and sighed. "Imagine me doing air quotes here because I can't right now. *Just friends* my ass. You don't care about Lark with Simon. Or Meriel with Dominic. We're *already in a relationship* so stop this silliness. Now, you promised me food and people will be arriving soon. So accept reality and please feed me."

She didn't need to look at him to know he gaped at her. Served him right.

"Molly, I care about you. A lot. But love is a big deal."

Oh, he would pay for this little bit of denial and for the way it hurt even though she knew it was a lie. And he knew it too, so she'd collect later, but that day she needed to just get through. She had to trust her gut and her heart.

Things were indeed scary. They were hard and dark and she wasn't entirely sure if or when they'd ever be normal again, or if they'd have to adjust to a new normal.

But she loved Gage Garrity with his frowny face and his awesome ass. She loved the way he listened to her. They bickered, but he respected her, which made all that bickering sort of fun and really hot.

Without another word, he handed her the television clicker and got to work on dinner. She tuned in to see just exactly what had happened all across the globe that day.

Chapter 27

GAGE stood at her office door and she took a moment to just look at him before he spoke. She knew by the look on his face that it would be something bad and she wanted that bubble of time to wonder at how magnificent the man was before it burst on the reality he carried.

He smiled when he realized what she'd been doing. "Hey."

Things had been tense between them since the night in his apartment when she'd told him she loved him. But the tension of the outside world had also grown far more quickly, so there hadn't been a lot of time to obsess over it. Mainly because she'd had to deal with the way some on the media had been spinning the news to make it look like all the attacks and persecution were the fault of the Others because humans felt threatened.

Threatened. She didn't see their homes and businesses getting burned down or bombed. The unfairness of it burned until she was filled with anger every waking moment. The entire world was totally illogical and while she did have a gift for swaying people to her perspective, she couldn't do the whole world and she couldn't change the minds of crazy people either.

More attacks. Only now Others were defending themselves and humans were beginning to realize Others simply weren't going to let themselves be shoved into camps without a fight. And that if they did fight, the humans might not find it so easy to win.

And this was before they even really had any idea what the Others were capable of.

"Okay, I'm done. Tell me."

"I should report you for objectifying my body."

She smiled back. "Yeah? G'head. But then I won't be able to objectify you anymore and then what? Your whole day will be absent of any objectification from me. That's what my mom calls cutting off your nose to spite your face."

"Good point." His smile went away. "Car bombs in Alaska. This time vampires."

"Oh shit."

The vampires had been wavering on leaving the Council of Others. They were sick of the violence. Impatient with the slow pace of the political and diplomatic process. And she didn't blame them.

"How bad?"

"This was an Elder. On his way to a local restaurant with his humans and a few of his staff. They set off what's essentially a roadside IED."

"So Alaska is suddenly Afghanistan? What the hell? What do the local vamps say?"

"They're pissed. Every vampire in that car and the one in front of it is dead. Their protected have also died."

Protected were the class of humans who served the vampires in dealing with the human world. They took a blood oath to protect them from harm and vampires took that stuff seriously. To kill one who is protected meant the vampires would be honor bound to avenge that death. And to kill an Elder? A vampire over five hundred years old? She had no idea what the cost to the humans would be. But it would be steep and she couldn't do a thing to stop it. And really, why should she?

"They just can't learn. No matter how many chances you give them, they just . . ." She broke off. "It's time to stop playing around." She stood and he handed her her crutches.

"I agree. But what exactly is it you're planning in that pretty head of yours?"

"I need to talk with Meriel. And the Full Council. Lark and you as well." Expertly she walked past him to Rita's desk and asked her to set up that meeting.

"Hey, why don't you let me wheel you wherever you're going in the wheelchair?"

She kept moving, heading toward the office Meriel and Dominic shared.

"The exercise helps burn off the rage."

"Molly, I'm sorry. I know you were hoping for . . . well, for a different result."

Goddess, he made her want to cry sometimes. Not always in a positive way, but at that moment she wanted to throw her arms around him and kiss him for caring.

"Don't be nice to me. I can't handle it right now."

He got in front of her, impeding her progress. "Why don't we get some lunch? Then you can get yourself together first."

"I don't have time for lunch. Being together is a luxury I can't afford. Things are falling apart. I've been drowning for three and a half months. I used to think it would let up, but I'm deeper and deeper. Going under is the new normal apparently."

Gage sighed heavily. "I hate seeing you this way."

"I hate being this way." She walked around him and headed toward Meriel's office.

She knocked, but it was Dominic who waved her in, a phone to his ear. He motioned for her to sit and she did, happy to be off her feet again.

Dominic hung up and turned to her. "I'm guessing you're here about the Alaska situation?"

"Yes." She was so very tired all the sudden and the emotion welled up.

Dominic got up and shut the door before returning. "Aw sweetheart, let it go."

She fanned her face. "I'm mortified. I apologize."

"I'm the boss and I do not accept your apology. It's unnecessary. What do you have to be sorry for? Having feelings? Getting overwhelmed by what has to be one of the most difficult jobs anyone could possibly have? Or being physically attacked on more than one occasion? Personally, I went out to the range this morning and shot off a few dozen clips and after that I boxed for another hour and I'm still angry."

"I wanted it to work."

He poured her a cup of coffee and placed it near.

"I wanted the good humans to outnumber the bad ones and stop this nonsense. But it keeps getting worse and I can't seem to stop it. I wanted to. I keep trying. And there are good people like Senator Sato and so many others who've worked so hard to protect us. I feel ungrateful and resentful for not remembering that sometimes."

"For what it's worth, I think good humans *do* outnumber the bad ones. But they're not making themselves heard enough over the bigots. And the outcome is what it is. We're being picked off. Our children are in danger. Our homes aren't safe. We can't drive without worry of roadside bombs now?"

"I used to feel caught between two worlds."

"And now?"

"I feel totally rejected by one and not completely accepted by the other. I'm not totally at home in either."

He held his mug up in a toast. "I hear you. I feel very much the same and this is my clan." His laugh was rueful. "I'm sorry. I'm sorry this has been what it has been. For what it's worth, it does get better. You get used to how a clan works. They get used to you. They do respect you, which is huge given how insular witches can be. It doesn't hurt that you're likeable and pretty too."

She snorted. "My old secretary, back at my old firm, would say, *'Well, at least she's pretty,'* when a woman was sort of dumb or incompetent."

Dominic choked on his coffee, waving a hand at her. "Not what I meant."

"I know, I was just teasing."

He shook his head as he got his breath.

"We need to draw a line in the sand now."

The words had been on her tongue for at least a month. But she held them back. Over and over. Hoping at some point that she could swallow them and not have to use them.

"Wow, that was liberating."

Dominic grinned at her. "Yeah?"

She nodded.

"I agree. So does Meriel. I was just on the phone with her. She's at a meeting but she's on her way back and we'd like to set up a meeting with you and the Full Council. I'm guessing that's why you're here?"

"Yes. And probably for the pep talk too. Thanks, Dad."

He started and then began to laugh. It was a wonderful laugh and she realized she hadn't heard it much. Pity that.

"You have quite a sense of humor a few layers down. Why don't you tell me what it is you're thinking?"

"We've been nice. We've been diplomatic. We've offered up various bits of information and education about ourselves. We've been open and honest about what witches are, what shifters and vampires are. The only things we haven't shared are that our powers seem to be growing since the Magister and that there are beings from the other side of the Veil and demons. And you know what would happen if we told them about demons."

He blew out a breath. "Yes."

"We've tried being firm. We've tried retreating a little to give them space. What we've gotten in return has not been hopeful. Bills rushing through both houses of Congress to put us in camps. To strip us of our citizenship. We've been run off the road, had our houses and businesses burned and vandalized. Riots. Assaults. Murders. Our children are bullied in schools, we're being fired from our jobs, discriminated against even in direct contravention of the Constitution. In other words, this particular path of media isn't working."

"You've done a great job. But you're right. I've seen you take a hostile room and convert it. But you can't do that to an entire nation. Or hell, maybe you could, but we don't have the ability to get to them."

"Gage suggested a reality show. It was a joke of course, but the *Real Housewives of the Others* or something like that. We do have Others selling their stories to tabloids now. Nearly all of it is utter nonsense and lies, but it makes us look bad either way."

She looked out the window for long moments. "I think we need to deliver a speech. A televised speech."

She outlined it for him and by the time Meriel and the rest of the Full Council had arrived, he was on board.

Chapter 28

"THANK you for coming. I know you've got enough to do with the recent bombing in Alaska." She bowed slightly to Franco.

"I'm hoping you're going to say something I like. If you don't, there will be war."

"Tomorrow at eight a.m. Pacific, I'm giving a televised speech that will also be broadcast on radio and Internet. In that speech I'm going to draw our line in the sand. The witches have had enough. We've tried diplomacy and it's gotten us nowhere. So now we show the fist in the glove."

From the corner of her eye, Molly noted Gage shifting in his seat. She hadn't said much to him. He was pouting that she hadn't filled him in on any of her plans. She usually did. But there'd been one meeting after the next at the clan and then this meeting had to be set up. In the midst of that, he and Lark had to deal with their own stuff. So it wasn't as if she could have anyway.

Nina Warden leaned forward in her seat. "The wolves are meeting right now and waiting to hear what you have to say, Molly. As many of you know, I was born human. I grew up in the human world and I was not made into a wolf of my own free will. I like to think that gives me a unique perspective on this issue. The wolves have been out for years now. We've had some problems here and there. We've been targeted by the Humans First people with leaflets and some generalized discrimination. But until recently we've never had the kinds of problems we all face now. Wolves will not allow our children to be harmed. We will not allow our Elders to be threatened. Our land, our pack is the lifeblood of our culture. Former human or not, we will no longer turn the other cheek."

Mia de La Vega, Molly's pilot and the wife of a high-ranking jaguar shifter in the de La Vega Jamboree nodded. "The wolves and cats are in accord here. You know I respect you, Molly. I've seen what you can do and it's given me hope. But you're sitting there with a cast on your arm, a splint on your wrist and a cast on your leg. They killed Elder vampires and protected. Police in some cities have begun using silver ammo. We will accept no further threat or violence from the humans."

Meriel had been listening quietly but she finally spoke. "Do you realize what you're saying?"

Helena Jaansen had been in a far corner guarding the room. She'd come up to meet with Lark and Gage. She stood forward.

"Gennessee is in accord with Owen, of course. I've been on this traveling road trip with Molly and the Others she travels with and with Senator Sato and the other human lawmakers. Not all humans are PURITY. Sato wants to do the right thing. He's a persuasive voice. He's principled and good. I know we have to do this, but I want to remind everyone that this is not—should not be—an *us versus them* situation."

"Should be or not, in the end isn't that exactly what it is?" Mia de La Vega shrugged. "I served in the military. I've been decorated multiple times. And still I had a police officer tell me I should be shot in the head and left to die in the gutter while we waited for Molly to arrive at the airport on her way from the hospital."

There was back and forth argument on this point for several minutes with passionate debate on several sides of the issue.

"No, it isn't exactly what it is. Let me clarify." Molly had let them go on a bit; it was good to let people speak and get things out of their system, but it was time to rein it back in and give the discussion some direction again. "My aim with this speech is not to divide humans and Others. That's already happening, I don't need to make it worse and I've worked my damndest to make it better. And failed. That's my failure and I own it. The aim of this speech is to draw that line. We will not be herded into camps. We will not be marked and tracked. We will not allow them to institute any of these ridiculous curfews and other things they want to do to curtail our rights. They need to understand that not only will we not allow that, but that we have the power—magickal and physical—to stop them.

"There are humans who support our rights. If a majority of them really felt like PURITY, we'd have been overrun. I watched the poll numbers and we came out looking far better than PURITY after the bombing."

Molly knew her magick flowed all through the room. Felt it touch shifter and vampire, felt it recognize witch and that particular flavor those like Simon and Faine, from the other side of the Veil, carried. She could control it now. It responded to her will without even a thought. She had no idea she could even do this a month ago and now she grew better at it every single day.

"But it's not enough. Our powers are growing. I know this. You know this. The humans don't need to know the full extent of it. But we are not cartoon witches. We have real power. And it's time the humans understood what that means. We will no longer be victims. And if someone tries to kill us, we'll try to kill them right back."

"Plus one for the *Firefly* reference." Nina winked. "I need to conference back with Lex and Cade. I move we take a recess to confer with our respective leaders and then meet back here to decide on next steps."

The others agreed and the room emptied, leaving her the space to let out a breath and the tension in her shoulders.

Gage was up, moving to her before he realized it. He saw the strain on her features. Even as he heard the resolve in her voice, he knew she paid a price for it. Knew this speech would be a final step out of her old life and into the world of magick.

He grabbed a sandwich from the stack near the doors and brought it to her. "Eat."

She looked up at him, smiling. "I thought you were mad at me."

She knew him so well. He'd hated that she hadn't come to him to bounce ideas off. Hated that she hadn't asked for his perspective when she so often did. Oh, he knew there'd been a time crunch and that things were hurtling forward at a scary-fast pace. But when he'd tried to comfort her back at Owen she'd walked around him and had sought out Dominic's counsel instead.

"Do I have a reason to be mad at you?"

"Give me the food and stop with that wily stuff. I'm too tired for it."

He handed her the box and she unwrapped the sandwich, eating slowly.

No one talked to him the way she did. On one hand it felt right to be so understood and also to know she wouldn't take any of his shit. On the other hand, it was raw. Exposed. She knew his flaws and thought she loved him anyway.

"No more coffee for you today. You're strung out."

She rolled her eyes. "I've got coffee in my veins now. Used to have blood until I moved to Seattle. That's what coffee shops on every corner will do to a gal. Anyway, your mom says I'm all right."

"She said your blood pressure was amazing for someone who is under as much pressure at you are." She'd also told Gage he was a damned fool if he didn't make a public claim on her. She'd scoffed when he'd told her, the same as he did Molly and everyone else, that he didn't have time for a serious relationship. It was like these people didn't know there was a damned war brewing.

Helena sent him a raised brow from where she sat with Lark.

"Do you want me to get you another?"

Molly put her hand over his and he shifted, turning his wrist to entangle their fingers.

"No, this is good. Thank you." She lowered her voice. "I read your report of the bombing. I hate that you blame yourself. It wasn't your fault."

"You're sitting here broken and bruised and you say that?"

"I'm sitting here, yes. So of course I say that. Why on earth do you think you can protect me from everything and that if you don't you're a failure? That makes me so mad."

"That makes two of us. Look, it's my job to protect. We've gone over that a million times."

"Yes, and every one of those million times I tell you it's outside of your abilities to prevent me from getting hurt if someone really wants to hurt me. I have a bodyguard because people want to hurt me. You do all you can, but even you can't possibly believe *anyone* is capable of preventing every single crazy person with an agenda from trying to kill me if they want to. You're awesome and all but you're not Superman. Hell, even Lois Lane got killed. Remember that movie? Superman had to fly backward around the earth to go back in time. Which was sort of dubious, but whatever. My point is, unless you have been hiding your awesome skill of flying and being able to control time, you're stuck with the reality that you can't be everywhere at all times. You can't stop it in every case, so what you need is to realize that and prevent it when you can and accept it when you can't."

He chewed on that a while. It burned in his belly that she could have been killed. For a number of reasons, he could admit. It tasted like failure and he didn't like failure in any guise.

She took her hand back and wrote some notes as people began to stream back into the room. She didn't like failure either. He saw it on her face when she spoke. This speech she was going to deliver would be a good one, he knew that much. But it would kill part of her to do it. That part that connected her to her old life. He knew it and wished he could spare her the pain.

He got up and left the room. He needed to walk off the anxiety that'd been riding his nerves for months now. That's when he literally bumped into Rose.

She smiled at him, clearly happy to see him. "I was just looking for you. I asked and they said you were in a meeting."

Rose hugged him and he hugged her back. That, of course, was when Molly came out of the conference room. She narrowed her gaze to where Rose's hand remained on his waist.

He hadn't done anything wrong, damn it. He waved at Molly, who rolled her eyes and made her careful way back toward the restrooms.

"What brings you back? I mean, I didn't know you'd even come back."

"I couldn't find a job, not a good one with benefits and stuff like I have here. And I missed things in Seattle. People."

"I'm sorry about the job thing. It's rough out there right now, for humans too. I'm guessing you didn't tell anyone you were a witch." He didn't go near the tentative step she tried to take back into a relationship with him.

"Yeah. Well, I'm not really a human now, am I? I . . . are you free? Do you want to go grab a bite or something? Catch up?"

"I'm not free, no." Not in either way she meant. He might not want to move in with Molly and start having babies, but he was with her. He didn't cheat and he had no desire to. Just looking at Rose then underlined the difference in how he felt about Molly versus anyone else he'd ever dated. "I'm in an important meeting. And I'm seeing someone."

Her smile fell. "Ah. Okay. Wow, that was fast."

Was it really? He met Molly in January. Early January and he'd been with her pretty much daily for three months. He knew her in ways he didn't know another soul. Even

Nell, who he'd been close with since childhood didn't know him the way Molly did.

As if he'd conjured her, she came back toward them and he smiled, waving her over. "Molly, there's someone I'd like you to meet." He may as well, because she'd be wondering who he'd been talking with and he didn't want her to worry.

She was pretty fast on her crutches. He'd joked with her that she'd overcome her crutches like anything else that might have gotten in her way.

She was at his side in moments, smiling at Rose, but clearly wondering who the other woman was.

"Molly, this is Rose."

She got it then. There was a slight shift in her body language, but her smile didn't falter, he gave her that.

"I've heard a lot about you, Rose. I hope you're back home for a good reason. That sounds odd. I mean, so much has been happening to so many that I hope you're here for something positive and not because you or someone you know was harmed."

Rose smiled and Gage realized Molly could charm most anyone. She could have acted like a bitch; some women would have. Goddess knew he did sometimes around Tosh Sato and he'd never even dated Molly. But Molly had been her normal gracious self and Rose got that.

"I was just telling Gage the job market is crazy and my job here paid more and had great benefits. And I missed being around other witches. So I figured moving back here was the best option. I saw you on television. More than once actually. You do a good job. I'm sorry you were hurt."

"I was just telling Gage that part seems to come with the territory, unfortunately." Molly looked back over her shoulder. "I need to get back in. Our break is over. It was nice to meet you, Rose. I hope to see you around."

She turned deftly and headed back into the room.

"That's her, right? The one you're seeing?"

"Yeah. I have to get back in there too. It was good to see you, Rose. I mean that."

"She's nice. I'm glad you ended up with someone nice. I need to run. But I'll see you around. The clan gave me my old job back. I'm starting again Monday."

She hugged him quickly, but there was a distance there now entirely appropriate for a friend. Gage found himself relieved that she was still as nice a person as she was before she'd gone.

But by the time he'd reached the doors to the conference room, his mind was fully back on Molly again.

She looked up, locking gazes with him and smiled before she went back to her conversation with Meriel. He liked that. Liked that she sought him out the way she did.

They needed to talk. Once this speech had been given and things calmed down, they'd go away. Maybe head to the coast to watch storms. He thought again. After the Magister, he didn't think he'd be up for storm watching for the next fifteen years at least. But maybe they could go to Hawaii or someplace sunny. Then they could talk.

Yes, that would be the ticket. He relaxed a little. Probably for the first time since that night she'd been attacked and then told him she loved him. He probably loved her too. Maybe. That was something else he could put off until after the speech.

Nina didn't waste any more time. "I spoke with Lex and then we spoke with Cade. We'd like to sign on to your speech tomorrow and Cascadia, along with National, will be issuing remarks of our own within half an hour of yours."

"The vampires also stand behind this speech and will likewise issue our own remarks if, after yours, we feel the need to."

"Likewise the cats."

Simon stepped forward. "Last week I went to Lycia and spoke with my father and oldest brother. We stand with Owen. Always."

Molly swallowed hard, licking her lips. Gage knew she was overwhelmed with emotion. She took a steadying breath and nodded. "I'll have a copy of my speech to each of you by midnight tonight. If any of you want to be present at the speech, I'll be giving it at the state capitol building. We do have friends in state houses across this country. I want to remind you all of that. We have those like Sato and Carroll at the national level too. Cops, mayors, governors. They're not all bad. The rest just need to understand who we are. It's my plan to make that happen. Thank you for your trust."

Chapter 29

HE looked over her place before he let her inside.

"I'm just going to get some work done." She went to her place at the small dining room table where she'd set up a home office of sorts.

He went to the couch and did his own work.

Molly needed to talk to Toshio. She'd known exactly what she was going to say in her speech for several weeks now. Each day she woke up and sent out a silent prayer that she wouldn't have to give it. And each night she went to sleep, thankful she got through another day.

But it was time and it couldn't be avoided any longer.

It was early evening in Seattle, so she knew he'd be settled in his home office. He picked up on the second ring.

"Hey, Molly. How are you feeling?"

"Physically I'm getting better. Can you talk?"

"Yeah, yeah. I'm alone. What's up? I heard about the situation in Alaska and I've been wondering when you'd call."

"I'm giving a speech tomorrow. I wanted to give you a heads-up so you can prepare for the blowback."

"Uh-oh. That doesn't sound promising."

"We can no longer go down the road we've been on, Tosh. My people can't sit by while they're being picked off one by one. You wouldn't, why should we?"

"I'm working on it. Every day. Carroll too. Our whole committee has been. Hayes isn't the majority. You know that."

"I do. And you know that's not what matters now. Because the majority are being silent. Which means people like Marlon Hayes *are* getting their way. And that's not going to happen any longer. We're not fairy-tale witches and Others. We are strong and we've been incredibly patient with all this nonsense so far."

"Are you declaring war?"

"We would still prefer a path through all this that is peaceful. We still have an open heart. We have, after all, lived side by side with humans for thousands of years. But we are not victims. Some are mistaking our tolerance for weakness and my speech is made to disabuse anyone of that notion.

"All this talk about camps and chips and taking away our citizenship. *No.* Not going to happen and you are not strong enough to make it happen. Maybe we should have been stronger and more vicious from the start, but we've been grieving our old lives. Wishing for the way it was before the Magister. And it can't ever be that way again. No matter how much I wish it could be. If this violence toward us continues, we *will* defend ourselves and our families. We will not tolerate losing our jobs and apartments. This will be at the heart of what I say tomorrow. As Captain Picard says when he's talking about the Borg, *the line must be drawn here.* Only he says it in a British accent and it's way scarier, but still."

"You know this will only give ammo to people like Hayes."

"They don't need it. They blew up cars today, Tosh. With humans in them. Humans protected by Elder vampires. Do you know what that means? You have no idea how hard it is to hold them back. They have so much more power than you can even conceive. And they've *been* holding back because I've asked them to. Each time I ask them and humans attack them I lose my credibility with them. That credibility is like credit. I was an outsider. I grew up in your world and they trusted me anyway. And I've let them down. Over and over. We can't afford to wait any longer. You know it. I know it."

He sighed heavily and she knew he paced, thinking carefully. And she knew that he'd have nothing else to say. She had no other options. To continue waiting for the humans to be nice after they'd repeatedly *not* been nice was suicide. How many times had a group waited and waited, only to be massacred?

"I know this is what you have to do. And I'm sorry because I know you don't want to do it."

She pressed her fingertips to her eyes. It didn't matter what she wanted. Things were what they were and she had to deal with it.

"Call me when you get the chance. I'll be watching it. I know you'll do great."

"I'll have my assistant send you the text when I go on. The Weres and vampires are also issuing statements after mine."

"All right then. Thank you for the heads-up. I appreciate it."

"You're our strongest ally. I owe you that much. I appreciate all you do for us."

"Look, it's my job, Molly. I was elected to represent the people in my state and this country. My constituents aren't just human any more than they're just white or black or Latino or whatever. This is wrong. You're doing your best in a messed-up situation."

"Thanks for the pep talk." She laughed.

"All part of the services I provide. Good luck, Molly."

She hung up and took a deep breath. When she opened her eyes it was to find Gage glaring at her.

"What now?"

"I can't believe you called him."

This again? "Really? And why is that?"

"Why does he need to know what you're up to? You lose the element of surprise that way."

"My job isn't like your job in that way. I can see why you might think so, and sometimes it might resemble it. But he's our ally. He needed to know so he could prepare. He's going to get a rasher of shit by the time I'm done. It was the right thing to do to tell him so he could prepare for it."

"You're telling the enemy what we're doing. They can regroup now, blunt whatever you say tomorrow."

"He's not our enemy, Gage. He's our ally. It doesn't matter if he supports what I'm going to say tomorrow, though he does. You do what you can in a situation like this. He'd have done the same for me. In fact he has. He's the one who sent me that legislation first. He shares all sorts of information with me. That's what you do."

Gage hated that she was so calm about the whole thing. Hated more that Sato had apparently comforted her and had given her a pep talk. *He* should have given her the pep talk, not Senator Sato.

"We have our own governance. That's what is important."

She sent him a raised brow but didn't lose her cool. "Don't think you can presume to tell me what's important, Gage. I know what's important. It's my job to know what's important. I went through our governance. I went through our process. I informed our people first. Then the rest of the Others. And then him. Because he's been such a staunch supporter of our cause, he'll face a lot of scrutiny tomorrow. It would have been rude not to have warned him. This isn't a secret attack. We don't need total secrecy and he's not going to tell anyone anyway."

"We don't need his approval. We don't need you going to Sato for his permission or permission from humans to take care of our business."

She slammed her fist down on the table, sending all her careful notes, pens and pencils flying. He flinched, knowing he'd gone too far.

"I have a job to do. I know exactly who I need to seek permission from and it's not the humans, or Toshio Sato. Or you for that matter." Her normally patient and somewhat annoyed tone had gone icy.

"You run to him all the time. You have plenty of your own people to talk to but they're not good enough for you."

Her eyes widened as that hit home.

"Not good enough for me? Really. You're going to stand there and say that to me? Fuck you, Gage. How dare you?"

He wanted to tell her he was sorry. He wanted to admit he sounded jealous and had gone too far.

He didn't want to admit the creeping panic that ate at his belly. The fear that she'd walk away. Didn't want to admit that this fight was different than the others.

He wanted to be the one comforting her but she hadn't sought him out. "I'm right here."

"Yes, not looking me in the eye lest I be emotionally open with you. God forbid. Also, in case you haven't noticed, you already knew I was giving a speech tomorrow. Tosh didn't. Just admit you're jealous! But you won't. Because if you did, you'd have to admit you love me. *I* can be nice to your ex-girlfriend, but you have to throw a tantrum over someone I work with. And you don't have the right."

"Don't have the right? What does that mean?"

"It means, Gage, that until you have the emotional maturity to just admit you love me and that we're in a relationship together, there's just no more of this *friends with sex* nonsense cover story. I'm not your mother; I can't make it easier for you to avoid being emotionally mature. If you don't want me enough to just admit you're being a jealous ass about Tosh because you love me and want me to come to you first, this is just a fucking lie."

"Why are you pushing this? Guys run from this sort relationship pressure from women."

"I'm not saying you have to marry me, so stop being such a whiner. I'm saying we're friends. If you want to know where a great place to get tacos is in Chicago, give me a call. I have a bodyguard. Faine is just fine to protect me.

I don't need another bodyguard, I need a man. *My man*. And if you can't be honest with yourself and with me enough to be that man, then I'm done with this game. I can't play anymore. It hurts too much and I have too much to do to have it always be between us."

She took a deep breath and he wished with all his might that she would stop speaking right then and there.

"I have a job to do. With or without your support. You know how much I value the support you've given me since the start. But if you can't admit your feelings, especially to save mine, I have to take a step away."

"You're right." He stood, gathering his things up. Inside his head, his brain screamed at him to stop. To not say another word unless it included an apology and a confession of how he felt.

But he didn't listen.

"We need to break things off. I can't give you what you need. I'll talk with Faine so that he knows I'm not here tonight. Good luck with your speech tomorrow." He left, slamming the door.

She stared at the closed door, tears coming to her eyes before she could lecture herself to stop crying. She hadn't expected him to break up with her. But in the end, she couldn't pretend to not be in love with him. Couldn't pretend they weren't a couple when everyone else knew exactly that except his dumb brain.

She managed to pick up all the things that had fallen when she'd slammed her fist against the table and then she used all her emotions to write the most difficult speech she'd ever given.

Chapter 30

HE stormed back downstairs, wanting to head to Heart of Darkness to find a woman to fuck Molly Ryan from his brain. But there was no Heart of Darkness. It was under construction after the bomb. And he didn't want anyone else in his bed.

So he headed to Nell's.

And found his friend with a baby strapped to her chest, a husband making spaghetti and a genuine smile at the sight of him.

"Gage! Come in."

Libby, their daughter, kicked and grinned, holding her arms out. Gage took the invitation and swooped her into his arms, dropping kisses all over her face as she giggled.

"Hello, beautiful baby girl. How are you?"

She grabbed his nose and then tugged on his beard.

"Nice to see some testosterone around here for a change," William, Nell's husband, said. "Stay for dinner, there's plenty."

"I think I'll take you up on that offer, thank you."

"Good. Now you can tell me why you have that look." Nell settled on the couch as Gage walked back and forth across the living room with the baby, patting her bottom gently.

"You're criminally good with babies. We should hire you as a nanny. She's been grumpy today."

"Everyone gets a grumpy day, Mom."

"Hm. How's Molly?"

He'd told her about Molly of course, but he was quite sure Meriel, who was also very close to Nell, had shared some as well.

"I just broke up with her."

"You did what? Why?"

"This job. Now. Everything is upside down. Every day we get death threats. Every event I take her to is full of pro-testers and people who want to harm her. People who want to harm Meriel. People who want to harm Dominic and the rest of the Full Council. The job used to be about dealing with problem witches and people who stole from the Font. Now it's dealing with loonies and kooks. Only they're elected officials and cops and stuff. With sniper rifles and bombs."

"You feel overwhelmed?"

"To say the least. Overwhelmed. Underqualified. I can't protect them all. Edwina was killed. Molly broke bones. You should see how she gets. You'd never know it when she's in the public eye, but once she gets behind closed doors, it takes a toll. She's afraid. The stakes are high. I can't be with her all the time and even when I am, well, I can't stop bombs, or a sniper's bullet."

"And you broke up with her for that?"

"She told me she loved me. She wanted me to say the same."

"And you're going to stand there holding my baby and lie, saying you don't love her? Because in all the years I've known you, Gage, you've never once talked about a woman the way you talk about her. You admire her. You respect her. She doesn't take your crap. She's your match on every level. You've never been a mimbo, so what, you're commitment-phobic now? Really? Is that a new thing? If so, it doesn't fit you."

Leave it to Nell to just say it like it was.

"I can't protect her. I can't make a commitment to her or anyone else because I can't protect her. It's my job and I can't do it."

She took a deep breath and watched him as he laid Libby down in her bassinet and set it to rock.

"I can't even believe you. We've been trying to get her down for three hours." William handed him a beer and went back into the kitchen. "Look, dude, until the second I met Nell I was a guy who never had any intention whatsoever of getting serious about a woman. I was, as my lovely wife puts it, a mimbo commitment-phobe. You're not that guy. You're a forever sort of dude."

"You can't protect her. Not totally." Nell joined them at the island in the kitchen. "Your job. Hell, her job too, is inherently dangerous. Especially right now and probably for the foreseeable future. You could walk out the door right now and get killed. She could get electrocuted or get into a car accident, or you know, one of these PURITY thugs could succeed and assassinate her. You cannot control everything.

"You're damned good at your job, Gage. You're a crack shot, your magick is kick-ass, you're physically strong and fast and your magick, like mine, like everyone else's from what I keep hearing, is only growing more powerful. And yet, none of us, not even the strongest of us like Meriel, can stop death when it's time. That's just how it works.

"There is no way to avoid what is meant to happen and so pretending you can control it will only lead to unhappiness."

William pushed a plate of spaghetti in front of him and the three of them ate for a time, talking about nothing more serious than babies.

He was getting antsy knowing she was alone back at the hotel and so he kissed Nell, thanking her for her advice, and went to the door.

"Gage, before today were you unhappy with Molly?"

Far from it. She brought him so much. More than he'd ever thought any other person could ever bring to him.

"No. But I'd sure as hell be unhappy if she died on my watch."

"Yeah? Well, you'd be even more unhappy if she died and you were broken up with her. So what does that prove? What does breaking up with a woman you're in love with do? Your problem, fear of losing this amazing thing, is about fear. You don't know what love really is until the thought of losing it fills you with so much fear you can't breathe. You already love her. She'll go when she's supposed to go. Being apart doesn't remove your fear, or your love. But you're both brokenhearted. So why the heck are you still here instead of groveling and getting her back?"

That was a good question. Ever since he'd walked out the door of her hotel room he'd been really sad. There was a hole in his belly where their connection belonged.

Even when he was annoyed with her, that connection burned between them, filling him, grounding him.

She was his woman, as most assuredly he was her man. Damn it. The question was, could he get past that fear and grab on or should he let go totally and let her find love elsewhere?

Chapter 31

MOLLY only hoped he slept worse than she did.

She woke up and rolled from bed, where she'd been alone for the first time in over a month. That had sucked and she hoped he was miserable because she sure had been.

Then again, she'd taken all that energy and written a great speech. So there.

She made herself a good breakfast and drank her coffee. She'd gotten used to having him around as she prepared. Bouncing ideas off him, having him listen to speeches and give her suggestions on how to improve.

She loved him. More than anyone she'd ever felt for in her whole life and she trusted that to get her through. Only it hadn't and he'd broken up with her. Chuck that in the failure file. Which pissed her off anew. He added something else to her failure list.

That sucked.

Luckily the mad burned away the heartache for the time being and when Faine arrived to escort her to the convoy of cars they'd drive down to the capitol for the press conference, she was less heartbroken and more pissed off. She'd take that.

Gage wasn't in her car and she didn't know if he was in any of the others either. She wanted to ask Faine but then decided she shouldn't care. But she did. So then she decided that if she asked she'd look sad and desperate, which did the trick.

She made calls and took notes and got about her day, pretending it was just another public-speaking gig. Until they got to Olympia and the roads were crazy backed up. There were dueling protests between the pro–civil rights groups and PURITY.

"Oh nice. God hates werewolves. Who knew God had time for such things?"

Faine laughed. "Imagine if they took their energy and channeled it into something positive. They could change the world for the better. Bitterness is a waste of time." He looked at her carefully. "As is regret."

"I know. But you can't make someone love you. Not these people, not anyone."

Faine squeezed her good hand. "It's going to be fine. I know this."

"Let's hope so. I'll settle for getting trough this without getting bombed or shot."

MOLLY approached the microphone and tried to swallow back her nervousness. All around her she had bodyguards, reminding her of why she was there. She'd had to wear a cape because her cast wouldn't fit into the sleeve of her coat. A cape like a superhero. Or so she told herself.

Off to the side she caught the golden-blond hair and knew he was there. She felt better and then wanted to punch him for making her so damned . . . dependent? Reliant? Addicted to his presence. Whatever. He was a poop head and she had to get through this so she could make him pay for breaking her heart like a dumbass.

"Ladies and gentleman, I'm Molly Ryan and today I'm

speaking on behalf of the witches all across the United States, be they clan or coven, as well as the Council of Others representing shifters and vampires. If you'll give me your silence while I speak, I'll open it up for questions once I finish.

" *'I swore never to be silent whenever and wherever human beings endure suffering and humiliation. We must always take sides.'* That's a quote from a great man, Elie Wiesel. And today it's more apropos than it's ever been in my lifetime. Four months ago, at the end of last year, a being manifested itself in this world. We know this being to be called the Magister. Humans have their boogeyman story to scare their kids into compliance on one thing or another. Others had theirs too, the Magister. Only our boogeyman was real and though it did not harm humans, thousands of Others simply turned into dust the day Clan Owen fought it and shoved it from this world.

"We lost so many that day. Without any notice for most of us. Countless brothers, sisters, friends, husbands, wives, children. And we barely had the chance to get used to the fact that these people were gone from our lives when humans, most of them scared, began to react to our presence, which we could no longer hide from human eyes.

"Since that day, we have been persecuted. We have been assaulted, murdered, attacked. We've had our homes burned down and vandalized. We've been fired from our jobs and kicked out of our homes. In some jurisdictions the police will no longer respond to our emergency calls and when there was a riot in our neighborhood in Indiana, when our peaceful gathering place was overrun with humans with guns and knives, who attacked the Others inside, when that spilled onto the streets and those humans set blocks of homes and businesses on fire, the police blocked fire trucks from going in to help.

"It was only Others who were arrested that day. Though we have surveillance video to prove our side of the story, that proof has been ignored until the Justice Department stepped in and made the locals obey the laws of this country and provide due process to its own citizens. Cars have been run off the road, including right here in Washington when the Borache family was assaulted. Both parents are now dead along with one of their children. Only one survives to face a world where no one seems to want to do anything to protect her.

"Then last week, bombs went off across the globe, all targeted at Others. I was caught up in that attack in Washington, D.C., as I was attempting to testify on a bill that will strip Others of their citizenship, implant us with GPS chips, forcibly sterilize us and put us in camps. Does that sound familiar to anyone? It should to anyone who took a history class in high school and studied World War Two."

A few people started to heckle and she used her magick to shut them up. The first time she'd ever really done that with such force and intent. And she let them know she did it.

"As I was saying. We have been there and we have done that. We have been burned at the stake. We have been drowned. We have been hunted with silver ammunition and left to die in traps lined with silver. We have been through your crusades, your *Reconqueista*, your Inquisition and your purges.

"We will not be your victims again."

She stood there, letting her words sink in.

"There will be no stripping us of our citizenship. We will not allow you to harm our children anymore. We will not march peacefully into your concentration camps. We will not let you chip us and track us and we sure as hell won't allow you to sterilize us. We will defend our property. We will defend our homes and our jobs and we will defend our persons. And what's more? *We can.*

"We've been patient with humans because we understand there is fear of us and what we are. We have offered to educate you. We have waited for your voices to overcome those voices of hatred and violence. I grew up in the human world. My mother is human, my grandparents are human. I know there are good men and women who disagree with what has been done in your names. But I need you to speak up because we aren't going to be victimized while we wait.

"There will be no pogroms. No purges. No marches into camps. If you try, you will meet resistance. And you will understand, far too late, that we have always had this power and lived peaceably with you while you have brought this war onto yourselves. We are not weak. We are not defenseless. We are strong and we are united. And we are fed up.

"I say this not to scare you. Not to start a war. But so that you understand we are not playing around. We prefer peace and diplomacy. You don't have to like us, but you don't get to kill us, not without risking getting killed right back. We are not your victims and we will prove that point if you make us."

She let go of the spell she'd been using to keep the hecklers quiet and the entire crowd erupted. Some with cheers, some with questions, some with tears and some with angry words.

"What is it you expect us to do now?" a local lawmaker asked.

"We expect you to leave us alone. We expect to enjoy the same rights and privileges as citizens that we have now. And we expect to carry out the responsibilities we have always carried out. We want to pay our taxes and complain like everyone else. We want to go to our kids' baseball games and track meets. We've tried to say all this over the last months. And you've ignored us. None of this would have been necessary had we not been backed into a corner."

"I should shoot you in the head right now! See just how powerful you are. You scum dare to threaten humans?" One of the PURITY people screamed.

She stared at him, hoping her face didn't betray the pounding of her heart. She knew there were shifters all through the crowd, witches with spells at the ready. Knew too that she had her own skills. But staring someone in the face who just proclaimed he wanted to shoot her was still shocking.

"I do dare, yes. Because you broke my arm, my leg and a rib. Because your hatred has killed children. Because you are a cancer in this country and we will no longer tolerate your threats. Do not come at us expecting us to turn the other cheek. We've turned it and you've bombed us. You've been warned."

Shoving broke out. One human pushed the one who'd just threatened to shoot her and the PURITY people waded in, fists at the ready.

"Will you create your own military like the humans have?" A reporter asked over the rising din.

They already had them, but there had been discussion of such a thing. Not that humans needed to know. The world had really split into an *us versus them* dichotomy and it hurt her heart. But it didn't make it any less true.

"We want to be safe. If the local police can't make that happen, we'll protect ourselves. We're not setting out to create a military of Others."

A woman off to the side nearly lost her feet when one of the PURITY thugs grabbed the pro-Others sign she carried.

"Stop! Someone is going to really get hurt." But no one heard as the shoving got worse.

Gage appeared at her side, speaking in her ear. "We've got to get you out of here, Molly. There's going to be a riot soon."

She allowed him to shield her, moving her down the steps as the rest of the hunters surrounded her, protecting her. She breathed Gage's magick in, even as hers rose to meet it.

He made her feel safe.

They got her in the car and slammed the doors, locking them as they managed to maneuver around the crowd. People jumped on the hood, banging on the windshield, and Lark threw a hand out with a blast of magick that cleared the guy off, sending him off to the side as they continued forward.

"Keep driving. Don't stop unless I say so," Lark ordered.

Molly shook, but wrestled herself back under control. She would not let them win. She would not let them see her upset. She would wait until she got back to her place before she let herself go.

"You did great." Gage spoke quietly to her, his arm around the back of her seat. She leaned into him briefly, letting herself take comfort.

"You all right? You kicked ass." Lark reached around to squeeze the non-casted leg.

"Not every day someone says they're going to shoot me."

Lark's face darkened. "That guy is an asshole who needs to be beaten senseless. Or rather, beaten since he has no sense to start with."

Molly put her head back and closed her eyes.

"Rest."

"Can't." She pulled her phone out. "Calls to make."

At least the calls gave her something to do to keep the shaking at bay until they got back to the hotel an hour later. News vans had parked out front so they went in the back way and took the freight elevator up.

Faine checked the room, as did Gage.

"I've got it for now if you want a break," Gage told Faine, watching her carefully. She was sick of being watched carefully.

Faine kissed her cheek. "I'm very proud of you."

She threw her good arm around him, hugging him tight. "Thank you."

He disappeared and she turned back to Gage.

"I'm going to run you a bath. Then I'll garbage bag up your cast."

"No bath. I can't get in and out on my own with the leg hanging over the side. I'll shower."

"Fine. I'll get it started." He looked her over carefully and walked down the hall while she got the duct tape and two garbage bags out.

BY the time he came back down the hall she'd gotten her leg in a bag and had taped it up.

"I've got the arm." She walked past him and closed the bathroom door behind her.

He allowed himself the full body shakes he'd been

holding back for hours. Christ. She could have been killed and if she had been, it would have been while they were mad at one another.

He got his Bluetooth in and began to make calls while he got her some tea, made her a sandwich and listened to be sure she didn't fall or have trouble in the shower.

The capitol police together with the Olympia police had managed to get things under control after nearly two hours of fighting. The news was talking about her speech in slightly awed terms. He wasn't sure how it would all turn out, but she'd hit it out of the park. Her speech had ridden the line between scary threats and olive branch.

He hoped the humans listened. For all their sakes.

She came out finally on a puff of Molly-scented steam. Coconut like the soap she used. She threw the plastic away and looked at the tea. "Thank you. I'm fine. You can go now."

He stepped to her, banded an arm around her waist and hauled her close. Carefully. Damn it, he was going to have to grovel like there was no tomorrow because there wasn't without her in his life.

"I'm sorry."

"Is the tea cold?"

He growled and she didn't even give him the raised brow.

"I'm sorry I broke up with you. I take it back. I never meant it anyway. I love you, Molly. I've loved you for a long time and I was a fool for pretending I didn't and for not saying it when it's been so true. I love you and I am sorry for hurting your feelings. I'm sorry for all the stuff I said about you calling Sato. I know why you did it and I know you weren't seeking permission and it was a low blow and I shouldn't have said it."

Some of her stiffness went away but he wasn't out of the danger zone just yet.

"I was jealous. Okay? I was jealous that Sato comforted you and made you feel better when I should have. I wanted you to come to me to share and it didn't matter that you didn't have the time to do it or that it was something you needed to address with him."

She kept quiet.

"Damn, you're a hard woman. Do you still love me?"

She nodded. "You think my love is so thin and flimsy that the minute you act like a jerk it goes away? If that was the case, I'd have been over you months ago."

"Ouch. I guess I deserved that. What can I do to make it up to you?"

"I need you to be honest with me. I need you to tell me what's bothering you. I need you to share with me because that's what you do to keep a relationship working. And it's a relationship. One that people will know about."

"I never hid you. I told Rose I was dating you just yesterday."

"This isn't dating."

"You're right, you're right. And so yes, of course one that everyone knows about because how can I not brag when my woman looks as good as you? I'm scared. Scared of losing you. Scared you can't count on me to protect you. Scared you'll look at a man like Sato and see one who is a lot more like you than I am and you'll regret loving me. I know you miss your human life and I worry you'll regret your choices and this life."

She kissed his chest, snuggling in and he let go of the panic and fear he'd been choking on.

"I could never regret loving you, Gage. Toshio Sato is a fine man. Intelligent and handsome, successful even. But he's not who I love. You're who I love. He's not who I want. You're who I want. I can't go back to my old life. That's been hard to accept, but that's reality. They won't have me. I lost it and for a while that held me back. But I have this life now. With you and this clan. I have friends. I have a man I love madly. I have these awesome, growing powers and sometimes I feel . . . guilty. Guilty for thinking they're so cool. Guilty for feeling guilty. I like being powerful. I like my magick. I don't regret this life. I regret that I had to lose my old one with so much devastation. But I don't regret that it brought me to you."

"I like the increase in my powers too. There's nothing to

be guilty over, your powers shut that heckler down today. I was amazed. You were also really hot and bossy. We're back together then?"

"I dare you to share your fears with me from now on. As a regular thing. That's the only way we can do this and be successful at it. There's too much pressure to add unnecessary relationship strain. If you're worried or jealous or mad, you need to say so. Or I can't take you back. Also if you break up with me like that again, that'll be the last time. A relationship has to be based on trust. I need to trust you not to take things that are so important to me and use them to hurt me. Being in a relationship with me isn't a game; it's not a tool you can use to manipulate me with. I won't stand for that."

"Deal. I'm sorry. You're totally right to be mad and hurt. It was so wrong of me. I love you so much, Molly. Please, let's make this work."

"All right then. I love you too. Now, pleasure me and maybe bring me donuts later. Tomorrow will be another fun-filled day at Clan Owen."

He grinned, walking her backward toward the bedroom. "The cast adds a challenge, but I'm up for it if you are."

"I totally am."

Turn the page for Lauren Dane's next

Bound By Magick novel

Coming soon from Berkley Sensation!

Chapter 1

HE tasted magick. Magick and blood rushed over his skin and through his system. His beast surged forward as he caught a human male by the back of the neck and threw him up against a nearby fence.

His beast raged within, aching to be let free. Aching to rip those who dared harm his protected to small pieces.

These humans had thrown firebombs into a community center that had been full of Others at the time. The parking lot had been full. Children had been playing on the field out back.

If it hadn't been for Clan Gennessee, who'd posted guards . . . Guards who'd noted the behavior of those humans who'd attacked them, who'd acted immediately and evacuated.

His fist made contact with a man's face, satisfaction roaring through Faine as the human crumpled to the ground.

The air was filled with the stench of the fuel used in the firebombs. With the scent of sweat and fear. His beast loved the latter.

Most of the humans were down, but what caught his attention was *her*.

She strode through the melee like a Valkyrie. Her magick sang with each step she took. Men fell all around her as she managed to use her fists and her power to push them back. Her face was a mask of fury and vengeance.

He blew out a breath as he took her in from head to toe. Helena Jaansen was magnificent.

She was totally focused as they fought the humans for a few minutes more before the threat they posed had been thoroughly dealt with. The police had not shown up yet, though some ambulances had arrived and those who'd escaped the building when it had been firebombed were being treated outside of the fray.

When it was over she put her fingers to her lips and whistled loudly

. Her men and women froze, turning their attention to her.

"I want a team working immediately to gather evidence. Get the kits from the van. John and Evan, I want everything on video. The police will arrive shortly. Do not impede them, but do not cede ground either."

"I'll keep an eye on these humans." Faine spoke and she turned her attention to him.

"Yes. Thank you. Feel free to break something if they try to escape." She turned away, issuing orders as she went.

The police rolled up seconds later, exiting their cars with their weapons drawn.

Helena approached them, her hands up. "Nice timing. Those responsible for trying to kill a community center full of people are all here, on the ground."

"On the ground!" one of the officers screamed at her.

Helena looked at them. "My hands are up. I am not going to get on the ground."

"We will shoot you if you don't comply."

"You can try. Or you can do your job and deal with this situation you avoided until you figured it was over." *Like cowards* hung in the air, unspoken, but not unheard.

She kept her hands up, but remained on her feet. "There's video of the attack. We've got a backup, just in case it gets *lost*. You're free to look at it. My people are guarding the room where the monitors are. It's in a relatively unscathed part of the building. Back door, up the stairs to your left. They know you're on the way, but they will continue to monitor as you watch. We'll wait right here with our hands up while you do."

"You don't give the orders here." The cop who stepped forward sneered. She was unmoved.

"Officer—" She leaned forward slightly, reading his name tag. "Officer Franklin. I'm Helena Jaansen and as you're too late on the scene of an assault called in twenty minutes ago, let me catch you up to speed. I'm not giving orders. I'm letting you know how it is. You can either protect us all, as it's your job, or you can refuse. In either case, I will protect my people. And you won't stop me from protecting children from these thugs. I have no desire to make this into an issue. But should you . . ." She shrugged. "I'm not a defenseless four-year-old just trying to jump rope. I can fight back."

Another law enforcement guy came up through the crowd. "Stand down, officers," he called out.

Franklin looked back, clearly intending to countermand that order, but when he saw the uniform and the big, yellow FBI letters, he stopped. "This is out of your jurisdiction."

"You can put your hands down," the FBI guy told Helena. She did, but she kept her body at attention.

"Firebombs are actually firmly in our jurisdiction. Especially when it's connected to a nationwide crime syndicate aimed at a certain group of citizens. That's right smack dab in our wheelhouse."

One of Helena's brows rose and Faine wanted to put his lips on it.

The FBI guy looked back to Helena. "You were saying there was video of the event?"

"Marian?" One of her people approached slowly, keeping her hands in plain sight. "Can you show Agent . . ."

"I'm Gill Anderson. Head of the new Cross Species Task Force."

"The what?" Officer Franklin and Helena said this in unison.

"We set up this week."

"Okay then. Marian, please show the agent up to the room with the monitors." Helena turned back to Anderson. "We have backups of the video, by the way. I was just telling Officer Franklin this."

"You don't trust us to be fair?" Anderson asked this after one of his agents went with Marian.

"I don't know you one way or the other. But I do know such evidence has been *lost* more than once since this mess started. And that makes me careful. Careful keeps people alive."

Anderson nodded. "Fair enough. Officer Franklin, please take the humans on the ground into custody. My people will conduct interviews at the station."

"You can't just jump in the middle of this!"

"I can. And I am. So, please get these men and women cuffed. Read them their rights and throw them in cells. Separately, please." Anderson turned back to Helena. "I'd like to interview you and your people as well."

"Fine."

Faine took up a spot next to Helena. She didn't seem to mind, but Anderson did. Too bad.

"If any of these assholes get *lost* on the way to the station, I'm going to be vexed, Agent."

"That would make two of us. Look, I'd prefer if we could start off on the right foot. I *am* here to help."

"I'm Helena Jaansen. I work for Clan Gennessee."

Anderson looked up into Faine's face. "Faine Leviathan. I work for her."

Faine caught the ghost of a smile flitting over her lips. Just a brief flash before it was gone.

"You're a Were of some sort?"

"Of some sort." They'd all decided not to reveal the existence of anything beyond the Veil. For the time being, no humans needed to know a damned thing about Lycia or the packs of Lycians, part man, part giant wolf, who dominated it.

Helena decided to forge ahead. The FBI guy didn't need to know any more about Faine.

"At four p.m.—prime after-school time, by the way—the guards noticed a group of humans who seemed to be casing the building."

"How did they know to identify that behavior as casing?"

Helena just shot him a look. "Really, Agent Anderson?" There was no need to let on just how well trained and militarized Clan Gennessee was, or the level of training of those Others who made up their new unified defense force. Or hell, even the existence of such a defense force.

"Go on. But don't think I'm not going to want to know just how well your people are trained."

He could want it until the sun burned out.

"They watched, notifying me and my people. One of the guards came out to get a closer look." Her mouth flattened briefly as he cast a look toward the body, covered by a sheet, that they'd moved out of the way of traffic. "He was attacked by two humans, shot in the head before he'd had a chance to react. The guards inside then began an evacuation out the back as those humans threw what we later ascertained to be firebombs through the front windows of the community center.

"By this point, we'd arrived, having only been in La Habra. They have automatic weapons, but we also have our own mode of protection. One of the men you took away is Gentry Fenton, one of the lieutenants for PURITY."

"How many of them were there?"

"Fourteen at the first." Faine broke in with his rumbly voice. Despite the stress and grief of the situation, it still made all Helena's parts tingly. "Then a van approached with six more."

Anderson interviewed her people, spoke to his own after they'd viewed the video and left two hours later.

PURITY had thrown twenty people with guns and bombs at a building full of kids and elderly people. It had been bad enough that some humans had gravitated toward the bigoted message of groups like PURITY and Humans First. But this sort of violence was a whole different level.

And rapidly becoming more common.

She wasn't sure how much longer things could go on without erupting into full-blown civil war.

Chapter 2

HELENA blew out a breath and turned to face her people. Covered in soot, blood and no small amount of dirty, they waited for her to give them orders.

Her gaze flitted over to the sheet and the two witches who'd been standing over it. She'd failed him. That Were who'd volunteered to be on her team. Who'd been doing his job and ended up dead for it. His pack members had shown up just a few minutes before and were preparing to remove his body.

"I'll be expecting your detailed reports. Tomorrow morning. Alix, Sam and Marcus, I want you to be lead on this. Get all the pertinent info to me. I need to speak with Gennessee, to brief her and the rest of the Governance Council about this. She'll then relay that information to the Owen."

The Enforcer from the South Bay Pack approached.

"I'm sorry for your loss. He was a good soldier." Helena carefully spoke, knowing grief was expected, but that wolves felt it was an honor to die protecting pack.

He inclined his head just slightly. "We appreciate the

honor you paid him by having your people watch over him. We'll be sending two replacements tomorrow."

She wasn't going to argue. She needed every body she could get. But it was hard, she knew firsthand, to put your people in the line of fire.

"Thank you."

"As my Alpha has made clear, we're in this together. We can't afford to let this break us."

She nodded. "No, we can't. But thank you anyway."

He turned, his wolves carrying the body away as they left the scene.

"Let's go. Get some rest. This all starts again in six hours."

Faine walked ahead, opening the passenger-side door for her. She allowed it because she was beyond exhausted.

"I need to go back to the office."

"You're about to pass out." He pulled away from the curb and away from the scene. But it was still in her head. The faces of all those Others who depended on her to protect them.

And the sheet covering the one she couldn't protect.

"I have a couch in my office."

"You and your sister are very much alike." He grumbled this under his breath, but she heard it and it made her smile.

"She has blue hair."

"The outside doesn't matter. Your insides are the same. Stubborn. Do you think you'll be more effective if you work until you literally just fall over? Who will you be helping then?"

"You know how long I've been awake because you've been with me the whole time. I don't see you getting into your jammies."

"Jammies?"

"Pajamas. The clothes people sleep in."

"I don't sleep in any clothes."

Christ.

But before she could really go there and imagine him, nearly seven feet of hard muscle and tawny skin, naked and in her bed, he spoke again.

"And I'm four hundred years old, Helena. I am Lycian.

I was bred to be up for days on end, fighting, marching, killing, all without sleep. You're a witch, and while you're powerful and fierce, you can't survive on two hours' sleep in two days."

"There were twenty humans in that group tonight. That means they're not flinching at sending their ranks to die. If I sleep, I'm not following up. How many people are going to die while I take a little nap?"

Failure wasn't something she liked at all. And in truth, she felt like she was drowning at least sixty percent of the time these days.

"You have people working three shifts. Trust them for six hours. Just six hours. You know you'll be far more alert and less inclined to make a mistake or miss something when you get some rest. Your magick will be stronger as well."

He was right. She knew he was. She'd used a lot of magick over the last few days. Her head hurt, her eyes felt like sandpaper and repeated adrenaline rushes followed by the crash afterward had left her muscles less and less responsive.

"Fine, but I'll sleep on my couch at the office."

"No need." He pulled up to a gate that slid open. "My place is right here. You can have my bed and I'll take the guest room. It's a big bed."

He was very, very bossy. But once she'd allowed herself to agree to sleep, her will to argue was gone.

The mini subdivision, now nearly full of Others, was pretty much an armed camp. Guard towers dotted the several-block area. High fences surrounded the entire subdivision. Barriers much like those that had been put into place outside public buildings in the wake of the 9/11 attacks surrounded those high fences to ward off any attempts at car bombs.

Many in the area now lived this way. It made her sad, but at least it kept them safer.

He pulled into his garage and she realized she'd never even been to his house before. She trudged to the connecting door as he turned off the alarm. "Wait here."

He went in first. She wanted to make a crack about how they'd just gone through eight different security checkpoints and two different alarms to get this far. But she'd seen so much happen in the last months after the Magister had come and turned everything upside down. So much death and destruction.

She kept her mouth shut and waited patiently until he came back to her. "Come on."

It was a surprise, how nice the place was inside. Faine worked so much that she didn't have any idea when he would have had the time to get the furniture and housewares inside.

"My sister."

She shook herself out of her thoughts. "What?"

"You were wondering how this place got decorated. My sister came from Lycia and she took care of everything. I'm not here that often, but when I am, it's nice to have a comfortable home to return to. A safe one."

He pushed a door open. She saw the massive bed, and may have sighed wistfully.

"I need a shower first. I'm covered in soot."

Another door pushed open to reveal a bathroom. "I'll get you some clothes. Towels are in that cabinet there."

And then she was alone to get rid of her filthy clothes, leaving them in a pile in the corner. She'd deal with getting a towel after she was clean, not wanting to get them dirty.

Hot water rained down on her skin as she made her way into the stall. She simply stood there, letting it wash over her for long minutes.

There had been far too many showers like this one. Where she'd stood and hoped all the death would wash off. But it was bone deep and she wondered when, if ever, she'd be able to let go of the things she'd seen—and done—over the last months.

She let the tears come as she scrubbed her hair. As she saw the soot and blood head down the drain. When she stepped out, she was grateful that he'd turned the heat up. Lycians, like shifters, had high body temps so quite often their homes tended to be cool.

But like his brother, Simon—her sister Lark's boyfriend? Mate? Whatever he was—Faine seemed to thrive on taking care of people he considered his to protect. Helena knew she'd become one of them.

She liked it, even as it chafed sometimes. It was nice to have someone taking care of her when it felt like pretty much every moment of her existence now was about taking care of everyone else.

He'd left a huge shirt on top of a towel. She hadn't even heard him come into the room. She hoped he hadn't come in when she'd been crying.

She had a reputation as an ice bitch. Crying ruined that image. Though he'd never say a word, he'd know all the same.

After a cursory towel-dry of her hair, she braided it quickly, put on the T-shirt that came to her knees, and shuffled into the bedroom where he'd left a pitcher of water and some snacks, and had even turned the blankets back.

She shoved some crackers into her face, gulped down three glasses of water, and lay back.

Once she did that, even as she felt herself falling toward sleep, she couldn't help recounting the last several days. One skirmish after another. Like a horror movie.

An assault by four kids at a high school in Fountain Valley. The shifter they'd attacked had handled it himself but they'd had to stop a near riot when the human parents of the bullies had shown up at the victim's house, demanding blood.

Vandalism in Garden Grove. A restaurant had had its windows broken out, anti-Other graffiti had been spray-painted on the walls. The interior had been totally destroyed and the food ruined.

A car set on fire in La Habra, which was where they'd been when they got the call about the community center in Whittier and had rushed over only to have to engage in an actual, no shit, pitched battle on the street with crazy people who thought it was totally okay to kill kids and the elderly.

She hated this world. Hated that people wanted to kill her simply because she was different. Hated that her friend Molly had been attacked and was now in a cast because of the rising threat of the human separatist groups.

These were her former neighbors. The kids she and her sister Lark had gone to school with. People she used to think were friends. The dividing lines had been drawn and the gulf between them got deeper by the day.

And now that Molly had given an ultimatum to the humans to leave the Others alone and stop trying to harm them or strip them of their rights as Americans, those lines kept getting drawn.

They were in a brief limbo period as Molly recovered, but soon they'd be on the road again and Helena would most likely be on the security detail for those Others who were travelling all across the country addressing crowds of humans, Others and legislators of all types. Trying to educate. Trying to mediate. Trying to stop an all-out war before it broke out.

But the edges of the world were torn and frayed. Helena wasn't sure how much longer things would hold before snapping.